THE HOUSE
AT THE
EDGE OF NIGHT

Catherine Banner

RANDOM HOUSE

NEW YORK

The
HOUSE
at the
EDGE
of
NIGHT

A NOVEL

The House at the Edge of Night is a work of fiction. All incidents and dialogue, and all characters with the exception of some well-known historical and public figures, are products of the author's imagination and are not to be construed as real. Where real-life historical or public figures appear, the situations, incidents, and dialogues concerning those persons are entirely fictional and are not intended to depict actual events or to change the entirely fictional nature of the work. In all other respects, any resemblance to persons living or dead is entirely coincidental.

Copyright © 2016 by Catherine Banner

All rights reserved.

Published in the United States by Random House,
an imprint and division of
Penguin Random House LLC, New York.

RANDOM HOUSE and the HOUSE colophon are
registered trademarks of Penguin Random House LLC.

Originally published in the United Kingdom by Hutchinson,
a division of Penguin Random House Ltd.

LIBRARY OF CONGRESS CATALOGING-IN-PUBLICATION DATA
Banner, Catherine.
The house at the edge of night: a novel/Catherine Banner.
pages; cm
Hardcover ISBN 978-0-8129-9879-5
International edition ISBN 978-0-399-58959-1
ebook ISBN 978-0-8129-9880-1
1. Families—Italy—Fiction. 2. Bars (Drinking establishments)—Italy—Fiction.
3. Domestic fiction. I. Title.
PR6102.A69H68 2016
823'.92—dc23   2015023813

Printed in the United States of America on acid-free paper

randomhousebooks.com

246897531

First U.S. Edition

Book design by Barbara M. Bachman

For Daniele

But islands can only exist

If we have loved in them.

DEREK WALCOTT

PART ONE

The

COLLECTOR

of

STORIES

...

1914–21

ONCE THE WHOLE OF THE ISLAND OF CASTELLAMARE WAS *plagued by a curse of weeping. It came from the caves by the sea, and because the islanders had built their houses from that rock, which had been the liquid fire of the volcano itself, very soon the weeping rang in all the walls of the buildings, it resounded along the streets, and even the arched entrance of the town wailed at night like an abandoned bride.*

Troubled by this curse, the islanders fought and quarreled among themselves. Fathers disagreed with sons, mothers turned against daughters, neighbors refused to speak to each other; in short, nobody had any peace.

This continued for many years until, one autumn, a great earthquake came. The islanders were woken by a shuddering at the heart of the island, an awful tremor. The earthquake rattled the cobbles in the streets and the dishes inside the cupboards. Buildings began to tremble like ricotta. By morning, it had knocked every house to the ground.

While the fallen stones mourned and wept, the islanders came together to decide what must be done.

A young peasant's daughter by the name of Agata had been visited by a vision of the Madonna, and developed ideas of her own about the curse of weeping. "Some sadness has seeped into the stones of the island," she said. "We must take the ruins and build from them a new town, and when we have done that great labor, the curse of weeping will be gone."

So the islanders, stone by stone, rebuilt the town.

FROM AN OLD TALE *of the island, in the version first told to me by Pina Vella, recorded at the Sant'Agata festival of 1914.*

I

HE WAS WOKEN BY A SCRATCHING AT THE WINDOW SHUTTERS.
Therefore he must have slept. "The baby is coming!" someone called.
"*Signor il dottore!*"

In his great confusion he thought they meant his wife's baby, and
was up and at the window in a knot of bedsheets before he recalled
that she was sleeping beside him. The face at the window was the
peasant Rizzu's, floating like a moon in the dark. "Whose baby is it?"
asked the doctor.

"*Signor il conte*'s baby. Who else?"

So as not to wake his wife, he went to the door. The moonlight in
the courtyard imposed on everything an odd clarity. Even Rizzu was
altered. The peasant had on his Sunday waistcoat and tie; he wore
them stiffly, as though nailed into them. "This is a mistake," said the
doctor. "I'm not under instructions to deliver the count's baby."

"But I was ordered to fetch you by *signor il conte* himself."

"I'm not under instructions to attend *la contessa* during her labor.
The midwife has had charge of her pregnancy all along. D'Isantu
must have meant you to fetch her instead."

"No, no, they already have the midwife. The count wants you, too.
Urgently, he said." Rizzu was puffed up with the importance of his
message. "Will you come? At once?"

"My own wife's baby is due very soon. I don't want to go far from
home if it can be avoided."

But Rizzu would not relinquish his mission. "The *contessa*'s baby is due right now, this very moment," he said. "I don't think it *can* be avoided, *dottore*."

"And the midwife can't handle it alone?"

"No, *dottore*. It's . . . a complicated birth. They need you, because the baby won't come out without those silver sugar-tong things of yours." Rizzu pursed his lips at having to speak directly of such matters; he had witnessed the births of none of his own nine children, preferring to think of them as having sprung out of the earth like Adamo *ed* Eva. "Will you come?" he said again.

The doctor cursed inwardly, for it was plain that he must. "I'll get my coat; I'll get my hat," he said. "I'll join you in the road in five minutes. Have you got your donkey cart or are we to walk?"

"No, no, *dottore*, I brought the cart."

"Have it ready."

He dressed in the dark. His watch stood at a quarter to two. He packed his instruments: forceps, steel scissors, a set of syringes—all of which he had prepared for his own wife's impending delivery—as well as morphine and magnesium sulfate in case of emergency. When this was done, he disturbed his wife. "How often are the pains waking you, *amore*?" he said. "The count's wife has gone into labor early—curse her—and I'm called away to attend."

She frowned at being woken. "Still a long time . . . let me sleep. . . ."

God willing, he should be able to deliver *la contessa*'s baby and be back in time for his wife's. Before leaving, he ran across the piazza and woke the ancient Gesuina, who had been the island's midwife until she began to lose her sight. "Signora Gesuina, *mi dispiace*," he said. "Will you sit with my wife? I'm called to attend to another patient, and my wife has been suffering labor pains."

"Who's the other patient?" said Gesuina. "Blessed Sant'Agata, is some other poor soul in the process of dying on this godforsaken island, that you have to leave her at such a time?"

"The count's wife has gone into labor early, and there are complications—they need me to bring the forceps."

"The count's wife, eh? And you've been called to attend her?"

"Yes, *signora*."

"From what I've heard, you've your reasons for preferring not to deliver *signora la contessa*'s baby." The old woman fell into a silence full of portent.

"What have you heard, Signora Gesuina?" The doctor was unable to suppress his irritation.

"Rumors," said Gesuina.

"Anyway, will you come and sit with her?"

Gesuina collected herself. "Yes, by Sant'Agata, of course. Where are you, boy? Let me catch hold of you, so I don't lose my footing on these troublesome stones."

The woman really was almost blind. Gesuina followed him across the square, holding the hem of his coat, and installed herself on a chair in the corner of the bedroom. He hoped the sight of the ancient figure would not alarm his wife if she woke.

Already it was past two. He kissed her forehead and left her.

Still cursing, he went in search of Rizzu and his donkey cart. Damn the count and his wife. She had refused to have him attend to her pregnancy, preferring the ministrations of the island's midwife. Why now this haste in calling him to the villa, at two in the morning? This complication of hers was probably no more than a twisted cord or a particularly violent pain, and there was no need of the forceps at all—and yet his own wife must be left unattended while he rode across town on their orders.

Rizzu was waiting, with his hat in his hands as though at Mass. They mounted his donkey cart, a fanciful contraption in green and yellow. Its painted panels told the stories of great battles, shipwrecks, and miracles belonging to the island. It was not a vehicle designed for haste. In a silence threaded with the blue crash of the sea, they traveled the sleeping streets. The moon burnished the palm leaves and lit the dusty back of the donkey. "Two babies due on the whole island," grumbled the doctor. "My wife's and the *contessa*'s, and both of them come at once. Who would be a *medico condotto*?"

"Ah," said Rizzu, who was not much inclined to express his opinion on the trials of country doctors. "It's a double blessing, though, *dottore*, isn't it? Two babies born on the same night—it's never happened on the island before."

"It's a double inconvenience."

They reached the count's gate at twenty past two. The doctor took his coat, his hat, his bag and stethoscope, and made off down the drive at a jog, the sooner to be finished with this business.

The count was standing sentinel outside his wife's bedroom in the modern part of the house. The electric glare on his face gave him a sweaty, reptilian look. "You're late," he said. "I sent for you nearly an hour ago."

"I wasn't under instructions to attend this birth at all." Irritation made the doctor forthright. "My own wife is in the early stages of labor; she's had pains on and off for days. It's damned inconvenient to leave her. And I thought *la contessa* wanted only the midwife in attendance."

"She did. It was I who sent for you. Carmela is in here; you'd better see for yourself."

The count stepped aside to allow the doctor to push past his bulk and into the countess's room. The electricity, newly installed, made everything pallid. The midwife was at work with a primal rhythm: *breathe, push, breathe, push*. But Carmela did not breathe, did not push, and he could see now that it wasn't just a matter of a twisted cord or a particularly violent pain. For a patient at this stage not to push was never a good omen. He did not often feel fear at his work, but now he felt it, dragging like a cold current across his shoulder blades.

"At last, you!" said the midwife in contempt.

A tiny maid quaked at the foot of the bed—what was her name? Pierangela—he had treated her once for bunions. "Bring me something to wash my hands," he said. "How long has the patient been like this?"

"Oh, Lord—hours, *signor il dottore!*" wept Pierang͏
soap and hot water.

"She's been suffering convulsions for an hour," corrected the
wife, "and then these fits of exhaustion when she seems to see nothing and nobody."

"When was the onset of contractions?" asked the doctor.

"Early yesterday morning I was called in. Seven o'clock."

Seven o'clock. For nineteen hours, then, they had been at this
struggle. "And it was a simple pregnancy?"

"Not at all." The midwife thrust a stack of papers at him—as
though it would help to read her case notes now! "*La contessa* has
been confined to bed this past month with swollen hands and violent
headaches. I'd have thought you would have known," she muttered.

"Swollen hands!" said the doctor. "Headaches! Why wasn't I
called?"

"*La contessa* refused," said the midwife.

"But *you—you* could have called me."

"*Signor il conte*'s mainland doctor saw her last week. He said it was
nothing. What could I do?"

"She should be delivering in the hospital in Siracusa, not here!"
The doctor rounded on the midwife and the terrified Pierangela. "I
don't have the tools to perform a cesarean section! I don't even have
enough morphine!"

"She refused to see you," said the midwife. "I suspected a pre-
eclamptic state, *dottore,* but no one ever listens to me in such matters."

This throwing up of hands enraged him. "You should have fought
to get her into the hospital," he said. "You should have insisted on it!"

Pierangela began a spontaneous lamentation: "Holy-Gesù-and-
Mary-Mother-of-God, Sant'Agata-saint-of-misfortunes-and-all-the-
saints—"

The knowledge of what had to be done came to steady his hands.
It always did, sooner or later. "Get everybody out of the way," he said.
"Prepare boiling water, clean sheets. Everything must be clean."

The water was brought, the sheets stripped from under the limp body of Carmela. The doctor sterilized a syringe, loaded it with magnesium sulfate, and injected it into her arm. The work led him now from task to task as though it were some ritual, the noon angelus or the rosary. He prepared morphine, steel scissors, forceps. "Find a needle and thread," he told the midwife. "Prepare swabs, prepare iodine. You'll find it all in my bag."

Carmela, in a moment of clarity, spoke. "I wanted only the midwife," she said. "Not you."

Without addressing her directly, the doctor said, "That can't be helped now. We need to deliver the baby as soon as possible."

He prepared the morphine and injected her slender arm once more. While Carmela sagged under the weight of the drugs, he lifted the scissors and planned his incision, making it first in the air. One neat inch-long snip. The sheets—where were the sheets? "Bring the clean ones," he ordered. "At once."

Pierangela stumbled about in consternation. "Everything must be clean!" raged the doctor, who had learned his trade in the mud and ice of the trenches at Trentino. "Everything. If the fits don't kill her, sepsis will."

Carmela, again lucid, met his eyes, and her own were sharpened with fear, the way he had seen a hundred etherized soldiers look during the war, when they surfaced. He put the back of his hand on her shoulder. Something altered in her at his touch, as he had known it would. She lifted her head and, with all the force of a malediction, said, "This is your doing."

"Give her more morphine," he told the midwife.

"This is your doing," Carmela said again. "The child is yours. Everyone suspects it but you. Why won't you look at me, Amedeo?"

He injected her without even glancing at her face, but he could feel the room tighten under the force of the accusation. As soon as Carmela sank again he knelt and made a single incision, reached inside for the baby, and turned it by a quarter. Then, with the aid of the forceps, he delivered it in one motion into the room.

A boy—already breathing. He cut the cord and deposited it in the arms of the midwife. "She still isn't safe until the placenta is delivered," he said. Then, in a slither, the whole mass of it came free, and everything was over in a confusion of blood and weeping.

Carmela began to revive in the following minutes, as he had known she would. She hauled herself up on the damp sheets and demanded the baby. Relief, and the burden of hiding it, made him nauseous. He went to the window. He looked down the avenue that led from the count's door to the road. He saw how the lamps among the trees made spheres of green light. He saw how, beyond them, the vista was melancholy, just the empty hillside and the black and endless sea. Everything was altered since he had last looked upon these things. The room was altered. Carmela was altered. He would not have recognized either.

When he had steadied himself, he returned to his patients. He checked Carmela's heartbeat, the baby's heartbeat. He stitched the incision he had made and swabbed everything with iodine. He presided over the burning of the placenta, the bloody sheets, the swabs and bandages. Only then did he allow himself to look properly at Carmela. Absorbed in contemplation of the baby, she was unaware of him now. Strange to think that the body which labor had so assaulted, which he had injected and incised and manhandled on the bed just now, had been whole and young when he had last seen her. *This is your doing,* she had said. *The child is yours.* He allowed himself one brief glance at the baby. A lusty boy with a puff of black hair—why, a baby at this stage could belong to anyone. It seemed as he studied it to assume the count's features, his jowly neck and protruding eyes.

But either way, she had accused him, and that was what mattered.

A great tiredness came over him now that his work was accomplished. The count came to the door, and Carmela was hastily wiped and covered. It fell upon the doctor to announce the birth. This he did, with more bravado than he felt, playing his own part, bringing forth the expected phrases: "A fine child . . . a strong boy . . . case of eclampsia . . . hope for a good recovery."

The count inspected the baby and inspected his wife, then gave the doctor a nod, and he understood that he was dismissed.

Unwanted now at the scene, he cleaned his instruments, packed them, and made his way through the dim passages of the villa and out into the light. The sun was breaking, with the quiet brightening belonging to the Mediterranean. It was just past six o'clock.

A figure came running between the palm trunks. Rizzu. "*Signor il dottore*," the old man yelled in exultation, "you have a baby boy!"

In his extreme tiredness, he did not at first understand. "A baby boy!" cried Rizzu again, startling the doves from the palm trees. "Your wife is delivered of a baby boy!"

Cazzo! He had forgotten. He met Rizzu at a run. "A very quick birth," said Rizzu, his modesty forgotten. "One hour, and Gesuina said she could have delivered the baby with her eyes closed!" The old man reflected a moment. "Which is just as well. Ha! Praise be to God and Sant'Agata, praise be to all the saints—"

The doctor refused the tiresome donkey cart, and went at a run through the waking streets. The cicadas had begun to sing. Light entered the alleyways and the squares. A hundred widows in a hundred courtyards were sweeping with a brisk, impatient sound. As he ran, he felt a great converging of the light inside him and without him, so that the whole world seemed charged with it.

The bedroom smelled of blood and exertion. Gesuina dozed, straight upright, on a chair at the foot of the bed. The baby was sleeping, too, hunched in the fold of his mother's waist. "I'm sorry, *amore*," he said.

"It was easier than I expected," she said, with her usual practicality. "All that dreading, and it was over in an hour! Gesuina and I managed very well without you."

He wiped off the last of the afterbirth. The child was a little stretching, mewling creature, as alien as a newborn kitten. He took the tiny weight of the boy and inspected the legs and arms, pressed the soles of the feet, separated the fingers and—with a thrill of pride—listened through his stethoscope to the birdlike beating of the heart. In the extreme joy that broke over him he waxed tender, even poetical. Oh, it was different to be a father than merely a lover—he saw it now! Why had he waited so long to beget a child? He understood that no other part of his life had mattered; all of it had only been a gathering of pace toward this hour.

But now there was the problem of the other baby. By afternoon rumors would be at large in every corner of the island, thanks to that witch Carmela—a miracle, twins born by different mothers, leaping into the world as though by agreement! He knew how they would talk.

His wife lay with the lassitude of a distance runner. He checked her all over, covering her with kisses—more than he would have given, true, if guilt had not been goading him. He knew that a storm of trouble was coming: The midwife and Pierangela had heard Carmela's accusations. A rumor like this would be enough to make an enemy of his wife, his neighbors, perhaps to drive him from the island. But just now all that he permitted to dwell within him was the light.

II

HIS OWN BIRTH HAD BEEN AN OBSCURE THING, UNCELEBRATED, unrecorded.

In the city of Florence, above the Arno River, lies a piazza of dim lights and marine shadows. On one side of this piazza is a building with nine porticoes, and in the wall of this building is a window with six iron bars: three horizontal, three vertical. The bars are darkened with rust; on winter nights, they take on the chill of the air, its damp, its fog. Behind the window, in those days, stood a stone pillar; on top of the pillar lay a cushion.

Here the doctor's own recorded life began, one night in January, when he was unceremoniously shoved through the iron bars. A bell rattled. Both naked and alone, the baby began to weep.

Footsteps approached from within. Hands lifted him. He was folded against a starched chest and borne away into the light.

When the nurses of the foundling hospital unwrapped him, they found that his body was still tender: a newborn, in spite of the size. A saint's medallion, snipped in half, was looped around his neck on a length of red ribbon. "It might be San Cristoforo," said one nurse. "See—two legs and three wavy lines, like water. Or some kind of southern saint."

The baby seemed to be in good health. They assigned him to a wet nurse for the night.

At first he was unable to suckle, but the nurse, Rita Fiducci, a dauntless woman, continued to push her worn teat at his mouth until he began to take great sobbing gulps. Sated, he slept. Rita rocked him and sang to him, a little scoldingly: "*Ambara*-bà, *cic*-cì, *coc*-cò!" A song for an older child, but this baby seemed far too robust to Rita for ordinary lullabies. It was a song that would return to Amedeo, at odd moments, all the days of his life.

The director, before leaving for the night, looked in on the new arrival. Five babies in one night! It was becoming an epidemic. A third of all children born in Florence now passed through the iron window of the foundling hospital, to be parceled up, named, fed, cured of their ills, and sent back out into the world that had abandoned them. The director opened a new entry in the great yellow book *Balie e Bambini* and noted the time of the baby's arrival, the wet nurse who had been assigned to him, and a description of the blanket in which he had been found ("blue, somewhat bloodstained") and of the medallion ("possibly San Cristoforo"). He also recorded the baby's abnormal size, ten pounds and eleven ounces, the largest the hospital had ever seen.

The director took the tin medallion, which he folded up in a square of paper and filed in the box marked "January 1875." The box was already stuffed with other trinkets in square envelopes: a perfume bottle on a silver chain; a paper silhouette of a lady cut down the middle; tin medallions halved and quartered, like tickets at a left-luggage department. More than half the children carried something with them.

He considered for a moment, then assigned the baby the name "Buonarolo." In the recent tide of babies—two thousand deposited in the previous year alone—the director, the chief nurse, and her staff had resorted to changing one or two letters at a time to fashion each child a surname: Thus tonight's five babies had become Buonareale, Buonarealo, Buonarala, Buonarola, Buonarolo. And "Amedeo" for a first name would suit this giant infant—a solid, God-fearing name. The director added it, then closed the book.

The baby woke again and sucked at Rita's teat, this time with a sense of purpose. Already unfurling within him was the great ambition of his life: to live, to grow up, and to find a home and a family.

———

NOT ONLY WAS HE the largest baby the foundling hospital had ever seen, he also grew twice as quickly as the babies Buonareale, Buonarealo, Buonarala, and Buonarola. It took two wet nurses to feed him, and a special cot had to be purchased and placed between their beds, rather than the usual white-starched cradle, because Amedeo fretted whenever he was placed in the cradle, already straining against its sides. He grew up by great leaps: "an ungainly little thing," his second nurse Franca said ("a blessed angel" was what Rita called him). Rita held him on her knee and sang "*Ambara*-bà, *cic*-cì, *coc*-cò," so that sometimes he forgot that she was not his real mother.

When he was a little older, Rita told his fortune from a torn pack of *tarocco* cards. The director caught her and forbade it. Amedeo remembered nothing about the fortune, but he remembered the cards and loved the stories furled within them: the Hermit, the Lovers, the Hanged Man, the Devil, the Tower. He begged for others. Instead of the card stories, Rita taught him a tale about a girl who became an apple, became a tree, became a bird. She taught him a story about a cunning fox. Afterward he longed for a little fox to sleep beside him on the stone floor of the dormitory. His thirst for stories grew. Franca taught him two: the first about a demon named Silver Nose and the second about a sorcerer named Body-No-Soul. After these stories, Amedeo had to shut himself uncomfortably up in Rita's bedside locker, in case the demon and the sorcerer should come for him, but he still loved the tales.

When he was not yet quite grown, Rita went away, and no one said anything more about her. For a while he was sent to the country, to a little house with a dirt floor, where he had a new foster mother and foster father. If you stood on the seat of the latrine and peeped through the window, you could see the bowl of smog that was the city of Florence, where he had been born, and the shiny serpent that was the Arno.

It cost too much to feed him, his foster mother said; she claimed the boy grew out of his clothes. He was sent back.

By the time he was six, there were mostly girls left in the foundling hospital, and Amedeo. The window where he had been delivered was shut up now. Babies had to be brought to an office in a basket, because that was what his nurse Franca called "civilized." Otherwise, she said, bad people abandoned their babies out of convenience. Amedeo, as he grew, wondered if he had been abandoned *out of convenience* (he took the phrase to mean "by accident"). He developed the habit of stationing himself on the steps beneath the closed-up window, in case his real mother should ever come back for him.

ONE AFTERNOON IN MAY, the visiting doctor found Amedeo there on his way to inspect the babies. Always, the visiting doctor had kept a special eye on Amedeo. The boy's abnormal size caused him pains in his legs and made him prone to all kinds of accidents, bringing him under the visiting doctor's care more often than the doctor would have wished.

"Now, my little man," said the doctor (who had difficulty addressing the children sensibly once they passed nine months), "no injuries in the past few weeks, eh? That's good progress. But what's to become of you?"

Amedeo, on this particular afternoon, had been troubled by a vague melancholy that now found a focus and a shape. He took the question rather more seriously than the visiting doctor had intended, and wept.

The visiting doctor was discomposed, in spite of himself. He rooted in his pockets and offered the boy in quick succession a violet pastille, a *lira* coin, a used theater ticket, and a handkerchief with the letters "A. E." on it (this last Amedeo wetly accepted). "There there," said the doctor. "They aren't quite your initials, but they'll have to do. The first one is right—an 'A' for Amedeo, see, for my own Christian name is Alfredo—but not the second. Can you read yet? I don't suppose you can. My surname is Esposito. A good name for a foundling like you; it means abandoned. Of course, one wouldn't be allowed to give that name to a foundling nowadays for fear of prejudice."

"Were you a foundling, too?" said Amedeo, leaving off his crying for a moment.

"No," said the doctor. "I think perhaps my great-grandfather was, since we don't have any record of him."

Again, the boy cried, as though personally insulted by the fact that the visiting doctor was not a foundling. "Take a violet pastille," urged the doctor.

"I don't like them," said Amedeo, who had never tasted them.

"What *do* you like?" said the doctor.

The boy, still crying, said, "Stories."

The visiting doctor cast about in his memory and brought forth a story that he half remembered his own nurse telling him. It was a story about a parrot. This parrot wanted to prevent a girl from betraying her husband, and managed this by means of a fantastic, ever-expanding tale. The parrot flew in the girl's window and told her this tale, and it kept her so absorbed that whole days and nights passed in its telling. Her husband came back and all was well. Or something like that.

Amedeo sat up, wiped his eyes, and said, "Tell me the story properly."

The visiting doctor could not remember it. But the next week he brought Amedeo a copy, transcribed into a red leather notebook by his housekeeper, Serena, who knew the story well, at least in the particular version belonging to her grandmother's side of the family, who were known to be formidable storytellers. Why he had taken the trouble of getting the story for the boy, he could not quite tell. The notebook had a gold fleur-de-lis on the cover. It was the single most beautiful thing that had passed through Amedeo's hands. Seeing his joy, the doctor made the boy a spontaneous present of it. "There," said the doctor, satisfied. "You can add more stories to it, or practice your reading and writing."

After that, Amedeo developed the habit of listening to everybody's stories—nurses, nuns, the priests of the Santissima Annunziata who passed by the steps of the foundling hospital, visiting benefactors—and whenever they pleased him, he recorded them in his book.

When they asked him, at thirteen, to which trade he should like to be apprenticed, he told them he should like to be a doctor. He was sent to a watchmaker. The watchmaker sent him back after three days: The boy's large fingers broke the tiny mechanisms. Amedeo was then sent to a baker, but the baker found himself tripping over the gigantic apprentice, and after several months of tolerating the boy he sprained his ankle in this manner and would tolerate him no longer. Next, Amedeo spent several months with a printer. This he liked, but he was returned to the foundling hospital on account of his unfortunate habit of pausing in his work ten times a day to read the stories, which was costing the printer clients and money.

And so the boy was without trade or calling. He was sent back to school, though he was really too old. Here he finally distinguished himself, finishing every year in first place ahead of the small sons of clerks and shopkeepers in whose ranks he labored. Still he persisted in his wish to be a doctor. He would be the first child from the foundling hospital, as far as anyone could remember, to study medicine, and the director consulted the visiting doctor Esposito for advice. "Could it be done?" he asked.

"It could," said Esposito, "if someone were to pay, and someone else were to take charge of his guidance and education. And if his clumsiness can be overcome, but I daresay it can if the boy puts his mind to it."

Under pressure from the director of the foundling hospital, a benefactor offered to pay for part of Amedeo's medical studies, another to supply his books and his clothes. Another two years were lost in military service, but when Amedeo returned, Dottor Esposito submitted to the inevitable (he had really become quite fond of the ungainly boy over the years), and allowed Amedeo to be sent home to live with him. The boy would board in the little box room at the back of the doctor's house, and eat his meals with the housekeeper Serena, and the doctor would oversee his medical education. The boy was almost twenty-one years old and could be expected to look after himself for the rest. The doctor arranged for him to attend lectures at the surgical school of the hospital at Santa Maria Nuova, and in the evenings to earn his keep by washing glasses in a bar between Via dell'Oriuolo and Borgo degli Albizi.

The arrangement was a success. The boy was accommodating, rushing to light the fire or rearrange the doctor's chair as he came in, in a way that the doctor, a bachelor on the edge of old age, found touchingly filial. Amedeo was also a satisfactory companion in conversation, on account of the fact that he studied daily every page of the newspaper and was working his way systematically through the doctor's library. All in all, Esposito was glad that he had taken the boy in. Sometimes, the doctor invited Amedeo to dine opposite him in his dark study, where he was accustomed to take dinner at his desk, surrounded by a mess of scientific periodicals. The doctor was a collector, and the study was full of specimens: butterflies, white worms in jars, sculptures of coral, stuffed Polynesian rodents, and other curiosities of nature that he had gathered during his long and solitary life as the last in a lengthy dynasty of scientific men. The boy was especially fascinated by a medical wax of the human eye, the surface peeled back to reveal the network of veins beneath, which stood on the hall table beside the umbrellas. Dangling alarmingly above the staircase on two wires were brushes from the mouth of a whale. Amedeo was not unnerved by these relics; on the contrary, he grew as fond of the collections as of the old doctor himself. And he privately resolved that one day he would have collections of his own: a parlor full of scientific specimens and a library full of books. His red notebook was filling up with stories, and his head with the longings of a half-educated man.

When at last he qualified (everything, in Amedeo's experience, took twice as long when you were a foundling), he became not a hospital surgeon like his foster father, but a *medico condotto*. In deference to his foster father, Amedeo took the surname Esposito. He could find no permanent job, but practiced his trade in villages where elderly doctors had died or overworked doctors had fallen sick. He had no horse or bicycle. Instead, he walked between the stone cottages in the rain-laden dawns and chill nights. On the hillsides below Fiesole and Bagno a Ripoli, he bandaged the broken ankles and gored shoulders of peasant farmers and delivered the babies of their wives. He sent letters of application to every village in the province, looking for a place, without success.

Meanwhile, he gathered stories with each year that passed. His vocation and manner seemed to invite confidences. The peasants told him of daughters lost at sea, of brothers parted who, reunited at last, mistook each other for strangers and slew each other, of shepherds blinded in both eyes who navigated by the sounds of the birds. The stories that the poor loved best, it seemed, were sad ones. And stories still held a kind of magic for him. Returning home in the gray dawn to whatever temporary lodgings he inhabited at the time, he would wash his hands, pour coffee, throw open the windows to the reassuring sounds of the living, and transcribe the stories into his red book. He did this whether the fate of his patient had been life or death, and always solemnly. In this way, his book became full of the bright vistas of a thousand other lives.

In spite of this, his own life remained narrow and shallow-rooted, as though he had never really begun it. A large and hawkish man with one straight bristle of eyebrow across his forehead, he was tall without being apologetic for his tallness, unlike most men of high stature. His height and the obscurity of his background made him out of place, a foreigner everywhere. When he witnessed the young taking photographic portraits in the Piazza del Duomo of Florence, or drinking chocolate at little bandy-legged tables outside the bars, he felt that he had never belonged to their species. His youth had passed and he felt himself to be at the beginning of middle age. He was a solitary man, grave of dress, reserved of habit, who spent his evenings in study of medical periodicals and his Sundays in his elderly foster father's parlor, discussing the newspaper, examining the newest specimen in the old man's collection, playing cards. As his hands moved, he remembered the *tarocco* tales of his childhood: the Hanged Man, the Lovers, the Tower.

The old doctor had retired now. He still visited the foundling hospital, which had modernized in recent years and whose children now slept in specially aired dormitories, and played on great terraces full of drying linen, built particularly for the purpose.

Amedeo continued to apply for a permanent position. He sent letters everywhere, to villages in the south whose names he had never heard before, to *comunes* in the height of the Alps, to insignificant islands whose inhabitants sent their replies by boat via neighboring villages because no postal service had yet reached them.

Finally, in 1914, one mayor sent back a letter by such roundabout means. His name, he wrote, was Arcangelo, his town Castellamare. If Amedeo was willing to travel to the south, there was an island utterly without medical assistance that might have a post for him.

The island was a crumb between the pages of his foster father's atlas; south and east of Sicily, it was the farthest Amedeo could possibly have ventured from Florence without reaching Africa. He wrote back the same afternoon and accepted.

At last, a permanent position. His foster father saw him off at the station, wept in spite of his intentions, and promised that in the summer they would drink a glass of *limoncello* on a terrace laden with bougainvillea (the doctor's views of the south were vague and romantic). "Perhaps I'll even move there in my old age," said the doctor. He had come to look on Amedeo not as a foster son but as a son outright, although he could not find within himself the phrases to say so. Meanwhile, Amedeo sought about for thanks, but could only shake the doctor's hand. Thus they parted. They were never again to see each other alive.

III

AMEDEO TRAVELED STEERAGE ON A STEAMER FROM NAPLES. IT WAS the first time he had been upon the sea, and he was dizzy with its hydraulic hiss, its vastness. He carried with him a trunk full of his medical instruments wrapped in bundles of straw, and a small leather case in which he had packed his few clothes, his shaving kit and pipe, and his book of stories. Also, a new Kodak folding camera, an unexpected gift from his foster father. Amedeo had resolved in Castellamare to be a different man, a man who had experiences of which photographs could be taken, a man who sipped chocolate on the terraces of elegant bars. Not a foundling, not a penniless jobbing physician. For he still inhabited the world as bare as he had come into it, with no wife, no friend except his foster father, no descendants. Couldn't life alter? Hadn't his life begun to alter already in making the journey here? He was almost forty. It was time to embark on the real existence he had always believed to be waiting for him.

Since boyhood he had felt himself to be set against the tide, and so it was now: Looking back, he observed that all the steamers leaving the port of Naples seemed to swing to the north as though drawn by some invisible compass, while his own ship cut against the waves and plowed south, churning white moonlight under its prow. The steamer took in Salerno and Catania, then docked in Siracusa. From here, Amedeo saw Castellamare for the first time. The island was a low and brooding thing on the horizon, no more than a rock on the water. To carry him there, he could find no ferry or steamer, only one fishing boat, which bore the ominous name *God Have Mercy*. Yes, said the fisherman, he could take Amedeo to the island, but for no less than twenty-five *lire* because with this wind it would take all evening.

An old man working at a pile of nets was drawn in by their conversation. He mumbled something about the island being a place of ill luck, plagued by a curse of weeping, and began a complicated story about a cave full of white skulls—but he was quickly hushed and sent away by the first fisherman, who believed himself on the brink of closing a deal.

So he was, for Amedeo was not superstitious—and since he was unaccustomed to the south, neither was he inclined to barter. He paid the twenty-five *lire*, and with the fisherman's help lodged his trunk of medical instruments under the thwart of the boat.

The fisherman rowed and talked, rowed and talked. The people of Castellamare, he told Amedeo, scraped a living by herding goats and picking olives. Also they fished for tuna, which they bludgeoned to death with sticks. And other fish, all types of fish, ones you could bludgeon and ones you could hook and ones you could gaff with a spear under the gills. Amedeo, who had been seasick since Naples, kept his mouth firmly shut while the fisherman expounded upon these themes. At last, they approached the stone quay of Castellamare.

The fisherman deposited him shortly after nine. As Amedeo watched the mast light of the *God Have Mercy* dip among the waves, a vast emptiness and silence settled around him, as though the island were uninhabited. Certainly, the few houses visible along its coast were unlit. The stone quay, which still held traces of heat, was scattered with petals of bougainvillea and oleander; a faint scent of incense hung in the air. Leaving his trunk, Amedeo went in search of some farm laborer or fisherman who might possess a handcart. But all he found was an old Arab *tonnara* with stone arches in which a few playing cards and cigarette butts lay scattered, and a white chapel, which also proved to be deserted. The altar bore the staring image of a saint Amedeo did not recognize; on either side of it were vases of lilies whose stems sagged in the heat.

Amedeo's letter from the mayor Arcangelo directed him to climb the hill, where he would find the town "past a stand of prickly pears and through a stone archway, on top of the rock." He was becoming used to the dark, and now he distinguished the outlines of a settlement hanging on the edge of the cliff: thin shuttered houses, the peeling baroque façade of a church, a square tower with a dome in blue enamel that reflected the light of the stars.

Amedeo could not carry his trunk up the hill. The only thing to be done was to make the ascent without it. He heaved it into the shelter of the chapel, which gave him some reassurance that it would be left undisturbed, and set out with only his suitcase. The road was stony and unleveled; on either side, lizards shifted in the undergrowth. The sound of the surf rose clearly through the dark, and looking down he saw that it pooled and foamed around the entrances of a hundred small caves. Farther up, the road twisted away from the coast and another part of the island came into view, flatter and more ordered, cut up into small strips of field and surrounded by the stone box houses of peasants. He passed under the shadow of an olive grove, between the somber forms of cacti. Sure enough, there was a stone archway here, faded and peeling. Now that he was at the summit of the island, in the full force of the wind, he saw that Castellamare was no different once you were upon it than it had appeared from a distance, still just a rock in a vast black ocean. To the north, the lights of Italy and Sicily shimmered hazily. To the south, the dark was uninterrupted.

The town itself had the blind stillness of a place unused to visitors. The main street was lit at intervals with blackened filament lamps, the side streets by assorted gas lanterns suspended from the balconies. A profusion of thyme and basil gave off a strong odor in the dark. He was obliged to go all over the town looking for signs of life. He passed a street of shops whose names were painted in black capitals on the plaster, a green-smelling fountain, and a belvedere with a vista of the ocean. No people. Just when he was beginning to despair, the sound of singing drew him. After some turns through unlit alleys, a wrestle with a low-hanging washing line, and an unfortunate encounter with a stray dog, he came up a long flight of steps to the edge of a piazza, and there he finally found the inhabitants of Castellamare.

The whole square was in a state of noisy chaos. Women bore fish overhead on great platters; wine slopped into glasses; the circus strains of guitars and *organetti* rose in the dark. A boy and a girl without shoes plied a barrow dangerously through the legs of the crowd. In one corner a donkey auction was in progress; around the creature, men, women, and children jostled and shoved, waving pink tickets. On a pedestal hovered a great plaster effigy of a saint, a woman with a coil of black hair and an alarming stare, fanned by a hundred red flames. Amedeo was soon to learn that he had arrived in the middle of the yearly festival of Sant'Agata. For now, it seemed only a wondrous, magical disorder unlike anything he had witnessed.

Into this disorder, as into a warm sea, stepped Amedeo. He passed through the scents of jasmine and anchovies and liquor, through snatches of dialect and accented Italian and high lamenting songs whose language he did not recognize, through the light of fires and torches and the hundred red candles that illuminated the ghostly saint. At last, emerging from the crowd with his suitcase clutched to his chest, he found himself before an extraordinary house.

A square building in faded amber, it seemed balanced on the very side of the hill, between the light of the piazza and the dark of the hillside and the sea. Its terrace was draped in great profusions of bougainvillea. At little tables, among the flowers, the islanders drank *limoncello* and *arancello*, fought and swore over card games, swayed to the whirling songs of an *organetto*. A sign in fanciful script proclaimed the words "Casa al Bordo della Notte": House at the Edge of Night.

A tiny old man approached Amedeo. Reeling slightly, this man looked up at him and said: "Who are you?"

"Amedeo Esposito," said Amedeo, startled into introducing himself. "I'm the new doctor."

The old man puffed himself up with delight. "The new doctor!" he said. *"The new doctor!"*

Amedeo was alarmed as the islanders surged around him, clapping their hands, thumping his shoulders, vigorously seizing his arms. It took him some moments to recognize this for what it was: a welcome. The tiny old man was crowing in delight. "Rizzu is my name," he said. "This bar is my brother's. The Rizzus are an important family on the island, as you'll see, *signor il dottore*. I'll fetch you a drink. I'll fetch you grilled anchovies and a rice ball and a plate of mozzarella."

The doctor had eaten nothing since Siracusa, and all at once began to be hungry. He sat. Liquors were poured for him, a table cleared. The mayor Arcangelo appeared soon after, a stout grocer who moved through the crowd with well-oiled charm, all smiles. He shook Amedeo's hand, clapped his shoulder, and welcomed him to the island. He then introduced the priest, who was narrow and went by the name of Father Ignazio and was also, Arcangelo said, a member of the town council.

After this hasty welcome, the mayor vanished, but the priest, with a grave cough, sat down near Amedeo. "You haven't yet been introduced to *il conte*, I daresay. The deputy mayor. This is the first time anyone but he has been mayor on the island, so you find us at a time of great modernization."

Amedeo, who had thought that there was no such thing as a count in any part of Italy in the twentieth century, was at a loss for a reply. "You'll encounter the count soon enough," said the priest. "Don't worry. Best to get it over with."

Rizzu returned, bearing plates, with an equally tiny old man whom he introduced as his younger brother and the owner of the bar. Rizzu heaved himself up into the chair on the other side of Amedeo, poured him more liquor, and began to explain the history of the island, and of the saint whose festival was now taking place in the square.

"I keep telling Father Ignazio he must speak to the pope about officializing Sant'Agata," he told Amedeo. "She's cured all kinds of illnesses. A curse of weeping one time, and another time an epidemic of typhoid. She saved the island from the invaders by bringing a storm of flying fish down on the enemy ships, and on a fourth occasion she showed her grace by mending the legs of a young girl who had fallen into a well, praise be to the saint. Why, there's the girl herself—there—Signora Gesuina—"

Amedeo looked—"No, *signore*, there!"—and at last understood that Rizzu was pointing to an ancient woman, swaying blindly to the wails of the *organetto*. "When did the miracle happen?" asked the doctor.

"Oh, a few years ago now," said Rizzu. "But we expect Sant'Agata to bestow another miracle any year now. At her festival we carry her statue all around the coast. Then, to reward us, she blesses the fishing boats, the planting of new ground, and all the babies born on the island. Seven this year—you'll be busy, *dottore*, I daresay!"

"And they'll all be named Agata," added the grave priest. "For I'm certain there's nowhere in the world with more Agatas than this island. There has been an epidemic of Agatas in recent years. It has now become necessary to refer to them by attribute: Agata-with-the-green-eyes, Agata-from-the-house-with-the-bougainvillea, Agata-daughter-of-the-baker's-sister—"

"'Agata' is the very best of names!" protested Rizzu, in drunken high spirits. He clambered down from his seat and went off in search of wine for the doctor, who didn't seem to like the island's liquors—for really he was drinking very slowly, thought Rizzu, and with unnecessary coughs and splutters.

Meanwhile, Amedeo delighted the crowd by taking out his book of stories and making a record of Rizzu's account of Sant'Agata, which had thoroughly charmed him. Like everything this night, it seemed enchanted and not quite real, and he was anxious not to forget it.

When the others had dispersed a little, Father Ignazio leaned toward Amedeo. "You'll have no peace, I'm afraid," he said. "We haven't had a doctor on the island since the first Greek sailors landed here two millennia ago. The islanders will be bringing you their bunions and piles, their sick cats and hysterical daughters, their whole backlog of medical complaints. And their stories. Many more stories. Be warned."

"You have never had any doctor on the island before?"

"None."

"What's the normal practice when someone is sick?"

Father Ignazio spread his hands. "For all serious matters, we send the islanders in a fishing boat to the mainland."

"And what about when it's stormy, or when no boat is available? I had some trouble getting here; there was only one man willing to take me."

"I have a few medicines which I can distribute," said the priest. "That good widow, Gesuina, attends the expectant mothers. We manage as we can between us. But no—it's a sad state of things. We'll be glad to have you here. It breaks my heart to bury the young when we've no medical man to tell us whether it might have been prevented."

"But why has a doctor only now been sought?"

In answer, Father Ignazio gave a melancholy, sonorous sniff. "It's a question of politics. The previous mayor was unwilling. He didn't see the need for a doctor on the island. Now the town council has changed—I'm on it, and the schoolmaster Vella—and Arcangelo is mayor now, and we get things done."

"Who was the previous mayor?"

"Il Conte d'Isantu," said the priest.

"This count everyone is waiting for."

"Yes, *dottore*. Of course, officially, he's no count any longer. But since the Unification the islanders—damned fools—have voted one d'Isantu or another in as mayor at every election. Except this time— God and Sant'Agata know why!"

"This *conte* has been mayor for years, and he did not see the need for a doctor? How many are the inhabitants?"

Father Ignazio said that he supposed about a thousand, though as far as he knew no census had ever been made. But here, the priest turned abruptly to the matter of Amedeo's lodgings. "You are to stay in the house of the schoolmaster Professor Vella and his wife, Pina," he said. "They must be somewhere about here—let me fetch them."

The priest got up from the table and returned some minutes later with the schoolmaster and his wife. *Il professore* was a man approaching middle age, who wore his hair greased sideways. He clapped Amedeo on the shoulder and said, "Ah, good, good, an educated man at last," which made the priest sniff. *Il professore* took possession of Amedeo, and began to recount to him choice facts from the island's history: "invaded by *eight* separate powers, imagine!" "and no church until 1500." At about three o'clock, drunk beyond talking, he toppled sideways from his chair.

The schoolmaster was escorted home. Pina, his wife, now came out of the shadows. *Il professore* had told Amedeo, confusedly, that the islanders were part-Norman part-Arab part-Byzantine part-Greek part-Phoenician part-Spanish part-Roman, and this was evident in Pina, who had black hair like ropes and eyes of a surprising opal color. She was drawn into the circle and exhorted to tell what the islanders called "the real story of Castellamare." This she did, in a voice hesitant but strong: a story of invaders and exiles, eruptions of liquid fire and ghostly weeping, mourning voices and caves full of the click of white bones—a story so dazzling that Amedeo would struggle to remember it properly when he woke the next day, and forever afterward believed that he had forgotten the most important part of it, that no telling could be quite as good as Pina Vella's.

Her story done, Pina excused herself: She must check her husband had got home safely; perhaps she would be back for the end of the festival, and certainly for the scattering of the flowers.

"Pina's a clever woman," said the priest, watching her go. "I baptized her, taught her her catechism. Too educated for this island, and for her husband—damned pity—but I can't persuade *il professore* to give up his job and let her take it. She'd do much better than he does, for the man's a terrible bore."

The old man Rizzu, who had reappeared for Pina's story, crowed again in delight. "Father Ignazio loves scandal," he said. "He's almost always causing it. He's the most unconventional priest we've had."

The priest seemed gratified at this, and swallowed his glass of *arancello* at one gulp.

A disturbance began to send its waves through the crowd at this moment—a kind of collective thrill. *"Il conte,"* said Rizzu. "Here he is at last."

"Ah," said Father Ignazio. "Another man for whom I have very little patience. Excuse me, *dottore*—I must make my escape."

Il conte, an ample man in a velvet jacket, came in sight beneath the statue of the saint. Amedeo was disconcerted at the way he worked the crowd, drawing attention and favor. Some of the islanders bowed and shook his hand; others brought forward gifts—a plate of aubergines, a bottle of wine, a live chicken in a wooden cage—which the count accepted before depositing them in the hands of his retinue. The scene did not seem to startle anyone else—though Amedeo noted that not everybody approached the count, or extended their hands in greeting.

The count, at last, came to rest before them. The priest had fled; Rizzu bobbed and bowed at one side of the table. Amedeo, gathering that it was expected, got to his feet, too.

The count said, "You, I understand, are the new doctor. I am Andrea d'Isantu, *conte*."

Amedeo made a hasty introduction of himself. *"Piacere,"* said the count, without pleasure. "This is my wife, Carmela."

A young woman with a bored aspect came out of the crowd. Her black hair was curled; she wore a hat with an upright feather of the style fashionable in Paris and London, at odds with the decades-old Sunday best of the other islanders. "Carmela," said the count, waving a hand in the woman's direction. "Bring coffee and spirits. Bring wine. Something small to eat, a pastry or an *arancino*."

Having spoken these words, the count drew out a chair, deposited himself in it, and fell into a calculated, brooding silence. "So," he said at last. "When did you arrive? Who met you at the quay?"

"About nine o'clock," said Amedeo. "And no one met me—

I made my own way. But I've been introduced to Signor Arcangelo, and one or two of the town council—Professor Vella and Father Ignazio."

"You're a city man, aren't you? A northern man? And what are you doing on this rock at the edge of the civilized world? Fleeing something, I suppose." The count gave a great bark of laughter.

Amedeo did not know how to answer this, except to say that he had been seeking a post as a *medico condotto* the whole length of the country, and had found one here.

"Well, I hope you'll make a living. Where do they come from, your family? Esposito—that's an odd sort of name."

"I have no family, except a foster father," said the doctor. He spoke clearly, for the fact did not usually shame him, though under the count's interrogation and the continuing heat of the piazza he had begun to sweat a little. He ran a finger around the stiff collar of his shirt.

"A man with no family?" said the count. "A man out of nowhere— an orphan?"

"I was brought up in the care of the Ospedale degli Innocenti in Firenze, a foundling hospital. One of the best," pride compelled him to add.

"Ah—I thought so by the name. Esposito. Abandoned."

Carmela reappeared, Rizzu and his brother in her wake, bearing trays with gold-rimmed cups, a saucer with a fantail of pastries and an unopened bottle of *arancello*. "The very best," Rizzu murmured, hovering about the count's chair.

"Carmela, pour the liquor." Again, the count did not look at his wife. She merely nodded, served the spirits to her husband, then seated herself at a little distance, with respectfully folded hands.

"We've ice cream and proper liquors at the villa, shipped in from Palermo." The count gave a mock sigh. "You'll find us a primitive people otherwise, I'm afraid, *dottore*. No proper electric light, no libraries. The sea air rots the books. An illiterate people, too—there's only myself who can read, and the priest, and the schoolmaster, and the grocer Arcangelo in his way. And Carmela, I suppose, though one never thinks of her as *literate*, somehow, with her fashion periodicals and French novels. Ha! I hope that foundling hospital brought you up with simple tastes, for this island would be a trial to any civilized man."

"The main mark of a civilized society," said Amedeo, who had only just formed the opinion, "I believe, is the employment of a doctor."

At this the beautiful Carmela—to Amedeo's consternation—let out a great shout of laughter. The count stirred his coffee and ripped apart a pastry. He attacked it with great bites, swallowed, wiped the crumbs from his mouth. "The employment of a doctor has never been prudent on this island," he said. "The new mayor and the council have got that all wrong. It's an expense we can't afford. I certainly hope you'll make a living here, but times are difficult and you may not last the year, I'm sorry to say."

A silence descended on the table. Amedeo met the eyes of Carmela, and was discomposed. She leaned forward a little. "You must join us at the villa for dinner," she said, her face lit with suppressed mischief. "You and my husband will find a good deal to say to each other."

"That's certainly kind of you, but I'll have very little time to spare once I take up my duties."

"Well, well—in that case, perhaps you'll survive," said the count. "At least you've brought no wife with you, or children—and with only yourself to maintain, and no time for social diversions, perhaps you'll do well enough, in a scraping, bachelor sort of way. It'd be no life for me, but perhaps you can manage it. How convenient to be a foundling, a man without wife or children, a man utterly unencumbered in the world!" Here he glanced at Carmela, who was still much amused.

"What about you, *signor il conte*?" said Amedeo. "Do you and *la contessa* have very many children?" For some instinct told him they were childless, and he hoped, unkindly, to needle.

The count, though, merely shook his head. "My wife is barren." Carmela bowed her head, and Amedeo could see the color spread across her neck at being publicly shamed in this way. By one stroke, the count had defeated her and silenced the doctor, and he began now to take his leave. He seized a final pastry, upended the last of his coffee into his mouth, and held out his hand again to Amedeo. "I hope you'll make a living here," he said.

"I certainly intend to," said Amedeo.

As *il conte* receded into the crush of islanders, Amedeo heard a melancholy sniff and, turning, found Father Ignazio at his shoulder. "There," he said. "You've survived your first encounter with *il conte*. From now on, everything is an improvement."

"I feel a little sorry for Carmela," said Amedeo.

"Yes," said Father Ignazio. "We all feel a little sorry for her."

DAWN CAME EARLIER THAN EXPECTED, with a gray brightening, and still the festival continued. Amedeo, too drunk to trust his feet and wishing very much to go to bed, sat between the priest and Rizzu while the whirling music grew ever more frenzied, the dancing ever more disordered. The card players were immersed in a round of *scopa* that seemed to have gone on for hours. Each time a winning player swept his cards from the table, the yells grew more raucous, the insults more good-naturedly extravagant. At the last round, Rizzu's tiny brother had leapt from his seat in triumph, holding his cards aloft, overturning a jug of *limoncello*. Meanwhile, among the dancers, a young man in the waistcoat and black jacket of a peasant was making a series of perilous leaps around the circle. Then all at once the dancers broke apart, the cards were gathered, and there was a great commotion in the square. "Damn — it's time for the flowers already!" said Father Ignazio, and rose from his chair. "As always I forget!" Weaving with surprising agility in and out of the crowd, he stopped before the statue of the saint. A group of young men hoisted it into the air. On all sides, shutters were banging open.

"What are they doing?" said Amedeo — but Rizzu, too, was gone. Amedeo found himself alone on the terrace of the bar.

The priest intoned a prayer. Then all at once a great unfurling took place, like some natural phenomenon, a wondrous rain of petals. From every upper window, women hurled basketfuls of oleander and bougainvillea, plumbago and trumpet honeysuckle, until the air was full of flowers. Children screamed and cavorted; the *organetti* and guitars took up a hymn; the saint's statue was borne swaying above the crowd; and in the confusion the flowers continued to whirl, thickening the air.

Out of nowhere, a thought came to him of the fine photograph it would make. He searched his suitcase and assembled the folding camera. He set it on the table and made his first picture, a grainy, underexposed shot of the bar, the piazza, the rain of flowers.

He developed the image weeks later, in the makeshift darkroom he established in the back of his closet at the schoolmaster's house (a useful hiding place, too, from the lectures of *il professore*). The flowers were just white streaks against gray, but nevertheless the clarity of the image startled him, a beautiful thing. It was the first photograph he had ever taken. Among the faces of the crowd he could make out the strangers of that night who were to become the daily figures of his life: Rizzu and his brother arm in arm before the bar, its lights blazing like caught stars; Father Ignazio beneath the statue; the dark shadow of *il conte*; Pina Vella at an upstairs window; and—aloof at the edge of the crowd—the beautiful Carmela.

Later, he would come to see this photograph as portentous, for within it, like the stories hidden in Rita Fiducci's pack of cards, were concealed the signs of his whole life to come.

BEYOND THE ISLAND'S SHORES, the world that year of 1914 was undergoing a long, slow heave toward war. Amedeo didn't realize it at first. The news of the assassination of the archduke in Sarajevo, which happened a few hours after that miraculous rain of flowers, took thirteen days to reach Castellamare—and meanwhile the island was so bright and alive that it seemed to him now the only real world. Yet it could not be denied that Amedeo was a foreigner here. As out of place as the giant in one of his tales, he was so tall that he was concussed several times merely going in and out of his patients' houses. The beds on the island were too short for a man his size; they had been made for the peasants of the nineteenth century, and he was obliged to push two of them together and sleep sideways until a special one could be built. (Years later, a special coffin would also have to be made to accommodate his height of almost seven feet—for he would remain, to the last, the very tallest man on Castellamare.) So he did not immediately fit, but still he felt himself, in some obscure, important way, to belong. For instance, when he woke at noon the day after the festival of Sant'Agata, he found that someone had carried his forgotten trunk of medical instruments up the hill and deposited it outside his door. Father Ignazio, from the first morning, sought him out to discuss the news from the continent—"You're a thinking man, Esposito, you'll have opinions." The elderly Rizzu brothers waylaid him on his morning rounds and plied him with coffee and rice balls. Within a month, his opinion was sought by the widows of the Committee of Sant'Agata (though he was not a religious man, and had scandalized them the first Sunday by not attending Mass) about the particular colors of thread to be ordered for a new banner dedicated to the saint. After he successfully extracted a sea urchin's spines from the foot of the fisherman Pierino, the Fishermen's Guild invited him to the *tonnara* for the ceremonial presentation of a tuna.

And there were a thousand petty town battles on which one must take sides (for already he had been persuaded onto the town council in an advisory capacity); there were several cases of typhus; eight babies due or imminent. When Italy entered the war, he was on his way to inspect the swamp to see whether it could be drained in order to reduce the risk of malaria, and somehow the swamp and the malaria seemed of more import than the declaration of war, this war here on Castellamare against pestilence and stagnant water a thing more worth fighting. The island seemed a separate country to him, not a part of the Italy in which he had passed his solitary youth.

On Sunday afternoons Father Ignazio taught him to swim, plunging ahead of him into the waves in a black woolen bathing suit. On the terrace of *il professore*'s house each evening, once the schoolmaster had fallen drunkenly asleep, Pina Vella told him every story belonging to the island.

"A small place like this is an oppression," warned Father Ignazio. "You don't feel it yet, but you'll come to feel it. Everyone who visits without having been born here thinks it delightfully rustic. I thought so, too, myself. But anyone born on Castellamare will fight by any means possible to get off the island, and one day you'll be the same. It hit me about the tenth year."

But Amedeo, who had always felt himself to be weightless, at risk of floating off from the earth altogether, now welcomed the solid heft of the place, the narrowness of its borders. He was amused at the way his patients knew all his business an hour before he did; he was unperturbed when the widows watched him from the wooden chairs outside their houses with narrowed, appraising eyes; he found comfort in the fact that it was possible, from the window of any of his patients' houses, to look upon the same blue line of the sea. The island was five miles long, and in his daily rounds he walked all over the face of it. He discovered the hollows where wild goats slept at noon, and disturbed the nests of lizards in the ruined houses outside town, so that they ran like water up the walls. Sitting outside old Rizzu's bar, he made a map of the island on a scrap of blotting paper, the old man nodding approvingly, pointing out flaws.

At the beginning of the spring, he sent a letter to his foster father with an invitation to drink *limoncello* with him at the House at the Edge of Night—for there really was a terrace with bougainvillea, he wrote eagerly, exactly as the elderly doctor had foretold.

But when summer came again, he did not sit with his foster father under the cool vines. Instead, a telegram ordered him away to the north.

IV

HE WAS SENT TO THE TRENCHES AT TRENTINO.

Shorn away from the island, two things became vital to him: the photograph of Sant'Agata's Day and his book of stories. Some of his fellow medical officers had brought their folding cameras with them, against regulations. He had left his own on the island, knowing there would be nothing he wanted to record. All he wanted was the existing picture, with which he would navigate his way home. He pinned it to the inside of his cap, to protect it from the mud. Always it was mud, and when it wasn't mud, ice, and when it wasn't ice, water, and when it wasn't water, gas and fog. It seemed a world composed of elements, where men were divided into their component pieces, men frothed, men screamed. At the surgical school of Santa Maria Nuova, he had received no training in how to put men back together.

In the inside pocket of his battledress, he kept his book of stories. The gold fleur-de-lis on the cover wore away; the leather became dull. But stories, he found, like the photograph, bore witness to the truth that there was another world than this. Chiefly, his duty was to remind his patients of this fact when nothing else could be done. To a shell-shocked captain in a mud-splattered field hospital, or a gassed infantry officer recovering his sight, he could merely ask about the man's home, his infancy, his family, and a spark would burn behind the eyes of his patient, a change would come upon him: Hesitantly, words would emerge, the patient's particular story unfurling by degrees, filling the space between them, a shared light against the dark.

He did not record these stories. He did not want to remember them. But sometimes no words came from the patient's mouth, and then he would tell his own stories instead, fanciful stories from his book of tales, stories that had evolved over centuries in the mouths of the poor, calculated to take one far from the gray world: the story of the girl who became a tree, became a bird; the story of the two brothers who met and did not know each other; the story of the tale-telling parrot. Across the whole region, he became known as "the story-collecting doctor of the field hospital in Treviso."

Occasionally, he told his patients about the island. Always the tale that burned in his own mind was the account he told himself of surviving this war and getting back to Castellamare. By the time it was over, Castellamare had become the only place he still believed in. Everything else had fallen behind the gray veil the war had interposed.

HE HAD A GREAT wish to see his foster father. As the war progressed and regressed, subjects had emerged that could no longer be spoken of between them, great gulfs in their experience that threatened to make them enemies. "Perhaps because you are a foundling," the elderly doctor had written, "you lack the natural patriotic feeling of your comrades, and this war is more difficult for you to bear."

"Perhaps because I am a foundling," wrote Amedeo, "I see its falsities more clearly."

He had received no letters from the elderly doctor for more than a year. Now, on the preprinted army postcards he wrote simply, "Love, Amedeo." The war ended, and still he was detained. There were troops with influenza, villagers with influenza. More variations of that same dying he had witnessed in the trenches: dying of the young and the healthy as well as the old and the weak, with swollen surprised faces and white-filmed eyes. It was 1919 by the time he got free, and he was forty-four years old. Riding the crowded train south to Florence, through villages empty and shuttered, he was seized with a feeling of waste so profound he could taste it, like a rot in his mouth.

Still, he would see his foster father, he would return to Castellamare, and life would begin again in some form or another.

He went directly to his foster father's house. A sticklike woman opened the door at his knocking, not the housekeeper he remembered. "Esposito?" she said. "The old doctor, you mean? He's dead. He was carried away last winter. Influenza."

His foster father's real relatives had already descended from Rome and carried off all his things. The woman returned to Amedeo only his bundle of army postcards.

She allowed him to walk through the rooms of the house. Gone were the snakes in jars, the masks, the whale brushes over the stairs. Only a few wires and squares of discolored wallpaper remained where the exhibits had once been suspended. "We've all lost people, you know," she said, slightly scoldingly, when Amedeo wept.

IN THIS GREAT DISORDER of mind he returned to Castellamare. It seemed that his previous journey, in the Neapolitan steamer, had taken place in a different life, and the war was the only real thing that he had lived: He had never dwelt with his foster father at the house like a museum, never been licensed as a *medico condotto*, never been apprenticed to the watchmaker or the baker or the printer, never been a foundling, never been born.

But Castellamare. He had lived that. The memory of Castellamare endured.

Father Ignazio had written to him when the war ended. "Things go very badly here," he had said. "Many of the young men are gone—at least twenty-seven at my count—and others still missing, and others threaten to leave in the general fever for America that now seems to be sweeping the island. The war has made this place more cramped, a good deal hungrier. You will find us much reduced."

Amedeo discovered from the priest's letter that Rizzu's brother was gone, departed for America. The bar was shut up, for no one wanted the place. Professor Vella the schoolmaster had been killed. Two of

Rizzu's grandsons had been killed. Only the household of *il conte*, who had been invalided out of Trentino in 1915 with a leg wound, was unaltered. Carmela, wrote the priest, had fallen out with her husband and left for the mainland shortly after his return, but she had been retrieved. Some matter of a lover. ("Be careful of Carmela," Pina would warn later. "This war has made her restless.")

In spite of Father Ignazio's letter, Amedeo had not expected to see the town itself so diminished. He arrived during the siesta hour, and the houses on the main street were shuttered. But some, he saw, were closed up entirely, their doors and windows boarded. Objects were abandoned outside them: a chair with a missing seat, a dry basil plant in a cracked pot. Two children played in the dust. Dimly he recognized them, children he had delivered, twins belonging to the Mazzu family. "Maddalena," he called. "Agato."

They came, tentatively. "Where is the priest?" he said, for a great wish had come over him to see his old friend again, to check that Ignazio at least was not altered. The children did not know.

Amedeo walked the route he had trodden his first night on the island. The House at the Edge of Night was shut up as the priest had written, its veranda sagging under the untended vines, its front steps already rife with weeds.

HE TOOK AGAIN HIS old room in Pina's house. He tacked the photograph of the island to the stone wall inside the closet. Pina was the only person on the island who seemed to walk straighter and taller since the war. After her husband's death, she had been appointed the schoolmistress. Late at night, the two of them sat up with Father Ignazio, around a bottle of spirits, making plans for the rescuing of the island from its abandonment. They needed to modernize. They needed a ferry service, a two-room hospital. They needed a second classroom for the school, a system of funeral insurance for the elderly. Il Conte d'Isantu had been elected mayor again, complained the priest, and nothing now changed on the island. D'Isantu was always on the mainland, pursuing his own advancement in some obscure way with friends in Catania, spending long months at his Palermitan estate, when here things needed to be done. The bar rotted, the missing did not return, and no one played *scopa* in the square or danced to the music of the *organetto*.

When Amedeo saw the beautiful Carmela again, some weeks later, it was reassuring to find her so unaltered. Waylaying him on the sea road, where she had been walking in her Sunday clothes, under a parasol, she made a pouting display of her displeasure. "*Dottore*, you've never come to pay us a formal visit," she said. "And they say you've been back a month. Things have been dull here, and I don't mind telling you. No clothes, no decent food. No visitors, during the influenza. But I'm glad you're back safely—and probably a war hero, too, unlike my husband."

Amedeo, who had not been aware that she cared one way or the other about his safety, sought about for a reply.

She invited him to go with her to look at the caves, which were a historical oddity he had never seen before the war. Still in the same mood of bemused curiosity, he consented. As soon as they were in the shelter of the damp dark, she began to kiss him, to caress him.

Reeling, Amedeo supposed that she meant to appoint him her lover as Pina had warned.

"Don't worry about my husband," Carmela murmured in his ear. "I've never loved him, and the whole island knows he's a tyrant and a fool."

Amedeo got free of her and excused himself, mumbling about the feverish Mazzu children and the elderly widower Donato he had promised to visit before noon.

For a fortnight she kept up her pursuit, intercepting him on his rounds in silent corners of the island. On the fifteenth day, he acquiesced and they made love on the cold stones of the cave. Why, he did not know, but she was insistent, and afterward he found that he did not, in fact, very much regret it. It was difficult to feel anything in particular.

Dressing in the dark, stumbling about, something clicked under his feet. Kneeling, he unearthed a cache of whitened bones.

"Don't be alarmed," said Carmela, with a laugh. "They've been here two thousand years. Did you think the caves full of white skulls were only a charming folk story? Go further in and you'll see them. The fishermen won't enter this cave, for fear of curses."

He stumbled away instead, into the light. They clawed the sand out of their clothes and hair; he fetched her parasol. Buttoning her underclothes, fastening the little waist of her jacket—which, despite her complaints about the lack of new clothes, still smelled of dye from the tailor—she was elegant once again. She took out a silver mirror and by the cave's dim light repinned her hair. She had an ability to compose herself that he found both alluring and frightening. He was damp with perspiration, disheveled, giddy; she had not even broken a sweat. She replaced her hat, adjusted the angle, and regarded him calmly from behind its visor of dotted tulle as though they were strangers again, all propriety restored. "Dottor Esposito, I've detained you," she said, "and you'll be late for your next patient."

On the way back up to the road, she showed him a second cave, in which there were not bones but hundreds of luminous white stones. These he recognized, for the island's fishermen nailed them to their ships as talismans. "We'll meet in this one next time," she said, "if you like it better."

They returned to the town separately, Carmela by the main road, he by paths and alleys, getting burrs stuck in his good wool trousers. Pina looked at him strangely when he entered the house, but had nothing to say.

AFTER THAT, CARMELA BEGAN to summon him to the caves once or twice a week, and then, when *il conte* was absent, to the villa. Amedeo found himself making a circle of the town on these nights, first talking to everyone, maintaining the pretense in his own mind that he was at liberty to choose whether or not to answer Carmela's summonses. The truth was he was not free; he never refused. But on such nights, his lengthy detours around town meant that he approached the villa only long after nightfall, when he could be certain that he would not be observed. As he made his journey, creeping up the avenue of palm trees, Carmela would appear in the window with a lamp. She would admit him silently to her room with its mock-baroque cherubs, its ceiling of peeling clouds, so as not to alert the servants to his presence. The count was thinking of installing electricity, she told him. For now their encounters took place in a dim light of pink and amber. Carmela dictated the terms of all their meetings, and always sent him away before dawn.

Once, he raised again the matter of her husband. "My husband is a fool," said Carmela. "I've been unfaithful before, you know. I even left for the mainland, but he got me back here. He said if I had another affair it would be the death of him. Well, good. I hope it is."

Her levity frightened him. "But, really, Carmela—"

"Don't worry about him finding out. He doesn't see anything. He hasn't looked at me in months. He's too busy being an important political man, and I'm glad to be rid of him. I'm not sure he spends his nights alone, either. No, it suits us both very well. He only found out about my last affair because I told him. Anyway, Amedeo, you'll hear him coming."

For the count had recently bought a motorcar, the island's first (and destined, in fact, to remain the island's solitary motorcar for thirty years). He'd had it shipped from Palermo, and unloaded at the little quay by ropes, with much gesticulating and shouting. Now he drove it about the island's dust tracks and stony roads, and from the driver's seat, sweating in his leather cap and goggles, he inspected the work of his tenants in the fields. The old men made the sign of the cross when *il conte* approached in his great metal box with its formidable coughs and growls.

Once, as Amedeo left Carmela's house at dawn and started out along the avenue, he heard around the bend the motorcar's gruff roar. With a painful clenching of the gut he threw himself into the grass, watching the motorcar churn the dust and illuminate the trunks of the trees as it passed by.

He seemed to be living a life not of his own devising in those days, an odd, dreamlike existence.

SANT'AGATA'S DAY THAT YEAR, too, was altered.

From dawn the heat was of a feverish, seething quality. The morning Mass, in a church so crowded not even a fly could pass between the shoulders of the islanders, was unbroken by a sigh of wind. Noon brought shimmering light and short shadows. Tradition dictated that the statue of Sant'Agata must be borne around every inlet and curve of the island's coast: along the edge of the fields belonging to the Conte d'Isantu, over the rocky crenellations at the island's head, through the bare villages of its southern coast, in and out of the sea caves (here at least the dark was cooler), and then into the port, where the statue was greeted with incense and a storm of flowers. But this year there were no young fishermen to carry the statue, and so the old men shouldered the burden. The statue weighed half a ton. On the procession around the coast the aged fishermen stumbled; wreathed in tidemarks of sweat, they had to be fortified with sips of wine and wiped with cold cloths. Coming to the end of their journey, the fishermen plunged with relief into the waters of the bay, but found that the surf was barely cool enough to satisfy them; it was listless, tepid, except around the rocks, where it seemed to froth and boil.

The ships were blessed, the year's three new babies baptized, and the islanders made the slow journey back up the hill. As the fishermen labored on the stony road, the sun at last descended. The islanders assembled in the piazza, relieved by the dark.

Old Mazzu dragged out his skinniest donkey to be auctioned, guitars were tuned and *organetti* dusted, and the widows emerged from Gesuina's kitchen, where they had been shut up since dawn, bearing plates of grilled anchovies and stuffed *zucchine*. But the House at the Edge of Night remained in darkness. There were no games of *scopa* on the terrace this year; no dancing; no drinking of *arancello*. The islanders were sober and in bed before dawn.

THAT AUTUMN, AMEDEO DECIDED to buy the House at the Edge of Night. He could no longer bear to see it standing empty, and now that the island was half emptied of its inhabitants, houses were worth less than salt. Even a *medico condotto* could afford one.

A light had gone out of Rizzu since his brother's departure. "That house is crumbling," he said. "It won't be any good to you. It's a bad-luck sort of a place." In the end, Amedeo could only persuade him to accept five hundred *lire* and a chicken for it, and he had to barter the price up.

Amedeo recorded the purchase in his red notebook and the date, the twenty-fourth of September, 1919. Now he had a home, and he hoped he could catch hold of the life he had been about to seize before the war interrupted. The house was indeed crumbling. He installed himself in the upstairs rooms and began to sand the walls and replace the sagging doors. He began collecting as his foster father had done. He gathered around him stories, artifacts, objects belonging to the island. Roman potsherds and coins, which the farmers threw away daily, he salvaged and bore carefully to the House at the Edge of Night. On the walls he hung tiles decorated in fantastic colors, patterned with sunflowers, fleurs-de-lis, the faces of lords and ladies. The images, some hundreds of years old, were painted in a hasty, swirling style that gave them the air of having only just dried. The artist Vincenzo had many ancestors who had painted more tiles than anyone ever needed, and Vincenzo dug them out of his cellar and gave them to Amedeo quite willingly—for the tourists had stopped buying them on his trips to the mainland, he said, and he was glad to be rid of them.

From the catacombs by the sea Amedeo brought back pocketfuls of white luminous stones, and lined them up along all the upstairs windowsills. Meanwhile, on the hall table, little trinkets belonging to

Sant'Agata accumulated, for these were often the currency in which
he was paid for the delivery of a baby or the setting of a broken arm,
by those of his patients whose treatment was not paid for by the mu-
nicipality. He gathered miniatures of the saint, holy water bottles, and
one statue in which Sant'Agata tore open her chest to reveal a heart
of red-daubed wood. For this statue, he felt both affection and fear.
He had never found comfort in religion.

But he seemed at last to have begun to grasp, to inhabit a real existence. He plunged into the sea each morning before making his
rounds—earning the ridicule of the fishermen, for no grown man of
Castellamare would have swum in the water like that, for amusement, at the very edge of autumn, as though he were drunk! Climbing the hill, salt prickling in the folds of his skin, he would pause to
pick up a white stone or a Roman potsherd to carry back to the House
at the Edge of Night. In addition to collecting, Amedeo kept records
of everything he purchased, as well as each improvement he made to
the house. The downstairs rooms were still damp and uninhabitable,
the upstairs bedrooms dark, their furniture mantled with dust sheets.
It was slow work at first. He was obliged to sleep under a tarpaulin on
stormy nights, and on these occasions he was something close to
happy.

During these first weeks of autumn, he began to make a system-
atic study of the island's stories, for with the general altered state of
the world, he had started to worry that the stories would be lost. It was
not only Amedeo who was preoccupied with the disappearance of
things. Stories poured forth, and all he had to do was go where they
could be heard, to the places his daily rounds naturally took him: the
dim upstairs rooms where widows pored over their rosary beads; the
dusty sheds of the fishermen; and the abandoned houses, rocky and
biblical, at the edge of the town that were haunted by the island's
children. Stories, it seemed, were to be found in dark places. Returning from these places, he transcribed the tales into his book.

He installed his old folding camera in the one dry room, the little
junk room under the eaves, full of old packing cases that had held,

according to their labels, Modiano cigarettes and Campari liquor. In front of it he hung a red curtain, as though the room were a photographic studio. In his mind the House at the Edge of Night was a great tall museum like his foster father's house, full of books and curiosities, and although he had no wife, no children, still he longed to photograph the descendants, numerous as stars, whose pictures would one day adorn the hallway and hang along the stairs.

During that hot autumn after the festival, he began to feel less satisfied with his association with Carmela. He had formed the habit of deferring to the fearsome Sant'Agata statue as he went in or out of the house, particularly if called to attend to a birth or a death, for, as irreligious as he was, he felt now that he would gladly accept good fortune wherever he might encounter it. It was the same desperation, the same grasping after life, that had led him to acquiesce to Carmela and to purchase the house—a feeling that his life must change. And yet sometimes the statue, on nights when his rounds had taken him to the lit window of Carmela's villa, seemed to greet him with sad, reproachful eyes. He sought a wife and a family, the statue seemed to scold him. And as yet what did he possess but this faltering connection with Carmela, which often, like the watery soup he drank on days when his patients had not paid him, left him hungrier than before?

In penance, he sought out his old friends—the priest, the schoolmistress, the men of the town council—and threw himself with fervor into the task of repairing the house.

One evening, sipping the syrupy remnants from one of the old Campari bottles on the overgrown terrace, Pina Vella told him the story of the House at the Edge of Night. "It's the second-oldest building on the island," she said. "The old people consider it unlucky. It was the last place where the famous curse of weeping still remained, all those centuries ago. The islanders tried to pull the house down. But the walls were too thick—they couldn't do it. It's survived four earthquakes and a landslide besides. It's won a kind of respect."

"Then how can it be unlucky?" said Amedeo.

"You can look at it in two ways," said Pina. "To survive such things a house must either be blessed by Sant'Agata or cursed by the devil—one of the two. That's what they say."

As for the old name "Casa al Bordo della Notte," she did not know where that came from. "Some of the old people think they can remember an Alberto Delanotte living here," said Pina.

"So it could be that the original name was Casa di Alberto Delanotte." Amedeo was a little discouraged by this unpoetic truth.

"But I prefer to think of the name as meaning 'at the edge of night,'" said Pina. "Because it *is*, if you look in both directions from here."

Amedeo looked. Illuminating the terrace was a single streetlamp, around which mosquitoes circled and inside whose panes lizards basked, sending their scuttling shadows across the tiles. Beyond it were the reassuring lights of the town, and in the distance the coast of Sicily, framing the island on either side, so that Castellamare could have been a peninsula, an outcrop of some greater mass. Look in the other direction, though, and all was sea and night, a vista of emptiness unbroken as far as North Africa. "It's an odd place to put a bar," said Amedeo.

"It was always a bar," said Pina. "The first count wouldn't let them have a bar at the center of the town, for fear of drunkenness and gambling. Before the Rizzus took the business over, the house was standing empty for years. Some of the old people will never cross the threshold. And there *is* some bad luck that seems to cling to the place. Look at Rizzu's brother. Two sons dead in as many years. You can see why people call the house cursed."

"It's this damned war that has been the curse," said Amedeo. "Not an old bar."

Pina said, quietly, "True."

Amedeo wondered if she was thinking of her husband. But Pina allowed herself to reflect only for a minute, twisting her cable of black hair in one hand, and then, straightening herself, she said, "Anyway, I must get home."

It had always been for *il professore* that she had had to get home. Amedeo wondered if she felt her solitude as he did, as she moved alone through the rooms of her old house by the church. On both sides her neighbors had immigrated to America. Even her beauty was of a handsome, far-off kind, as forbidding as a Greek statue. Perhaps this was why no suitor had approached her since Professor Vella's death. Her elderly father had been the island's schoolmaster at the turn of the century, Amedeo knew — Professor Vella had married Pina on the old man's death, inheriting both girl and schoolroom. Now she had no remaining family on the island except the fisherman Pierino, who was a sort of distant cousin.

Afterward, draining alone the dregs of red liquor, he wished that he had unburdened himself to her a little, for Pina was always so composed, a woman stronger than the walls of the old house. He wished that he had told her how the war had opened a grayness inside him, a grayness that he had sought to fill with the affair with *il conte*'s wife, with the purchase of the crumbling house, but which still yawned and gaped on nights like this. Fitting that he now inhabited the House at the Edge of Night, for his own spirit these days could be precisely divided — half of it light and fathomable, half as dark and deep as the ocean.

ONE NIGHT IN LATE OCTOBER, his friend Father Ignazio intercepted him outside the church. "Come and drink a coffee with me, *dottore*," he said.

Amedeo was on his way to examine the infected eye of the Mazzus' goat (for he was treated indiscriminately by the islanders as both physician and veterinarian). But the priest's words were an order, not an invitation, and so he followed his friend under the austere arch of the priest's house, and into its courtyard, a dark place green with the scent of oleander bushes, a courtyard that never seemed to get warm.

Father Ignazio poured coffee, arranged cups and saucers on the little rusting table, and addressed Amedeo sternly. "It's time there was a wedding on this poor island," he said. "That's what I want to discuss with you."

Discomposed, Amedeo sat, stirring his coffee. "You and Pina," said the priest. "I may as well come out and say it directly. The girl's got a great affection for you—anyone can see it. And look at you, a bachelor of nearly forty!"

Amedeo was forty-four, but did not say so. "I'd like to see her married again," said the priest. "She's lonely, especially since you left her house to go and knock about in that old Casa al Bordo della Notte."

Amedeo, uncertain how to reply, said at last, "I still see Pina very often."

"Yes, but why not see her every day? As man and wife. Amedeo, you'd be a good husband for Pina. You wouldn't nag at her to give up thinking and reading, as less enlightened men would. She'd be willing to marry you, I'll bet ten thousand *lire*—though I can't say for certain that she loves you. But she'll come to, Amedeo. Her husband has been dead three years. It was a poor match to start with, made because of some family connection over a house and a lemon grove, not out of love. She's an outstanding woman, Amedeo—loyal, resourceful. She's young enough to bear children, with some luck. Why do you hesitate?"

Amedeo drained his coffee and examined the grainy depths.

"Unless there's another woman," said the priest. "I can't deny I've heard some strange rumors, these last few months."

"No," said Amedeo. "There's no other woman."

"Then consider it at least. It grieves me to see the two of you moping about in your great crumbling houses, both alone."

Pina. He walked away dizzy with the strangeness of it.

That afternoon, he inspected the eye of the goat on the Mazzus' farm, receiving a sharp bite on the thumb for his pains. Mazzu always paid Amedeo in food, having no other currency, and he walked back to the town with his pockets stuffed with hazelnuts and white truffles from the Mazzus' olive grove. He checked a bad case of constipation on the Dacosta farm, and called in to inspect Rizzu's two smallest grandchildren, who were suffering from an itching complaint of the skin. He found them, still scabby, wrestling in a heap with an assortment of their brothers and sisters. He would be treating them all by Friday, no doubt. Always, children everywhere on this island. It gave him a pain in the chest, so that he could hardly look at them directly. Disinfecting the small, hot backs of the youngest Rizzus, comforting their tears at the sting of the iodine, he felt dizzy for a moment in the unseasonable heat, when really it was his own longing for a child that all at once overwhelmed him.

He went to Pina's house and walked in without knocking. Pina was at the stove, her hair pinned up, preparing a chicken. He waited, dry mouthed, attempting a polite smile. At last, he knelt at her feet (she had no living father or brother to ask for permission), and asked her to be his wife. "Or at least consider it," he said, his courage failing.

Pina, to his surprise, consented immediately and with tears in her eyes: "I don't need to consider; I already have my answer; oh, Amedeo!"

They agreed to be married at once. On the last day in November, Father Ignazio bound their hands before the statue of Sant'Agata and the whole island.

IT WAS PINA WHO was responsible for the first recorded photograph of Amedeo. A few days after the wedding, she ambushed him with the folding camera at the top of the stairs. "Stand still!" she cried. "Stand still! Let me capture you!" Amedeo, startled, posed a little self-consciously with one hand on his waist. Just back from his morning rounds, he had yet to put down his medical bag. He had with him also his book of stories—the widower Donato, whom he had treated that morning, had just finished recounting to him a tale about his aunt's visitations by the saint during the festival of 1893. In the photograph Amedeo seemed aflame with happiness, possessed by it, his whole being angled toward the woman behind the lens. For Pina, it turned out, possessed within her the depth of passion he had been lacking all this long while. He had not found it in Carmela. He had found it in the schoolmistress with a face like a Greek statue; it was here.

They had made no wedding journey, though in honor of his new bride he had set aside all work except emergencies for five days. After the wedding, Pina, with her small neat trunk of belongings, her crates of books, had followed him to the House at the Edge of Night, which was now beginning once more to be habitable. The house was fragrant with the purple scent of bougainvillea, its rooms sonorous with the noise of the sea. Happiness hung in the air, hummed inside the walls; now it seemed a thing that was attainable. That first night, Pina had climbed through the house, exploring every half-forgotten, dust-sheeted room, throwing open every window. Amedeo followed in her train, picking up the pins that fell from the rope of her black hair. Then, at the top of the house, suddenly mischievous, she removed her bridal crown of oleander and set the rest free. The glossy ropes of it filled the room with their perfume, and he found himself seizing them in great handfuls. They pursued each other through each room of the house. It seemed for the first time to be a place of joy again, as it had been before the war.

By some good fortune, there were no serious illnesses that week, and they passed it blissfully undisturbed. He was thankful that he had never brought Carmela to the House at the Edge of Night, that he had now broken all ties with her. He resolved to be a better man. And to his gratification he found that as his passion for Pina grew, during those wondrous days of makeshift honeymoon when they ate their dinner off old cracked saucers and out of coffee cups like fishermen at sea, and never opened the shutters until noon, and made love wherever they found themselves—on the newly sanded floorboards, on the dust-sheeted sofa in his study, on the straw mattresses in the spare bedrooms—during those days, the memory of Carmela became smaller, less significant, like something seen through a gray veil, belonging to another time, to his life before the war.

But Carmela had not been easy to break with. She had turned vindictive at the news of his engagement, had threatened to reveal their association to her husband unless Amedeo submitted to her advances one last time, and a last, and one more. Reluctantly he had continued to play the part of her lover, breaking the thing off painfully, gradually, rather than all at once as he wanted to do. He had last visited the caves by the sea—it caused him hot shame even to confess it to himself—on the eve of his wedding. Then, at last, in the darkness full of the spray of the churned autumn ocean, he had managed to break with Carmela for good. On his wedding night, Pina wondered why he sneezed so, in what damp place he could have caught such a cold.

Shortly after their wedding, Pina became pregnant. And in the joy of this news, the affair with Carmela was forgotten; it became something he regarded dispassionately, as though it had never happened to him at all. He did not want to consider it. For when he did, a dark fear possessed him that Carmela might at any moment take it into her head to tell her husband the truth. He gave thanks that the count was always absent in those months, and absorbed himself instead with Pina.

Had he felt some dim sense of foreboding at the news that Carmela, too, had given thanks at the shrine of Sant'Agata, for the conception of a child? He could not now remember. Everything in those days had been fogged by his love for Pina, and his own happiness. But by continuing to vacillate between the two of them—out of weakness, out of fear of scandal!—he had somehow got into this predicament. He had hoped that the affair with Carmela would go unnoticed on the island. Now he saw that it could become a thing of monstrous size, impossible to shake off, a thing that could pry his whole life apart.

V

BY NOON ON THE DAY OF PINA'S BABY'S BIRTH, IT WAS RUMORED across the whole island that the doctor had delivered two babies, one his wife's and the other his lover's. It was the greatest scandal ever to sweep Castellamare. It was also the most thrilling entertainment, and several people took the day off work especially to follow its development.

When Pina heard, she wept, turning her face to the wall. She refused at first even to nurse her child, so that Amedeo was obliged to carry the wailing baby from room to room. The count raged in the streets, making an exhibition of himself; the priest and the mayor had to be summoned to coax him out of the public square; and Carmela, despite the exhortations of her friends, her midwife, and her servants, sat up in bed and refused to retract her story. For the first time in her marriage, she had the upper hand over her husband, and she was not about to relinquish it. Her baby, she repeated, was Amedeo Esposito's. She and the doctor had been lovers for half a year, only ceasing their meetings the night before his wedding day. "If the baby belongs to my husband," she said, "why have we been married six years with no child, so long, in fact, that he accused me before the whole town of being barren?"

This, no one could answer—least of all Amedeo, who cursed himself for never considering the possibility that the difficulty had been *il conte's*.

In the circumstances, one path of action presented itself.

"I never met with her," he insisted (his desperation lent the words a certain credibility). "I never did any of those things she claims, as God and Sant'Agata are my witnesses!"

Pina would not be consoled. Carmela would not retract her story. In the House at the Edge of Night, all was disorder and weeping.

Amedeo was thankful when his duties allowed him to flee the house. The sound of his beloved Pina sobbing now permeated the walls at nights (he had been banished upstairs to sleep on the damp sofa, under the tarpaulin). Yet soon, during those first days of his son's life, he began to feel himself unwelcome not only in his own home but in certain corners of the island. When he went to the ancient Signora Dacosta's door to check her rheumatic knees, the old woman merely answered that she was "quite well, thank you, *dottore*," and closed it, clearly still limping. Gesuina, he noticed, slammed her shutters with unnecessary force whenever he crossed the piazza. The grocer Arcangelo, with whom he had sat on the town council since before the war, excused himself when Amedeo entered the shop and sulked in the back room until he was gone.

Meanwhile, the fishermen reported that the count's doctor friend had been summoned from the mainland. With bottles of wine and boxes of Palermitan marzipan, he came. The two of them could be heard late at night raising their voices on the terrace of the villa, the count drunkenly roaring, the rich doctor consoling. Carmela, apparently, was shut up in her room with the baby, and the count would not see her.

On the third day, the mainland doctor examined the baby and, after some consideration, declared his characteristics to match those of *signor il conte* in every way.

Amedeo knew that it was possible to draw blood from a child and from the suspected father, to ascertain their blood type and (somewhat unreliably) to test the paternity that way. The mainland doctor, clearly, did not read the latest medical periodicals. But in the light of this evidence, the count now underwent a violent reversal.

"She means to shame me," he raged to his friend. "I see it now.

The whole thing was calculated to shame me. She means to take my son from me, and make me the laughingstock of the island, by claiming an affair with this Esposito, this bastard doctor with holes in his shoes with whom she has hardly exchanged a word in her life! I won't stand for it. Bring me the child."

The baby was taken from Carmela's breast and brought wailing to his father. The count kissed him and made much of him, and after some thought chose for him the name Andrea, his own first name. "There," said the count (who was holding his son at arm's length because the boy was now frothing in an unappetizing, milky fashion). "Take him back to his mother. It's settled. The boy is mine."

The news spread around the island that the baby was the count's after all. There had never been any affair between the doctor and Carmela, and the whole thing was a slanderous lie on Carmela's part designed to discredit her husband.

But most of the islanders preferred the first story. Rizzu had come to life again in his wonder over the week's events. "It's a miracle of Sant'Agata," he told the priest. "Two babies, born on the same night! A miracle. The miracle we have waited and prayed for since the start of the war—longer—since the saint mercifully cured the legs of Signora Gesuina!"

Father Ignazio, who was pruning the oleander bushes in his yard with his soutane rolled up, merely raised an eyebrow.

"Twins—miraculous twins!" continued Rizzu in his rapture. "Twins born by different mothers on the same night, to the count's barren wife and to Pina, a woman far too old to bear a child."

"Pina is hardly more than thirty," said Father Ignazio. "And it's not a miracle for two babies to be born on the same night, merely a matter of statistics. It's never yet happened in my time on the island. It was bound to happen sooner or later. I've seen both children, and they don't look alike."

Something troubled Rizzu. "Look, *padre*, do you believe this tale about Amedeo and *il conte*'s wife carrying on with each other in the caves by the sea?"

"No," lied Father Ignazio, and inadvertently hacked a dozen buds from the oleander bush.

The next day, the doctor himself came to visit. Amedeo wept with his head bowed, and Father Ignazio found himself playing the uneasy role of comforter, when really it was Pina whose side he inclined to in this matter. "There," said Father Ignazio, thumping the doctor's shoulder. "There, now. You'll have to hold your head up, you know, Amedeo. When a rumor takes hold in a place this small, with nothing else to talk about, it can be the ruin of a man; it can drive you from the island, if you let it."

"It's Pina I mind about," said Amedeo. "It isn't what everyone else is saying, it's that Pina believes I did those things."

"Talk to her," said Father Ignazio. "Tell her the truth about it, one way or the other."

Amedeo raised his head. "*Padre*, the truth . . ."

But here Father Ignazio raised his hand. "No, no," he said. "I've never been your confessor. I know you aren't a religious man. I think it's better that you make your peace with Pina, and leave the rest of us in the dark about the matter. Don't add to her humiliation."

When Amedeo got home, Pina was sleeping, with one hand stretched above her head, exposing her nightdress and the brown curve of her right breast. Her eyelashes were wet; her rope of black hair, unwound, spread itself over the pillows. He could not now remember how he had loved Carmela—if, indeed, he had loved her. A great homesickness overcame him for the first time since he had set foot on the island.

But at last he had a son. He had not been allowed to hold the boy since that first morning. Now, he took the baby and bore him away to the top of the house. So tiny the boy was. His hands, his pink little face, his small barrel of a chest rising and falling.

He longed to offer the boy some gift, some token. And so, in a whisper, he offered the first thing that occurred to him: He told his boy the story of the island.

——

THE FIRST NAME GIVEN to the island was Kallithea, he told his son, by a group of Greek sailors in search of a homeland. The name could mean "most beautiful" or "auspiciously burning." Either was a possibility, for the island was volcanic; the sailors of Siracusa claimed to have seen it glow and shoot up flame. Now, it shone like a beacon and the travelers steered their ship by its light. As they made safe passage across the waters, the island's summit smoldered and went out.

The travelers landed and passed the night in a series of square caves cut out of the cliffs. The island was a place of black water and many stars. In the early hours, the moon came out and illuminated the sea, and the travelers were woken by a clear sound of weeping. It seemed to surround them, to come from the rocks of the island itself. Groping in the dark, they found hard white skulls and heard under their feet the click of bones. The caves were not caves but tombs. Clearly, something terrible had happened here.

The new islanders prospered, but for one thing: They were disturbed each night by the sound of weeping, which provoked in them troublesome dreams. Gradually, the situation became so unbearable that the islanders decided not to sleep at all. So the first settlers in their town of stone huts became a wakeful people. They gathered on nights full of flame and stars, and sang and shook tambourines to drown out the weeping. But whether it was the wailing voices or the isolation of this place with its black sea and many constellations, all their songs were melancholy. No one could write a joyful song, not even the greatest of their poets. Even now (the doctor told his boy), the folk songs of Castellamare sounded to the stranger so mournful that, if you listened to them long enough, they might turn you mad.

(Hesitantly, murmuringly, so as not to wake Pina, the doctor sang to his boy the most beautiful and least melancholy of these songs.)

He had been going to tell his boy the rest of the story, how the curse of weeping was lifted: how a girl named Agata, a peasant's daughter, saw visions of the Madonna; how the islanders, stone by stone, rebuilt their town. But here the boy stirred and let out a cry, and Pina, downstairs, awoke with her son as though by instinct. "Amedeo!" she called. "Where is my son?"

He caressed the boy's face. "Time to go down and talk to your mother," he said.

Pina, when he entered the room, was still for a moment disoriented—he could tell by the way she languidly smiled at him, as she had on her first morning in the House at the Edge of Night. Then she recalled their present trouble, and her face altered. "Give me my baby," she said.

He put the boy in her arms. The arch of her shoulders made him unwelcome, but he remained. "Pina," he said. "I need to speak to you. I've done wrong by you, Pina."

Now she did not weep but was straight and unyielding. "Yes," she said. "You have."

He became beseeching. He had not meant to, but he did. "Pina," he said. "*Amore.* Tell me how I can make it right."

"It's the lying I mind most of all," said Pina, hard-eyed and quiet.

So he told her the truth.

It was a long time before Pina had anything to say. "You've disgraced me before everyone," she said at last. "Our neighbors, our friends, the whole island. Do you think you can behave so badly and expect everyone to forget it? This isn't a big city like Firenze. Once people know a thing, they remember! There's nothing else to talk about. Now, everyone will know—and their children's children—how you went with another man's wife on the eve of your own wedding."

"I'll make it right," he said. "It's you, Pina, I love. I'll show it to be true."

"Can't we go away somewhere?" she said. "To the north, to Firenze! Can't you find another position, in some big town where we know nobody?"

"And leave the island?" said Amedeo. In spite of himself, he shed tears of self-pity. They struck the baby like great raindrops, making him look up in wonder. "Isn't there some other way, Pina? Ask me anything except that."

Pina dismissed him.

THAT AFTERNOON, ARCANGELO'S TEENAGE SON appeared on his bicycle on the dust road above the Rizzus' farm. Amedeo was in the Rizzus' kitchen, inspecting the children's skin infection. The boy took flight down the hill in a fog of dust, and, propping the bicycle outside the gate, removed his hat and entered the kitchen. "You're wanted, *signor il dottore*," he said. "A special meeting of the town council."

After Amedeo had finished bandaging the children, he made the climb back to the town. On the slope between the prickly pears, the dust was silken, the heat like a weight on his back. Arcangelo, sweating, waylaid him on the steps of the town hall. "You're to wait outside," he said.

"What do you mean, 'outside'?"

"In the lobby. You aren't wanted at the meeting. We've your position to discuss." Arcangelo took out a handkerchief and polished his forehead. "After this week's events, we need to consider your situation on the island. Therefore *il conte* has called for a special meeting, and you're to wait outside for our decision."

The count's motorcar drew up with a retch. Up the steps came the count in his mayor's sash and suit of English linen. Without a word to Amedeo, he caught Arcangelo by the elbow and drew him into the darkness of the building.

Quick in pursuit, alight with fury, came Father Ignazio. Amedeo met him halfway up the steps. "What's this?" he said. "You're discussing my position. I was told only to come to a special meeting; I wasn't told anything about this."

"I've only just heard it myself," said Father Ignazio.

"Am I merely to wait outside?"

"We'll fight it out, Amedeo," said the priest. "I certainly intend to."

On the varnished bench in the entrance of the town hall, Amedeo waited. From within he heard shouting, roaring voices: the count's voice and—to his surprise—the priest's. "Damn you!" he heard the priest shout. "Do you think you'll find someone else to take his place? And what about when the Mazzus were laid low with that fever last Christmas? And the idea of draining the swamp—not a child's succumbed to malaria since! Why, your own wife would be dead now, d'Isantu, and your newborn boy, if it weren't for Amedeo Esposito!"

With a great banging of doors, the men of the council emerged into the dusty half-light of the entrance hall. Amedeo got to his feet. For the first time on the island he felt stooped, wrong-footed, as though his great height made him vulnerable to attack. The priest was red in the neck, his soutane flying. "They've stripped you of your duties!" he said. "The damn outrage of it, the indecency! I'll deal with these *stronzi* no longer!"

Arcangelo came forth, bearing an oily apology. "As deputy mayor it falls to me to inform you that you have been suspended from your offices as doctor and public health officer. The good character of the public officials in a town like ours, you must understand, is of first importance."

Amedeo began to sweat, as though stricken with a fever. "Give up my duties? But nothing's been proved against me! I'm accused of no crime!"

"Even so," said Arcangelo. "There have been suspicions."

"And what about the patients I'm in the middle of treating? The Dacosta girl, Agata, and Pierino's nephew's broken leg, which I was to take out of its cast tomorrow afternoon so he misses no more of the tuna fishing season?" Stupidly, he thought also of the Mazzus' goat. In three days, its eye would again need lancing.

"How long am I to be forbidden from carrying out my duties?"

"All I know is, we can't allow you to occupy a position of trust in this town without further consideration."

Amedeo, shamefully, asked, "And what about my pay?" For his

savings had been depleted since the wedding with Pina, and the baby was ten days old.

"That also will be suspended," said Arcangelo. "My best advice would be to look for a position beyond the shores of this island. We're all very grateful for what you've done here, but better to leave without causing a scandal."

This island was the first place he had loved. But he saw now that it could also be a small place, a mean place. How could they remain, unless by some miracle of Sant'Agata they learned to survive on its sunlight and its water? Amedeo walked home by a long route. He could no longer imagine a life away from this place.

"There may be hope," said Father Ignazio that evening. "For Lord knows it was difficult to find you, Amedeo. There may not be anyone else willing to take the post. An island so cut off from the modern world, so inward looking. Not everyone could survive here."

But the count disappeared to the mainland on "political business" the following afternoon, and returned six days later with a spectacled youth, pale as an Englishman, who had been found to take the post of doctor, temporarily, until a new physician could be appointed. This young doctor had a certificate from the university in Palermo, and was the son of a friend of the count's who had once been a kind of duke in Punta Raisi. He was installed in an empty house on Via della Chiesa, and instructed to take over Amedeo's duties at once.

For five days, Amedeo remained in his house, existing on the food the widows of the island brought him, and the four chickens the Rizzu family had sent as payment for the curing of the children. Pina still talked of leaving the island. But she was kind at heart; she could not help being so. Seeing how he moped and suffered, she relented and began to allow him at least to see the baby, whom she had named, at last, Tullio. During these days, he became inseparable from the boy. He carried him everywhere, curled against his shoulder or folded in the crook of his arm. In the face of their misfortune, Pina seemed to straighten the way she had after the war. On the sixth day, she summoned their friends to the house: Father Ignazio, Rizzu, even the disapproving Gesuina. ("I don't support your carryings-on, *dottore*," Gesuina announced, "but it's plain this island can't be left without a proper physician. Why, only a devil would try to drive you away!")

"We must lodge an appeal," said Father Ignazio. Passing the baby between them in the dim lamplight of the cavernous kitchen, they drafted a letter to the government in Rome. Father Ignazio folded it in an envelope and put it inside his soutane to be sent with the fisherman Pierino, Pina's cousin, to the mainland post the next day.

SEVERAL DAYS LATER, just after nightfall, there was a tapping on the window. It was Signor Dacosta, his hat in his hands. "*Signor il dottore*, little Agata is sick again," he said, "and the new doctor says it's nothing but croup. But she's had croup already—you remember—and it wasn't like this."

After some deliberation over the morality of his position—for he had been clearly forbidden to practice—Amedeo fetched his coat and hat and followed Dacosta out into the night.

The Dacostas' farm was the poorest on the island, between the dry southern side where nothing grew and the recently drained swamp. He found the child tossing drily in her tangled bedsheets, beside her sleeping brothers and sisters. He had suspected for some time that the girl was afflicted with asthma. He ordered a bowl of hot water to be brought, and made a tent of damp sheets over her head. "Lean forward on your elbows," he exhorted her. "Breathe."

Gradually, in his arms, Agata gained her breath again.

"I'll not call that new fellow a second time," said Dacosta. "He didn't know anything about that trick with the sheets."

"She would have been fine either way," said Amedeo. "Just frightened."

"That damned *cazzo* of a new doctor, frightening my child!" raged Dacosta. "I won't stand for him. Thank you, *dottore*—I knew you could be relied on. And I don't care whether you've been screwing with every woman on this island," he added.

———

IN THE FOLLOWING DAYS, he began to feel the tide shifting once again in his favor. For, confronted with this new outsider, the island-ers now began to see Amedeo as one of their own. Others broke ranks and came secretly, by alleys and back ways, to summon Amedeo for their sick relatives. But these were the island's poorest, the costs of whose treatment had been paid always by Amedeo's salary from the *comune*, not out of their own pockets. These patients could not afford to pay him in money. And their gifts of vegetables and spindly chick-ens were not enough to keep any man's body and soul together, never mind a wife and child.

"We could go to Firenze," Pina said. "We could live in an apart-ment in the city, and have hot running water and a newspaper seller just down the street, and listen to the bells from the Duomo every morning, and later we could send the baby to a proper school, and a university. No one from Castellamare has been to a university. I don't know if it's right, to bring up a child on this island. Won't he just leave us? Won't he go away to some city or some war, and we'll never see him again? I would have done," she concluded bitterly, "if I had been a boy."

"Give me time and I'll make everything right," Amedeo said, to distance himself from the day when he would have to think about leaving the island.

ON THE FIRST NIGHT in October 1920, he began to consider the house. It had been a bar; it could be so again. He summoned their friends. "What about the House at the Edge of Night?" he said. "It could be reopened. I could reopen it. I could make a living that way."

Rizzu spoke up: "But the place is falling down."

"It could be restored," said Amedeo. "I could restore it."

"*Ai-ee*," said Rizzu. "No one would come to this old place."

Father Ignazio had been considering; now he spoke. "I'm not

sure," he said. "It's an idea. D'Isantu is trying to drive you off the island. You'll not get your old position back while he's mayor. But he
can't do anything about your living here if you find some different
occupation. If Arcangelo is mayor again, or someone else, you can
perhaps be reinstated and things can go back to normal. Why
shouldn't you have some different trade until then?"

It was Pina that Amedeo was waiting for, Pina whose approval he
needed. In her eyes he thought he saw passing sadly the bells of the
Duomo and the newspaper seller on the corner, the apartment with
streams of hot water and the university for their son. At last, she looked
up and nodded.

By this nod, he understood that it was possible she still loved him.
"I'll make it right," he promised. "I'll make all of it right. Rizzu, show
me what must be done with the bar."

"THIS USED TO BE THE COUNTER," said Rizzu, gesturing to an old
board propped against the wall, furred with dust. "Here were glass-
topped cabinets with pastries, rice balls, chocolates. My brother was
going to install a machine for ice cream, but he could never afford
the down payment. Then here were the tables, ten of them. Also behind the counter he had cigarettes, liquors, matches, *aperitivi*, pep-
permints, Leone violet pastilles, toothpicks, replacement blades for
razors, ladies' silk stockings (too expensive—no one ever bought
those), and American chewing gum. He used to make sandwiches for
people, and prepare coffee in little cups without handles. Those cups
must still be stored away somewhere in a back room; you'll not have
to buy new ones. Our old mother, God and Sant'Agata have mercy
on her soul, used to make all the rice balls and pastries and carry
them up the hill at five in the morning, and my brother would sell
them all day. The best rice balls on the island, better even than Signora Gesuina can make."

Amedeo, who had no idea how to make a rice ball and doubted

whether Pina had, either, merely nodded and wrote all this down in his red book.

"And he had newspapers from the mainland," said Rizzu, with pride. "From Sicily. He paid Pierino the fisherman to bring them over in his boat. They were only a week old—or sometimes two, in stormy weather. People came here to read the latest news. At first he charged ten *centesimi* a read, but people said that was mean-spirited."

Amedeo brushed the dust from the mirrors behind the counter. "Casa al Bordo della Notte" emerged on each one, in a twirling, fanciful script. In the windows, beyond the mess of bougainvillea, the sea seemed to hang in the air, crossed by the black diamonds of the fishing boats. "It might be possible," said Amedeo.

Each day that winter he labored, sweeping and scraping, his lungs full of the dust of the place. He felt, obscurely, that he was invested in a labor as great as that of the first islanders who had rebuilt the town stone by stone, to quell the weeping in the walls.

Gesuina, feeling her way around the kitchen, taught Pina how to make rice balls and pastries, and how to tell when a coffee was perfectly strong or a cup of chocolate suitably smooth. "You're to remember all this, girl," said Gesuina, "because when you've got to my age you only say a thing one time."

Pina wrote the recipes down in her clear schoolteacher's hand in an old exercise book, then put it firmly into the hands of Amedeo. "This is your bar," she said. "I will have enough to do with looking after Tullio, and the next baby when it comes. You make the pastries and the rice balls." But though she spoke firmly, he saw when he opened the book how precisely she had recorded each recipe, how neat and careful all her observations in the margins ("drain rice thoroughly, and not too much salt"; "an extra half-spoon of lard, cooled, if the pastry is too elastic"). Seeing this, he allowed himself to hope a little.

And she had begun to talk of another child. This gave Amedeo another vestige of hope.

He had allowed Pina her own way in everything. First, the boy's name. Tullio had been her father's name, and Pina liked the Latin sound of it. ("A name for a man of importance," she said.) Also this matter of a second baby so quick on the heels of the first. Flavio, he was to be called—she had already decided. The third, Aurelio. After her two uncles. Then perhaps, she thought, a girl.

One day when Amedeo was immersed in the business of fixing up the bar, scraping the spiderwebby filth from the ceiling, Carmela passed, pushing her new baby carriage.

Amedeo hung motionless on his ladder. As he watched, the baby squalled. Carmela lifted it from the carriage to comfort it and Amedeo saw a little scrunched hand, a smear of black hair, a face pale and distorted with weeping.

The child looked to him like a sallow, ill-favored thing. He thought with pride of his own Tullio, who sucked lustily and had already put on four pounds. Amedeo found it difficult to think of Carmela without cursing her. He was glad when she passed out of sight.

He and Pina and Tullio were existing almost entirely on the charity of their neighbors. Amedeo—who had never sawn a plank or nailed a floorboard in his life until the purchase of the House at the Edge of Night—did everything alone. Sometimes when he ascended the ladder he felt a little weakness in his head, a mild dizziness. He gave the best of the food to Pina, so that she and the child should lack no strength. Once, as she served the soup, she had rested one hand on the back of his neck and his whole skin prickled with gratitude. It had never happened since, but it gave him his third reason to hope. Surely when the bar was finished she would begin to forgive him.

With a few *lire* borrowed from his friends, he ordered supplies from the mainland—coffee, ingredients for the pastries and rice balls, a few boxes of cigarettes. As soon as the business began to make money, he would order more. He contracted the fisherman Pierino, as a favor to Pina, to bring parcels fortnightly on his boat, promising to pay him when the bar broke even. When the first supplies arrived, he was discouraged at how few and sparse they looked. He worked in the kitchen until three that night, making plates of the rice balls and tiny pastries. As a boy, his hands had been too clumsy for the watchmaker's shop, but they had extracted bullets from the entrails of wounded soldiers, delivered premature babies no bigger than his palm; he made them work for him now.

On a windblown day in March 1921, the House at the Edge of Night opened for business.

PART TWO

MARIA-GRAZIA

and the

MAN FROM THE SEA

. . .

1922–43

A KING'S DAUGHTER WAS TO WED A RICH SEA CAPTAIN, WHO had claimed her as his prize after rescuing her from a sea monster. But the real rescuer had been the cabin boy, whom the wicked captain had thrown overboard, and now the king's daughter wept and wept. For she had promised to marry the cabin boy, and given him a ring, and now he was gone, drowned in the ocean.

"ON THE DAY OF the wedding, the mariners in port saw a man emerge from the water. He was covered from head to foot with seaweed, and out of his pockets and the holes in his clothes swam fish and shrimps. He climbed out of the water and went ambling through the city streets, with seaweed draping his head and body and dragging along behind him. At that very moment the wedding procession was moving through the street and came face-to-face with the man wreathed in seaweed. Everyone stopped. 'Who is this?' asked the king. 'Seize him!' The guards came up, but the man wreathed in seaweed raised a hand and the diamond on his finger sparkled in the sunlight.

'My daughter's ring!' exclaimed the king.

'Yes,' said the daughter, 'this man was my rescuer and will be my bridegroom.'

The man from the sea told his story. And, green though he was with seaweed, he took his place beside the bride clad in white and was joined to her in matrimony."

———

A LIGURIAN STORY, *first told to me by the widow Gesuina, whose cousin once lived in the Cinque Terre. By virtue of her telling and retelling it, there are now many versions on the island, though the story is incomplete, and Signora Gesuina could remember neither the beginning nor the ending. This fragment I took, with Gesuina's permission, from Signor Calvino's book of folk stories published in 1956.*

I

IN THE BAR'S SECOND MONTH, CARMELA HAD COME TO THE DOOR
with her baby in her arms. Amedeo, glancing up from the counter,
became aware of her with a shock like a sudden gust of wind. He had
almost forgotten her appearance, yet there she stood, *il conte*'s beautiful wife, his former lover, the shape of her like water poured into a
vase. The bar's half-dozen customers turned in their seats and stared.
"I'm here to speak to Signor Esposito," said Carmela.

Amedeo felt the eyes of the whole place on him. But Pina placed
a hand on his shoulder, jogging the fat Tullio on the other hip. "*Signora la contessa*," said Pina, "he—we—have nothing to say to you."

Carmela laughed—the same laugh, full of insult, bewitching, that
had greeted him on his first night on the island. "Let him decide that,
signora," she said.

But Pina stepped forward, bearing Tullio before her. Carmela
reached for the sickly Andrea and heaved him in front of her, too, as
though in protection, and Tullio, catching the other baby's eye,
smiled a great wet smile.

"You are not to visit this bar again," said Pina. "Not you, or your
husband, or your son. Haven't you made enough trouble on this island?"

Carmela sought Amedeo's eyes, but he turned away from her and
studied the blue line of the ocean, painfully aware of the hot noise of
the blood in his ears. Carmela left at last. As she crossed the piazza he
allowed himself to look at her, and through the glass she seemed at
once an ordinary-sized, unremarkable person, struggling with her

heeled shoes on the cobbles, balancing the baby. Pina, hauling Tullio higher on her hip, said, "We won't see any d'Isantu in this bar again, as God and Sant'Agata are my witnesses."

Nearly half a year after its opening, the bar began to break even— and that same summer, Pina at last invited Amedeo back to her bed in the stone room beside the courtyard. "Let's talk no more about Carmela d'Isantu," said Pina. Amedeo wholeheartedly agreed. He felt that from now on he would do anything Pina asked of him.

By the end of that year, very few of the customers in the bar spoke about Carmela any longer within Amedeo's hearing. Pina, a woman who always kept her word, had two more sons in quick succession, which she named after her uncles—Flavio and Aurelio. By the time the last was born, the affair with Carmela was no longer talked about on the island. "For this island has a heart again with the House at the Edge of Night open," said Gesuina. "And that's the truth of it."

Pina had produced her three boys with remarkable efficiency, all of them within the space of four years, and now she devoted herself to their upbringing. Years later, when Amedeo tried to remember that time, he found that the boys were all mixed together in his mind, a jumble of grasping fingers and warm, milk-smelling hair. He spent long hours at his post behind the counter, soothed by the clicking of glasses and dominoes, the scent of bougainvillea, the rattle of *lire* in the cash register. In those years, he began to believe that he lived now a better life than he ever had as a *medico condotto*. When he saw the young doctor, Vitale, trudge past the window with thinning hair and worn trouser knees, he tried to repress his satisfaction.

Though Amedeo was banned from practicing medicine, still there were those who called on him for help, arriving shiftily by the court-yard door or leaning over the counter of the bar to make their whispered requests: "*Signor il dottore*, my Gisella is still suffering with her arthritis"; "*Signor il dottore*, that young Dottor Vitale hasn't set my niece's collarbone properly after she fell from that high ladder—I'm sure of it, it's clicking in and out of place when she tries to wash the dishes—will you take a look?" And some of the islanders, like the

Mazzu and Dacosta families, openly mistrusted the new doctor's judgment and came to the bar to obtain Amedeo's opinion on every cough and fever. These islanders still referred to Amedeo quite openly as *signor il dottore*, calling Dottor Vitale only *il ragazzo nuovo*, the new boy.

This presented a dilemma. The man was qualified, Amedeo assumed, but he lacked a certain gravity, and he had almost no experience—he had never splinted a man's broken femur in a waterlogged trench by candlelight, or delivered a baby on a straw-covered floor. And when in doubt—Signor Mazzu had told Amedeo this with the deepest disgust, leaning over the counter to hiss the accusation as though reporting some scandal or infidelity—when in doubt, the young doctor pulled great books out of his attaché case and consulted them! *Books!* Dottor Esposito had never needed to carry a great book about with him!

"Yes, but I consulted books," said Amedeo. "And medical periodicals, and all kinds of written matter."

"But not in front of your patients! How is anybody to trust him? Books—there's something indecent about it!"

Eventually Amedeo resolved the matter by dispensing advice for free with coffee and pastries, over the counter of the bar, or—for more serious cases—within the cool dark of his study at the top of the house, packing away his medical instruments afterward in an old Campari liquor case to avoid suspicion. Since he was paid principally in vegetables and eggs and the occasional live chicken, he reasoned with himself that to continue to advise the islanders like this was not the same as practicing medicine. For the purposes of conscience he was now merely a bartender—and if he offered the occasional benefit of his advice, he was certainly not the first in the history of bartenders to do so.

In those years, they began to live more comfortably. The house was still crumbling, but now he had the money to turn the current a little, to fix new hinges to the shutters and paint over the damp patch in the corner of the boys' room that had previously kept him awake whenever they coughed or sighed. Pina's relative Pierino, who worked as a fisherman when there were fish to be caught, and the rest of the time as whatever anyone in the town would hire him for, cleared the weeds from the veranda and repaved it with old tiles salvaged from the kitchens of the ruined houses outside the town walls. These tiles, red and deeply mottled, seemed to possess maps of the world beneath their surfaces. They pleased Amedeo, and he had Pierino install them in the washroom of the old house, too, which would eventually, he hoped, be converted into a modern bathroom with the hot and cold running water to which Pina aspired. Amedeo trained the bougainvillea and it bloomed profusely, so that each time the swinging door of the bar opened or closed, the rush of hot air that entered carried its perfume.

When Tullio was four, Flavio a fat toddler, and Aurelio still an infant, Pina fell pregnant again.

This child was different. Amedeo had not seen Pina suffer with any of her pregnancies the way she did during this one. For the first time she began to be flattened, oppressed by it. Her ankles swelled so that she hobbled; her hands were arthritic and stiff; she no longer ate properly, only in small mouthfuls from the plates of the boys. She fell accidentally asleep across the bed on hot afternoons, so that shrieks and roars would summon him at a run from the bar to some distant part of the house where the boys, left to their own devices, were making joyous war. Then he would have to prize apart Flavio and Tullio, or retrieve the bawling Aurelio from beneath the laundry basket where the others had stuffed him, or pick cicadas from their hair.

Clearly this was not a state of affairs that could continue.

"We must do something about the children," he told Pina one night. "They can't carry on this way." But Pina was languid and dreamlike; in her sickness, she did not seem aware that the boys were beginning to run wild. Still beautiful, her face had an insubstantial quality now that made him afraid to look at her. Always, before, she had been as solid as a Greek statue.

Eventually, Gesuina agreed to help Pina mind the babies, and

Rizzu agreed to help Amedeo in the bar. "Not for the money," said Gesuina. "Out of love. But the money I'll accept, too." She was almost completely blind now, but resourceful, and she found her way about. She could lull Aurelio to sleep in minutes, croaking island songs over his cradle. If the two elder boys fought, she would creep up behind them and floor them with an alarming roar of "*Basta, ragazzi!*" After Gesuina had done this four or five times, they stopped fighting altogether. Then, once she had the boys under control, Gesuina became kind, and plied them with sugared *ricotta* and fresh figs she peeled with her own hands.

So between them, Gesuina and Pina kept the boys in some kind of order and Rizzu and Amedeo kept the bar open, and the pregnancy progressed into the autumn. Because Pina craved the dust from the ground and the twigs of the orioles' nests that fell from the poplars into the courtyard, Gesuina predicted that this child would be a girl: "Odd cravings," she reasoned, "always mean a female child." The old woman had her own kind of logic that could not be argued with, and they began to refer to the child as "she."

Amedeo planned that his fourth child would be delivered in the hospital in Siracusa. His medical equipment was outdated and some had had to be thrown away due to rust; he had not opened a medical periodical since 1921. Plainly, he could not deliver a child. He had delivered two of his boys, but this was a responsibility he felt he could not bear for a third time.

"When the baby is due, we'll go in Pierino's boat to the mainland," he said, as he lay beside Pina early in November, brushing out her ropes of black hair, caressing her aching shoulders, while the first winter storm troubled the windows. "I'll take you there and you can stay there until the baby is born."

It was all arranged: Rizzu had a cousin on the mainland at whose farmhouse Pina could stay, and the farmer's wife would be paid twenty *lire* a day to act as Pina's nurse. When the time came, the farmer and his wife would take her to the hospital in a neighbor's motorcar.

But when he explained this plan to her, Pina would not agree. "Is it Gesuina's superstition?" said Amedeo. "It's quite safe to have a baby in the hospital, you know. You mustn't listen to what the old women say. Gesuina's never been in a modern hospital in her life, and she's frightened of the electric lights and the doctors in white coats and the smell of disinfectant—that's all."

"It's not that," said Pina. "I don't mind about the hospital. No, it's just a sense I have."

He knew better than to laugh at these notions of Pina's. Hadn't she predicted the births of Aurelio and Flavio—two more boys, she had said, and then perhaps a girl? "I know that my baby will be born here on the island, like her brothers," said Pina. "She'll come at her own time, before we're ready. I know that for certain."

Pina was right, as it turned out. The baby came suddenly, in a rush of water and blood, eight weeks too soon.

THE FIRST THING HE HEARD of it was Pina screaming, "Ai-ee, ai-ee!"

They had installed a curtain between the bar and the kitchen during the chaotic early days of her pregnancy, so that he could listen for sounds of strife among the boys. Now Gesuina came hobbling through it. "Where are you, *dottore*?" she said.

"Here," he said. "Here."

"You'd better shut up the bar at once and go to poor Pina."

The customers began an excited clamor. But Gesuina banged a steel pan against the counter, tipped the domino players off their chairs, and ejected them into the rainy piazza, closing the blinds firmly against their curious eyes.

In the kitchen, Pina was standing in a pool of water, gripping her stomach with both hands. "*Amore?*" he said, taking hold of her, but she shook him free. She began to roam the house. All he could do was follow her. Up and down the stairs, through the kitchen, into the bar and then out again, leaving a trail of blood wherever she went. This he followed, desperately questioning: "When did the pains start, *amore*? And for how long? And how severe? And are they the same as with Tullio, and Flavio, and Aurelio, or different this time? Tell me, *amore*. You're frightening me—you're frightening the boys."

Indeed, the toddler Flavio had hauled himself up by the kitchen doorframe, watching with big eyes. Somewhere in a back room, Aurelio shrieked for attention, utterly forgotten.

"It's too soon," Pina wept. "She's coming too soon. I have to stop the labor pains or she'll die. She's supposed to come in February and it's barely December now."

But Amedeo could see quite plainly that there was no stopping this baby. "Lie down, *amore*," he said. "Try to push. There's nothing to be done now but to deliver the child."

Gesuina nodded. "Breathe," she exhorted. "Push. Breathe, *cara*. Push."

"No!" wailed Pina. "I won't push! I mustn't—I can't!"

"I'll fetch the statue of Sant'Agata!" cried Gesuina, and went shuffling off into the hall.

But before they could do anything more for her, Pina collapsed with a great heave under the domino table. Amedeo put out his hands and delivered the child.

"She's breathing!" he said. "Pina, she's breathing."

"Look how small she is," Pina wept. "How small. How weak. Amedeo, she won't live and it will break my heart!"

"She'll live," he said fiercely, as he rubbed the child dry. "She'll live."

Still, something in him clenched in fear when he examined the baby properly. He saw how lightly veined her head was, how pink and translucent the barrel of her chest. He had delivered very few children this tiny, and nearly all of them had been stillborn. In the hospital in Siracusa, he admonished himself, they would have known what to do. It was no good now—how could this child make the sea crossing, in winter, in Pierino's fishing boat? She would live or die here on the island; that was certain.

"What about a name?" he said, as he opened his shirt and pressed the trembling child against his chest, the only warmth he could think of to offer her in that moment of confusion.

"I can't name her," wept Pina. "I can't look at her. Not yet; not if she isn't going to live."

NOTHING HAD PREPARED HIM for this fourth child. The baby was too weak to suck at Pina's breast. She had to be fed instead from Aurelio's silver christening spoon in tiny droplets. Pina could not stop crying, as though all the strength in her had broken. He closed the bar and took charge of the child himself, for now he found his world had narrowed, until the only thing in it was his daughter. He carried the baby about in the crook of his arm and at nights sat awake beside her cradle, under which he placed an old warming pan full of almost-extinguished coals—for the child had been born into the rain-blown island winter, and every draft seemed designed to kill her. The baby barely cried. Her head was still veined and her ears bruised from the shock of her delivery. On these nights when neither of them slept, he told the baby every story he knew.

He told her the story of the girl who became an apple, became a tree, became a bird. He told her the story of the parrot who kept a young wife safe by spinning for her a never-ending tale. He told her a story of Gesuina's about a boy who made a pact with the devil to save his father's life. The boy's father got well, and the boy went about the world and grew rich and successful, a great king, and he began to love the world so much that he forgot his pact. In ten years, when the devil came for him, the boy did not want to go. On those unreal nights in the room at the top of the house, the only sound the far crashing of the sea, Amedeo began to believe that all of these stories were in some obscure way the story of himself and his daughter, that they were locked in some ancient struggle that had been repeated and repeated like the struggles in those tales.

He told her, as he had told baby Tullio, the story of the island. Of the caves, and the curse of weeping, and the girl Agata, the peasant's daughter, who had cured it and become their saint, patron of misfortunes.

Amedeo, who had never been religious, now found himself overcome with superstition. Thoughts of the afterlife had never troubled him; now he was impatient to baptize the child. "You name her," said Pina. "I can't bear to name her myself, not if the Lord and Sant'Agata are going to take her from us afterward."

His thoughts inclined toward heavenly names: Angela, Santa, Madonnina. He settled at last on Maria-Grazia. The name had been Pina's grandmother's. He gave his daughter Agata as a middle name, in case the saint saw fit to throw him down some scrap of good fortune in return. In the first nights of his child's life, he was surprised and a little ashamed to find himself praying to the statue. "Holy Sant'Agata," he prayed, "if this is some punishment for my sins with Carmela, chastise me another way. Take something else from me for the wrongs I have committed on your island—not this little daughter."

In his great desperation he thought that he would more easily bear the loss of his wife, his sons, than this fragile child he barely knew, this child who should still have been in Pina's womb with curled fingers and closed eyes.

The boys sensed that something was amiss. They had stopped their rampaging on the stairs and their battling with sticks in the courtyard. Once, during the first days, they had accidentally woken the baby by throwing a rubber ball against the wall of the nursery, and their father's rage had been so great that he had frightened everybody, even Gesuina. He had flung the ball out of the window into the prickly scrubland. Since that day the boys had played more quietly in the courtyard, and even the smallest, Aurelio, seemed to be aware that his sister was hanging in the dark space between life and death.

Meanwhile, the bar remained closed, and Gesuina kept the neighbors, with their gifts of baked aubergine and their hunger for gossip, firmly out of the way. Even so, it became widely known that the fourth child of Dottor Esposito and Pina Vella was in the process of dying.

When the baby was ten days old, Amedeo had his friend Father

Ignazio come and baptize her. Afterward, the family assembled around the baby's cradle and he took a photograph. The picture was to remain undeveloped until the crisis of the baby's first months was over. Forever afterward, when he passed the picture on the stairs, it had the capacity to bring him to a sweat. There she was—yes, she had really been so small and frail!—with her eyes closed, her fists curled. Every time his daughter slept soundly, he was seized with fear and rested his head very gently against her chest to hear the soft suck of her breathing.

He continued to neglect the bar, though they had reopened it in a faltering way at the end of the winter. He could not bring himself to mind about anything except his daughter. The girl would sleep soundly only when she was in his arms, would take milk from the spoon only when he held it. Rizzu began to man the bar on afternoons, Pina when she could persuade the boys to play quietly behind the counter, and at nights—when his daughter was always most unsettled and Rizzu worked as a watchman for *il conte*—Amedeo trusted the customers to get their own liquors and boxes of cigarettes, and leave the money in a small box on the till.

Rizzu nailed a postcard of Sant'Agata with a bleeding heart to its lid. "To shame everyone into honesty," he said. "No islander of Castellamare would steal anyway, of course, but especially not when confronted with the blessed face of the saint." Rizzu garlanded the box with rosaries for good measure, drilled two holes in its top and stuck them with huge, wax-dripping candles, and he borrowed from Father Ignazio a small wooden crucifix to tack to the inside of its lid, in case any thief got as far as actually opening it.

Whether because of the blessed visage of the saint or out of fear for burnt fingers, no one stole from the box, everyone paid the correct sum for their liquor, and the bar—haltingly—remained open.

It took his daughter until the end of January to gain the strength to suckle properly, by which time Pina's milk was dry. But the baby could suck a little from a bottle with a rubber teat, and she began to appear larger and more solid even to the unbelieving Amedeo. Still, her life proceeded in fits and starts, an uncertain thing. A cough delayed her for another fortnight, and when the cough cleared her skin became jaundiced. Amedeo carried her out onto the veranda and held her across his lap in the sun, shielding her eyes with a folded handkerchief, until her skin lost its yellow tone.

He weighed his daughter every morning in the brass scales behind the bar counter. At last, one morning in February 1926, he felt a change in the balance, a light fluttering, and the next day the brass dish dropped. The baby had begun to grow in earnest.

By spring she was gaining weight just like his other children. In the summer she smiled; soon afterward she rolled over and began to attempt to crawl.

He saw that there was something wrong with the development of her legs. He had suspected it, but he could see it plainly now that she was no longer frail in every other respect. She could manage only a dragging movement, hauling herself about the floor by her arms like a lizard. She would require leg braces at the very least. But that did not matter; none of it mattered, if only she would live. Reluctantly, he returned to his duties behind the bar counter, but he kept the baby with him, letting her crawl about on a blanket, or sleep in his arms as he served pastries and poured coffee, in a kind of makeshift swaddle that earned him the ridicule of the peasants and the admiration of their wives.

Maria-Grazia, against all expectations, grew into a joyful, self-contained child. When she crawled about the floor she laughed softly to herself. Everything pleased her: the sun; the great bunch of keys belonging to the House at the Edge of Night, which her father hung on a string so that it twirled above her; a branch of the bougainvillea that Gesuina brought in from outside with its petals still chilled. The bar's elderly customers fussed over her, promising her their prayers and their grandchildren's cast-off clothing. They also tried to feed her with sugared *ricotta* from their fingers and pieces of browned pastry if Amedeo did not keep an eye out.

It took him until her first birthday to believe that she was not going to die. By that time, it was so evident to everybody else that even he had to accept it.

So things began to return to normal. Still, Pina was shaken; he was shaken. Something in both of them had altered during the months of their daughter's struggle—now a quite ordinary island song could bring tears into Pina's eyes, and Amedeo felt the same tenderness barely suppressed in him, as though something had broken, or softened, some carapace that had once made him less permeable to the world. Pina told him one night that she had forgiven him the affair with Carmela, blotted it out entirely. "We'll have no more children," she said, caressing his wrist in the dark. "I don't think I can live through such a time again."

Amedeo, on the whole, agreed. Four was enough—especially three boys who were so warlike and a daughter who would need special treatment. For although she was boisterous and stout now, still an aura of miracle was to remain about Maria-Grazia, a sense that the life she possessed was a fortunate one, blessed by the saint, one that should never have been lived.

ON EACH OF THEIR CHILDREN'S BIRTHDAYS AMEDEO TOOK A PHO-
tograph. He saw within the sequence of pictures belonging to his
daughter a struggle unfolding, a fierce soul like Pina's battling the
circumstances in which she found herself. In the first photograph,
Maria-Grazia sat bandy legged on Pina's lap, the deformity in her legs
plain to see. But in the second photograph, look how she stood
already!—clinging tightly to their hands, buoyed by her parents'
pride. By the third picture, she had succeeded in balancing upright
by herself. On each leg was a boot with a metal brace that extended
to her knee and ended in a leather band. The leg braces gave her an
odd stance, poised, like a wrestler in combat. The doctors in the hospital in Siracusa had told him that the child must wear these every
day for the next ten years. They would be specially adjusted each autumn.

At night, there was another brace that held the feet in position
more rigidly, against a steel bar; this would be worn until she was
eleven or twelve, at least, perhaps longer, and replaced with a tighter
one as she grew. Maria-Grazia never cried when the night brace was
put on, though her eyes narrowed a little. She could not move in this
night brace, not even to turn over, and if she needed to go to the bathroom she was obliged to call out to her mother or father to carry her
there. Sometimes, from their stone room downstairs, they did not
hear her calling—and in the morning they found her lying patiently
among wet sheets, enduring the ridicule of her brothers. She never
once complained about this humiliation.

In the fourth photograph, Maria-Grazia stood in her wrestler's pose in front of the ocean. This one made his heart hurt a little, for he knew that her brothers were at that moment capering among the waves, beyond the frame. The leg braces could not be worn in the sea; even the salt air of the island made them rust, so that they had to be rubbed with glass paper and treated with olive oil.

Of all the photographs, the fifth was his favorite. Here he felt that Maria-Grazia, in spite of her difficulties, had begun to assert herself over her brothers in one important way: While they blundered and struggled their way through school, she was fiercely intelligent. In this photograph, Maria-Grazia was submerged in study of one of her brothers' schoolbooks, her hair—which was braided in a black rope to match her mother's—resting lightly on the pages, her pale amber eyes fringed like Pina's with lovely bristling lashes. Absorbed in private delight, she smiled at whatever it was she read: history, mathematics, the *Iliad*—who knew? The child was a prodigious scholar.

At first the schoolteacher, Professor Calleja, had refused to enroll Maria-Grazia in the school, believing that the weakness of her legs must be matched by a feebleness of the mind. When Pina received the letter informing them of the fact, she took Maria-Grazia by the hand and half walked, half hauled her to the schoolroom. There, Maria-Grazia stood before the blackboard and the bewildered Professor Calleja, who stood in a corner working at the ends of his mustache. At Pina's prompting, Maria-Grazia demonstrated her ability to count to a hundred, add, subtract, multiply, recite the poetry of Luigi Pirandello, and describe the patterns of the stars that were visible above Castellamare, all of which she had learned from a concerted and independent study of her brothers' schoolbooks. When Professor Calleja refused to be convinced, Pina seized a copy of *La Divina Commedia* at random from the pile on his desk and pressed it on her daughter. "Read, *cara*," she exhorted. "Read!"

Maria-Grazia knew how to read, and she did so, stumbling a little over the mainland Italian, the odd poetry of it, pronouncing the words without understanding them: "Midway upon the journey of our life, I found myself within a forest dark, for the straightforward pathway had been lost. Ah me! How hard a thing it is to say—"

"Very well," interrupted Professor Calleja, unwilling to be entirely generous in the face of this defeat. "She can begin school in the autumn and we will see how she proceeds. If her marks are good enough, she'll stay—otherwise not." Reluctantly, he even agreed to allow Maria-Grazia to borrow the copy of *La Divina Commedia* in order to finish reading it before school began.

Pina carried her daughter home on her shoulders, crying tears of anger and pride.

The sixth photograph had been taken on the eve of her starting school, an occasion more important even than her birthday or name day to the child, who trembled all the evening before like a blown vine. In the photograph, Maria-Grazia wore proudly over her leg braces a schoolgirl's white *grembiule*. In her arms was a packet of new books tied up with string. Her brothers had had to share, and in truth had opened their books so little between them that the savings had been justified. But all Maria-Grazia's books were brand-new, ordered from the mainland and delivered to the island in Pierino's boat from the bookshop in Siracusa, wrapped carefully in brown paper.

Her brothers tried to be kind, in their way, dragging her along with them in their noisy games, defending her against the children who kicked her leg braces and stole her books. But a rift had begun to open between them. The boys had their own urgent concerns. Tullio, a great giant like their father with a mess of black hair and the same formidable eyebrows, had developed a consuming obsession with the workings of motorcars. Aurelio, the closest brother in age to her, stocky of form, earnest of intention, swam and swam. Her middle brother Flavio, whose looks were dark and severe, like those of their mother, Pina, shut himself up in his room and made protracted experiments with a brass trumpet. It was clear to the boys that Maria-Grazia was the best-loved child. And it was clear to Maria-Grazia that neither love nor learning could remedy the fact that she was a different sort of person from her brothers—a person who, while other children roared and hit things with sticks and cavorted in the sea, sat primly on the sand in leg braces, reading books about the stars.

"Your treatment is progressing well," her father would tell her, consolingly, on such occasions. "Next year you can take off your leg braces for short periods to swim."

Maria-Grazia knew that by then all the other children would swim faster or else would be tired of swimming, but she did not say so.

Preoccupied with her loneliness, her father encouraged her friendships with the bar's elderly customers, and with the stray cats that roamed the courtyard at nights. One evening Maria-Grazia ran to the counter in tears and led her father to a cat's nest, where a rather off-putting black kitten, matted with its own excrement, was giving out a pitiful "*Miu, miu, miu.*" "He's sick," Maria-Grazia wept.

Stooping, Amedeo found a wound in the kitten's side, hot to the touch. "He's got an infection, *cara.* There's very little we can do unless we can get his wound clean, and he won't be willing to stay still long enough for us to finish the treatment."

"Fix him, Papà."

A good number of the bar's elderly customers had followed them out into the dusk, and now gathered round, tut-tutting in pity—even the town's confirmed cat haters. "Fix him," said Maria-Grazia. "Papà, get your medical bag and fix him."

"*Cara*, I don't know about that."

"Fix him," echoed the old people reprovingly.

The mother cat watched from a bush, her tail beating a wary rhythm.

Amedeo, against his better judgment, allowed his daughter to coerce him into bringing his medical bag down from the room at the top of the house. "Fix him," Maria-Grazia continued to weep, as Amedeo worked. "Don't let him die." Amedeo finished the job, laid the clean kitten back in its nest, and detached the mother cat from his shoulder, claw by claw.

His daughter's tearful gratitude knew no bounds. And when, three weeks later, she brought the kitten to him and showed him its wound, neatly scabbed over, and the tame way it licked her hands, it was all he could do not to weep himself. "His treatment is progressing well," she said. "Like mine."

It was true. Maria-Grazia was to remain small all her life—the only descendant of Amedeo who was not a giant on the island—but otherwise there was no sign, except for the leg braces, that her parents had ever feared for her survival.

NOW THAT AMEDEO BEGAN to be concerned not with Maria-Grazia's survival but with her future, he became aware that an alteration had taken place in the world. News from outside reached them only foggily at the best of times. The financial troubles in America had been a subject of conversation in the bar for a while; the elderly *scopa* players had marveled over photographs of rich families camped out in motorcars, sleeping under tarpaulins. ("To think, *americani* living like us poor folk! Just as well my 'Ncilino never left for Chicago after all!") But the island's solitude had saved it from serious trouble. Except for ordering a few cigarettes from the mainland now and again, the islanders of Castellamare had no dealings with the economies of great nations. As Rizzu said, there would have been no motorcars to camp in if the island had suffered a depression, excepting *il conte*'s, and nowhere to go in them anyway, and the only thing any islander possessed a stock or share in was the Committee of Sant'Agata or the Fishermen's Guild.

Now, though, a tectonic shift had occurred closer to the island's shores. During the chaotic babyhoods of his children, the changes in Italy had reached Amedeo only faintly. Like the dim sound of breakers from the caves by the sea, the world outside had never seemed as important as the world inside the walls of his house. The year Flavio was born, there had been some disagreement over the voting (due to a rather alarming vomiting episode of Tullio's, Amedeo had lost track of the time and made it to the polls only after they were closed). Listening to the furious discussions in the bar the next day, he had grasped the gist of the disagreement. It seemed that no one on the island had intended to vote for the *fascisti*, except *il conte* and perhaps Arcangelo. To remedy this, *il conte* had posted two of his agents at the doors to the town hall on election night, armed with sticks. By this means, *il conte*'s peasants had been persuaded to recognize that the island was a ship from which *il conte* could eject all mutinous passengers. When it came time for *il conte* to count the votes, the *fascisti* had received a majority.

A while after this, the mainland newspaper *La Stampa*, which came to them all the way from Torino, had been full of the murder of a socialist deputy, a Signor Matteotti, and then for a time they couldn't get hold of that particular newspaper. When it came back into circulation it had nothing more to say about Matteotti after all. Amedeo hadn't much minded about it at first, because the only newspaper his customers cared about was *La Gazzetta dello Sport*.

He remembered these things happening, of course. He remembered that for a while, those who had voted for the *fascisti* and those who had not had refused to speak to each other, which had made that year's Sant'Agata festival an awkward matter. When it came time to elect the local mayor, the islanders voted not for *il conte* or for Arcangelo, but to reopen the nominations to another candidate—an outcome unheard of on Castellamare. Then, not long after, the town council had been disbanded anyway, by order of *il duce* from Rome. Now there was to be no mayor and no elected representatives, only a single *podestà*, which made the standoff between the *fascisti* and the other islanders seem somewhat irrelevant. As the new *podestà*, *il conte*, declared in his first address from the steps of the town hall, they were all *fascisti* now.

There had been some muted protest. A small party, in the dead of night—fortified by Amedeo's liquors—had torn down the new Fascist flag and the portrait of *il duce*'s bald head from the entrance of the town hall. Rizzu's teenage nephew Bepe and the fisherman Pierino, who had encountered Communism briefly during the war, began to sing "The Internationale" whenever Signor Arcangelo was passing (they did not dare sing it at the count). Then, one night, these two *"comunisti"* were seized on their way home by two of *il conte's* agents, roughly shaken, and forced to drink a pint of castor oil. After that, no one complained about becoming *fascisti*—at least not in the open. For, as Gesuina said, "We've all got to live together after this, you know."

"This is northern nonsense," raged Rizzu over the counter of the bar. (He still worked for *il conte* occasionally as a porter and night watchman, but his patience with his old employer had worn thin since the ambush of Bepe.) "No one on Castellamare has ever bothered about politics until now. These are Italian matters, not ours."

"It will pass in a year or two," said Gesuina. "If it's our cursed fortune to be ruled by other people, it might as well be this Duce as the Spaniards or the Greeks or the Bourbons or the Arabs or anyone else who's had a turn. We'd all better just ignore him and go on with our own affairs."

By this logic, the two old people reconciled themselves to the new situation, and for a while things were quiet again in the House at the Edge of Night.

Then, shortly after Maria-Grazia had started school, *il duce* imposed himself forcibly on Castellamare.

News reached the bar early one afternoon that two officials had arrived on the island in a motorboat and had demanded to speak to *il conte* about the matter of a prison. The prison was not intended for the islanders (for no serious crime had ever been committed on Castellamare), but for prisoners of *il duce*. *Il duce's* prisoners were routinely exiled to such remote outposts, said the officials—to the butterfly-shaped island of Favignana in the west and the smoking volcanoes around Lipari. Castellamare had also been chosen as fitting for this purpose.

The two officials of *il duce* were housed in the guest wing of the count's villa. They drank noisily on his terrace every night. After three days they went away and nothing more was said about the prison. Three months later, a group of workmen from the mainland arrived in a motorboat and began to repair the ruined houses outside the city walls with rocks and tarpaulins ("Work that could have been done by Castellamare men!" said Rizzu). The prison would open at the end of the summer. Eight Fascist militiamen, two *carabinieri*, and a lieutenant from the mainland would accompany the prisoners to the island, and in anticipation they were leased several of the empty houses belonging to *il conte*, at a specially reduced rate.

"We've never needed any *poliziotti* on the island," said Gesuina, who was now firmly set against the current developments. "Guards! A sharp smack or a talk with a boy's grandmother has always been more than enough. How will I know if they're spying on me when I walk about the town, me with my poor eyes?"

That summer the first of the political prisoners arrived, in a gray ship from Calabria, sporting wild beards that terrified the children. They made the long climb from the port in a single line, chained together so that they had to step as one, like the caterpillars on the stems of the bougainvillea. One or two who trailed at the back had brought their wives and children. These prisoners were installed in the half-repaired houses, and now every night the bugle call of the *fascisti* could be heard at five o'clock, summoning the prisoners to the rooms where they were shut up until dawn. *Il conte* had made clear to his tenants and his peasants that the prisoners were not to be approached or spoken with.

After watching the prisoners march up the hill in chains, Pina went about straight-lipped with anger, and behind closed doors she raged against *il duce* and his prison and his warlike ranting in the newspapers and the presence on Castellamare of his odious guards. Therefore when the boys Tullio and Flavio, aged nine and eight, came home from school in miniature black shirts, carrying toy guns (the most beautiful toys ever to pass through their hands), she marched them to the schoolteacher Professor Calleja's house and hurled the guns at him through the kitchen window. "What do you call this?" she demanded.

"It's called the Opera Nazionale Balilla," Professor Calleja tried to explain, shielding his head from the missiles. "It's a youth organization—a sporting organization—the children are all encouraged to join and become *Balillas*—not just your boys, Signora Esposito. Just like the Catholic Scouts."

"There are to be no *Balillas* in my house!" raged Pina, ignoring her boys' wails at the loss of the toy weapons. "There are to be no guns in my house! Didn't the last war take enough from this island? If my sons want to join the Catholic Scouts with Father Ignazio, they can join the Catholic Scouts!"

But now the Fascist guards were a constant presence, roaring with their motorboat off the scattering of rocks the fishermen called Morte delle Barche, setting up pickets at street corners, loafing about the town—and little could be said in the open. The guards called at the bar regularly for cigarettes and strong black coffee. Amedeo kept his head low, and occasionally slipped a rice ball or a slice of mozzarella to a prisoner, too.

But when Pina saw a prisoner loitering miserably in the street (they were given five *lire* a day to get by, she had heard—less than the day wage of the humblest of *il conte*'s peasants), she invited him in and offered him bread, pastries, and coffee, seating him at the best table.

The prisoners were allowed to work, but there had always been exactly enough work on the island for the islanders, and no more. All the same, Pina paid three of them to repair the broken veranda. The men worked slowly, talking about philosophy and art in schoolbook Italian, and put the wooden beams on back to front. The fisherman Pierino raised his eyebrows when he saw the work. "I don't think much of that," he said. "It looks like you had *il conte* do it, or the schoolmaster—one of those clever men who wouldn't recognize a roof beam or a door lintel if it came up and struck them over the head."

"These prisoners are educated men back in their hometowns, Pierino," Pina said. "One is a journalist from Trieste, the second, Professor Vincio, a university lecturer in the faculty of archaeology at Bologna, and the third, Mario Vazzo, is a published poet."

"That explains it," said Pierino, and offered as a favor to his cousin to put the veranda back the way it should have been free of charge.

Amedeo began to grow uneasy at all this, for Pina was making them conspicuous among the islanders. But it was hopeless to confront her once an idea took hold. He immersed himself instead in the rearing of his children and hoped all this was merely a passing squall that would strike the island with its first heavy drops and then move on to vent its fury elsewhere. It was easy enough to distract himself with the boys. In order to get them through their final years of school, they had to be coaxed away from catching lizards in the scrubland or kicking stones around the piazza. Amedeo and Pina tested them on their mathematics and history and French, supervised their studies in the atlas, and read to them from improving works of literature. Catching the boys to perform these ministrations was a task in itself. And then there was his daughter—his most promising child—propelling herself about on her stiff legs, always questioning, always asking: "Papà, why do the lizards hide inside the streetlamps? And what makes the sea go in and out? And why do hairs grow on Gesuina's chin like an artichoke?" Her legs had to be exercised every evening, and the braces fitted. On cool nights, to build her strength, he took her on slow walks around the city wall to the belvedere, where she hauled herself onto the railing and pointed out to him the patterns of the stars. She was best in her class at school, to Professor Calleja's irritation, so far ahead of the others that even with the reduction *il professore* made to her marks ("To stop the girl getting self-important"), he could not prevent her from coming first.

"You might go to one of the universities on the mainland," Pina told her daughter. "You might become someone educated, a scientist or a poet."

She also encouraged her sons to think in this manner, but with less conviction. Instead, to persuade them of the delights of a proper education, she enticed them with pictures of great bustling squares full of ice cream stands and great rivers of city lights, in her old schoolmistress's atlas. Yet none of the three boys would have been caught within ten miles of a university, for they loved the waves and the wild scrubland and football games in the piazza, and none of them could endure being shut up in a classroom. Maria-Grazia, however, loved books with a sacred fervor, like a fisherman's love for the ocean, and her parents privately delighted that they had produced one intellectual child.

The problem with an intellectual child, though—as Amedeo began to realize in the years that followed—was that she understood things, witnessed things, kept her eyes stubbornly open, as Pina did. And just like Pina, she could not be persuaded to look away.

III

IN THE SUMMER OF HER NINTH YEAR, MARIA-GRAZIA WITNESSED FIVE things, each of which was to alter her life to come. Indeed, these five events would seem to her afterward so important that until the day she died she would recall them in odd magnification, like scenes viewed under clear water, the sharpest pictures belonging to her childhood. The first thing she witnessed was an argument over a misplaced vote.

Walking home on that dusty afternoon, Maria-Grazia was consumed with longing for the first weekend's swimming. The previous summer, her father had taken her down to the ocean at last and taught her to swim like her brothers. Feeling her legs move in the water, without hindrance, she had let out a scream of pure joy. But swimming had ruined the land for her; now it seemed stale and cumbersome to walk on earth at all. She felt that she had been born in the wrong element, like the mermaid girl in her father's story, for her legs in air felt as heavy as though they were moving through water, her legs in water as weightless as air.

Limping home after her three brothers from school that afternoon, her legs were tiresome to bear. She had learned to recognize days when the joints of her knees would creak all day and her calves with their metal braces move as heavily as limbs at the bottom of the ocean. Why couldn't she have been born a sea-dwelling animal?

Halfway home, her brothers ran ahead and left her. They fled, exulting at their freedom from "that *stronzo* Professor Calleja" (as Flavio put it). Always her brothers had to be racing, roaring, hitting things. They would be making for the Rizzus' farm. During the Christmas break from school, her brothers had invented a game with the three youngest Rizzus, a game they called *nemici politici*, which filled them with wicked joy. In *nemici politici* the players were first divided into two bands, the *fascisti* and the *comunisti*. Then the *fascisti*, armed with sticks and empty gasoline canisters, had to hound the *comunisti*, the political enemies, from one end of the island to another, threatening in terms as obscene as possible to beat them with sticks and dose them with pints of castor oil. It was an exhilarating game, sometimes violent, like all her brothers' pastimes, and it often ended in a black eye or a skinned knee. Then their father was obliged to get his medical equipment out of the Campari liquor case and repair her brothers.

On these occasions, their mother would become fierce and inquisitive, and Maria-Grazia would retreat with her cat, Micetto, to the courtyard until the fussing was over.

As her brothers tumbled out of sight into the scrubland, she resumed her painful walk and reached the terrace of the House at the Edge of Night at about one o'clock, just after the church had finished chiming its Ave Maria. Gripping the tendrils of the bougainvillea, she hauled herself to the top of the steps. Here she paused, for she could hear the cat Micetto.

She propelled herself about between the tables and at last found him, folded up in a loop of the vine. Painfully, she got to her knees. "Come, Micetto," she called. "Kit, kit, kitty! *Micetto, Micettino!*"

Something had badly frightened the cat. When she hauled him out he was stiff tailed and crying like a baby. "Here, Micetto," she whispered. "There now, Micetto. Calm."

Maybe some old witch had kicked him again, she thought, the heat making her irritable. "I told Mamma and Papà to keep you in the courtyard," she murmured into Micetto's fur. "It's not safe for you out here."

The cat had his own methods of breaking and entering. Worming himself up the fretwork of the back gate, he had been known to get as far as the latch and pull it back with one paw, so as to gain entry to the kitchen and feast on cold chicken. Once, he had got in at the window of the bar at night and eaten until he was so fat and sated that he fell asleep inside the glass counter, curled up in a plate of *salami*. But she feared he had a reckless side, like her brothers: He was forever getting into the courtyards of the most cat-despising islanders, where he would be smacked with flyswatters and hit with brooms; he was constantly seeking to fling himself under the wheels of *il conte*'s motorcar. Maria-Grazia bundled him up in her arms.

The piazza was quiet. *Il conte*'s car stood under the single palm tree, ticking in the heat. The only person about was a prisoner, loitering by Gesuina's house. Could he have kicked the cat? Though her Mamma always said the prisoners were important men, clever men from the north, they frightened her a little. Once, Tullio said that he had seen two of them out on the veranda in the early morning, picking up the cigarette butts the islanders had dropped, blowing on them and putting them in their pockets. Her brothers found this a great joke, but to Maria-Grazia it was not funny, it was awful.

Climbing the steps had been a difficult process, and it was only when she pushed open the swinging door that she became aware that the bar was full of shouting. At the counter, *il conte* and the stout grocer Signor Arcangelo were making a scene about something. They were dressed in their black shirts, which her mother always said privately that they put on when they meant to cause trouble.

"You should have kept the ballot paper you didn't use!" *il conte* was shouting. "As proof that your vote was in line with the party! Do you want the *fascisti* thinking we're all Bolsheviks here?"

"I've done nothing wrong," her father was saying—his voice was raised, too, the back of his neck, which was all she could see of him, mottled with agitation. "I merely went to the ballot box yesterday afternoon at the town hall, cast my vote—such as it was—and came home."

"Come along now," said Arcangelo, soothingly. "Let's be sensible. I'm sure you kept the ballot paper you didn't need, Signor Esposito. Just bring it out to show us, and we'll leave you to carry on your business and say no more about it."

"I thought ballots in this country were supposed to be secret," said her father. "At least in the country, the Italy, in which I grew up."

That was strange, for Maria-Grazia had never thought of her father as belonging to Italy, only to Castellamare.

From the doorway, her mother, Pina, said, "What's all this noise?"

Signor Arcangelo spread his hands. "Signora Esposito," he said. "It's all a misunderstanding. I've said already to your husband and *signor il conte* that I think things are getting rather out of hand."

Her hands and cheeks a little floury from preparing lunch, Pina advanced. "What's all this noise?" she said again.

Arcangelo adopted again his consoling tone. "*Il conte* and I were the returning officers for yesterday's election, which means—"

"I'm aware of what a returning officer does nowadays," said Pina. "You seem to forget I was a qualified schoolmistress before my marriage, Signor Arcangelo."

"Of course. Well, in the line of duty, *il conte* and I found that certain individuals on this island, regrettably, voted against the list of candidates published by the Fascist Party, putting the white 'No' paper into the ballot box instead of the tricolored 'Sì' paper."

"As is their perfect right," said Pina, and *il conte* gave a great huff like a sea lion.

"Therefore," concluded Arcangelo, as if no one had said anything, "we have decided that it will be safest to check for proof of loyalty among every man of voting age on the island—just to make sure that we are aware, as it were, of who is unhappy with the Fascist candidates, so that we can endeavor to reassure them."

"I see," said her mother. "And you thought you'd check which way my husband voted, in case he's one of those who voted 'No.'"

"Precisely, Signora Esposito."

"Amedeo," said her mother. "Do you still have the unused ballot paper?"

Her father looked down for a minute, and eventually, sulkily, said, "Yes, Pina."

"Then go and fetch it," she said, "and let's put an end to this silliness."

"I'm quite sure that your husband has voted 'Sì,'" said Arcangelo, who was quivering like a *ricotta*. "I've always thought highly of your family, Signora Esposito, and of your poor deceased father, you must know. Therefore I'm sure that Signor Esposito has voted 'Sì.'"

"Naturally," said her mother, "I hope that the opposite is true."

A pained little silence. Maria-Grazia knew by it that her mother must have said a very shocking thing.

Her father came back through the curtain, holding a white card in his hands. "Here," he said, putting it down on the counter. "I voted 'Sì.' Here's the 'No' paper left over—you can see plain enough that the 'Sì' one went into the ballot box."

"There," said Arcangelo, puffing. "That's very satisfactory, Signor Esposito, and I don't see why you made such a fuss about showing us in the first place. Everyone else has been obliged to show theirs—you're no different, you know."

Then all at once her mother became angry—or perhaps she had been angry all along. "Please leave our bar," she said. "We've nothing more to discuss with you."

With a slamming that startled Micetto out of Maria-Grazia's arms, *il conte* and Signor Arcangelo left.

When they were gone, her mother took the white card and crumpled it, as though it were some shoddy piece of work belonging to one of her pupils. Then she said, "'Sì' to the *fascisti*? I'm ashamed of you."

Il conte's car roared outside. Micetto! She could hear him. She banged open the door and—stumbling, cursing the leg braces—launched herself down the steps of the veranda. Here Maria-Grazia lost her balance and dived into someone's stomach, sending the air flying from his lungs in a great huff. "*Ai-ee!*" she screamed, fearing Arcangelo or *il conte*. "I'm sorry, *signore*—"

The prisoner set her upright. "Don't be scared," he said, in formal Italian, as though he were speaking from a book of poetry. "I caught this *gatto selvaggio* trying to throw itself into the road. I think it belongs to you."

And he held out the screaming, fighting Micetto in both hands.

This was where her mother and father found her ten minutes later, playing with the cat in the company of the prisoner, a poet whose name was Mario Vazzo and who knew all kinds of songs from the mainland and pretended not to notice when Maria-Grazia cried a little and then rubbed her nose on her sleeve. In this way, neither Pina nor Amedeo knew that she had heard anything at all about the vote. But in her heart, Maria-Grazia stored up the scene for future contemplation.

THE SECOND THING MARIA-GRAZIA witnessed that year was the beating of the fisherman Pierino.

It was a few nights later—or else the same night—that she woke quite suddenly because her father had not come, as he usually did, to put on her night brace. She maneuvered herself onto the edge of the bed, into the square of moonlight from the window, and worked the pains out of her calves. The bar had closed for the night and downstairs, in the kitchen, Mamma and Papà's voices were going up and down, up and down like a motorboat engine, as they often did these days. Flavio was coughing. He had been peaky all the previous winter, suffering with a protracted bronchitis for which their father had not been able to order the proper medicine. Maria-Grazia heard him hacking and hacking in his room above hers, playing his trumpet only in wheezy gasps. Now, he was trying to swallow his coughs, which meant he did not want to be overheard.

After eight years of exercises, she could walk a little without her braces. She went sideways to the top of the stairs. Here she almost tripped over her brothers, who were lined up along the steps like *sarde* in a can, their heads through the bannisters, listening.

Flavio, dark and fierce, attempted to glare her away: "You'll make a sound, you with your metal pins—you'll give us all away!"

"But I haven't got them on," said Maria-Grazia. "And you're the one coughing."

"You can stay if you promise to keep quiet," said Tullio. Maria-Grazia got to her knees beside Aurelio. Nothing could be heard of what her parents were saying, only the rise and fall of their voices.

"*Cazzo!*" said Tullio. "They've gone into the bar. They must know we're listening."

Flavio said, "And that's *your* fault for making a noise!"

"It isn't her fault at all," said Aurelio, her kindest brother, and gratitude brought a sudden sting of tears into her eyes.

She did love them, her brothers, but ever since she could remember she had been aware of loving them, adoring them, far more than they ever loved her. Even Aurelio. Always she felt herself to be trailing behind: trying to keep hold of their attention, cross with herself for wanting it. Now, succumbing to the same trap, she boasted, "I heard them earlier. Mamma thinks it's shameful that *il duce* changed the rules so that you can only vote 'Sì' or 'No' in the election. That's what she said—shameful—I heard her myself. She said it isn't *democrazia* at all."

Flavio rounded on her. "What is there except 'Sì' or 'No'? 'Sì' for the *fascisti*, 'No' if you don't like them. If you ask me, *il duce* gets a bad press in this house."

Now she saw that she had hurt his feelings. Flavio had won prizes for his dedication to the *Balilla*. At nearly thirteen, her middle brother's voice was unruly and his face obscured under an embarrassing constellation of acne, but at the *Balilla* meetings he became a fierce firer of rifles, a fervent singer of patriotic songs. He was invited to special meetings where he played his brass trumpet while Professor Calleja marched about, and Dottor Vitale, drafted in as *il professore's* assistant after the swelling of the numbers, beat a great bass drum. Pina kindly pretended to admire Flavio's medals, then consigned them to the back bedroom with their father's collection of historic potsherds, but Flavio—undaunted—only brought home more. "Maybe you're right, Flavio," said Maria-Grazia, trying to make amends.

But Flavio only hunched crossly away from her. Her brother had been in a bad mood all evening. He had come home late, a little tired and drawn, carrying his brass trumpet in one hand. His coughing had been too much at the *Balilla* meeting—*il professore* had sent him home.

Tullio pressed his ear to the tiles and said, "Listen—I think I can hear somebody else."

"That prisoner Mario begging for work again," said Flavio.

"No. Shh. One of the neighbors."

Sure enough, whoever it was, they were speaking the dialect of the island—for no northerner could lament like that, on and on like a river, without pause, without end.

"Oh, it's probably just old Rizzu, come to get drunk with Papà," said Flavio. "We won't hear anything sensible now."

And indeed, the argument was over and all they heard now was a lamenting voice. "I think it might be Rizzu's nephew Bepe," said Maria-Grazia. "It doesn't sound quite like Rizzu himself—and anyway, he's supposed to be working at *il conte*'s tonight."

But her brothers had lost interest, and they all went creeping to bed. Maria-Grazia, however, was decidedly awake now. In her legs, liberated from the stifling night brace, was a feeling like electricity, a feeling of being shockingly alive. Perhaps this was how it felt always to have ordinary legs like her brothers'! Sitting up in bed, she heard her father's footsteps ascending the stairs. She waited for him to come and fit the night brace, but his shadow crossed her door and continued. She heard him climb to the small room at the top of the house, pause there a moment, and come down again at a run. Edging her door open by a crack, she saw that in one hand he carried his medical bag, and around his neck hung his black stethoscope.

Her father was leaving the house. Out of nowhere, the feeling of strength left her, replaced by a powerful fear. Hauling herself up on the curtains to look out into the moonlight, she watched her father cross the courtyard and disappear.

Maria-Grazia sat very still for a moment, then got up and followed him.

She could not have said what was in her mind as she descended the stairs, made her way across the stretch of moonlight in the courtyard, and pushed open the gate. By this time her father was a long way ahead and she had to run, keeping her legs stiff like Flavio's wooden soldiers so as to manage the slight uphill without falling. She caught only the flash of her father's shoe around the corner of each alley, the swing of the leather bag. It took her almost five minutes of concerted effort to catch up to him. It was when her legs buckled that she realized why running was a greater effort than usual—she had not had her night brace on, and in her panic she had left the house without putting the ordinary ones on, either, the ones she was never supposed to remove. And here she was running after her father, silent as Micetto.

At least the alleys were narrow here, and she placed both hands on the walls to propel herself forward. Past the shops, past the fountain that always smelled of green weeds, even in summer, around the side of the church where there was nothing to hold on to and she almost toppled. Sure enough, her legs had begun to tremble now as though she were suffering a high fever. But her father, mercifully, came to a stop at this moment, outside the skinny house that belonged to Pierino the fisherman.

Pierino was family, her mother had told her once. Their cousinship was so distant that they no longer remembered how they were connected, but sometimes at Christmases the two families sent each other a bottle of *limoncello* or a *cassata* cake with an affectionate label. But Maria-Grazia had entered Pierino's house only once before. After Mass, Pierino's wife, Agata-the-baker's-daughter, had called her in to be prayed for, because of her legs, and reluctantly she had submitted to the papery hands the old women laid on her forehead, the soporific chanting of their Ave Marias and Our Fathers. On the front of the house Pierino had rigged several washing lines for the sheets and pinafores belonging to his eight children, so that while the women prayed for her in the hot stupor of the upstairs parlor the house itself seemed to swell and catch the wind, the sun flickering through its sails like a ship on the sea.

Now, the washing lay limp, the house shuttered.

Her father went to the side door. Before she could call out to him, he was admitted, leaving behind only the scent of the basil plants disturbed in his passing. Shut out, Maria-Grazia wished all at once that she had not followed him.

She hauled herself up by the windowsill and looked in at the kitchen window. Her legs were almost used up. But she was seized with a fierce determination to see what was happening inside the room.

What she saw was candlelight, like a funeral vigil. Neighbor men whose names she knew only dimly: fishermen and peasant farmers. Mazzu, Dacosta, Terazzu. On the empty kitchen table, Pierino lay on his back, his chest hair thick with petrol as it had been one evening last summer when his motorboat engine cracked clean in two, dousing him with the liquid. ("Twenty buckets of hot water it took," his wife, Agata-the-baker's-daughter, had complained. "And he still stank of petrol at the end of it—I could smell it everywhere about the house; it got into my cooking, the parlor furniture, the eggs of the chickens in the yard—")

She could see that old woman now through the glass, standing at Pierino's head, and Pierino's youngest daughter, Santa Maria, at his feet. And there was her father, stooping to keep his head from hitting the ceiling. Someone turned on the electric light. The streaks on the fisherman's chest shone, and Maria-Grazia understood at once that they were not streaks of petrol but of blood. Someone had whipped his skin raw.

Her father spoke—and though the glass absorbed some of his words, others passed through clearly to the alleyway where she clung in terror. "When?" said her father.

"Two hours ago," answered Agata-the-baker's-daughter. "He voted 'No,' *signor il dottore*. It was he who did it. If only, by the grace of Sant'Agata, he hadn't taken it into his head to vote 'No.'"

Her father began swabbing Pierino's chest with a clear fluid, pausing to pick out little pieces of grit that glittered in the lamplight and which he set aside in a butter dish. As her father worked with his tweezers, Pierino's chest rose and fell. Her father began to wind Pierino in bandages, the fishermen assisting—they heaved Pierino up as they heaved their nets full of *sarde*, then laid him gently down again.

"Who did this?" her father said.

Agata-the-baker's-daughter was overcome and turned away, burying her face in her hands.

With a rumbling came the voice of old Rizzu. "They carried him up here and threw him in the alley," he said. "Signora Agata heard the thump and came out, thinking it was the stray dogs making trouble, and instead she found her husband thrown down here in the dirt like a sack of old rubbish, and whoever did it had run away—that *figlio di puttana*! I've given in my notice to *il conte*—I've had enough of his friends and their politics."

"Was it *il conte* who did it? Or Arcangelo?"

But here a murmur: "No . . . no . . . not *il conte*. Not Signor Arcangelo."

Pierino woke with a cough. He began to twist on the table. Her father held him down and continued bandaging. Pierino twisted for several awful minutes before he lay still again. Now, her father went to work on his head, cutting the hair from the scalp with a razor blade. A wound emerged, slitted like the inside of a blood orange. Her father began working at the edge of this wound with his needle, getting the red juice from Pierino all up his arms.

Maria-Grazia could not loose her fingers from the windowsill. Terror had stuck them fast. Instead, she began to make up a story for herself about how it wasn't really Pierino's blood at all coming out of Pierino. About how it was petrol after all, or else the harmless blood of a fish. The youngest fisherman, Totò, who could pull in twenty small tuna in an afternoon and still dance all night with a girl on the veranda of the bar—this fisherman had once come up the hill at dawn drenched in blood like an executioner. He had battled a tuna bigger than himself for a day and a night, he claimed, and sure enough the other fishermen followed him into his mother's kitchen, singing, bearing the corpse of the tuna on a stretcher above their heads.

They had also been drenched in blood, and Totò's elderly mother had fainted clean away at the sight of it before she could even scold them for messing her kitchen tiles.

But Maria-Grazia knew that this story was not the real one, not this time. Pierino was old. Only a young man like Totò could battle a tuna.

She could see now that her father had almost finished fixing Pierino. He drew the broken seam of the fisherman's head together as neatly as her mother, Pina, repaired her brothers' split knickerbockers. He had been sewing a long time. While she watched, the gray light of dawn illuminated Pierino's gray skin, and reflected in the glass, making the scene recede a little. At last, when her father had finished sewing, he spoke again. She did not hear everything, only a few words at a time, in the silences between the waves of the sea—for this morning the sea was restless. On an ordinary day Pierino, in his vest and greasy tweed trousers, would have already been hauling his nets and his lobster traps down to the shore.

"Some hemorrhaging in the brain," Maria-Grazia heard. "Unsure how far . . . difficult recovery . . . rest and good care . . ."

And Agata-the-baker's-daughter sank down over her husband, as though she wore some great chain around her neck. When Maria-Grazia's father came out of the door, he moved just as heavily.

"Mariuzza!" he said, when he saw her at the windowsill. "What are you doing here? What's wrong?"

Her legs were trembling; they could no longer support her. She did not know, once she let go of this windowsill, how she would get back home, and—suddenly sorrier for herself than for Pierino or Agata-the-baker's-daughter or even her poor, tired father—she began to cry. Her father stepped forward and took her in his arms, prying her hands off the windowsill as if he were unsticking a *riccio di mare* from a rock.

"Gesù, Maria-Grazia!" he said. "What's wrong?"

"Papà, I thought bad things were going to happen, so I came to look for you and then I got stuck here, because my legs wouldn't work anymore. I didn't mean to spy. I thought you'd come back out and find me."

"How long have you been here?" her father asked, shaking her a little. "What have you seen?"

Maria-Grazia found herself sobbing more violently than ever. "Just five minutes," she said. "Just five minutes. I didn't see anything at all."

"What have you seen?"

"Nothing. Nothing."

Her father hugged her and rocked her. At last he put her down, took a good look at her, and said, "Where are your braces?"

"I haven't got them."

"Maria-Grazia! You walked all this way on your own two legs, without the braces?"

"Yes, Papà. I'm very sorry for it."

But her father lifted her up and—in spite of the stink of blood and exhaustion still clinging to him—he swung her around and around in pure joy.

Riding in her father's arms through the waking streets, she began to feel a little better. Her father said that they must go secretly, that some people wouldn't want him fixing Pierino, and so he carried her not by the main street but through the alleyway belonging to the Fazzoli family, their washing flapping coolly in her face as her father bore her along. Soon her father was lowering her into bed again. "Is Pierino going to die?" she said.

"No. Go to sleep, Mariuzza. Listen to the sea."

She dragged herself to the surface once, anxiously, to ask about school. But her father merely smoothed her forehead and said, "Shh. Shh. There'll be time for school tomorrow. Sleep."

The sleep that came to her was dreamless, and as overwhelming as the breaking of waves.

THE THIRD THING MARIA-GRAZIA witnessed that year of her ninth birthday also had to do with her father.

Now it was almost the end of summer; the bougainvillea was scorched and straggling, the dust overpowering, and tempers worn. Sitting on the veranda one afternoon with Micetto, she became aware of a disturbance in the piazza. Her brothers had been immersed in the daily football game that was carried on, with a rolling exchange of participants, from the end of the siesta hour until eleven or twelve at night. But now the game had broken up, and voices erupted. Raising her head, she saw that her brothers were at the center of it all. Flavio and Filippo, Arcangelo's younger son, were shoving each other hard and exchanging curses. The boys became a current that surged and receded, hurling insults, flinging stones. Then Filippo seized his ball and launched a string of spit in Flavio's direction, which fell short and landed in the dust. Tullio and Aurelio hauled their furious brother toward the House at the Edge of Night; the rest of the boys scattered. Tullio and Aurelio got Flavio as far as the veranda of the bar, where he shook them free and ran up the steps.

She was learning this summer to keep out of sight. She gathered up the cat and retreated behind a frond of the vine.

"I never heard what he said," Tullio was hissing at Flavio. "And we *won't* let you go after him. Get ahold of yourself, Flavio. If Mamma sees you she'll know you've been fighting and there'll be trouble. Tell me what Filippo's been saying."

Flavio was working himself into a frenzy. "He's been spreading damn lies about Papà," he cried at last. "He and everyone else — but Filippo's the worst. He's been telling everyone that Papà did shameful things in the caves by the sea with *il conte*'s wife, Carmela. Years ago, before we were born. It isn't true — I won't believe any of it!"

Maria-Grazia saw Tullio step away and sit down at the nearest table, resting his head on his palm as their father did whenever he was seized with some difficult thought he wished to pursue to its conclusion. Flavio paced the veranda, and at last began to beat upon its beams in frustration. Aurelio, with a little whimper, went up and shook him by the shoulder.

"It isn't true," declared Tullio solemnly at last. "Of course it isn't.

But someone means to shame our family. Someone wants to make fun of Papà because of that damned election they've all been talking about. Someone has it in for us, *ragazzi*."

"It's that bastard Filippo!" Flavio could not bear this rational discussion of his enemy. "Not *someone*, him! *He's* the one whose head needs smacking! *He's* the one who needs his ankles broken! If you hadn't stopped me, I'd have done it myself!"

The swinging door opened and there was Pina. "*What's* this I'm hearing? Flavio? Tullio?"

Her schoolteacher's inflection was enough to make Tullio start up out of his seat, but Flavio continued to rage. "Mamma, boys from school have been saying things about Papà and we've got to go and knock some sense into them, that's all. It's no one's business but ours, not yours or Papà's—"

"Not my business! If I catch you fighting once more, Flavio, I'll *make* it my business—you'll stay home and mend socks and gut chickens and peel potatoes with me all summer, without going out to play at all."

But though the others bowed their heads and shuffled, Flavio's fury was unbending. "Mamma, you don't know what they've been saying! They've been gossiping that Papà did bad things with *il conte's* wife. They've been saying he was screwing with her all over the island, behind the bushes and in the caves by the sea, that *puttana!*"

Pina didn't give Flavio a slap, didn't even acknowledge his bad language. "Lower your voice," she said. "Lower your voice at once, Flavio!"

"No!"

"You will lower your voice."

"I won't!"

All at once, her anger was a force of greater strength than his, and beat his into submission. "I'll not have you talking like this in plain hearing of our neighbors!" she raged at her sons. "I won't stand it! Come inside at once, all of you—where's Maria-Grazia—the *risotto* is sticking to the pan while I have to deal with you!"

"Is it true about Papà?" murmured Tullio.

"Of *course* it isn't true—of *course* your father didn't do those things—why do you think I'm so angry—haven't you got enough intelligence between the three of you to know what's true and what isn't—"

Even Flavio, fists clenched, submitted as she manhandled him in through the door. In the piazza, all that remained was heat and silence.

Cowering behind the vine, Maria-Grazia—despite the awful sick feeling in the bottom of her chest—was certain that her father was innocent.

NOT LONG AFTER, ANOTHER RUMOR began to circulate on the island. According to this rumor, Flavio had been seen skulking home late on the night of the beating of Pierino. When Professor Calleja was asked at what time he had dismissed Flavio from the *Balilla* meeting, *il professore* was definite: well before nine o'clock. Flavio hadn't got home that night until ten, and Pierino had been found at exactly the same moment—his wife, Agata-the-baker's daughter, confirmed it.

A grim object was discovered one morning, shoved in among the bougainvillea branches on the veranda of the House at the Edge of Night, a thing her father tried to hide from her but Maria-Grazia still saw, with awful clarity: a great horsewhip, its flails crusted with dried blood.

This was the fourth scene Maria-Grazia witnessed, the shaming of her brother. Over the years, the islanders would tell many stories about what had happened on the night of the beating of Pierino. The tale about Flavio was the first, and she was the first of the Espositos to hear it, whispered in the schoolyard behind her back with mischievous intent.

Flavio Esposito, the rumor went, had been dismissed early from the *Balilla* meeting, had taken the concealed path between the prickly pears, and had reached the road at about half past nine, when

Pierino had returned from the ocean, alone, a little drunk after a day's good catch. Climbing the hill from the *tonnara*, Pierino was unaware of the Esposito boy shadowing him.

At the dark corner beside Pierino's house, under the flapping laundry, Flavio had attacked—for everyone knew the doctor's son was a good little Fascist, a favorite of Professor Calleja. But, really, the boy had gone too far this time—a dosing with castor oil would have been enough, and besides, wasn't Pierino some kind of cousin of his mother's? The whole thing was shameful. With a well-timed blow to the head, Flavio had rendered Pierino senseless, whipping him across the chest as he fell. Then he must have come home by the byways and *vaneddi*, and—shoving the whip in among the vine branches— had climbed the steps of the House at the Edge of Night and returned to his parents with his brass trumpet in his hand, for all the world like an innocent boy.

"I didn't do it!" cried Flavio, when his father held the whip before him. "Someone's put it there to shame me—to shame us—to make everyone think I was to blame! I've never seen that whip in my life. Why would I beat Pierino? He's family. And Professor Calleja dismissed me at half past nine."

But when their father shook him by the wrists, demanding he tell them at once who might have spread such a wicked rumor, Flavio could not say.

News came that *il conte*'s groom had noticed just such an ancient horsewhip missing from *il conte*'s stables. He could not say when it had been stolen, for it had hung there, laced with cobwebs, for a hundred years, and he never paid it any attention. Only now, suddenly, he realized it was gone—had been gone perhaps for six months. Couldn't the Esposito boy have crept in and stolen it after leaving the *Balilla* meeting that night?

"How could I have taken it?" cried Flavio. "How could I, when I've never even set foot in those stables? And what about my brass trumpet? I had it with me the whole time. How did I beat a man senseless with a whip in one hand and a trumpet in the other?"

Besides, neither Santa Maria nor Agata-the-baker's-daughter had heard coughing in the alleyway that night, and Flavio was still racked with the same cough that had troubled him all year.

Meanwhile, poor Pierino was in a bad state. He could no longer speak or move his right side. When his wife and daughters spoke to him, tears fell from his hangdog eyes, but he said nothing. Death lay upon him now; it seemed only a matter of time. His silence, to many of the islanders, was further proof of Flavio's guilt.

One of the elderly *scopa* players dared to voice these suspicions too openly one evening in the bar. Then Amedeo rose to his full height. "It was not my son," he said. "My son had nothing to do with that shameful attack. Someone means to frame him as a criminal, when he's never done anything wrong. When I find out who it is they'll leave this island, for I'll chase them off myself. How can you believe such a wicked lie?"

No one dared repeat the accusation after that. And, a little ashamed, those islanders who had allowed the story to get out of hand in their imaginations now remembered that it was the good doctor Esposito, after all, who had treated Pierino, that the fisherman and the schoolmistress were distant cousins. But the tide of opinion on the island never turned back fully in Flavio's favor; the rumor had left a stain on him, indefinable, impossible to remove. Feeling this, Flavio shrank away inside himself and swore to leave.

THE FIFTH THING THAT Maria-Grazia witnessed was harder to comprehend, a thing she would only come to understand a quarter of a century later. She saw the prisoner-poet Mario Vazzo, at dusk, his hair oiled, his shoes held together with fishing wire from the old *tonnara*, turn to leave at the bugle call of the *fascisti*—and then he hesitated, caught her mother's wrist, and pressed into her hand a single fallen bougainvillea flower.

This, too, Maria-Grazia stored up in her heart.

IV

IT WAS THE BEATING OF PIERINO THAT LED, INDIRECTLY, TO AMEDEO'S reinstatement as doctor on the island.

That autumn, an opposing rumor gained strength, crushing the grim one about Flavio. Someone whispered in the bar that Dottor Vitale had refused to treat Pierino's injuries. That was why Amedeo had been called, in the dead of night, and why the former doctor was still overseeing Pierino's recovery and not the one who was supposed to be in charge. This rumor spread into every corner of the island by nightfall. The following day, poor Dottor Vitale found himself utterly without patients.

Meanwhile, a disorderly queue of sick and injured islanders had formed on the steps of the House at the Edge of Night.

"I can't treat you," remonstrated Amedeo over the coughing and groaning of his would-be patients. "I'm not the doctor anymore. You must all go back to Dottor Vitale, who knows about your treatments and keeps all the medicines."

But the death chime of Dottor Vitale's reputation had sounded.

Something in Amedeo had altered on that awful night of the beating of Pierino. It was not the fisherman's injuries that caused the change. Amedeo had sewn together dismembered soldiers at the Piave River; he had seen men blown apart, men whipped raw by shrapnel and flame. Always he had been able to separate these things from his own real life, which was a thing lived privately, behind the doors of the House at the Edge of Night. But when he had emerged from that bloodstained room to find Maria-Grazia standing at the window—his Mariuzza, the purest and best of his children—then, in anger, the political portion of himself had woken and shook itself, fierce like a bear out of hibernation.

Now he found himself becoming by degrees a political man.

He allowed Pina to employ the prisoner-poet Mario Vazzo to work afternoons in the bar (the guards prevented any prisoner from working any later than five). They transmitted his wages directly to his wife and child in Milan, who—Mario said—had suffered nothing but trouble since he was taken, moving from apartment to apartment, the child beset with a series of colds and fevers. Sometimes, sitting at the bar, the prisoner-poet composed fragments of melancholy verse on paper napkins, which he later abandoned, and Pina gathered these, proud that a real poet, an educated man, was serving behind the counter of the House at the Edge of Night.

No one else had an educated man working for them, for no one else had employed any of the prisoners. Indeed, many people made it known that they thought it a damned shame that a northern man, a man with a respectable five *lire* a day, should be employed in preference to one of the island's own. But Pina had decided, and Amedeo deferred to Pina in all things in the end.

Mario Vazzo had luxurious curling hair, which, in his new poverty, he slicked with olive oil. He questioned Amedeo about the island's legends, and spent many days poring over Amedeo's red book of stories, researching what he called an "epic verse drama." (Rizzu snorted at this, and Pina retaliated by calling Rizzu a *filisteo*, and for a while there was very nearly war between them.) Pina would allow none of the islanders to mock Mario Vazzo, and though many of the elderly peasants and widows could not take entirely seriously a man who had made his living by scribbling on napkins, soon he was afforded a kind of respect by his association with the former schoolmistress. Besides, he was fascinated by the legends belonging to the island, an interest Amedeo was keen to foster, and which flattered everyone. Pina had told the poet, early on, the story of Castellamare. "There must be some explanation for it," he said. "That noise like crying. All those white skulls."

"So there must be," said old Rizzu. "But it won't be any earthly one. This island's a mysterious place."

All this, the poet wrote down. When the *fascisti*, his guards, entered the bar, the prisoner-poet vanished out of sight behind the curtain.

To remedy this, Pina began a campaign of passive resistance, merely taking note of what the guards liked best—violet pastilles, Modiano cigarettes, a particular brand of Palermitan *arancello*—and failing to restock it, until the guards found in exasperation that they could get nothing they asked for. "*Mi dispiace*," Pina would say. "The war in Abyssinia has disrupted the supplies yet again, *signore*." The *fascisti* repaired instead to Arcangelo's shop, which never seemed to have the same troubles with its stock.

All of these actions were Pina's, true, but Amedeo no longer wished to look away from what was happening to their island. Always, his wife had been ahead of him, from that very first evening when he had pursued her through the house, picking up the pins from her hair. She was ahead of him now, and she was, as always, right. Besides, Pierino had been her last living relative, however distant. She insisted on sending parcels of food weekly to Agata-the-baker's-daughter, despite the depleted supplies in their own house, for the fisherman's family were struggling now with Pierino out of work.

One morning the islanders woke to find Dottor Vitale gone. Now that the island was without a doctor, there was little that *il conte* and Arcangelo could do to stop the islanders coming to the bar for treatment. And if Amedeo occasionally treated the injured and sick among the prisoners, too—well, he was scrupulous about hiding his instruments and covering his traces, and the islanders swore they knew nothing.

So Amedeo resumed his practice of medicine. Besides, *il conte* had his arthritic old war injury, Arcangelo his indigestion, and though they were too proud to come to the doctor directly, they soon began to send their sons for bottles of pills from Amedeo the same as everyone else.

DURING THE SIXTEEN YEARS since Tullio's birth, Amedeo had not stopped watching the boy's phantom twin, Andrea d'Isantu, for signs of similarity. But the two boys, though born almost in the same minute of the same night, had never been alike—and to his knowledge, had never spoken to each other except when school or *Balilla* activities demanded it. Neither was Andrea like *il conte*, however. The boy had been a sallow child, pinched looking, more like a poor man's son, with none of the luxuriant fatness of the count. Now, at sixteen, the boy's thinness had become something more coiled and potent. Andrea's marks at school, his sons reported, were impeccable (second only to those of Maria-Grazia, who was beginning to overtake him). He had excelled in the *Balilla*, and had graduated now to the *Avanguardisti*, where he beat even the zealous Flavio at sports and shooting, and he was to be sent away to a mainland university where he hoped to become active in the *Fasci Giovanili di Combattimento* and then become a party man.

Amedeo tried to make conversation with Andrea when the boy came to collect his father's aspirin tablets every month, but Andrea was oddly self-contained. "My own sons tell me you are making fine progress at school," Amedeo would say, and Andrea would merely reply, "Yes, *dottore*, I am making progress, thanks to Professor Calleja." Or, "And how does your mother feel about your departure for university in a year or two?" he would ask, guilty at speaking Carmela's name aloud in case he gave some hint of lingering feeling, but the boy would merely say, "Fine, thank you, *dottore*. She understands that I wish to better myself by going to the mainland."

This Amedeo knew to be a lie, though a polite one, for whenever he had seen Carmela with the boy—at a distance, during village festivals, or riding about in *il conte's* motorcar—it was clear that she adored her son. In public, she would cling to his arm for support, or brush imaginary mosquitoes from his hair. This attention Andrea endured with the same clear-eyed equanimity with which he endured everything, allowing her to caress him and make much of him, without feeling the need to shake her off as other boys might have done. He was politer and more composed than his father, and better liked on the island, and yet also—in some obscure way—he was felt to be more dangerous. "You know where you are with *il conte*," said Rizzu. "That's why I could stand working for him for twenty-six years. He shouts when he's angry and laughs when he's glad, and you know then whether to keep out of his way or suck up to him for a favor. He was like that even as a boy. His father was a better landlord, but he's easy enough to read, the current *signor il conte*. Whereas it's anyone's guess what that Andrea with his sharp eyes is thinking. He's polite enough, but I daresay he'll turn out to be a harsher master in the end."

Still, Amedeo had little time to think about Andrea, for his own sons were getting to an age when he needed to find occupations for them.

He had loved his boys—fiercely, heart-achingly—as small children, but sometimes now he was troubled by the youths they had become. They seemed to belong more to the world beyond the House at the Edge of Night than they did to him and Pina. He had not known bringing up children would be like this, a slow process of losing. The dark Flavio, his middle son, was the most worrying one. He had developed an odd fascination with the *fascisti*, which had divided him from his mother in recent years. He had insisted on pinning a portrait of *il duce* above his bed until Pina took it down and shoved it away in a drawer; he practiced Fascist marching songs every evening on his brass trumpet. Now it seemed Flavio was perpetually running about the island in his *Avanguardisti* knickerbockers and black fez, swarming up mounds and into ditches, firing guns. Outside of the *Balilla*, Flavio was close as a *riccio di mare*: dark, sallow, reserved of manner, grave of habit, just as Amedeo himself had been as a young man.

The bristle-browed Tullio, in contrast, seemed unable to stop talking. Leaning on the veranda, with thick black hair like his mother's and Amedeo's great stature, he charmed the girls on their way home from Mass, exchanged cigarettes with the fishermen, won the confidence of the elderly *scopa* players, and, in short, was admired by everybody. But Amedeo was uneasy at this self-assurance; it seemed a thing too big to be contained by a five-mile island. Tullio spoke incessantly of America, where some cousin of the Rizzus lived and was said to drive a big motorcar and own a refrigerator, having hauled himself spectacularly out of the Depression. It would not be long, Amedeo feared, before Tullio, too, launched himself across the sea. Amedeo, on more than one occasion, had had to extract his eldest son from the bougainvillea, where he had been discovered entangled in the embraces of the eldest Mazzu girl, scandalizing the elderly *scopa* players, and he rode his bicycle so fast about the island that Pina feared he would come into some fatal collision with *il conte's* motorcar.

The youngest of Amedeo's sons, Aurelio, did not talk about leaving the island, chiefly because he was still mired in the painful and protracted process of attempting to complete his final years at school. This youngest boy, Amedeo felt, was most completely his. Aurelio would still sometimes sidle up to him demanding to hear the latest story from the red book, still sometimes consent to sit beside his sister on the veranda and tease the cat, Micetto. Aurelio had a good round face and a voice that still occasionally plunged endearingly out of his control. But even he, Amedeo knew, would tire eventually of catching lizards in the scrubland, of diving into the same patch of ocean from the same bank of rocks each summer weekend, of the endless football game in the piazza. Amedeo saw the way his youngest son followed the elder Tullio about, imitating his swagger, copying his greased hair.

Now he feared, in his heart, that he needed some pretext to keep his restless sons from leaving the island. And so he immersed them in the life of the bar, teaching them how to make coffee and chocolate as Gesuina had taught him almost twenty years ago, keeping them up late at night cooking rice balls and pastries, and enticing them with a modest share of the profits to spend on whatever they wanted: chocolates and football cards and presents for the various neighborhood girls who hung about the veranda on Saturday nights, hoping for a glimpse of "the Esposito boys." All three walked with a swagger as they imagined American movie stars did, and oiled their hair like the prisoner-poet Mario Vazzo.

THE TRUTH WAS, Amedeo's work as the island's unofficial doctor was becoming all-consuming, and he was glad to have the boys' help in the bar. In those days, people came to the back of the house to have a tooth pulled or an arm bandaged, and to the front for sweet wine and strong coffee and a game of cards, sometimes both in the course of an afternoon. From the terrace of the bar, recovering patients and other customers could sit under the chaos of vines and sip coffee or liquor while contemplating the bar's singular position: in one direction, the whole bright and seething expanse of Europe; in the other, the vastness of the sea.

One day he came upon his daughter weeping on the veranda steps. "What is it, Mariuzza?" he said, covering her in kisses. "Is Micetto sick?"

"No, no," she said crossly. "No, Papà."

"Then what? Do your legs pain you?"

"Papà, my legs haven't pained me in three years."

He supposed that was the truth. "Then what is it?"

Maria-Grazia gave a cross little huff. "Why do you never let me help in the bar? You let Tullio and Flavio and Aurelio help. Why don't you let me go to the *Piccole Italiane* like the other girls, and do the marching, and the camping, and the singing? All the boys went to the *Balilla*. I can sing, Papà. And I can help in the bar and do sums and give customers the right orders much better than Tullio, who's always got his face stuck in his magazines with pictures of cars, or Aurelio, who barely knows up from down!"

Reeling a little at this outpouring of discontent, Amedeo said, "But you don't want to help in the bar, do you? You're a clever girl—you might go on to become an educated woman. And you don't want to go to those Fascist Saturdays, do you, and those camps?"

"My legs are *fine!*" roared Maria-Grazia. "And everyone else goes to them! I'm the only one on this whole island who doesn't!"

With that, she retreated in a rage behind the curtain of the bar. He heard her steps go away from him through the house—still slightly uneven after all those years in braces—and stung with a mixture of exasperation and love.

Was even Maria-Grazia to become adolescent and recalcitrant? He felt he could not bear that. Later he went to her and, soothing her with pet names and the choicest pastries from the bar counter, agreed to allow her to attend the *Piccole Italiane* on a trial basis.

As it turned out, the trial was short. The *Piccole Italiane* would not have her. Professor Calleja felt she could not keep up with the others, that her weak legs hampered her.

Racing up the bar steps in a storm of tears, Maria-Grazia shoved away her father's questions. "I don't want to hear anything about the *Piccole Italiane* anymore!" she cried. "I'm going to leave for the mainland and become a nun!"

It was the poet Mario Vazzo who enticed her out again in the end, serenading her so charmingly that she relented, a little angry with herself, and came back down.

"I'll send your mother to talk to that fool of a teacher Calleja," said Amedeo. "She'll soon put him right."

"I don't want to hear anything more about it, Papà," said Maria-Grazia.

He had intended to speak to Pina about it, but the next day, the newspapers were full of the German führer, *il duce*'s great friend, and his war in Poland. Though *il duce* was to dig in his feet and vacillate for another year, it was this war that soon became the only thing anybody could talk about. And it was this war that was to lead Amedeo's sons, one by one, away from the island.

V

SHORTLY AFTER TULLIO'S NINETEENTH BIRTHDAY, ALL THE BOYS OF his former school class were sent letters ordering them to the mainland. Here, they were to undergo a medical examination. Tullio returned from this examination with a new city haircut, and possessed of private thoughts that made him quiet and inward looking, though he had never before been a pensive boy. He had been pronounced medically fit, and a few months later a green postcard arrived ordering him to report to the barracks near Siracusa.

Tullio considered for half a day, lying on his back in the bedroom full of the football medals and tin cars of his boyhood, instructing his brothers not to disturb him. But that night, when his friends congregated on the veranda of the bar to discuss airplanes and machine guns, Italy's cities and far-off mountains, he was lost. After the bar closed its doors that night, he stood before his mother and father and announced his decision. "I mean to go," he said. "I'd feel all my life that I'd missed the real thing if I didn't. And, anyway, I don't have a choice, so we'd better all be as cheerful as possible about it."

His willingness to go cut Pina to the core, though she had planned from his infancy that he should have a life away from the island. It seemed indecent that he did not weep or struggle, that he waved grinning to them from the fishing boat that bore him away. "All of them will be taken," she wept. "Why, by Sant'Agata and all the saints, did I ever wish for three sons?"

Tullio sent them a keepsake photograph of himself in his regimental uniform. He sent them fortnightly letters, in which he alluded only vaguely to his location. They believed from the dust that fell lightly from the pages that it was somewhere hot like their own island, Libya or Abyssinia, not the cold north—and for this at least Pina gave thanks.

When Flavio received his green postcard, he was already packed, prepared, and performing daily pull-ups and push-ups in his bedroom so as to be "battle ready." He mailed an eager, unpunctuated letter from the barracks three weeks later, complete with a matching photograph, and that was the last they heard from him.

On the awful day in 1942 when the youngest, Aurelio, left the island, Amedeo stood at the bar counter without speaking, his hands wide apart, bracing himself by its support the way Maria-Grazia, years ago, had braced herself on the stone sill of the fisherman Pierino's window—and neither she nor her mother could think of a thing to say.

Aurelio, in his photograph, looked tearful and a little boyish, with a shaving rash on his neck.

The boys' regimental photographs were added to the display along the hall, and sometimes when Maria-Grazia came downstairs softly in the mornings, she found her father standing before them.

Meanwhile, she overheard her mother and father crying, a thing she had never witnessed before. It woke her in utter disorientation one night. "I should never have encouraged them to leave," she heard Pina weeping. "I should never have told them about the mainland, about the universities and the cities and the *palazzi!*"

And her father: "Who has succeeded in keeping their children? Even the Rizzu boys have been ordered away now, and they had to be dragged off by the recruiting officer. How could we have kept them here?"

"All the same, *amore,*" Pina wept, "they won't come home. I know it—they won't come home."

And now her father's voice, too, became high, lamenting: "I

should never have made that bargain with the saint! I should never have gambled Maria-Grazia's life against theirs! What have I done, Pina, *amore*—what have I done?"

No one could get out of him what he meant by this—not Pina, not his daughter. But it was as though her father knew already that the boys would not come home.

THE NEWS OF TULLIO'S disappearance arrived by telegram. He had gone missing in Egypt. The news that Aurelio was missing in the same battle came a week later: The two boys, Tullio, the eldest, always leading, and Aurelio, the youngest, always following, had vanished together. The news about their middle boy, Flavio, came three months afterward, though he had vanished at almost the same moment.

There followed a longer letter in which Amedeo was informed that Flavio had been awarded a medal by *il duce*, for service against the British in Egypt. This medal his sergeant enclosed, because it was all of Flavio that had been found during the retreat.

Holding the disc of metal in his hands, Amedeo broke, and so did Pina. With stooped shoulders, he ordered the customers away from the bar and shut its doors. "It will remain closed," he ordered, "until our Tullio and our Flavio and our Aurelio are found."

He retreated to his study at the top of the house, where he polished and repolished Flavio's medal, as though trying to scrub out the relief of *il duce* emblazoned on its bronze face. He became once again submerged in stories, with a kind of drugged distraction. Meanwhile, Pina, who had been summoned back to teach a little at the school now that Professor Calleja was fighting at Tripoli, did her duty calmly, but moved through the house as though asleep, too, troubled no longer by anger or passion or fierceness or—in fact—by anything at all. To Maria-Grazia it seemed that she was living now not with her mother but with the ghost of her mother, and with a vague, helpless double of her father who moved about like an old man, shoulders bowed.

The House at the Edge of Night was locked up. On the mirrors behind the counter, on which the bar's name was emblazoned in twirling, fanciful script, rust spots began to bloom and lizards crawled, leaving behind them trails of four-fingered prints. The bar, like all things on the island under the influence of sun and dust, returned with alarming speed to its perpetual faded amber, so that seen from a distance it was like the sepia photograph of a building.

Maria-Grazia finished her growing up in this reverential silence. They were both broken, her mother and her father, and she tended them with gentleness. But inside her a storm was raging. She was *not* broken: She was almost seventeen and full of tightly wound life, and here she was compressed between the two of them with their grief and their silences, with scarcely room to breathe. She did not want to believe, as they did, that her brothers were not coming home—that Tullio would never again be discovered entangled with some girl behind the bougainvillea, that Flavio would never again trumpet one of his Fascist marching songs. Worst of all, Aurelio, who (though she had never told her parents this, and refused to let herself remember it except very occasionally) had crept to her room in the early hours before his departure and wept, racked with silent fear, in her arms. Aurelio, always her kindest brother, was like her at heart, she knew—he had never wanted to leave the island, had loved its shuttered noons and its roads weighted with heat and silence. For Aurelio, this small world had been enough, and yet he had been sent far away across the sea, to be lost among the deserts of Africa. If she allowed herself to think about it she might, like her parents, simply refuse to inhabit her life any longer. So, for her own survival, she decided not to believe that they were gone.

The summer after Aurelio left, *il conte*'s agents had come to the House at the Edge of Night with a written offer to buy the bar. "Why not?" said Amedeo, throwing up his hands.

"What will Tullio and Flavio and Aurelio do, if we sell the bar while they're away?" cried Maria-Grazia. "Have some sense, Papà!"

"The accounts won't balance," said Amedeo. "I haven't the strength to open the place again."

Then Maria-Grazia, exhausted with her parents' weeping, took charge. She had finished school with the highest marks—eights and nines, even tens in arithmetic and Italian. Without opening her prize books (Pirandello, Dante, and a volume of Fascist poetry), she put them away and the next morning occupied herself with the salvaging of the bar. If her mother and father could not take care of the House at the Edge of Night, she would.

She opened its doors and began trading in a reduced way, staving off the financial ruin that had begun to hang over them like the air of defeat hanging over the whole country. Chasing the lizards away from the mirrors, which they now considered their territory, she saw reflected in the glass the impossibly blue line of the ocean and allowed herself to dream of the day when her brothers would cross it as war heroes with medals on their chests. Then, perhaps, she would be an educated woman, but not yet.

She could no longer get the cigarettes or matchbooks that once had come from the mainland, the packets of chewing gum or the bottles of liquor. A shipment of *arancello* had been bombed in the Strait of Messina; the pistachios for the pastries, which came from Sicily, could no longer be bought because the Sicilian peasants, starving under the loss of half their manpower to the war effort, had foraged and eaten them all. At the beginning of the war the wives of Castellamare had hoarded the remaining mainland food: cans of fruit and hot chocolate from Arcangelo's shop, packets of *biscotti*, fat *salami*. Maria-Grazia could no longer get coffee for the bar, and drinking chocolate had long since been out of the question. The baker no longer supplied anything but the hard, rustic bread belonging to the island, and—when the supply of flour became sporadic— very little of that, and most of it dry and gritty. The island's pigs grew thin, and the butcher had taken to cutting their ham into petal-like slices in order to sell more for the same price. Everything that could be harvested that summer of 1942 was harvested as usual, but afterward the most desperate peasants went out into the fields as they had in the nineteenth century and gleaned what was left, and others took to roaming the hedges and abandoned orchards, foraging for wild "grandfather" oranges, the warty fruits that had been left on the trees since last year and were sometimes succulent and sometimes dry as sand inside. The peasants also foraged little bundles of "greens," which were really just weeds and shooting plants, but could be tied up with string and sold in the marketplace. They gathered bucketfuls of the great *babbaluci*, ground-snails they found under rocks after wet weather. They dug nuts from among the thorny grass of *il conte*'s uncultivated hunting land.

By the end of the war, they would all be eating snails and greens. For now, Maria-Grazia instead served approximations of the former glorious pastries; homemade *arancello* and *limoncello*, which she bought directly from the island's elderly widows; and what she christened *caffè di guerra*: hot water with a dusty trace of coffee. In a faltering way, complaining loudly, people continued to come to the House at the Edge of Night, if only for the company. Maria-Grazia, in the latter years of the war when all the railways were bombed and the ports occupied, would invent fantastical dishes for the customers out of what was left, a homemade *limonata* utterly without sugar, chicory coffee, bread-and-tomatoes, bread-and-onions, bread-and-greens.

Very little in the way of material goods could be brought from the mainland, because of the constant passage of warships around the island and the fact that there was nothing to be had. But occasionally extraordinary things washed up. One night the fisherman 'Ncilino, Pierino's son-in-law, brought word of a crate of wireless radios, in full working order, available for discreet purchase to the highest bidder. Maria-Grazia waylaid him on the way back from the sea and demanded to see the radios. Two or three were waterlogged, one had a smashed dial, and another was undamaged. "If you can get me a battery for it," said Maria-Grazia, "and if it works, I'll buy it."

The bar was becoming outdated, as Maria-Grazia knew, and in a fit of recklessness that kept her awake for several nights afterward, she spent the whole of her first two months' profits on the radio—outbidding even Arcangelo, who had wanted it for his shop. Once 'Ncilino had obtained batteries by some means known only to himself, the radio came alive.

She set it up on the counter. She loved the BBC station, which they picked up occasionally from Malta ("If the wind is right," claimed Gesuina), and any station that played jazz music and orchestral music, so different from the wailing songs of the island, that were all she had ever heard. But cannily she kept the wireless tuned instead to news of the war. Now that the bar was hers, and now that the wireless radio might at any moment blare tidings of their sons and nephews and grandsons, people thronged to the bar and gathered round the wireless radio, in spite of having to pay one whole *lira* for *caffè di guerra* and gritty bread with a few greens arranged on top.

"I would have charged you more for that radio," said 'Ncilino ruefully, "if I'd known I was selling you the only wireless on Castellamare. But there you go, Maria-Grazia, you're a clever businesswoman and I can say no more about it. Who would have thought you'd become so shrewd, you with your leg braces always clanking about?"

Maria-Grazia knew how she had always been viewed on the island. She knew that she was, at best, "that poor girl in the leg braces," at worst, "the cripple child"—though she had stopped wearing the leg braces when she was fourteen, and tired now only when she walked long distances, or uphill. In the end she had not thrown away the braces, but stowed them in the old Campari liquor box in her father's room under the eaves, among the other family relics. She sometimes felt the phantom weight of them, and it seemed the rest of the islanders, too, still believed them to be fastened around her ankles. In fact, it had taken the blind Gesuina almost three years to realize she no longer wore them, for the simple reason that no one had bothered to tell her. "I couldn't hear them anymore, of course," said Gesuina, who was nearly ninety and had to be led to and from the bar each morning. "But I thought it was just my hearing going, too."

At the beginning of the war Maria-Grazia had been fifteen years old. That year a change had come over the male youth of Castellamare, a kind of fever: Even the most innocent of her female classmates had begun to be desperately claimed by the boys who would soon be leaving, as though all of them were laying down a deposit on future wives and sweethearts. For weeks the girls and their lovers had hung about in alleys and in the caves by the sea, to return at dusk with necks mottled like the skin of flounders, earning scoldings from their grandmothers. But no boy came to claim Maria-Grazia, and as she sat on the steps she understood bitterly that her own place on the island was still a separate one. She would always be a different kind of person: a person to be prayed for, not fallen in love with.

For these and other reasons, Maria-Grazia now failed to realize the simple truth that would have been evident in a larger town: that she was beautiful.

Yet, during these years of the war when great gray ships flung tidal waves onto the shores of the island, when ceaseless planes like mosquitoes—British, some said, and others German—traversed the great blue sky overhead, she saw that from her stewardship of the bar came a grudging, hard-won respect. For everyone saw how she managed the business, carefully, like the captain of a fishing vessel, steering it from ruin and loss into safer waters. She spoke kindly to the elderly *scopa* players and the widows of Sant'Agata; she charmed the retired fishermen as completely as her brother Tullio had. And no one could deny that she stood on her own feet for eight hours each day, ten hours—as straight and tall (or almost) as any other girl on Castellamare.

Only at night did she allow herself to weep, brushing the cigarette butts and bent *scopa* cards from the floor—and not out of self-pity, but from the sheer exhaustion of these long days of work and solitude and endless waiting.

VI

THEN CAME THE DAY OF THE SHIPS.

Like a miracle, boats began to gather at the edge of the horizon, great gray ones like churches and tiny ones no bigger than the fishing boat of Pierino. The young fisherman Totò's sister Agata, who in his absence plied the deep waters with the same fearlessness as her brother, in his boat the *Holy Madonna*, arrived in the bar later that afternoon, her nose and cheeks a little scalded. Agata reported that she had got close enough to the ships to hear that the voices on board were speaking "some kind of funny *inglese*." "How many ships?" asked the elderly *scopa* players. Agata reported that there were over a thousand of them by her count—"*Cazzo*, perhaps thousands and thousands!" And, she added, judging by all the guns and the cannons, they weren't amassing around Sicily for a tourist visit to the Greek temples.

At this a cheer went up—for the islanders had long since abandoned any pretense at Fascism or socialism or any other -ism, and instead favored anyone who might cut short the war so that their sons and nephews could come home.

Totò's sister, whom everyone referred to as Agata-the-fisherwoman, drained two glasses of water and two of *arancello* through lips as dry as the soil of the island. "I'd wish them better weather for it," she said. "It's fiercely hot out there, but there's a *bastardo* of a storm coming, and they'll be seasick before they land, those *inglesi*, for I've heard most of them have never been upon the sea at all."

Of course, there was no sign of a storm, but every ancestor of

Agata-the-fisherwoman had possessed the same prodigious gift for predicting the weather, and no one contradicted her. Shortly after, sauntering like a boy in her baggy men's trousers and flat cap, Agata-the-fisherwoman left to return to the sea. "Clean your mouth out, young woman!" Gesuina called after her. "I don't want to hear your *bastardo* and *cazzo* in here again, thank you!"

"I'm sorry, *nonna*," called Agata, abashed.

The customers crowded around the wireless radio, which was playing a Fascist marching song. Maria-Grazia tuned it to the BBC station. This station had something to say. Maria-Grazia listened, but the English voices had nothing to say about ships or the Mediterranean. "They're talking about the English weather," she said.

"Do you think there really is going to be an invasion?" said one of the elderly *scopa* players.

"They wouldn't tell us about it if there were," said Rizzu. "But will *our* island be spared—that's the real question? Will they leave Castellamare alone, or will we have to take up our pitchforks and our tuna gaffs and fight?"

"I doubt the English or the Americans have very much use for Castellamare," said Father Ignazio from the corner, "even considering, of course, its strategic location in the Mediterranean and its evident natural charm."

"*Ai-ee*, but we've been invaded and invaded since the first baby drew breath to cry on this island!" mourned Gesuina. "And it'll be our cursed misfortune to be invaded again—begging your pardon for disagreeing with you, *padre*."

"That's quite all right," said Father Ignazio, and covered his face with his handkerchief. The priest was becoming an old man now, and spent his afternoons dozing on the veranda of the bar. But even he could not sleep through the continuing uproar of this particular day.

Maria-Grazia knocked on the door of the stone bedroom beside the courtyard, and the room at the top of the house. "Mamma," she said. "Papà. Wake up. They say the *inglesi* and the *americani* are coming."

Her father roused himself at once and followed her into the bar. But here the marching songs were still playing, the ceiling fan still whirring, and all looked as it had every day for the last year. And so her father returned to the top of the house and to his book of stories. Around six o'clock, just as the heat was leaving the courtyard and the piazza, he called her up to him. "Maria-Grazia, you're right," he said. "Look at the horizon."

Her father was bent over an old pair of binoculars that had once been Flavio's, a *Balilla* prize. Now that the heat haze had lifted a little, the ships were quite plain. Along the edge of the sea they were gathering, arrayed like raindrops on a wire.

All of this unsettled Maria-Grazia a little—made her wander from room to room and out onto the veranda, when she should have been minding the bar's counter.

Standing there beneath the cool mat of vines, she heard the voice of a child. She searched under the tables and unearthed the girl Concetta, who was trying without success to entice Micetto out from the bougainvillea. "He doesn't want to play with me," said Concetta.

"Come inside for a glass of *limonata*," said Maria-Grazia. "Or an *arancino* if you're hungry."

"Everyone in there is pushing and shoving over the wireless."

"I know, but come with me. I'll find you somewhere to sit out of their way."

Concetta, Arcangelo's daughter, was a child who seemed to belong to no one; neither her father nor her mother knew what to do with her. Dirty of face, draggled of hair, she roamed the island like a boy, catching lizards in her pinafore and hitting things with sticks. The girl suffered from violent seizures—as a child of three, she had fallen down in the piazza and convulsed until foam came out of her mouth, and ever since then she had been afflicted. Though Amedeo had examined her and diagnosed an epileptic condition, the town's old women insisted on capturing her as she roamed about the streets, and hauling her to the church where they would say endless Ave Marias and Our Fathers for her troubled soul.

Recently, to escape their ministrations, Concetta had taken to hanging around Maria-Grazia at the bar. "Yes, please, a *limonata*, please," she said, getting to her feet to expose a front entirely coated in the white dust of the veranda. "After that a rice ball. Or two?" she added, hopefully.

Maria-Grazia set a glass and two *arancini* on a napkin before her at the bar, and hoisted the little girl onto a stool. With great satisfied sucks, Concetta devoured the rice balls and drained the lemonade. She was Maria-Grazia's most appreciative customer. Concetta could not remember the fat rice balls from before the war, which had had the unquestionable advantage of being made with real rice and not rolled-up bread with grit in it; she was unaware that *limonata* was not meant to make you wince and suck your teeth but was supposed to be a sweet thing.

"There," Concetta said, with satisfaction. "That's better. I had a pain in my stomach from being so hungry all day."

"Where have you been today?" said Maria-Grazia.

"Over by the rocks and in the caves," said Concetta. "And with the goats at the Mazzus'. But they were boring today because it's so hot. All they would do is lie and wave their ears."

"You take care when you're about by yourself on the island," said Maria-Grazia. "There are lots of ships out in the sea right now, getting ready for something that's happening in Sicilia." She hardly knew what she was warning the girl against.

"I don't worry about the ships," said Concetta. "Unless they do something interesting like start fighting. Then I'll go and watch." She gave her empty glass a last great suck. "Why doesn't Micetto like me?"

"Oh, he's fierce like that with everyone. You mustn't worry. He's got a wild nature, not like us."

"*I've* got a wild nature," said Concetta, with perfect truth.

AS MARIA-GRAZIA SAT BETWEEN her father and mother that night at the kitchen table, oppressed as usual by their separate silences, a

storm approached. She heard it in the uneven crashing of the breakers, the snapping of the leaves of the palms. "Agata-the-fisherwoman
was right," she said, watching clouds mass at the window.

"What?" murmured Pina.

"A storm."

That night, in her childhood room with its prim pressed-flower
pictures, its home-developed photographs of Micetto, and its school
certificates with yellowing edges, she could not get to sleep. This
wakefulness infuriated her. She felt goaded by it, as if by a mosquito.
Why would sleep not come? Outside, great winds tore through the
palms, making Micetto yowl. Someone's shutters rattled on the other
side of the piazza.

She went down and retrieved the cat, as she always did in bad
weather, but he would not settle to sleep on the end of her bed. Instead he ran round and round her room, fur bristling, until she was
obliged to put him out again. Then, for the first time in his life, Micetto bit her. "*Micettino!*" she scolded, but the cat was quivering
under the oleander bushes, entirely wild.

When the storm quietened for a moment, she thought she heard,
above the clouds, the high whine of planes.

SHE MUST HAVE SLEPT a little because she was woken—all at once—
by a great thunder as though the house were falling to pieces around
her. "Mamma!" she called. "Papà!"

Blindly, in the dark of the stairs, she and her father found each
other. "What is it?" she cried.

"Gunfire," said her father. "Heavy guns."

"Here?"

"No, *amore*. Further off than they sound. They're bombarding the
coast of Sicilia."

She ran with her father to the top of the house. From there, the
sea spread out beneath them. Great lights and explosions pierced the
dark, and when the night was lit up she saw a wall of smoke obscuring

the stars, like the boundary along a forest fire. Those tiny houses that had always stood as vaporous as something in a dream across the water had vanished under rolls of cloud. Plumes of water flew up, plumes of sand. And all over the surface of the ocean bits of wreckage were heaving, assaulted by the waves. "Airplanes," said her father. "Those poor men in their airplanes must have been wrecked in the storm."

"Do you think any survived?" she said. "Couldn't we send out ships?"

"They're too far off."

Meanwhile, the island was thrown into confusion. Someone, startled out of bed, had got to the church before Father Ignazio could stop them and rung an invasion bell. Mazzu and his sons had gathered their pitchforks and hunting rifles and were in their boat and halfway out of the quay on a rescue mission before the rest of the fishermen stopped them: It was no good; in the heavy shelling they would certainly be sunk. Meanwhile, a crowd had gathered in the piazza and a group of *il conte*'s peasants had hauled out the statue of Sant'Agata. Gesuina and the other widows were addressing prayers to it, while the *podestà, il conte* himself, faintly ridiculous in his nightshirt, wool socks, and chapped boots left over from the Great War, was running about giving orders.

It was rumored that the prison guards had boarded their gray motorboat and fled, leaving the prisoners unguarded. Sure enough, when *il conte* went to summon the guards to reestablish some kind of order, they were nowhere to be found.

All that night, the great gray ships kept coming, disgorging men as small as grains of rice onto the coast of Sicily. And as the light came up, another great wonder appeared—ships like water creatures that drove straight up the beach and out of sight onto the distant shore.

Morning brought a lower rumbling, which suggested the *inglesi* and the *americani* had broken through into the depths of Sicily. There was nothing to do but open the bar, and this Maria-Grazia did. When she raised the blinds, she found a crowd of neighbors already outside, impatient to follow the proceedings on the island's only wireless.

All morning, to the sound of great guns, Maria-Grazia did a steady trade. Meanwhile, the wireless had nothing new to say, did not seem to know that a battle was taking place at all. Even when Pina came home from school at lunchtime, she could get nothing from the BBC station, which was too fast and too crackling for her to make out.

Thus it was that when the miracle of the man from the ocean took place, no one witnessed it except the girl Concetta.

ALL MORNING, EXHILARATED BY the popping and thundering of the battle on the Sicilian coast, Concetta had roamed the island in search of a better view. By noon, she had reached the remote end of Castellamare, where the scrub dropped down to the caves. Now the sun was like a weight on her shoulders, and she took refuge in the first opening in the rock. The caves had never frightened Concetta, though she had heard about their strange weeping. She didn't believe in any silly Greek ghosts.

At noon the sea was oily, listless, blurry on its surface, Sicily just a faint shadow like water vapor. How she wished she had a pair of binoculars like those *Balilla* boys! What a glorious din and smoke it all made!

Concetta did not know what war was, but she certainly liked its noise and its chaos. Both appealed to her natural sense of things. She had always regarded the world about her warily, never sure if it was entirely safe. In her six years of life she had been doused with holy water and warded with the sign of the cross, subjected to endless ambushes by pious old ladies brandishing effigies of Sant'Agata, and bullied through the rosary by her father, when all she wanted was to run free and to be left alone! To Concetta the world was a rock in a hazy blue ocean and it had never occurred to her that it should make sense. She didn't know her age or the names of the other islands, and she agreed with her mother that the stars and the tides of the ocean were a great puzzle, just like her sickness. A world for clever people like Professoressa Vella and *il conte* to read about in books, not a world that ever intruded on her own.

But now, across the sea, something was intruding, and Concetta felt a light chill of fear pass over her. She hunched down in the entrance to the cave, small like a stone, and waited.

The thing had begun as a space between waves, a blackness. Something so tiny it could have been a dying fish or an empty glass bottle. Now it was larger, more like a hunk of wood. No one but Concetta watched it approach. Slowly the dark thing crested each wave, vanished, reappeared. Sometimes, blurrily, it broke apart and became two; at other times the heat haze made it rise up, like it was performing a feat of levitation. Once it put out a tentacle, or a leg, or an arm perhaps, as though reaching for something. That was when the girl realized, with a shock, that it was alive, or half so. How else could it make those strange motions in the water, flailing like a dying *medusa*?

Now it came a little closer, and she saw that it had two arms that moved with purpose, drawing it on across the water. When it was a few meters off the shore, among the rocks the fishermen called Morte delle Barche, it stopped and rode the waves: up and down, up and down. Then it raised an arm and heaved itself out of the water with a sudden surge of purpose, making alarming, watery yells.

Concetta, without realizing it, had come forward out of the cave in her fascination. The creature in the ocean, she now understood, had seen her on the shore and was signaling. Concetta's arms felt heavy as wood. In the back of her throat she could taste the strange tang, like the castor oil her father rubbed into the shop counter, which always came before a seizure. It was only now that she knew for sure that she was frightened. The sea creature forged on through the breaking waves. It drew near to the submerged rocks, and the harder waves here dragged it in and then out again, in and then out, until it was thrown up against the triangular rock that they called Canetto. This rock it seized in desperation. Making a tent of her folded hands on her forehead, Concetta squinted and saw that the sea creature resembled a man with skinny shoulders, a barrel chest, long arms like a monkey, and a face white as *ricotta*.

Concetta's toes curled with wanting to run. The creature, gathering up a last surge of strength, shoved itself off the rocks and plunged again into the water. It went under a couple of times before its feet could gain a purchase on the fine sand just off the shore. Slowly, it began to emerge, by faltering steps, plunging and rearing in the waves, making a sound like drowning.

"*Hé!*" it called. "*Hé!*" And then an explosion of nonsense. The creature wore green. In its hand it grasped a gun. It waved feverishly, still pouring its nonsense language.

"*Salve, signore*," said Concetta, for by now she was almost certain the thing was human and not animal.

The man heaved up out of the shallows, water streaming off him. Then with a great thump he landed in the sand, stretched out at the edge of the water, and moved no longer.

Standing in the shelter of the edge of the cave, Concetta felt the fit loosen its grip and pass over her, leaving the blue sky less oppressive and the heat less thunderous—and all at once her fear lifted, too.

By tiny steps, like those she used to capture lizards in the scrubland, Concetta approached the man. She knelt beside him. The man's hair was yellow, like the hair of a dog or a cat. His skin was so fine that in places you could see a little blue and gray coming through from underneath. Or perhaps he was just very cold. Blood dripped from somewhere under him and made a perfectly round hole in the sand. A crab edged out of the shade and began working at this hole rhythmically, with both pincers, an old woman knitting. When she had taken a good look, Concetta said, "Who are you?"

"*Wiliu helpmee*," said the man. "*Wiliu helpmee gogetelp plenwentdown.*"

"Speak properly," said Concetta, a little sternly. "Speak dialect, or Italian. Let me look at your shoulder. I've seen Dottor Esposito work and I know how he does it."

But the man gave a yell and swatted Concetta away, babbling more of his foreign words at her.

"I can't help you if you won't speak properly," said Concetta.

The man was going to sleep. When she was sure that he didn't have anything else to say, Concetta got up and started along the shore to the town.

CONCETTA CLIMBED THROUGH the prickly pears and scrub grass, following paths of her own, and emerged on the edge of the piazza a little after two. The houses were all shuttered at this hour for the siesta. Not even the priest, Father Ignazio, was about. Concetta climbed the steps of the House at the Edge of Night and heaved open the swing door. In one corner, the ancient Gesuina dozed over the wireless radio. The doctor's daughter sat behind the counter with a fat book propped against the coffee machine, under a ceiling fan that spun and spun without cooling.

"Here's Concetta," said Maria-Grazia in the way she always did, a way that made you feel important.

Concetta drew herself up to her full four feet and said: "There's a man. He's sleeping by the ocean. You'd better come, Signora Maria-Grazia, right away."

Maria-Grazia let her book fall to the counter. "O, Dio," she said. "You've found a dead body."

"No, he came out of the ocean. Swimming out of the ocean. Dressed all in green. He's got hair like the Mazzus' dog, funny yellow hair, and his face is white as *ricotta*."

The doctor's daughter got to her feet. "Where did you leave him, Concetta?"

"By Morte delle Barche, outside the caves." Concetta considered for a moment whether there was anything she'd forgotten to tell Maria-Grazia. "He's got blood coming out of him. And a gun."

Gesuina woke with a snort and said, "What's that? A man with a gun? *Ai-ee*, it's the invasion!" With alarming speed, she rose and shuffled out of the bar, in search of reinforcements.

"Come with me," said Maria-Grazia, and she took Concetta by the hand and turned the cardboard "Chiuso" sign around in the bar's door. "You'd better tell my father everything you've just said, and quickly, before Gesuina starts gossiping."

AMEDEO OFTEN SLEPT IN the afternoons, on the bald velvet sofa at the top of the house, and recently he had found himself plunging deeper, and staying down longer and longer, so that it became difficult to surface. Often, by the time he woke, the sun had arced over the island and fallen, and the world outside was a twilit one. But today he had barely closed his eyes when he was dragged up with a start. Here was his daughter shaking him, and the girl Concetta, Arcangelo's girl, barefoot and filthy in a white dress translucent in the sunlight, her legs coated in sand. "What is it?" he said, more irritably than he intended.

The girl Concetta began at once to tell a confused story about a ghostly pale man appearing from the ocean, dressed in green, with hair like straw—

"He's injured," said Maria-Grazia. "He may need your help, Papà."

"And he was talking a funny language," said Concetta, who had just recalled this fact. "A nonsense language. Like this: *Wilu helpee wilu helpee.*"

Amedeo, properly awake now, sat up and met his daughter's eyes. "Does anyone else know about this?"

"Just me," said Concetta, puffing up a little with importance.

"And Gesuina, who overheard," said Maria-Grazia.

Amedeo reached for his medical bag, which was always ready now. He packed extra swabs, extra bandages, and a precious shot of morphine, which was a little out-of-date but would be infinitely better than nothing if the man were in a bad state. "We'll need a few people to come with us," he said. "Ignazio, and a couple of strong fishermen—Bepe, and Totò's sister Agata. Fetch three clean sheets in case we need to carry him, Maria-Grazia."

Maria-Grazia ran and stripped the sheets from the beds in her brothers' empty rooms.

Together, the three of them crossed the town and knocked at the priest's door. The streets were quiet under the oppression of cicadas and heat. Father Ignazio came right away, and together they woke Rizzu's nephew Bepe. He emerged at once, too, sticking his head out of the upstairs window of his house behind the church. "There's an injured man who needs help," called Amedeo. "We need people to carry him. Will you come with us?"

Bepe retreated; they heard him running down the stairs. When he opened the door, Father Ignazio caught him by the shoulder. "It's a foreign soldier," said the priest quietly. "We don't know what the position is with *il conte* and the town council if we help him, but we're going to anyway. If you would prefer not to be in on it, then go back inside."

Bepe nodded, and disappeared into the house. He re-emerged with his hunting rifle over his shoulder. As they left the town they called for Agata-the-fisherwoman. Agata had not been sleeping; she was under the trumpet vine in her yard, knotting a new net, while her dog, Chiappi, lay prone on top of her feet. Agata listened for only a moment before bounding from her chair, dragging the dog by the collar.

Concetta was usually frightened of Chiappi, but not today. Today she ignored his bad-tempered, sleepy growls and said, "Everyone, listen—I know the quickest way."

"Then lead us to the patient, Concetta," Amedeo said.

Concetta led them by her own path, through the cacti, under the fence of the Mazzus' vineyard, and down the rough slope to the caves. The doctor, the priest, Maria-Grazia, Rizzu's nephew Bepe, and Agata-the-fisherwoman ran in grim single file behind her.

It was the most exciting thing that had happened to Concetta in her life.

———

THE FOREIGNER WAS LYING under the full force of the sun, turned on his side a little. One hand had left a great scratch mark across the sand. His torn shirt flapped open, exposing a great wound on his shoulder which expelled blood with a steady rhythm. Maria-Grazia hung back as her father checked the man's breathing and pulse, and gripped his arms and legs for signs of injury. Then he ordered the others to move the soldier into the shadow of the caves. Maria-Grazia, without knowing why, stood aside and did not assist them. Her father knelt beside the man and began to rip off his battledress. "*Padre*, get me swabs and iodine," he told Father Ignazio. "We'll keep the morphine unless he needs it urgently. It's almost my last. Is anyone's English good enough to speak to him? Maria-Grazia, yours?"

"No!" she cried in alarm. "I can't speak to him, Papà."

The man woke a little and made a half turn on his back in the sand, groaning. "Mariuzza," called her father. "Come here and support his head, will you? See he doesn't move while I apply these bandages."

Maria-Grazia did not want to approach, but she did. Kneeling, she took the foreigner's head in her hands. His hair felt like her brothers', tousled with salt and warm like Aurelio's after swimming. She looked down into his face and found that it was not distasteful, as she had expected it to be, but open and a little upturned, appealing, like a boy's. When she moved the remains of his shirt aside, a heavy disc of metal fell from the pocket and landed in the sand. Concetta seized it with delight. "What's this? Is it mine? Can I keep it? Is it from America?"

"I don't know, *cara*. Give it back to the man. Maybe his country gave it to him for bravery, like my brother Flavio's medal from *il duce*, and if so it's probably precious to him."

The man reached out with one hand, grasping a little with sandy fingers. "See," said Maria-Grazia. "He wants it back. Let him hold it—maybe that will make him feel better."

Concetta dropped the medal into the foreigner's palm, but the foreigner let the medal fall and continued to grasp for something until—at last—he found Maria-Grazia's arm. Maria-Grazia recoiled a little, but the foreigner did not let go. He worked his way along the arm until he found her wrist, and held it. He continued to hold it all the time her father was swabbing and disinfecting.

Meanwhile, Concetta disappeared into the cave and returned with one of the lucky white stones. She dropped it into the man's pocket and put the medal around her neck. "There," she said. "A fair exchange. He can have that lucky stone instead and I'll keep this."

"Is he going to live?" said Maria-Grazia, when the man was bandaged and a little water fetched from the Mazzus' spring had been tipped into his mouth from the priest's cupped hands.

Her father, who never said one way or another until a patient was firmly out of danger, merely rubbed his forehead with his handkerchief and said, "We need to get him up to the house and out of this heat, anyway."

"He's from the north, where they have snow," said Agata-the-fisherwoman. "This heat is probably enough to kill him."

"Get the sheets ready," said the doctor. "You two at the head, Agata and Bepe—you're both stronger—and Ignazio and I at the feet."

"Look over there," said the priest, under his breath, as they hoisted the man in the stretched sheets. "Here comes the town nuisance brigade in their black shirts—watch out, *dottore*."

Sure enough, along the beach came an officious little party: *il conte*, the grocer Arcangelo, and *il conte*'s two land agents.

"Lord have mercy on us all," said Agata-the-fisherwoman. "Excuse me, *padre*—but if Arcangelo gets talking, we'll be here until the war ends. Let's get going."

This they attempted, but still the little party came blustering across the sand. *Il conte* stopped with his boots touching Amedeo's shoes. Sweat dripped from his nose. "What's this?" he said. "An enemy soldier! Seize him, men. The other members of the town council are on their way, Signor Esposito, and you'll be compelled to surrender him to us."

The doctor said nothing, but he turned the stretcher party a little so that he and Bepe stood between *il conte* and the foreigner. "Arcangelo! Men!" said *il conte*. "Seize this enemy soldier. Apprehend him."

"He doesn't look like he'll last the night, *signor il conte*," said Arcangelo, twisting his hands. "Maybe we had better just let the doctor take care of him. Why don't we let the doctor—"

"This man is not the doctor," raged *il conte*. "He's just the bartender. I'm surprised I have to remind *you*, Arcangelo, of that fact!"

"Then, since I'm no doctor," said Amedeo, "you'll have no objection to my taking this injured foreigner home with me. To my bar, which is private property and nothing to do with your *fascisti* friends or your damned war!"

Il conte reeled in fury.

"Please," said Maria-Grazia. The soldier's hand around her wrist was becoming hot and dry, as though he was suffering a fever. "Please. Let us take the man up to the town. He's a prisoner of war either way, at least until we know who's won in Sicilia, and we have to treat him fairly. Especially now the *inglesi* and the *americani* are just across those waters. If anyone comes looking for him and finds he wasn't treated by a doctor . . ."

She would never afterward know what had compelled her to make this speech, but her father gave her one quick nod when it was finished.

Il conte waited a long time before he stepped back, but at last he did. They went with the makeshift stretcher at a jog across the sand, Concetta still wearing the medal, the foreign soldier groaning, and Maria-Grazia gripping him by the hand.

"PINA!" YELLED THE DOCTOR as they deposited the foreigner on the kitchen table, sending peaches rolling. "Come here! I need you to speak English!"

"What is it?" called Pina.

"I need you to talk to this man in English, *amore*, and find out what's happened to him. Fetch me the smallest tweezers, Maria-Grazia. And another bottle of antiseptic. All the grit and sand in his shoulder needs to come out. We'll see if he needs the morphine then. Pina! Come here and speak English for us, please!"

At the threshold, Pina halted and drew back a little. "Who is he?"

"We don't know. A foreign soldier. He was washed up on the beach. I need you to ask how he was injured, what happened, where he's from, and if there's anyone else who needs rescuing. Maybe the fishermen can take out their boats if so, though I doubt there's anyone left."

Pina, whose English had always been more a matter of theory than of practice, sat down with a thump, stared at the man in bewilderment, twisted her braid in one hand, and finally said, haltingly, "What your name? Who are you? Is there any person else?"

Concetta wrinkled her nose. "That's not English!"

But the man had turned his head at Pina's voice, and now he began to murmur.

"Robert," said the man. "Carr. Robert Carr. Paratrooper. No one else."

"What does he say?" asked Amedeo.

At last the man had loosened his grip on Maria-Grazia's wrist. His eyes opened. They were the coldest eyes she had ever seen, a blue like the northern ice in her brothers' picture atlas, and that coldness and strangeness made her recoil a little, though there was nothing unpleasant about it. "Grazie," said the paratrooper Robert Carr, "Grazie mille," and promptly fainted.

ON THE KITCHEN TABLE of the House at the Edge of Night, Amedeo picked the grit and sand from the paratrooper and doused him with iodine. Meanwhile, Pina had roused herself from her trance for the first time in months. She boiled water and fetched clean sheets and opened the shutters of Flavio's room. Here on the bed the half-conscious Robert Carr was laid, still groaning. Amedeo set up watch at his feet, armed with Bepe's hunting rifle, which the younger man had left behind in case the remaining local *fascisti* should choose to pay a visit.

But the local *fascisti* were walled up in the town hall, furiously discussing their plan of action. For if the war was really over, then sheltering one of its victors might not be so impolitic after all.

Meanwhile, Gesuina and Bepe and Agata-the-fisherwoman had unleashed a storm of gossip on the island. "What's his name?" everyone was asking. "Who is he?"

"Wobbit, I heard."

"Wobbit. That's an odd, heathen sort of a name."

"No, no, Robber."

"Rob-a-Car. From America."

"I heard England. Near Buckingham Palace and Kensington Gardens Park."

"I heard he's a spy."

"Nothing of the sort—he's a Protestant."

"I heard he's got a machine gun, and there are twenty others roaming about the island ready to attack us as soon as night falls."

But dusk came, and no band of *inglesi* armed with machine guns came swarming up from the scrubland or appeared at the edge of the piazza. Instead, the *inglesi* and the *americani* passed the island at a distance, in a second wave of ships, with great guns, to bombard the coast of Sicily again. A fishing vessel, the *Holy Madonna*, was sunk in the bombardment and came to rest on the seabed between the island and the mainland. Agata-the-fisherwoman—who had gone out in search of more paratroopers to rescue—was hauled to safety by a passing crew of Sicilians just in time. Concetta, dancing up and down with glee, the captured medal around her neck, shrieked at the firework display that the warring armies had made of the sky above Sicily, its lights beautiful and fierce as shooting stars.

VII

THE DISTANT BOMBARDMENT WOKE ROBERT—WOKE HIM TWISTED in the bedcovers, scrambling for his gun with one hand.

Dusk. A cool room. Shelves grimed a little with dust, on which stood an odd collection of objects that together gave off a powerful odor of someone else's life. Unfamiliar football trophies, a collection of toy swords each on a separate square of brown felt, a disintegrating teddy bear with a pointed nose. A papier-mâché Etna, its slopes furred with dust thick as snowfall, wooden soldiers swarming over it. A pennant with the fasces symbol—this he recognized. A photograph of a group of dark, skinny boys in shorts and white vests, chests barreled out, receiving medals at a sports day. A photograph of the same boys in the uniform of some military organization: fez and knickerbockers. A photograph of a woman with a rope of black hair—this woman he dimly recognized as one of his rescuers. Robert, dry with sunstroke, his tongue clogged with thirst, lay back on the sheets with their scent of foreign soap, and considered his situation.

Somehow here he was, in a dark stone room, surrounded by all the trappings of someone else's childhood. Dimly, he knew that infernal noise of war was coming from wherever he was meant to be. He remembered very little. Now into focus, nearer, on the wall above the bed, swam a stern portrait of Mussolini. Robert made a concerted effort to locate the point at which his memory gave out.

Firstly, the camp in El Alamein—that he remembered well enough. A little before they boarded the glider, the sergeant had come into the tent, bearing a mess tin full of water, strutting with suppressed excitement. A little had dripped on the back of Robert's hand and he remembered noting that it was warm in that heat, like blood. "We're being mobilized," said the sergeant. "For home, they say."

Robert, who did not mean to be rude but was a scientific man to his core, said, "Who said so? And are you sure they know what they're talking about?"

But the sergeant became defensive at this, and refused to say anything more.

Still, a festival atmosphere had begun to reign in the camp. Robert remembered a little now about El Alamein, the light most of all, the way it burned you, made everyone screw up their eyes involuntarily at its touch so that they went about all day scowling.

Yes, El Alamein he remembered.

In the glider, as the American tug hauled them upward through air that was already, he could feel, a little choppy, he was handed a booklet called A *Soldier's Guide to Sicily*. Opening it at random, he read halfheartedly from the darkening pages: "Sicily in summer is decidedly hot. . . . The bulk of the inhabitants are Roman Catholic and much addicted to Saints' Days. . . . Morals are superficially very rigid, being based on the Catholic religion and Spanish etiquette of Bourbon times; they are, in actual fact, of a very low standard, particularly in the agricultural areas." It was too dark by now to read the booklet, so he stowed it inside his battledress and resigned himself to the fact that they were not going home.

He had repeated to himself the odd formulas he had devised to keep proper thought at bay during the interminable glider flights. For instance, that this would be his 79th jump. That between them, the men inside the glider had jumped at least 1,975 times. That their current airspeed was 115 miles per hour. Their current elevation 3,500 feet. Of course, these last two were speculation, but he had a pretty good feel for the plane now, for the heft of it as it moved through the air, the catch of the cable as the tug hauled them skyward, the elastic snap of the tug releasing. This instinct was sometimes a comfort—on calm jumps, in smooth weather—and sometimes a worry, like today, when he could not help knowing from the moment that they launched that something was a little off.

Then the storm hit them side on. He remembered the jolt of it, knees smacking his chin. A few of the men were cantankerous at that jolt, cursing the tug pilot, not realizing this was the prelude rather than the main act. But he, Robert, had known at that moment with awful certainty that they were going down.

Strange, because he did not remember actually descending, only the smack of the water when it came up to meet them. Then the feeling of plunging and yawing under the waves, the way the body of the glider buckled. How some of the men were hacking with clasp knives and bayonets, others had got hold of a wooden hammer and begun beating the roof. And the absurd thought had come to him from nowhere that the Yanks called their gliders, beige and unwieldy, "flying coffins." Then a hole rent itself in the canvas, and through that hole he had dragged himself, struggling and kicking blindly, the sea pouring in past him, his only urge the one for air and light. The splintered air brake, flapping off the wing, had ripped open his shoulder on the way up.

Straight as a knife he plunged, through water howling like the wind, to emerge on the surface of a churned black sea. He found himself utterly alone.

He remembered the rest only in brief moments—he had been losing blood, no doubt. How he had clambered onto the torn wing of another glider, and a great breaker had spun him full circle, slapping the air out of him. How exploding shells plunged wave after wave of air into his ears. How he had yelled for a far-off landing craft, drifting barge-like on the surface of the water, to come and take him. How when at last he reached it and pulled himself up by the ramp he found no one, only a great hole dragging it under by degrees, a sergeant, dead, on his face in the stern. He had let the man drift away from him. And later, when the sun came up, he had swum dream-like through calm waters, the sun a forceful hand on the back of his head. A rock had risen up ahead of him; it resolved itself, miraculously, into an island. Then he heard the voice of a child. He remembered crawling up a ramp of scalding sand. Lying flat under the sun while a crab worked at the sand, getting its claws bloody. How he had thought he was dying, had almost resigned himself to his death, when they came for him with the makeshift stretcher.

And now here he was, bandaged and feverish, in a room belonging to a foreigner's son.

Again he tried to move, and became aware of his shoulder. Pain like a net paralyzed his whole right side. He tried to get the bandages off with his left hand and his teeth, to see the extent of his injuries, but soon, shuddering, gave it up as a bad job. Instead he shuffled along the bed and drew back the curtains, dislodging a fine dust-like sand from their folds.

Between the slats of the shutters, a swaying paradise appeared before him. Olive groves, palms, the kind blue line of the sea. No sign of the battle he was supposed to be fighting. He would learn later that this room faced away from Sicily, and he was really looking back the way he had come, toward North Africa. Now, on the evening of his rescue, it only added to the wonder of the place. He could have been anywhere: in the South Seas, the Pacific, the setting of some boyhood adventure.

But they had spoken some kind of Italian. Dimly, he remembered that. The man with the alarming eyebrows, the woman with a few words of English, and the girl who had held his hand—all three of them had addressed him in Italian. With his good left hand he attempted to feel inside his battledress for *A Soldier's Guide to Sicily*, but found both book and battledress gone. Instead he was wearing someone else's nightshirt, an unnerving, billowing thing like the robe of a nineteenth-century ghost.

Someone's shadow crossed the doorway. Looking up, he saw the girl descend the stairs. The evening trapped her in its stillness. And a second miracle took place. Robert, who did not know that Maria-Grazia was the girl with the leg braces or the girl whom no one had fallen in love with or anything about her except that she was beautiful and had held his hand—Robert, who was usually a scientific man but just now was tearful with gratitude, a little delirious with fever, and under the influence, though he did not know it, of a formidable dose of morphine—Robert, seeing Maria-Grazia turn the corner of the stairs, did the inevitable and began to fall in love.

Footsteps. Into his eager gaze came not the beautiful girl but the doctor with the eyebrows. The man entered the room, put down a glass of water on the nightstand, then glanced at the stairs. "*Mia figlia*," he said firmly. "Door-tair? Daugh-tair?"

"Daughter. *Sì, sì.*" Robert nodded furiously to show that yes, yes, he had understood.

"My wife speak leetle *inglesi*," said the doctor. "*Io, no. Mi dispiace.*" He put a glass of cold water into Robert's hand, and closed Robert's fingers on it firmly. "Dreenk, dreenk."

Robert drank. "I had a booklet," Robert said, when the doctor released his grip. "A little booklet. English. A *Soldier's Guide to Sicily.* With some Italian words in it."

The doctor's eyebrows quivered with effort. Eventually he shook his head—no, he did not understand.

"A book? A little book?" Robert tried again, making a pantomime of opening and closing with his good hand. A few words of school Latin came back to him. "*Liber?*" he said. "*Liber?*"

"*Ah! Un libro!* Yes." The doctor left the room and returned some minutes later with a stack of books. "*Ecco—scrittori inglesi.* Shak-e-speare. Charldicken. Like thees you learning *italiano*, yes?"

It was no good attempting to ask for the booklet again. Instead, Robert allowed the doctor to deposit on his lap what seemed on closer inspection to be *A Tale of Two Cities, David Copperfield,* and *The Complete Works of Shakespeare,* all in Italian. "Wife," said the doctor, with evident pride. "Tea-chair."

"Teacher?" said Robert, and the doctor nodded. "But I know these books," said Robert, ashamed to find himself close to tears. "Why, I could read these in Italian and know every damned word of the English."

The doctor, catching Robert's enthusiasm if not his meaning, nodded eagerly. "Yes, yes," he said. "English."

Emboldened, Robert gestured at the room around him and attempted the question that had troubled him since he woke. "*Filius?*" he said, making a guess at the word. "Son? Where is he?"

But here the doctor's eyebrows descended. "*Morto,*" he said. He held up three fingers. "*Tutti e tre figli. Morto, morto, morto.* Disappear. War. Probably dead. All three son."

Cradling the familiar books in his arms, Robert, with acute shame, found himself weeping. Great sobs racked him, made breathing impossible. He could not seem to stop it. The awful noise he was making drew the woman and the girl. The family was not discomposed by his fit of weeping; the woman merely gripped him by the shoulder with little murmurs of concern, while the daughter ran to fetch him more water. He took it with gratitude and drank. "Don't be ashamed," said the woman, when at last he was finished. "I want please to say this: You must not be ashamed. We all here lost someone. We all here know how it is to lose."

The woman trembled a little; her urge to say what was on her mind seemed at last to have unlocked her voice. "There," she finished. "I have said. Maybe I not speak English so good, but I decide I must say." She lifted the weight of the books and set them down on the nightstand. "Now you please sleep. And when you little better, you start to read these books and learn Italian. Not worry. My husband will guard with the shotgun in case the local *fascisti* try to come, but I don't think they come no more."

Indeed, it began to become clear to the islanders of Castellamare in the following days that the star of the local *fascisti* was rapidly declining. *Il conte* and Arcangelo had put away their black shirts and disbanded the *Balilla*. Then, stirred by unfounded rumors that the *inglesi* would take away their sons' medals and army keepsake photographs and the letters informing their wives and mothers of their brave deaths in battle, all kinds of people crept out into their yards and fields and knelt in the earth to bury these relics out of sight. Even

Amedeo took Flavio's medal one night, wrapped it in a scrap of leather, and hid it under the great palm in the courtyard.

The moon made the palm's leaves waxy, unreal, and silvered the fur of the sleeping Micetto. As Amedeo turned to go inside, brushing the earth from his fingers, he found that his grief had lost its edge a little, like the turning point of a fever, abating just enough to be borne.

PINA BEGAN TO RELAY to them fragments of the foreigner's past. He was an Englishman, not an American, she said—which, in Amedeo's view, explained his flustered stammering whenever Maria-Grazia was present. He was twenty-five—two full years older than Tullio would have been. Though Pina had to consult the dictionary, and even then wasn't quite sure about it, she thought he had used the English word "foundling" about himself. "A foundling!" cried Amedeo in delight. "Why, then, he's already an Esposito!"

Pina looked at him with narrowed eyes. "*Amore*," she said. "He isn't your son."

But how could he not see the boy, somehow, as restitution? He had even begun to become daringly, tremulously hopeful that at least one of his boys might come home once the war had officially ended. For if this boy had been rescued, so might his have been, by some kind Englishman on some foreign shore.

In the days that followed, the islanders, too, began to regard the foreigner lying wounded in the doctor's house not as a curse but as a blessing. If the soldier's English comrades arrived, or the Americans with their jeeps and flags, wouldn't they see how well the islanders had treated their brother, caring for him as one of their own? And, besides, wasn't it a miracle of Sant'Agata, to have delivered to them at the end of all this fighting a drowned man out of the ocean? Now, from morning until night, the town's widows arrived at the door of the House at the Edge of Night, bearing platters of baked aubergine and bottles of homemade liquor for the foreigner. The fishermen delivered freshly caught *sarde* on their way back up the hill each evening. And even a few of the girls, girls whose sweethearts were absent, turned up in the lipstick in which they had not been seen since before the war, and asked Maria-Grazia if they could have a glimpse of the soldier.

Maria-Grazia sent these admirers packing, though she would not have admitted to herself that there was anything in her heart but indignant concern for the Englishman's recovery. "He doesn't want to see you," she could not resist calling after them over the counter, a little too low for the girls to hear. "He's out of danger right now, but one look at your painted faces would be enough to bring his sickness back again."

And Gesuina—who had always believed it a great injustice that poor, good Maria-Grazia got the worst of everything among her classmates—woke from her slumber and gave a shout of delight.

But the truth was, the English soldier was not out of danger. Amedeo, as he sat over the young man's bed, felt himself to be engaged in the same struggle he had endured during the birth of each of his youngest three children. The boy's temperature peaked and dipped. He was troubled by a raging thirst. The shoulder itself wept, refused to heal. "Bathe the wound in water blessed by the statue of Sant'Agata," suggested Gesuina. "That should do it, right enough."

"What I need," said Amedeo, "is more sulfanilamide tablets."

Gesuina pursed her lips at this irreligious talk, shuffled off, and returned with a Sant'Agata medallion to hang round the Englishman's neck, a lucky stone in the shape of the Madonna, and a bottle of holy water from last year's festival.

To Gesuina's great gratification, the wound began to heal. Little by little, the young soldier seemed to be fighting off the infection—until, one morning, Amedeo uncovered the shoulder and, with a nod of satisfaction, found it cool and dry. "It will itch a little," he told the Englishman, bandaging the wound. "Don't touch it." For it was his custom to talk to his patients constantly, whether or not the boy understood. Robert grasped enough to sense that the news was good and said, "*Grazie. Grazie.*"

"It's time for you to get up out of this bed," said the doctor. "It will do you good to sit out a little on the veranda, or in the bar, and get some sea air."

The Englishman nodded and said, "*Mare, Mare,*" having understood that one word: sea.

MANY OF THE ISLANDERS had regarded the shuttered window of the foreigner's room with suspicion. But now that he at last emerged into the town, they found to their surprise that they liked him. His lack of language made him oddly attentive and deferential; he would nod along obligingly with even the most outlandish opinions, murmuring only "*Sì, sì, sì.*" He hung about Maria-Grazia in the bar, and he had a flattering habit of rushing to pull out the chairs for the customers or diving to retrieve the lost cards of the elderly *scopa* players, emerging red and flustered and just like the picture they had in their heads of an Englishman. He was attempting to learn Italian, and this provided much daily amusement: The day on which he confused the word for "year" with the word for "anus" was to become legendary on the island. ("I'll never forget it," Rizzu would weep with laughter, years later. "That young man asking how many *ani* Signora Gesuina had, and the look on her face! *Ha!*")

What was more, both Micetto and the girl Concetta loved Robert, and as Gesuina said, with grudging approval, "If that wild creature and that wild girl will take to him, anyone will."

Robert found that, under this strange sun, unable to communicate more than two words with Maria-Grazia, his love was like a fever of its own, immoderate, a constant provocation. If he knew she had passed on the stairs, he would rush to stand in the air she had breathed, gasping for a trace of her perfume (which was dry and a little like oranges). If she touched something on the bar's counter he would surreptitiously pick it up, for the simple pleasure of touching it, too.

Robert serenely believed that no one had noticed his adoration. Unable to contain his passion, he even began to speak to her of it. She would come to his room with a jug of water or a book, and as she leaned over to deposit it, he would say, in an ordinary voice as though he were merely thanking her, "Let me make love to you, here, at once, before your father wakes up from his siesta." Or, as she swept the corners of the bar after closing, he would begin by talking to her about the radio broadcast or the weather, and end by informing her that she was the most beautiful woman he had seen, that the air itself through which she moved was holy.

It was thus that Maria-Grazia—who really spoke perfectly good English, only she had been too shy to admit it in the first place—became aware with a shock of joy that he loved her.

Robert, noticing her blushes, wondered if perhaps something in his tone had given away a trace of feeling, and he resolved to be more matter-of-fact in his declarations. But not to abandon them—for he could not have done that, any more than he could have stopped adoring her. It was part of the miracle of this island, part of the very air he breathed here.

HUNCHED OVER THE STATICKY BBC broadcasts for news of his comrades, Robert heard that the push into Sicily had been successful, that the Italians had surrendered, and that the Germans had been driven back to Messina. Now that his shoulder was starting to heal, he began to be preoccupied with getting back to his regiment. At least, the fragment of him still dimly motivated by duty was preoccupied. The greater part of him wanted to remain in Castellamare, lulled by the waves and the whirring of the cicadas, boldly declaring his love to Maria-Grazia—to remain here, and forget there had ever been a war.

But gradually, this vacillation began to be a kind of misery to him. Either he must leave now, or he would not leave at all, and that would cause difficulties of its own. One day, during the siesta hour, Maria-Grazia came to his room where he was sleeping a little fitfully, the wireless radio beside him receiving only static. Kneeling beside the bed, she took his hand and poured out a stream of Italian, her narrow eyebrows as soulfully tilted as her father's bristling ones. He understood nothing, but it was all he could do not to take her in his arms and tell her the words that had been the first Italian he searched for, feverishly, in Pina's school dictionary, *"Ti amo. Ti adoro."*

Instead, he listened while she spoke to him: She seemed to consider, remonstrate, double back, and finally beseech—then at last she fell silent, apparently satisfied, and dropped his hand.

Without another word, she climbed the stairs to her own room. He heard her moving about (that tread of hers, always slightly uneven). He heard the quick strokes of a brush through her hair, her clothes falling lightly to the floorboards. The bed sighing as she accommodated herself; it was an ancient thing, like all the beds in this house, and too short for Maria-Grazia, who would curl herself slightly to fit into it, her lovely eyes languid, her black braid resting as heavy as rope on the pillow.

Sometimes, when the braid swung over her shoulder as she maneuvered a tray of pastries or swept the corners of the bar, he longed to take it in both hands and kiss its glossy length.

If he didn't leave now, how would he ever reconcile himself again to the war he was supposed to be fighting?

He had prepared a note in Italian, days ago—inadequate, he realized now, to the Espositos' kindness. His tongue felt as heavy, as feverish, as it had during his illness. He laid the note on the nightstand and took his gun and left while they were all still sleeping.

Outside the church, he ran into Father Ignazio. The priest eyed the gun thoughtfully. "Where you go, Robert Carr?" he said at last, but Robert pretended not to understand his English, and with smiles and nods made his escape along an alley. He took Concetta's shortcut, through the scrub and between the prickly pears, reaching the road by this means unobserved. He went at a jog past the Mazzus' farm, supporting his shoulder with one hand because really it was not as strong as he had thought, and hotter with pain, now that he was in the open air. He almost wished that he had allowed the priest to intercept him. The Mazzus' dogs barked, flinging themselves to the ends of their chains, but no one stirred from behind the shuttered windows.

When he was almost at the quay, he heard quick footsteps at a distance. Maria-Grazia, running. The very thing he had dreaded, for now he would be obliged to explain himself. He watched her approach, the cat Micetto streaking in her wake, Concetta scrambling through the scrub yelling, "Wait, Maria-Grazia! *Wait!*" Maria-Grazia stopped before him. And now, from her mouth, poured a great tide of English: "You leave," she said. "Why you leaving now, Robert? We all want you stay. It's grace that brought you here, everyone think so. Grace of Sant'Agata. Why you leaving just for get killed in another battle?" She gave a dry sob. "I thought you coming up to my room. That was what I ask of you. And instead you turn and leave—it was something I do or say, Robert? You make my mother and father very sad now. You make all of us sad."

Robert said, a little roughly, embarrassed, "You're speaking English."

"Yes, yes. I always know to speak English. Only I was too shy, before. Today I ask you, in Italian, to come up to my room, and instead you go and leave us."

"Why didn't you ask me in English, since you speak it?"

Maria-Grazia, eyebrows fierce, said, "Why you no tell me you love me in Italian, since you know it? I see you leave that page open on your table, again and again."

"Well, I'll tell you so now," said Robert, still more roughly than he had intended. "*Ti amo. Ti adoro.* But I have to go."

"Your shoulder isn't healed. You not able to fight anybody with that shoulder, Robert—you will die."

"It's healed enough for me to walk until I find my regiment."

Maria-Grazia wept. "You will die," she repeated. "Everyone think so. I wish to God and Sant'Agata that the wound reopen—anything that stop you going back to that war."

"I'll go," he said. "I'll go, and I'll come back. Haven't I said I love you?"

Maria-Grazia followed him along the dust road, weeping.

At the quay, he discovered a curious thing: Not one of the fishermen—Bepe, or 'Ncilino, or even Agata-the-fisherwoman in her borrowed boat—was willing to carry him to Sicily. All of them flatly refused, standing guard over their oars and shaking their heads. Agata-the-fisherwoman launched a stream of dialect at him with such ferocity that he recoiled. "Why is she angry?" he asked Maria-Grazia, almost tearful at the way Agata, one of his rescuers, had turned on him. "She not angry," said Maria-Grazia. "But she not willing to take you, either."

"What does she say?"

"She say you cannot leave now that the war is over," said Maria-Grazia. "She say you're good luck to us, you bring good luck. She say they catch nothing but good *sarde* and large tuna since you come here—that's just her superstition, of course—"

But Agata-the-fisherwoman had not finished. "What's she saying now?"

"She say . . . she say this island, it lose enough good men already."

Robert, driven a little mad by all this, decided there was nothing to be done but to swim to Sicily. Holding his rifle above his head he made a run and launched himself from the quay. Maria-Grazia, the fishermen, the girl, and the cat stood in a row watching him, stunned at last into silence. He got as far as the rocks, grunting at the pain in his shoulder. At this point, he was forced to lower his rifle.

Dimly, he heard shouts behind him. When he turned, he saw a great crowd assembling at the end of the quay. There was the doctor, Amedeo; and Pina, and the priest, Father Ignazio; and Rizzu's grand-daughter leading Gesuina by the hand; and the elderly *scopa* players; and even the grocer Arcangelo, who had barely exchanged three words with him and until a month ago had been a Fascist. "The townspeople declare," Arcangelo called across the water, hesitantly, whispering to Pina for a translation, "that if you not stay of your own free will, *il conte* and I will be forced to make you—*come si dice?*—prisoner of war. Come back now, won't you please, Signor Carr?"

As Robert trod water, gasping in the spray and the salt air, a little dizzy at this exertion, the hot pain in his injured shoulder narrowed, intensified. He raised his hand. A sticky residue messed his fingers. The wound had opened and begun to weep. It wept until the three fishermen, Bepe, 'Ncilino, and Agata, had forged through the water, taken him in their arms, and borne him safely to shore.

PART THREE

THE CITY

of the

DEAD

...

1944–53

THERE WAS ONCE AN OLD WOMAN WHO TOOK IT INTO HER HEAD to put a curse on a king's daughter. "You shall never marry," she declared, "until you have found the Dead Man, and watched over him for a year, three months, a week, and a day."

The girl grew up, and the curse remained. Though she had many suitors, and was very beautiful, never did she meet one whom she liked well enough to make her husband. "Father," said the princess at last, "it's no good. It's plain to me that I cannot marry until I find the man whom I was cursed to marry, for no one else will do. Therefore I intend to go out into the world, and seek the Dead Man."

The king, her father, wept, but the girl would not be dissuaded, and the next day she saddled her horse and packed her bags and went out into the world in search of the Dead Man.

After journeying for many years, she came to a great white palace. The door was open, and the lamps were lit. A fire burned in the fireplace. The girl entered, and went from room to room until, at last, she found a dead man lying before the hearth in an upstairs chamber. "Now here is my bridegroom," said the princess. "And I must watch over him a year, three months, a week, and a day, until he awakes."

So saying, the princess flung herself down on the tiles before the hearth, and waited for the Dead Man to awake.

———

A TALE BELONGING TO *Venice, also told in the* Decameron *and by Signor Calvino in his book of tales, which somehow found its way to Castellamare during the second war. It is my belief that it must have come from one of the northern prisoners. First recorded when Signor Rizzu retold it to me in 1942.*

I

THE WAR BURNED ITSELF OUT THAT SUMMER WHEN MARIA-GRAZIA and Robert became lovers. The following spring, when Sicily had been occupied for eight months and the fishermen had begun, tentatively, to venture further out upon the ocean again, an unfamiliar boat appeared at the horizon. Running to the top of the house, Concetta and Maria-Grazia inspected the sea through Flavio's binoculars and found the boat, the fisherman rowing, and two American soldiers in tin helmets.

The late arrival of the Americans on Castellamare was an oversight. The island should really have been occupied months ago. But in the chaos that engulfed Siracusa, the Sicilians had simply forgotten to mention to the occupiers that the small island on their horizon was inhabited at all. It was only a long time later that a colonel, bent over his aerial photographs with a magnifying glass, made out a grainy smudge to the southeast of Sicily. Blowing the picture up, the colonel found the gray blocks of a quay and a red bloom that might represent houses. He made inquiries at the market below his office window. *Sì,* *sì,* said the Siracusans, *sì,* Castellamare was inhabited, there had even been a prison camp there, many clever men from the north, four or five guards.

The next morning the colonel dispatched a boat across the water to investigate.

The Americans—a sergeant and a lieutenant—had offered the elderly owner of the *God Have Mercy* a single dollar bill to transport them to Castellamare. They landed shortly after four, in a bestial spring heat. The fisherman docked at the empty quay and pointed the way between the olive groves and cacti to the summit of the island. Then he sat down in the bottom of the boat and began laying out a hand of solitaire on the thwart, announcing very firmly his intention to stay behind.

"It'll be a damn hot climb," said the sergeant.

"We'll find someone with a motorcar on the way up," said the lieutenant.

The fisherman pursed his lips. "No motorcar here," he said, with the disdain of the city dweller for the village. "No refrigerator, no television, no wireless radio. Nothing here. You understand, *americani?*"

Slogging up the hill, the *americani* understood. In the fields the tendrils of the vines were just pushing out, reminding the sergeant of home and the fields of California. In the distance, close to the sea, a line of laborers moved as one, the chopping of their mattocks against the dry earth audible even from this height. Beside them, on the dust track, was the tiny form of an unexpected motorcar. "Shall we double back down there?" said the sergeant. "Ask those people?"

"We'll try the town first," said the lieutenant, who couldn't face another climb in this heat.

But they found no other sign of human life until at last they passed under the peeling archway into the town. The arch had become a kind of blackboard for slogans of all political persuasions. "Viva Il Duce!" and "Viva Mussolini!" were almost obliterated now, replaced with the names of the heroes of half-liberated Italy: "Viva Badoglio! Viva Garibaldi! Viva il Re!"

The lieutenant nodded approvingly. "No Fascists here," he said.

"Leastwise not anymore," said the sergeant.

The fisherman from Siracusa had been wrong about another thing: There was a wireless radio. After some searching, they located it outside the bar. Here they found a strange assortment of people: widows, elderly card players, two or three fishermen, and a British soldier, drinking coffee and arguing over the BBC news report.

"Where is the rest of your regiment?" the lieutenant asked the British soldier. "We weren't told this island had been captured already by British forces."

Robert put down his coffee and got to his feet. "It hasn't," he said. "I'm the only one. I was washed up on the night of the ninth of July. I got separated from my regiment when the tugs ditched us into the sea, and I've never seen any of them since."

The sergeant had heard about the landings from his brother-in-law, a tug pilot: how the wind and the rain had confounded the tugs, forcing them to ditch the gliders too early; how the British paratroopers had been scattered among mountains, plunged into rough water, discarded in vineyards a hundred miles behind enemy lines. In the days that followed, those who could still fight had fought where they found themselves; those who were still floating about on bits of wreckage had been picked out of the sea and shipped back to Tunisia. Some of the Tommies had been so incensed at the Yankee tug pilots that they had to be confined to camp. "Goddamn mess," murmured the sergeant. "We heard about all that."

Now, the British soldier said: "Number Six Guards Parachute Platoon, Third Battalion, First Airborne Division. Do you know if any others got out of their planes? That's what I keep thinking. I dream about it at nights. Did any of the others get out?"

"We only got to Sicily six months ago," said the lieutenant. "I don't know anything about that." He glanced from the British soldier to the old men at their card table, the widows murmuring in the corner, and the two fishermen who had set aside their newspapers and were now regarding the two soldiers with benevolent interest. "I thought there was a prison camp," he said at last.

Pina was summoned. She led the soldiers along the main street, to the collection of ruined cottages where the prisoners had once been housed. Too shy to speak in English before these foreigners, Pina explained instead in formal Italian that the prison camp was gone. "She says this was where the prisoners were kept," translated Robert. "There wasn't any proper camp except this. Then, she says, when the fighting started, the Fascist guards all left. It was just at the time I landed on the island."

"What about the prisoners?"

"There's a university lecturer. One or two socialist deputies. The rest have gone, too." Even Mario Vazzo had gone—returning to the mainland in search of his wife and child.

"What about the local government? Are there any of them we need to deal with? The mayor?"

Robert shook his head.

By now, half the islanders had got wind of the American soldiers' arrival. They crowded around the American liberators, clapping them on the shoulders. Someone began a cheer of "Viva l'America!" Concetta wriggled free of Maria-Grazia and emerged at the front of the crowd to peer up at the foreigners. "It's all damned strange," said the lieutenant, who had hoped to take the island in grander style. "We were told there was a prison camp, four or five guards."

"Yes, yes," said Robert. "She says there was a prison camp, but it's all gone now."

"Bring the *americani* back to the bar for a coffee," said Rizzu. "Offer them something to eat and drink."

The American soldiers were led back through the streets as guests of honor, which mollified the lieutenant a little. At the House at the Edge of Night, they refused Maria-Grazia's *caffè di guerra*, but did consent to sit down at the bar, under the ceiling fan, where they asked that the island's former *podestà* be summoned at once.

Rizzu, riding proudly in the front of the motorcar for the first time in his life, brought *il conte* from the fields. *Il conte* made a stiff bow to the liberators. "Can you understand English?" asked the lieutenant.

Il conte, who had never been much of a scholar, was obliged to shake his head. Robert and Pina were called upon to translate. While *il conte* turned red and looked at his knees, the American soldiers declared the island captured and *il conte* relieved of his duties as mayor. *Il conte* shuffled forward and, after a tense moment when rage seemed to swell in him, he subsided, and consented to shake the soldiers' hands.

Then the Americans turned to the problem of what should be done with Robert. "We'll take you back to Siracusa," said the lieutenant. "Get you a good meal and a transfer back to your regiment."

"I can't go," said Robert. "I tried to leave, to get back to my regiment, already. It won't work. The wound in my shoulder began to bleed again when I left the island."

"*Sì, sì,*" added one of the villagers, an elderly woman with blind eyes that showed only a white film. "*Un miracolo di Sant'Agata.*"

"What'd she say?"

"She says it's a miracle of Sant'Agata."

"Come on now," said the lieutenant. "Enough of this. We'll get you off of here and into a proper hospital, if you're wounded. We'll get you evacuated to Tunisia. Or sent home to England if that's what you want."

But Robert shook his head.

Amedeo was ushered forward by the crowd of islanders to give a medical report. Yes, yes, he agreed. There was nothing to be done about Robert's shoulder but wait for it to heal. A period of rest; it was advisable not to move the patient from the island at this delicate stage.

"Let me see your shoulder," said the lieutenant. Robert unbuttoned his shirt and exposed the scar, now silvering over.

"That's healed pretty good," said the lieutenant. "There's nothing wrong with that."

"But not when he leaves the island." Maria-Grazia came forward, twisting her rope of black hair, speaking clear English. "Then it bleeds again."

The islanders, murmuringly, agreed. The lieutenant remembered the field guide to Sicily they had been handed before disembarking at Messina. *The bulk of the inhabitants are Roman Catholic and much addicted to Saints' Days.* The British man seemed to have some kind of a hold on them. "The fighting must have turned him a little nutty," he muttered in the sergeant's ear.

But the sergeant was clearly spooked and inclined to disagree. "I ain't so sure about that," he said. "I heard about other miracles in this war, from my brother-in-law Harvey who flies planes."

"Come on." The lieutenant tried again, addressing only Robert. "Wouldn't you like to come with us back to Sicily and have a proper meal and see a doctor and find out what's happened to your buddies?"

But Robert shook his head. He could not go with them to the mainland and would not submit to medical treatment in an army hospital. "I can't leave," he said. "This is the only place where my shoulder can heal. This is the only doctor who can cure me."

Here, for the first time, the sergeant was moved to speak up. "His shoulder's busted anyway," he said. "Seems to me it don't make no difference if we leave him or if we bring him."

"A deserter's a deserter," said the lieutenant. "We can't just leave him here."

THE LIEUTENANT HAD EXPECTED more resistance on the Englishman's part, but in the end Robert went with them. What he had not expected was the procession of islanders who followed them down the dust road to the quay, lamenting, protesting in dialect, and in some cases even weeping openly, clinging to the Englishman's hands. The lieutenant, sweating, leading the pale and sullen Robert by the elbow, wished he'd never been sent to this island. It made matters worse that his sergeant, a superstitious young man who had been raised in a shack in California, obviously sided with the Englishman.

On the quay, the islanders waited in silence for the *americani* to take Robert away. The lieutenant felt some kind of announcement should be made. Clambering up on the thwart of the *God Have Mercy*, he addressed the islanders. "We'll take good care of your friend," he said. "We'll see he gets treated right."

The islanders continued to stare in silence while Robert and Maria-Grazia exchanged one single, brief embrace. Then the fisherman cast off, with the *americani* and the Englishman on board. The islanders, a sad crowd, remained on the quay for a long time, watching the boat depart.

"Hell of a place," said the lieutenant.

"Bad omen, if you ask me," said the sergeant.

As the fisherman plied the choppy waves of the open sea between Castellamare and Siracusa, the Englishman gave a low murmur. Black blood was blossoming from the wound in his shoulder. The lieutenant fumbled in his first-aid kit and brought forth a Carlisle dressing from its plastic wrapper. "Here," he said. "Put that on your shoulder. We'll see you get medical attention when you're back onshore."

Meanwhile, a memory came to the sergeant unbidden: how, as a boy of fifteen or sixteen pulling in the harvest on a ranch near Soledad, he had seen a man fall from a wagon onto a pitchfork, how the man had bled until there was no blood left in him.

He was glad, when they deposited the soldier at the English field hospital, to have nothing more to do with him.

FROM SIXTY-SIX GENERAL HOSPITAL, Catania, Robert, still bleeding, was evacuated to Tunisia and from there put on a hospital ship bound for Southampton. On the journey he was confined to his bunk, and could drink only a little beef tea. His wound would sometimes begin to heal, but every few days it began to bleed once more. Robert's temperature rose and fell; he was troubled by persistent headaches. This was an infection no ammoniated mercury or sulfanilamide tablets seemed to cure; it seemed to run deeper, to have taken root in him.

His regiment—what was left of it—was training farther north, but Robert could no longer be deployed anywhere. While his comrades of the Number Six Guards Parachute Platoon floated down over Arnhem, Robert lay in a bed with gray curtains, sometimes recovering, sometimes declining, and dreamed of Maria-Grazia. Of her embraces on hot afternoons when the rest of the town lay drowsing behind shutters, when they had held their breath so as not to disturb the great silence of the island. Of the thick rope of her black hair. Of the calm of waking beside her in that room with the palms at the window, the blue line of the sea. Whether these things had happened or had only been imagined, he could not now tell for sure. The whole world seemed a submerged place in which great chunks of time were swallowed up and yet days themselves dragged listlessly. But still he clung to the belief that he had been her lover once, and would love her again.

He listened to the wireless, understood that the war was drawing to a disordered close. That a pair of great bombs had been dropped in Japan, whole cities flattened, an awful thing. Then surrender. Hitler dead, Mussolini dead. Soon, he knew, soldiers would be returning in ships, on trains, a great exodus across the known world in all directions, their enmities abandoned, like the migration of birds toward home.

MARIA-GRAZIA RECEIVED A POSTCARD with a photograph of a red-brick English hospital on the front, in the autumn of 1945. Addressed only to "Maria-Grazia Esposito, the House at the Edge of Night, Castellamare Island," it somehow found her. "*Sto pensando a te,*" it read. "I am thinking of you." By this, she knew that Robert had survived.

THE GIRL CONCETTA WOKE HER BEFORE IT WAS YET LIGHT. "MARIA-Grazia, come down!" she called, her voice setting up an echo in the courtyard. Maria-Grazia surfaced from strange dreams, dreams of black caves, of falling. She fumbled for the window latch and put out her head. "Concetta?"

A light rain had fallen; the sky was dense with stars. "Maria-Grazia!" called Concetta. "Wake up! It's rained and the *babbaluci* are out. If we go now, we'll get the best of them."

Maria-Grazia dressed in the dark and descended the stairs, past the shadowy photographs of her brothers. In the courtyard, drizzle was still hanging in the air; the night seemed saturated with it. Maria-Grazia picked up two metal pails, a little slime-ridden on the inside from the last time they had gone out to gather ground snails. Others would be out already, she knew: the Mazzus, whose harvest had been poor this summer; *il conte*'s underemployed peasants. "Let's go to the ruined houses," said Concetta. "No one else looks there. The *babbaluci* hide in the cracks in the walls, all stuck to each other in a ball. I've seen them. Come on, Maria-Grazia."

Concetta, who had never been known to suffer from fatigue or low spirits, ran alongside Maria-Grazia through the wet dark. In the piazza, the peasant laborers were already stirring. Some were standing about waiting for *il conte*'s agents to drive up in the motorcar and hire them as day laborers—it was what they had always done when there was too little work. But some of them were gathering now for a different purpose, looking furtive, bearing red flags, under the direction of young Bepe. "What are they doing?" said Concetta.

"Protesting," said Maria-Grazia. "Come along—leave them."

The trouble between the peasants and *il conte* had first started when Bepe had gone to visit his cousin in Palermo. He had come back agitated, running up the steps of the bar the night after his arrival with a Palermo newspaper under one arm and a store of righteous indignation in his heart. "There are new laws," he announced to the peasants and fishermen sitting around the *scopa* table. "I've only just heard. My cousin told me about them. Land reforms. They've been in place for a year or more, but no one told us about it. But the new laws apply to us here, too, just as much as anybody else in Italy! We're to get a proper share of our grain and olives from now on, not the usual quarter *il conte* offers us. And those of you who aren't tenants or sharecroppers aren't supposed to stand about in the piazza each morning waiting for work—instead, you're to be given a proper contract. And any land that isn't cultivated is ours to take and occupy! Even *il conte*'s unused land is ours!"

The peasants gathered grudgingly around Bepe's newspaper, unwilling to be taken in. But sure enough, the mainland newspaper confirmed what Bepe had said—and what was more, if the new laws weren't properly followed, claimed Bepe, *carabinieri* from the mainland would come and make *il conte* follow them, because the new minister for agriculture was a Communist and had said so.

"Yes," confirmed Maria-Grazia from behind the counter. "It's been in all the newspapers here, too, only no one reads anything in this bar except *La Gazzetta dello Sport*."

"There's one important thing," said Bepe. "We have to form a cooperative before we can occupy the land."

"A what?" said the tenant farmer Mazzu, with suspicion. "I'm not cooperating with any of you."

"We have to form an organization," said Bepe. "That's all I mean. And we have to go out and occupy the land together. That way the government will listen to our claims. And"—Bepe whipped an expanse of red cloth from under his jacket—"we'll carry this Communist party flag when we go, and stick it in the soil on a little pole. There's a lot of uncultivated land, when you think about it—*il conte's* hunting ground, and that stony bit to the south no one ever bothers with. Which used to be common ground," he added, and one or two of the older peasants, remembering, stirred with an old indignation.

Gradually, by degrees, Bepe went about the island and made himself heard. The year before, no one's harvest had been good; half the island was in debt to *il conte* and his agents. On the day that *il conte* and his wife left for their estate in Palermo, fleeing the late summer heat, Bepe at last succeeded in tipping the other peasants into action. The following Monday morning, the men—accompanied by their wives with great cooking pots on their heads and an excitable straggle of children—forayed out to claim *il conte's* unused land. The stony field on the south of the island, occupied until now only by wild goats and nests of lizards, was divided into strips with lines of taut fishing wire, and planted with autumn wheat.

At lunchtime, *il conte's* agents, armed with hunting rifles, rode up on donkeys. "You're to leave this land alone," they ordered.

The peasants left, but came back when the wheat sprouted, and subversively thinned the rows.

No one knew what would happen when the heat broke and *il conte* returned from Palermo. But now again the peasants were marching out to the fields to claim his unused land: the hunting ground this time. Concetta followed them for a few paces, drawn by the noise of Bepe's muted *organetto*, until their ways parted. Concetta and Maria-Grazia's path took them down the bare hillside, while the procession of peasants wound on along the road, the lights of their cigarettes brief fireflies in the dark. In their wake the music faded; all was darkness and rain. Maria-Grazia and Concetta, pushing through wet grass and clumps of thistle, reached the abandoned houses where the prisoners had once been kept. Sure enough, kneeling down among the rubble, Maria-Grazia found the *babbaluci* everywhere, poking out their heads.

Maria-Grazia felt a pang of regret as she dropped the snails into the bucket. Concetta kept a gleeful count: "Fifty-one, fifty-two, fifty-three . . ."

"We'll make a stew," said Maria-Grazia. "With oil and wild parsley and garlic, and a little pepper."

With the dawn, the ruined houses shrank to ordinary proportions and the snails began to dig deeper underground. The two of them worked side by side without speaking, racing the sun and the day's heat, until one pail was full. "Maria-Grazia," said Concetta, gazing into the bucket of snails. "What do you think has become of Signor Robert?"

Maria-Grazia stiffened a little at this question. "What makes you ask that?"

"Nothing especially. But what do you think has become of him?"

"I don't know. He's still in England, I expect. I showed you the card he sent."

"That card," said Concetta, "didn't have much to say, and it came more than a year ago."

"I expect his shoulder was hurting again, so that was all he could manage to write."

"Can't *you* write to *him*?"

Maria-Grazia shook her head. She had written to the hospital a year ago. No news, they told her. The patient had left. They did not know where he had gone.

Concetta lifted a snail and watched it put out its horns and retract them again, as though it were dancing. "Can't we go to England to find him? On a boat, or an airplane. Me and you, Maria-Grazia?"

"Oh, Concetta, you know what that would cost. *Lire* and *lire*. Anyway, he'll come back as soon as he can—I'm sure of it."

The child disappeared behind the wall. Maria-Grazia heard her muttering to herself and scratching in the earth. The girl would be searching for the smaller snails, the *attuppateddi*, who lived an inch underground. "Don't put the *attuppateddi* in with the *babbaluci*," said Maria-Grazia. "They'll only fight like last time, and the *at-*

tuppateddi are bitter—they'll have to be soaked for a day or two in bran to get out the bad taste."

"Mmm-hmm," said Concetta, by way of grudging reply.

They worked until the sun was overhead, and all the remaining *babbaluci* were gone, buried in their crevasses and holes, the *at-tuppateddi* sunk deep underground. Concetta, covered in earth up to the elbows, dropped the last handful into her pail. "Can I eat one or two now?" she pleaded. "I don't *mind* them raw."

"Oh, Concetta—wait until we cook them."

Only as she straightened, hoisting the first pail, did Maria-Grazia become aware of someone standing a short way behind them, throwing a shadow across her back.

Perhaps it was because Concetta had just mentioned him, or because such things had happened a hundred times in her secret imaginings—but for a moment, as she turned, she was convinced it was Robert. Instead, here was a man in ill-fitting foreign clothes, with a dented cardboard suitcase and a face like one of her brothers'. A face a little compressed and lined but known to her somehow, with its spread nose and dark features and thick eyebrows under a mass of well-oiled hair. It dawned on her in a rush of terror: "Flavio! Dio, is it you?"

"Maria-Grazia," said the man like her brother.

"Oh, Flavio. Is it really you, not your ghost?"

"Of course it is."

"Where have you been? We were told you were missing in North Africa."

"Aren't you going to greet me?" he said.

But when she embraced him, he held off a little, stiff and unyielding in her arms. "You were expecting someone else," he said. "When you turned and saw me, you were disappointed."

Now she found herself in tears. "No—it's just the shock of seeing you. Come home to Mamma and Papà—"

"Aurelio and Tullio? Are they back yet?"

"We haven't heard from them."

She took his wrist and led him, Concetta stumbling behind with the buckets of snails.

Inside the town walls a few people seemed to recognize Flavio and murmured a *"salve"* or a *"buongiorno."* But no one approached. Aware of this, she talked a little too eagerly: "I'm so glad—and you'll see things are just the same here—we've your medal, too—"

Concetta, struggling behind them, let go the buckets and called, "Hey! *Hey!*"

Maria-Grazia turned. "Sorry, *cara*—it's too much for you to carry. Give me one of those."

Flavio put out his hand for the other. "What is it?" he said, drawing back a little from the roiling heap.

"Snails."

"For eating?"

"What else? To tell the truth, there hasn't been much to eat lately. But thank God and Sant'Agata for the fishermen—I'm sure the people on mainland Sicily are starving much worse than we are, miles from the ocean in those dry stony places."

She noticed all at once, when he took the bucket, that the fingers on his right hand were gone, except the first one and the thumb. She felt tears threaten. "What happened to your hand?"

"Oh." He looked at his hand both ways, first the front, then the back, as though it were new to him. "Shot off," he said eventually. "But there's nothing to say about that, and I'd rather not."

All the way up the main street she tried not to stare at them, the poor lost fingers that had once danced over the keys of his brass trumpet, sounding bright notes.

Outside the house, she stopped and set down the bucket. "Let me go in first," she said. "Let me tell them."

Flavio nodded and stood stiffly, holding the bucket of snails.

While he waited, he allowed himself to be soothed by the drafts through the mat of bougainvillea, lulled by the familiar hiss of the sea. He heard the low murmur in the bar, the familiar music of voices.

He heard his father's voice, his mother's. His sister again now: "He's here. He's standing outside. My brother, back from the war."

He heard, unmistakably, his mother's screams of "Tullio? Aurelio?" Only after calling the names of both the others—and a foreign name that he did not recognize at all—did she say, at last, "Flavio?" Flavio heard this, and knew all at once that he would not be happy again on Castellamare.

AFTER THE WAR ENDED, many of the young men had returned to the island. Some carried medals bundled up in suitcases; others returned in the ill-fitting civilian clothes of strange countries, smelling of foreign shaving foam and cheap hair oil. Just after Christmas, while the *presepe* with its life-size figures of the Madonna, the infant Christ, and the stooped San Giuseppe still stood outside the church, *il conte* had received the news that his son, Andrea, with a shattered knee, was returning from a prison camp in Indiana. At the celebration of the *Epifania*, his mother, now middle-aged, arrived at the church, leaning on *il conte*'s arm. Carmela wept before the statue of Sant'Agata, raising her arms and declaring out loud her thanks to the saint. ("For all the world," said Gesuina, "as if she were a common island woman.") After that day, Carmela seemed at last to grow old like all the other islanders, her clothes just as tired and inelegant, her face just as worn.

While Andrea was still imprisoned in America, other islanders had also received letters and telegrams with Red Cross stamps and foreign postmarks, and a wave of boys had returned. But there had never been any letter for Pina and Amedeo. This unexpected return of Flavio jarred the House at the Edge of Night, a shock as great as his disappearance had been.

In fact, a crumpled Red Cross letter arrived a day or two after Flavio, delivered by Pierino's son-in-law to the door of the bar. Pina's cry woke the whole piazza, startled the orioles out of the trees, and brought her husband and daughter diving down the stairs—for she believed, for a moment, that it was news of one of her other boys. Instead, it was merely the missing communication they should have received about Flavio. "We are pleased to inform you," it read, "that your son Flavio Esposito has made contact with us in anticipation of his release from Langton Priory Prisoner of War Camp, Surrey, England. During his time in Britain he has received treatment for an amputation to the fingers of the right hand and for psychological disturbances sustained during his service in North Africa, at the Addington Park War Hospital, Croydon, and also at the Belmont Prisoner of War Hospital, Sutton. He is recovering well, and in reasonably good spirits though not able to write at present. If you wish to enclose a message for him by return, we should be happy to convey it to him." The letter was three months old.

Flavio was not able to say what had happened in the intervening time, and when "psychological disturbances" were mentioned he grew drawn and sullen and refused to say anything at all.

"Do you think they mistreated him?" wept Pina in the privacy of her bedroom, late that night.

"The English are good people," said Amedeo, who had only ever met one Englishman, the soldier Robert. "They will have taken good care of Flavio. And now he's back home, he'll recover—you'll see—good sea air, the family, the familiar faces."

But in truth, Flavio seemed to find nothing familiar. After the initial greetings on the veranda of the bar, he had moved away from his mother, as though she were an overaffectionate stranger, and climbed the stairs to his room. Here he had found his portrait of *il duce* and his brass trumpet gone, a stranger's razor and shaving foam on the nightstand. Pina had rushed to clear these traces of Robert away, to bring out fresh sheets and haul open the dusty curtains. But Flavio had sat on the edge of the bed, turning over each object on his nightstand as though it were unknown.

Afterward, Pina was able to put back Flavio's belongings exactly as he had left them, for in the years after his disappearance and before

Robert's arrival she had wandered and rewandered the rooms of her sons on sleepless nights, examining every tin soldier and school certificate. Only the portrait of *il duce* was left out of sight, rolled up in a drawer. Flavio's brass trumpet in its case was placed on the table at the end of the bed, his favorite toy soldiers and football cards on the nightstand. "Mamma, he's twenty-five now," said Maria-Grazia, observing this. Amedeo went out and dug up Flavio's medal from under the palm tree in the courtyard, and put it into his son's hands. "I can get those earth stains off," said Amedeo. "I buried it to keep it safe—that's all." Flavio said nothing; he merely lay down and went to sleep—a sleep so deep that he did not surface properly for over a week.

Meanwhile, they crept about the house, as though a wild creature lay dormant in the room above them.

In the days of Flavio's slumber, Pina took up position on the veranda of the bar. Though the customers made a tiresome cacophony in her ears, though Maria-Grazia circulated with trays of glasses and attempted to draw her out of her silence, Pina ignored them. She sat at the edge of the veranda with her back firmly turned, watching only the ocean. During these days, looking at her mother's lonely back, Maria-Grazia began to realize that Pina was close to becoming an old woman. Her rope of hair, which in Maria-Grazia's mental picture of her mother was still black, had weathered, losing its thick luxuriance. Her shoulders were sloping hillsides, her spine a straight ridge, as though the old Pina were hung on the frame of the young one. There she sat, and waited for her son to wake up and come down to her.

Maria-Grazia supposed her brother would want the bar back now, and, privately, she began to search the newspapers for prices for a ticket to England—for couldn't she go and find Robert, and leave the bar in Flavio's hands? But the prices were so high—a whole month's profit for the House at the Edge of Night—and even supposing Flavio were up to running the bar, where would she begin in the vastness of that gray country of her imagination to search for Robert? Why hadn't he instead come back to her?

Pina went to bed only reluctantly each night, after the bar had been shut up, and each morning she rose again before dawn, splashed her face with cold water, put on her best clothes, and went down to the veranda to wait for her son to wake. Sometimes the cat Micetto, tame at last in his extreme old age, sat just out of her reach, flicking his tail, bearing her company.

IN THE MIDST OF all this, when everyone was preoccupied with the return of the soldiers, Gesuina's spirit left her.

She was sitting in her customary chair in the corner of the bar, by the wireless radio. She died so silently in her sleep, with her hands so neatly folded, that no one noticed immediately that she was gone. The *scopa* games continued; the dominoes clicked in the drowsy silence; the coffee machine, elderly now, too, hissed. It was only when the girl Concetta went up to Gesuina, tapped her on the knee, and yelled "Hey!" to wake her, that she felt a chill in the old woman's bones.

"She didn't scold me!" wept Concetta. "There's something badly wrong!"

Amedeo was called, and knelt down before her. "Signora Gesuina?" he said.

The old woman made no answer, but her face as it rested seemed composed into a faint smile. The smallest mirror from behind the bar was taken down and held before her open mouth. It remained clear, reflecting only the blue line of the sea.

WHEN THE ISLAND HEARD the news, its grief was immeasurable. Gesuina was the first person to die on Castellamare since the rash of deaths from the war, and now her departure afforded the islanders a shelter beneath which to mourn all those other more terrible losses. Shops were closed, black armbands dug out of drawers, and those who had wept behind closed doors for other griefs—had pummeled their pillows as though mad, had lain wailing on the floors of their kitchens for days on end, had rubbed their faces with ashes—all those islanders now went about the streets without shame, mourning in moderation, with wet handkerchiefs and red eyes.

The old woman, in her tiny coffin, was buried in the cemetery beyond the Mazzus' vineyard. Here every islander had been buried since the first Greek settlers died. Gesuina was allotted a grave under the cemetery's single cypress tree, which she would occupy for a twenty-year season before the bleached bones would be gathered, prayed over, and put into a little white alcove in the cemetery wall. Father Ignazio led the procession and sang lamenting Sant'Agata songs. The grief of the island had no bounds. In the blare of sunset with which they buried the old woman, Father Ignazio watched them weep and understood that they wept not for Gesuina but for everything that was changing, everything that was gone. Sometimes grief needed a focus, an object—this the old priest knew. The count attended the funeral, with his wife, and laid a handsome wreath of trumpet vine on Gesuina's grave. The old woman had delivered into the world almost every islander who now mourned her, even *il conte*.

III

WHILE THE WHOLE TOWN WAS BURYING GESUINA, FLAVIO AWOKE AS
from a spell. Stirring in his boyhood room, he opened his eyes and
felt the great exhaustion of the war ease its weight. His hair was matted, his mouth sour. He had a pain in his bladder from sleeping so
long. It was twelve hours since he had last surfaced to make a drowsy
stagger to the bathroom. He hauled himself along the corridor and
emptied a stream of foamy piss into the toilet bowl. Here he had once
jostled with his brothers, rising in the dark before school to shave
their baby chins with razors of their Papà's, to grease their hair with
olive oil like the prisoner-poet Mario Vazzo, feeling themselves already too big for the island. He pushed open the bathroom window
and stood for a long time looking out.

Some kind of procession was winding in from the fields. Was it
Sant'Agata? But no—he was confused—Sant'Agata's festival was always in June, and now it was autumn, soon winter. One of those land
occupations, probably. He worked his face with the remaining finger-
tip of his right hand. Still the sense of unreality persisted, as though
he were looking at a cinema reel of the island projected on a wall, not
the real thing. None of it came to him right. He had felt it from the
first moment the fisherman from Siracusa had set him down on the
quay, in his English charity clothes with his cardboard suitcase under
his arm.

Flavio returned to bed, lay back on his pillows, and retraced that
journey, trying to recognize in it some pang of homecoming. He had
climbed the hill slowly, by the path through the prickly pears he had

always taken as a boy. His prison-camp belongings rattled in the case with each step: his razor, still rusted with English damp, his English playing cards, his English Bible. He had not known what to do with the Bible. To abandon it seemed sacrilegious; to throw it away was unthinkable. So he had carried it back to Castellamare when he was discharged, where it was to spend the next fifty years gathering dust in the room at the top of the house, its front cover inscribed with his prison-camp address.

Flavio had not expected a welcoming committee at the town hall. But as he climbed the hill and passed under the peeling archway that marked the entrance to town, he understood that he was to receive no welcome at all. One or two children, half-grown since he had last seen them, glanced up at his approach and fled. He caught sight of the old mayor Arcangelo, who merely ducked out of sight into an alley, with a pained expression as though to communicate to Flavio that it would be impolitic for the two of them, the ex-Fascist and the former star of the *Balilla*, to speak to each other.

Then he had stumbled away from the town again, toward the ruined houses—until at last, with a shock, he came upon his sister, a woman with a line down her forehead and no leg braces anymore.

When she embraced him, the perfume of a grown-up woman had hung around him in the air.

She had led him to the bar, and Flavio found everything altered, everything strange. His mother was diminished, his father a reedy-voiced old man. He had become confused then under the force of memory. Where were his sister's leg braces? Where was the kitten? Then he had discovered a stranger's belongings in his bedroom, the trumpet tarnished, the portrait of *il duce* gone—and before memory could get a proper hold on him, he plunged into sleep.

NOW, HE GOT UP. He put on a shirt and trousers from the mothballed interior of his chest of drawers, descended the stairs, took a glass of water. His mother came in and worked off her schoolmistress's shoes.

The others followed: his father, his sister. "What was the procession?" said Flavio. "I saw it from the window."

"A death," said his mother. "Signora Gesuina."

Gesuina. The woman had tended him in his youth, had fed him sugared *ricotta* and peeled figs. He tried to coax forth a few tears, which came at last. His mother approached and rubbed him a little between the shoulder blades. "My Flavio," she murmured. "My Flavio. You've come back to me now, my boy."

He let her work a curl free from the front of his head. "What was it like in the camp?" she said. "Did they treat you well, those *inglesi*?"

What could he say? That they had given him decent food, of a stodgy, puddingy sort? That they had put a black suit on him, with a gray spot on the back and one on the ankle, to show them where to shoot if he should run away? That they had let him work on a farm, only not at first? At first, he had still been what they considered a Fascist. How could he change his mind all at once? Nevertheless, four of the prisoners, including Flavio, had eventually been allowed to work at a great dark farmhouse surrounded by baying dogs, making the long walk each winter morning through a coppice stiff with ice. At the farmhouse, one Christmas, they had been allowed to sit around the farmer's table and eat roast goose and little roast potatoes and miniature cabbages with a bitter taste which the *inglesi* called "sprouts," laughing when he wrinkled his nose at the overpowering foulness of the things. Should he tell his mother about that? How they had worn coronets of paper for an afternoon, and drunk indigestible English beer? Or the hospital—should he tell her about the hospital? How, in the psychiatric ward when the lights were turned out, you only had to listen to locate each separate bed by its mumbling and groaning, each one an island of weeping in the dark. Which of those things should he select and dust off and bring forth? He was tired; he didn't know.

"They treated me well enough," he said. "Everything was all right." Still, this insatiable thirst. He downed more water. His mother seized his glass and filled it again, as though desperate to be of use.

———

IT WAS ALL HE could do to keep awake in those first days. He told his sister he would take back the management of the bar, but in truth he could barely carry a tray with such a great piece missing out of his right hand, could not now remember how to make the coffee and the pastries. Had he ever known? For Flavio, now, to go about the business of daily life was to only half inhabit the world, for in a deeper chamber of his mind the war was playing and replaying, sapping his energies as though he were still fighting it. It came over him quite suddenly. For example, he would smooth out the sheets on his bed before sleep, and before him instead the desert would ripple, the wind scouring its surface. Or he would raise his hand to shave and see instead a slick of blood—feel again how his guts had curled when he raised that same hand in the dark to find one finger, two fingers, three fingers gone, shot away entirely. The fingers had been unsalvageable (though he had scrabbled in the sand for them with his left hand, turning up only hard stones). They came under fire again; they had to move on. "*Vai, vai!*" the sergeant screamed. Flavio had hobbled along, doubled over, pressing his bleeding hand to his stomach, the fingers abandoned miles behind them now, trampled by English boots. The pain came only afterward, rolling over him hours later.

Sometimes, now, he would be behind the bar counter, wiping a glass clean with his good hand while his thumb and his one remaining finger kept it anchored, and he would hear the rattle of machine gun fire and turn, startled, to find beyond the door only the harmless rattle of cicadas, the blank blue line of the sea.

He had been told a little about the Englishman Robert Carr. The man had slept in his bed, and—judging by his sister's sad glances out to sea—also in Maria-Grazia's. Shortly after reinstating himself in his childhood room, Flavio had found a little pamphlet forgotten under his nightstand, A *Soldier's Guide to Sicily*, sea-wrinkled, a single strand of blond hair between the pages. Then the Englishman must have known what Flavio knew: the infernal light of the desert, the charge up a dune's flank, the roaring, the thunder. The Englishman knew, but he was gone, and from the stories the islanders told about him he had been welcomed as a hero, while Flavio, with his missing fingers and restless eyes, was a person no one seemed to know what to do with anymore.

ANDREA D'ISANTU RETURNED two weeks after Flavio Esposito. *Il conte* was determined that his son should receive a welcome more resounding than that afforded to any of the other returned soldiers. He ordered his peasants early to work that morning, in their Sunday clothes, and had them lined up along the avenue of his villa, holding oleander garlands. His wife procured the services of the village band. Their numbers were sadly diminished since the war; several of them lamented this fact, assembling in the bar for a dram of courage before the performance.

Flavio's mother urged him to go along with his brass trumpet. "How can I play?" he asked her, as she thrust it at him, "when I've got no fingers to play it with?"

"Play anyway," she urged him. "Play as well as you can with only your left. You used to play so nicely, Flavio, and you see the band needs more players."

As Flavio remembered, she had never much liked his brass trumpet. He went, though, sullenly, some childhood obedience persisting in him. As he stood before *il conte*'s villa among the elderly musicians, sweating in a borrowed jacket, he saw *il conte*'s motorcar approach, plowing the dust of the road before it. In the passenger seat rode the returning soldier, still thin as a pine tree, looking neither to the left nor to the right.

As Flavio mimed the notes the others sounded, a curious sensation came over him: moving the stumps of his right hand, it was as though the fingers came to life again; he could feel them pushing and resisting against the stops as they had when he was a boy. When he looked, nothing. And yet he felt them, the ghosts of his fingers, playing the trumpet in the air.

Some altercation was taking place between *il conte* and his son, meanwhile, *il conte* murmuring and wheedling, and his son protesting, "I won't! I won't!" And then a great eruption: "I won't be made a fool of by you, you *stronzo*, you *figlio di puttana!*"

An ass—a son of a whore—never had any islander of Castellamare talked in such terms to his father. Flavio was seized with a kind of horrified admiration. Andrea d'Isantu left the car, slamming the door behind him. He came up the drive at a furious strut, limping with a cane. While the band struck into their first verse, he passed them and limped on. Past the band, past the peasants, past the servants, and around the corner of the villa. He vanished, leaving them all looking ridiculous in his wake. *Il conte*, caught in undignified pursuit of his son, beat a hand in the air at the musicians, made them stop.

The musicians waited in the hot silence, but no one else came. An embarrassed servant brought the band a jug of *limonata* eventually, and half a bottle of *arancello*. They stood on the scorched grass before the villa and drank, and then they went home.

AFTER THE FAILED WELCOME COMMITTEE, Andrea d'Isantu remained shut up in his father's villa. His mother had called the priest for him, his father the mainland doctor. Andrea sent both away.

"He's sore at losing the war," murmured Rizzu, in the bar. "That boy must have been a real Fascist."

But Flavio, who had got a good look in Andrea d'Isantu's eyes before he vanished, understood that the truth was different. Flavio had stung with a kind of recognition as *il conte*'s son passed—as though the two of them were fellow initiates, brothers, sufferers of the same shameful disease.

Now he assembled his scraps of memory concerning Andrea. Flavio remembered once playing "Giovinezza" on his brass trumpet for the visit of some dignitary; Andrea had sung. Andrea had possessed a startlingly high voice, nasal, very pure, unbroken even at sixteen. No one considered mocking it. In general, he had been left utterly alone by the other children, protected by the suits of foreign clothes in which he came to school, by his habit of speaking proper Italian to the teacher, saying *"grazie"* with an "e" instead of the normal *"grazzi"* belonging to the island, *"per favore"* instead of *"pi fauri"*—"Like a character from a textbook," Tullio said. Andrea had walked to school alone, and on hot afternoons the old man Rizzu collected him in the donkey cart, or the agent Santino Arcangelo, the grocer's elder son, in *il conte*'s motorcar, swerving all over the road, sounding delighted beeps to clear the other children out of his way. Andrea had completed his last years of school alone in the library of the count's villa.

But here he was now, back from the war with a sick look in his eyes.

The next time Flavio caught a glimpse of him, after the failure of the welcome committee, was toward the end of autumn. There he was, limping through the edge of Flavio's vision with his walking cane. In the other hand, he carried a few storm-battered trumpet vine flowers. The bones in the boy's knee had shattered, Flavio had heard; it had taken five operations in an American hospital to put him back together. Andrea paused a moment by the green-smelling fountain and lowered his face to the orange mouths of the trumpet vine. Flavio watched, rubbing the itching stumps of his fingers. At length, Andrea raised his head, turned, and said, "What do you want?"

Flavio said, *"Salve,* Signor d'Isantu."

"But what do you want? Why do you stare so?"

"Mi scusi," said Flavio. "Only I heard you were also captured in Africa, during the war."

"Come here."

Flavio approached and stood before him. *Il conte*'s son had his father's manners and his father's protruding, insolent eyes. He raised the flowers like a toast. "For my mother. She loves them. We have none on our estate. She's been a little difficult since I returned, a little demanding, so I go for long walks to gather them, and that way she gets her flowers and I get a little peace. They're almost finished now."

Flavio offered up a sentence or two about his own mother: how she had arranged his football cards on his nightstand, had forced on him his brass trumpet—as though he could still play that thing, with all his fingers shot off! "They can't help thinking we're just the same, these damned mothers and fathers," said Flavio, becoming strident in his urge to be understood. "They don't know anything except this island, the sea, fishing boats, village gossip, the damned Sant'Agata festival . . ."

For everyone on the island seemed a child now to Flavio, all of them very cheerful and simple, like the inhabitants of some previous century. He found Andrea nodding: Yes, the count's son understood this also. "You don't have to tell me I need to get out of this place," said Andrea. "This *isola di merda*. I'm dying here. You, too."

Thus, a peculiar friendship began.

AS THE ISLAND BEGAN to heave itself upright the following year, to shake off the dust of war, a fever for weddings swept Castellamare. Every Saturday, handfuls of rice strewed the main street; at every Sunday Mass, Father Ignazio was obliged to read the banns, so that he began to confuse the names of last week's newly joined couples with this week's expectant brides and bridegrooms. On still nights, village boys with their guitars and *organetti* could be heard at a distance, serenading the new couples under their windows, beating on the doors of the parents' houses where they passed their cramped, embarrassed wedding nights. The florist Gisella had never done such a trade, and the hedges and courtyards were stripped of trumpet vine and white oleander in the furious demand for bouquets, so that it seemed that summer had not come this year, or had passed early, without any flowers.

As the last of Maria-Grazia's classmates, Giulia Martinello, danced in exaltation down the steps of the church with her husband, young Totò, pinned firmly by the arm, Maria-Grazia was seized with a melancholy so profound that she could taste it, the way you could taste a storm coming in off the ocean. Pinioned in her smile and her too-small Sunday clothes, flinging rice in the faces of Giulia and Totò, she understood that this summer marked three years since the *americani* had taken Robert away across the sea.

At first, her mother and father had carried on their backs, as she had, a great grief at the loss of the Englishman. But she had refused to mention him—had turned away when they spoke his name—until they had given up and retreated, hiding it away in some chamber of their hearts where the memories of Tullio and Aurelio were also incarcerated.

So no one talked about the Englishman any longer, except the girl Concetta and old Rizzu. "We all loved the *inglese*," the old man told Maria-Grazia one afternoon in the bar, seizing her by the hand. "We all loved Roberto Caro. But a marriage is a marriage, and it's time we were finding someone for you, Maria-Grazia."

"You're wrong about that, *nonno*!" cried Concetta, upturning Rizzu's coffee in her rage.

"What's wrong about it?" quavered Rizzu. "There'll be no one left if poor Mariuzza waits any longer!"

"Maria-Grazia's waiting for Signor Robert," said Concetta. "She must wait until Signor Robert comes home."

"There'll be no one left," mourned Rizzu. "There'll be no one left, Mariuzza."

"There's no one left already," said Maria-Grazia.

It was true. The rash of weddings was subsiding as quickly as it had come on. In loyalty to Robert, she had held herself aloof, even when half chances at happiness had been offered her. She had lowered her eyes when she served the young fisherman Totò, who had given up hissing at her as she moved about the bar and gone in pursuit of Giulia instead, securing her hand with admirable efficiency in just ten days. She had treated the middle-aged widower Dacosta with a daughterly, bluff cheer until he stopped hanging about at the counter of the bar offering her his views on politics and farming, and took his coffee alone at the corner table instead, the newspaper before his eyes. Even Dacosta had married again now, finding a wife among his second cousins on the mainland when he had visited the previous winter. There was no unmarried man that she knew of on the island except the priest and old Rizzu. Jokingly, Rizzu made a pantomime of proposing to Maria-Grazia with a ring-pull from one of the new American soda cans the bar stocked now, singing in his splintered old voice the most romantic of the island's songs.

It was meant to cheer her, but Maria-Grazia turned away with tears in her eyes, feeling herself mocked before them all.

AT THE COLD END OF AUTUMN, she came out onto the terrace to gather the dirty glasses and found *il conte*'s son, in an English linen suit, lounging against the veranda. Since the incident over the voting in '34, never had *il conte* or any member of his household approached the House at the Edge of Night. The enmity between *il conte* and her father, an unspoken thing, had its own force, which must be respected. "Good evening, Signor d'Isantu," she said, all the same. "May I offer you a table?"

"No. I'll not set foot on your terrace. I'm only here to see Flavio."

"I'll fetch him."

Andrea, used to being obeyed, said, "Come here a moment."

Maria-Grazia set down the glasses and wiped her hands on her apron.

"You're Maria-Grazia, aren't you? I remember you from school. The clever one."

His attention held her hostage. A narrow face, black oiled hair like his father's, interrogating eyes. Every muscle of him gave off an odd intensity. He dragged himself a little closer on the silver-topped walking cane, and she felt a sudden tenderness, remembering the frustration of her own leg braces. Now she stood straight and tall, and he was the one who was spoken of by everybody as a cripple, in hushed tones. Eventually, when he had appraised the whole of her, he said, "You've changed since the war."

Maria-Grazia, who did not know how to reply to this, said nothing. At an upstairs window, Amedeo looked down on the two of them, the boy at the edge of the veranda and his beautiful daughter, and knitted his eyebrows in a single line, wondering what trouble Andrea meant to cause.

THE FRIENDSHIP BETWEEN FLAVIO and Andrea d'Isantu had begun to be noticed. They had been spied by the elderly Mazzu taking walks together around the circumference of the island, Andrea beating at the scrub grass with his cane, Flavio gesticulating in the air with his wounded hand. They made an odd pair, the count's son and the son of his enemy, the doctor. Several times, Flavio had invited Andrea to sit with him on the veranda of the bar. But Andrea d'Isantu refused to set foot on Esposito territory, in deference to his father. So Flavio moved a table into the neutral space under the palm tree in the piazza, a meter or two beyond the bar's boundary, and the matter was resolved. Here Flavio sat with his friend and engaged in fierce discussions over bottles of *arancello*.

Neither Pina nor Amedeo approved of the friendship, and nor did Carmela and *il conte*.

Meanwhile, Maria-Grazia heard the way her brother and Andrea d'Isantu talked about the island: *Isola di merda*, they called it—narrow, gossip-ridden, an island of inbred goatherds and pickers of olives. Though she herself had flung accusations at the island a hundred times in her heart, she sprang to its defense now to hear it maligned out loud; she burned with suppressed rage as she cleared the tables. She felt abashed in Andrea's presence, constantly wrong-footed. Several times, collecting dirty glasses or arranging plates before the customers on the veranda, she looked into the palm tree's black shadow and found Andrea d'Isantu looking back at her, a gaze that seemed to come from the depths of a mirror, matching her own. As she moved about the veranda his eyes followed her, going everywhere she went.

She remembered him at school, laboring at a desk set apart from the other children's in tribute to his father's status, with blocks of concrete under the legs to elevate it above the others. Some idea of Professor Calleja's to get into *il conte*'s favor. Andrea d'Isantu, neck smarting, had bent his head over his mathematics problems at the humiliation, and to Maria-Grazia his slicked hair and skinny neck had seemed the loneliest thing in the world. The separateness of the two of them, he with his expensive clothes and Latin diction, she with her clanking, creaking leg braces, had never been enough material from which to forge a friendship. But now his eyes followed her, and hers sought him out, with a kind of rhythm, repeating and returning.

He looked at her as though they shared some complicity, the two of them.

Early one morning in December he came to the bar asking for Flavio again. A rain like wet ropes was falling outside. Andrea stood with the water running down him. "Flavio isn't up yet," she said. "I'll fetch him."

In this rain, there was nothing to do but invite him in—courtesy held sway over everything else on the island, even old feuds. "Wait inside," said Maria-Grazia. "Come into the hall for a moment. You'll be soaked through."

"I'll wait here."

"Please, Signor d'Isantu, come in."

But here Andrea was adamant. He knew the story of how Pina Vella had driven him from the bar as a baby in his mother's arms, and pride compelled him to maintain his position now, even in the force of this downpour. "I'll not come in," he said. "I'll not set foot in your bar. I'll wait here beyond the steps."

Rain poured down on him, battening his hair monkishly to his pale forehead, making great well buckets of the pockets of his English suit. All at once, Maria-Grazia was seized with a fit of rage at the absurdity of the feud, this pride, the waste of a good suit of clothes! It wasn't to be borne any longer. She threw her cable of hair over her shoulder and stamped her two feet on the wet veranda. "I've never heard anything so silly!" she cried. "Come in when I tell you! What— are you going to stand in the rain?"

"I will," said Andrea.

"You won't, you *stronzo!*"

Never had anyone on Castellamare spoken thus to *il conte*'s son. Winded, puffing a little, he opened his mouth to resist. But before he could repossess himself of the power of speech, Maria-Grazia had hauled him by the arm so fiercely that he became unbalanced, stumbling on his weak leg. "Come on," she said. Dragging the furious Andrea behind her, she gained the shelter of the entrance hall of the House at the Edge of Night, muscled *il conte*'s son inside, and shut the door. "There," she said, shaking the water out of the pockets of his suit. "That's enough of that nonsense."

Andrea, utterly discomposed for the first time in his life, said, "There's no need—there's no need—" while water dripped from his pockets onto the red map-of-the-world tiles.

Now, all at once, Maria-Grazia was a little abashed at what she had done. For a moment, the two of them regarded each other. "Wait here, please, Signor d'Isantu," she said at last. "I'll fetch Flavio."

Andrea stood, shuddering, ill at ease. Maria-Grazia ascended the stairs, and his eyes ascended with her.

"Flavio!" she called, beating on her brother's door. "Your friend is here! Signor d'Isantu!"

Flavio, with a great moaning, awoke. "I'll be down in a minute or two—tell him to wait."

"He's waiting."

But now Andrea's presence at the bottom of the stairs was a dark weight, like a cloud over the ocean. Maria-Grazia retreated to her own bedroom, astounded at what she had done. Her brother was blundering about in the room below her, waking—that room she still thought of as Robert's. She still remembered the little noises belonging to the Englishman: the protest of the bedsprings as he turned, the coughs he made, foreign sounding, the thud of his book on the nightstand as he readied himself for sleep.

The postcard from Robert lay in its accustomed place on her nightstand. She lifted it caressingly, looking for unseen meaning in those few inadequate words.

With a shock she realized that Andrea d'Isantu had climbed the stairs. Now, huffing from the effort, hauling his bad leg in both hands, he was here, at the very door of her room. She dropped the postcard and retreated to the window. "Flavio's room is downstairs—on the landing—not here—"

"I wanted to apologize," said Andrea. "You're right—this feud is a silly thing. All of it." He bent, keeping one leg straight, to retrieve her postcard from the floor. "*Sto pensando a te?*" he said.

"It's from a friend—"

"Your Englishman. Flavio told me." His shrewd eyes, a little mocking, held her hostage. She kept herself taut and stern under his gaze, feeling like an old spinster warding off some perilous suitor. She hugged her own elbows, leaning back against the knobby front of her chest of drawers. Once—she recalled it dimly, like something that had only been narrated to her secondhand—Robert had pressed her against these drawers, made love to her, bracing her against its edge so that when they were done they found two circles printed on the small of her back.

Andrea held out the postcard, which now, she saw, bore a wet thumbprint where he had gripped it. But as she reached to take it, he caught instead her wrist and held it there before him, as though uncertain what to do with it now he had possession of it. "When you took my arm just now," he began at last. "Since I came back—since the war—not one person's touched me—not my mother, not my father. Just you."

All at once her father filled the doorway; she had not heard him climb the stairs. He advanced, big with a rage she had never seen in him before. "What's this?" he cried. "Leave hold of my daughter!"

Her father came forward and with one swift blow broke the boy's grip on her wrist.

"Out!" he cried. "Out!"

Andrea retreated before the yells of the incensed Amedeo, his cheeks inflamed. "You are not to see my daughter," roared Amedeo. "You are not to pursue my daughter. You are not to speak to her."

Flavio, roused, sprang from his room and followed his friend down the stairs in a sweat of embarrassment.

Now, in the room still ringing a little with what had just taken place, Amedeo rounded on Maria-Grazia. "What were you doing with *il conte*'s boy? What was he doing in your room?"

"I wasn't doing anything. He came for Flavio—the rain—I had to invite him into the house to wait—"

"It's some damned game he's playing—it's some wicked game—"

"He came by mistake. He was looking for Flavio."

Amedeo gripped her by the elbows. "You are not to have anything to do with *il conte*'s son."

But that night, when Maria-Grazia tried to sleep, her dreams were odd and disordered—dreams of the forceful Andrea pinioning her against the chest of drawers as Robert once had, or pressing her up against the wall of the caves by the sea, so that the marks on her back were the imprints of skulls. She woke and washed in cold water, and went down into the bar. When she unlocked the door and stepped out onto the veranda, Andrea was waiting there, a single trumpet vine flower in his hand. The way the light slanted, the flower glowed as though it were a light source of its own. "I made a poor impression yesterday with your father," he said, "an ugly impression. Can I make amends?"

In the space during which she hesitated, unsure of how to rebuff him, Andrea took her wrist and closed the flower in her palm. It recalled to her the moment when she, a girl behind the bougainvillea, creaking in leg braces, had beheld the poet Mario Vazzo pressing a single trembling vine flower on her mother, Pina Vella, without understanding the meaning of what the prisoner-poet did. Now, she understood it.

She put the flower in a glass of water on her nightstand, and when she looked at it she had a feeling like nausea, but not exactly unpleasant. Her father, when he saw Andrea's gift, threw water and glass from the window so that the vase exploded in a thousand needles. For weeks afterward they were treading on crushed glass as they went about the veranda, and Andrea remained at its edge again: banished, pensive, sallow of face, constantly watching.

Maria-Grazia had never seen her father behave in such a manner. She heard him raging in a whisper at Flavio behind the curtain of the bar some nights, wound in a knot of fury: "I don't trust that friend of yours with Maria-Grazia—not one bit, not even a little!"

ONE EVENING, AFTER THIS had gone on for several months, her father called her up to his study. Here he took her hand, kneaded it between his own great wrinkled ones, smoothed her hair, and spoke at last. "Would you like to leave the island, Mariuzza? Do you want to go somewhere else? Is that what troubles you?"

"Leave the island," she murmured, thrown off-balance by the question.

"You could go to university, or train as a teacher," her father said. "Go to a big city, Roma or Firenze. You've been shut up in this house for so long, taking care of your poor Mamma and Papà in their old age." The attempt at jocularity fell flat between them, leaving a painful silence.

"Why do you ask me?" she said. "Is it something I've done? Does Flavio want the bar?"

"No, *cara*. Nothing like that. You've never done anything but be a blessing to us." Her father gave a great sigh and went on, "But Andrea d'Isantu—"

Indignant rage brought tears stinging to her eyes. "What about him?"

"*Cara mia. Principessa.*" He stroked her hands, but Maria-Grazia would not be consoled.

"I've done nothing wrong," she raged. "Nothing happened, Papà."

"You've heard the rumors about Carmela d'Isantu and me. You can't be ignorant about what happened between us, before you were born."

Loyalty compelled her to turn away from him, maintaining silence, watching a great liner move along the horizon with slow grace, lit up like a city in the distance. "Look at me, Mariuzza," said her father. "Don't be ashamed. It's I who should be ashamed, for I was the one who did those things—though God knows I wish I could lie to you and tell you I didn't. I can't stand the thought of being diminished in your eyes, *cara*. But I must speak. Look at me, Mariuzza."

She looked at the books on the shelves—books of folktales, old leather-bound medical periodicals—at anything rather than her father. "I thought they proved Andrea wasn't your son," she murmured at last. That was the story she had heard, whispered behind her back in the schoolyard—that a doctor had come from the mainland and done a special test. At the time, the rumor had only bolstered her fierce conviction that her father was innocent.

"That test isn't worth anything," said her father, with an impatient click of the teeth. "That's no sure way to tell. *Cara*, I don't like the way he looks at you, following you about with his eyes. It's no good, that look. It means trouble."

"No one else looks at me," she said. "No one else notices me. No one else on this damned island cares whether I live or die."

"I've heard of this phenomenon before." Her father had adopted his doctor's tone—she couldn't bear it! "In my practice on the mainland, when I was a young man, there were a half brother and sister who were separated as children, brought up in different houses at opposite ends of the village, who began living as man and wife, but it's a danger, Mariuzza. In such cases there can be a powerful attraction—not to mention the legality of the affair, the scandal in a small place—"

Humiliation brought her near weeping.

"Does it shock you, what I've confessed?" asked Amedeo. "Does it make you think less of me, *cara?*"

"No," lied Maria-Grazia, her face turned away.

"What about Robert?" said her father gently. "We all loved Robert." Here his voice came apart a little, but she felt in her misery that she could not bear it if he were to cry, too, and so she shook him off and went farther away, and said, with as much indifference as she could manage: "Well, what about Robert? We haven't seen him in four years."

"What about Robert, you say? Cristo, Dio! You loved him, Maria-Grazia, didn't you? But you've never once spoken his name since he went away. He came to us out of the ocean—like a miracle, like a son! Don't you love him, and he you? Isn't he coming back?"

Rage, in the end, brought the infuriating tears to her eyes. "Ask *him* if he's coming back!" she wept. "Ask *him* if he loves me! I've waited, haven't I? For four years I've waited! Now I'm to be humiliated, a laughingstock, an old spinster in everyone's eyes, the only girl left alone! I loved Robert! Why won't you all see that I loved him—that I waited and waited and waited for that worthless *stronzo*, and he never came back for me?"

Her father reached for her, but she fled him, inconsolable. She escaped the town by the nearest route, tumbling down through the olive groves, and lost herself among the caves by the sea.

ANDREA D'ISANTU, AMEDEO DECREED, was never again to enter the House at the Edge of Night. *Il conte* had also curtailed Andrea's freedoms, and later that year arranged for a friend from the mainland with five daughters to spend Christmas at the villa. Andrea escaped while they were all having dinner on the first evening, and threw sand at Maria-Grazia's window. "Maria-Grazia!" he shouted, drunk. "Why won't you see me? Dio, are you trying to drive me insane?"

Maria-Grazia, with the weight of her father's warning on her chest, could not bring herself to open the window. From behind the curtain she watched instead, mute, as Andrea turned away, hunched over his walking stick, and crossed the piazza. At its four corners windows were opening, neighbors peering—alone in the frosted dark, Andrea seemed to her the loneliest person on the whole island, as solitary as that schoolboy had been, elevated above the others on his throne of four concrete bricks.

Rumors raced around the island and were back at the House at the Edge of Night before morning. The count's boy had been sick since the war—that everyone knew—but still doubt persisted in the minds of some of the islanders. Mustn't Maria-Grazia have done something or other to encourage him? Descending the stairs to the bar, she knew by the abrupt silences of the customers, the shuffling glances, that it was what everyone had been talking about. And she overheard ugly things in the following days: "He's quite besotted with her, Signora Carmela says—refuses to marry any of those city girls," "In love, *gesummaria*, with a girl who might be his sister for all any-one knows," "I've heard of this—my cousin on the mainland knew someone who married a first cousin—children with legs like octo-puses, heads like *medusas*, with twelve fingers and five eyes—"

Andrea attended the Christmas Mass, between his mother and father, the city girls processing in his wake. From the front of the church, facing down the whole island, he twisted and fixed Maria-Grazia with his dark, uncompromising gaze.

Now, the elderly *scopa* players and the women on their wooden chairs outside the houses gossiped about her quite openly. The whole island seemed to have become a mass of lowered eyes. She was tainted like Flavio was, like Andrea; the desert dust of their war had left its trace on her, too. In those last days of 1948 she cried in frustration, pummeling the mattress of her narrow room in silent grief. Andrea was said to be sick. He no longer drank with her brother under the palm tree, no longer took his solitary walks around the island, and those peasants who still worked for *il conte* whispered that he had hung up his walking cane, taken to his bed, and refused to speak to anybody anymore.

None of this would have happened if Robert had come back for her. He had betrayed her so completely by his leaving, by his years of silence, that she felt sometimes that she simply could not care about him any longer. Andrea was right about one thing: This was an *isola di merda*, full of gossip, full of shame. She could not stand it. As 1949 began, her twenty-fourth year, she developed the habit of hoarding banknotes from the till and stuffing them down the back of her bed in an old Campari bottle. When she had enough, she'd be gone from this place.

IV

THAT YEAR, SHORTLY AFTER *EPIFANIA*, CARMELA PAID A VISIT TO THE House at the Edge of Night. She must have made her way in when the house was still sleeping, for Maria-Grazia, rising early with the dissatisfaction that had possessed her since the beginning of this trouble with Andrea, found *la contessa* already waiting for her at the bottom of the stairs. There she stood in her faded Paris suit the color of aubergines, her Sunday hat with its visor of dotted tulle purchased before the first war. It was the first time that Carmela had crossed the threshold of the House at the Edge of Night in twenty-eight years, since Pina had ejected her and her baby from the bar and sworn never to let them return.

"Signora d'Isantu," said Maria-Grazia, coming to rest in the sunlight at the turn of the stairs.

Now Carmela spoke, her voice as thin and windblown as that of the late Gesuina. "Signorina Maria-Grazia," said Carmela. "You have to help my son."

Maria-Grazia found her heart constricted, her breath slight. "What's wrong? Is he sick? I'll wake my father—I'll fetch his medical bag."

"No, no, no," wept Carmela, shaking her head. "Don't fetch Amedeo. It's you I need."

"Tell me what's the matter."

"He's sick," said Carmela. "He's sick for love of you, Signorina Maria-Grazia! All year he's been growing worse. He won't leave his bed, he won't eat, his tongue is dry and white, his eyes are yellow. I fear I'll lose him. Won't you give him some hope? My boy is dying for love of you."

As though she were an actress lifting a mask, Carmela pushed back her veil, and Maria-Grazia saw that tears had washed the kohl from *la contessa*'s eyes, and her cheeks underneath were gray-smudged like a bandit's. Pity moved Maria-Grazia. She took Carmela by the elbow and led her into the empty bar. Taking down two upturned chairs, pulling the blinds against the intrusive eyes of the early customers loitering in the piazza, she left the sign at "Chiuso" and began to rouse the coffee machine. "No, no," said Carmela. "Something stronger—more fortifying—that *limoncello* Rizzu used to make, if you've got any left?"

Really, Carmela must be a little beside herself, thought Maria-Grazia, for that *limoncello* had been exhausted a quarter of a century ago. Instead she fetched a different bottle, and set two glasses between them. The clock above the counter stood at just after seven, but all the same, Carmela swallowed her dram of liquor in one bracing gulp and, like a woman in mourning, consented at last to sit down, feeling her way onto the edge of the chair.

"*Signor il figlio del conte* can't set his mind on marrying me," said Maria-Grazia at last. "It's not possible. From what I've heard, anyway, Signora d'Isantu, it wouldn't be right."

Here Carmela turned acidic, flashing her eyes with bitter amusement. "I know how they all talk about me. It's not true, what you've heard."

Maria-Grazia found herself timid with hope: "Not about my Papà . . . or . . . or the caves by the sea?"

"Yes, yes, that's all true. I don't mean that." Carmela dismissed this with one downward motion of her white-gloved hand. "But Andrea isn't your half brother. At least, I don't believe so. That's what I'm here to tell you. Maria-Grazia, I believe there's no barrier to your loving him. There's no barrier in the eyes of God or the law to the two of you being married. That's what I came here to say."

When Maria-Grazia made no answer, Carmela reached forward

and plucked at her sleeve. The *contessa* had an odd musk about her, a perfume of despair that hung about them in the air. "My boy is threatening to leave the island if you don't," she finished.

At last, carefully, Maria-Grazia said, "How can you be sure he isn't my half brother?"

"I'm convinced of it, *cara*," said Carmela. "It's true what they gossip, that my husband and I had never been able to conceive. But *cara*, he hardly tried." Here Carmela gave one quick, disparaging laugh and reached again for the *limoncello*. "My husband put it about that I was barren when we were first married, until the whole island knew about it. It suited him, I suppose, to make a mockery of me and avoid his duties at the same time. The truth is, *he* never wanted *me*. It was a marriage made by arrangement, an affair of land and *palazzi* parceled out between our families. Never consummated—or hardly, nothing worth speaking of. I must be frank, *cara*—excuse me. The truth is, my husband never wanted any woman. Well, not until I began seeing other lovers. Then, I suppose, some lordly instinct came over him and he'd come back to me for a while. That was the only way to make him care anything about me. It was only after the affair with Amedeo that he wanted me, *cara*. Only after someone else did. So you see"—here Carmela caught Maria-Grazia's sleeve again— "Andrea isn't likely to be Amedeo's child. You're free to love him— you must. I allowed those rumors about the boy being Amedeo's—God knows why, some instinct for mischief, some wish to get the better of my husband—but it isn't true. At least, I don't believe it."

Maria-Grazia looked into the misted depths of the *limoncello*. "But you don't know for sure," she said at last.

Again, Carmela plucked at her wrist. "He has his father's weak ankles, *cara*. The same attacks of constipation once a fortnight. When the damp winds come in from the north, they both get agonies like needles in their knees, in their old war injuries, in just the same place. I've watched them together for twenty-eight years. I'm certain of it."

"But you can't know for sure," persisted Maria-Grazia.

"No," said Carmela. "I can't know for sure."

When Maria-Grazia maintained her silence, Carmela reached forward again and caught hold of her sleeve. "Please, *cara*, give my Andrea some hope or he'll be gone—I know it—I know he will, and leave me all alone here, with no one but my damned husband for company in this whole godforsaken town."

"You can't command me to love him, just like that!" cried Maria-Grazia, panicked in the face of the *contessa*'s grasping, her desperation.

"No, no, Signorina Esposito. No one's commanding you—I didn't mean that. But won't you give him an answer? Give him an answer at the end of the summer, when you've had time to think about it. Say six, eight months—ten if you wish! Take all the time you want to think it over, and let him court you, let him visit—"

But Maria-Grazia was overwhelmed: "No, no—I don't want him to visit—I don't want him to court me—hasn't there been enough scandal already?"

"Very well, then I'll order him not to visit you until you've had time to think it over. As long as you need, *cara*. Six months, a year! I'll order him not to come near."

"And what if I have no answer by that time?"

But here Carmela dissolved again: "He's threatening to leave—he'll be gone, my only boy—"

"Very well, *sì, sì*," said Maria-Grazia, who felt all at once that she could not bear another attack of weeping. "I'll think about it—I'll give him an answer in six months."

"Tell no one I've been here," said Carmela, gathering her purse, buttoning the little aubergine-colored jacket, dabbing methodically under her veil to blot the black rivers of kohl from her face. All at once she seemed herself again, the same cool column of a woman whom Maria-Grazia had only before encountered at a distance—passing her with lowered eyes at the Communion rail, or standing aloof at the saint's festival, dressed in clothes that had been new before the first war, a veil always covering her eyes.

"I won't tell anyone," said Maria-Grazia.

"Someday years from now, when I'm dead . . ." murmured Carmela.

"I won't tell."

Carmela took her wrist again, with a cool pressure. "You've a kind face, *cara*," she said. "It's a relief to me to tell someone, after all these years shut up in those empty rooms, speaking to no one. And you've given me hope, for I see that you could find it in you to love him, *cara*. Tell me the truth. You could."

"*Sì*," admitted Maria-Grazia. "I could."

Carmela gripped both her hands. It was a smooth grip, uncalloused as a child's, the kind of grip achieved only through a lifetime spent in white gloves. Then she was gone, so that Maria-Grazia, lightheaded, watching her recede across the piazza, believed for a moment that she had only dreamed the encounter. The piazza was calm again. The palm tree's shadow moved listlessly across the tiles of the veranda, marking time like a sundial's needle. The lizards crept out from the cracks in the houses to seek the day's sun.

But Maria-Grazia found herself raging in a whisper as she went about the early morning business of igniting the coffee machine, rolling the blinds up, arranging the chairs. What claim did this Carmela have on her? Was she, Maria-Grazia, to become the repository of everybody's secrets? What was it they wanted from her, they with their shames furled within them, their guilty eyes, piling upon her these troubles that had occurred before she was born?

And yet the thought of Andrea sleepless, tormented, pained her as the fear for Robert once had. Did this mean love, or only pity? She could not love Andrea the way she had loved Robert. She knew that to be the truth; she had used up all her capacity for that kind of adoration. And yet Robert was gone and Andrea was here, and was sick with love for her. No one else had ever paid her that honor. For Totò and for the widower Dacosta she had been merely a potential wife, replaceable. Perhaps Robert had long since replaced her, too, with some English girl, some sweetheart from before the war. Not Andrea d'Isantu.

A tenderness persisted in her when she thought of his shattered leg, recollecting the shame of her own weak ankles, her own limping gait. And hadn't they really been companions since their youth, when she considered it: she and *il conte*'s son, both friendless, united by the same dark intensity, the same solitude, the same studious hunch and high marks? Four years behind him in school, she had felt herself always to be following in his wake, for when she outstripped her own companions, Andrea's grades were the ones drawn out of the teacher's cupboard for comparison. Professor Calleja would murmur, "Now, Esposito, let's see how d'Isantu fared in this exam." The schoolmaster had kept a running average of her marks alongside Andrea's. By his final year, her average had outstripped his. When Andrea was informed, he had merely smiled a little, inclining his head. She had seen this at the time as ungenerous. Why hadn't he consented to shake her hand? But might it not have instead been a kind of deference, the same deference with which he had tremblingly presented her the flower?

At the end of the summer she would give her answer. Until then, she would do her best to drive both of them, the Englishman and *il conte*'s son, utterly from her mind.

EVEN THE ISLAND WAS UNSETTLED, dissatisfied, in those days. It had once been a volcano. Though the islanders knew this, the volcano had lain quiet so long that they often forgot. And then sometimes it behaved oddly, smoldering with faint recollections of its past. Once or twice a decade a hole in the ground would open, releasing a jet of smoke, singeing a vine, or turning a mountain goat to a black heap of bones. At other times, warm water would well under the rocks at the edge of the ocean, moved by invisible currents. Then, if you plunged your head under the surface, you could trace a line of bubbles escaping from some chasm in the island's side. But these things were expected. The island, after all, was known to be a place of miracles.

The volcano had never erupted; its crater lay somewhere under *il conte*'s villa. But it did shift itself sometimes, sending out shocks and tremors. Nineteen forty-nine was one of those years. The ceiling of the House at the Edge of Night opened with new cracks that January. By March, it was possible to lie on the floor of the bar and hear a sound like groaning coming up from the earth. This Concetta reported with delight, stretched flat as a sea star on the tiles, hissing at everyone to be quiet so she could listen. "An earthquake's coming, Maria-Grazia!" she announced. "An earthquake's coming!"

The child still had a disconcerting appetite for chaos and violence. "Sant'Agata preserve us from any earthquake," Rizzu admonished her. "I'm too old for that." And he attempted to terrify Concetta with fantastical tales of the former earthquakes, when all the houses had been floored except the House at the Edge of Night and old Mazzu's farm and *il conte*'s villa, when great tidal waves off Sicily had assaulted the shores of the island, like the tale of Noah and his sons, and the islanders had fled to higher ground.

Concetta refused to be terrified. "Imagine!" she cried, eyes lit. "Everything gone! My father's stupid shop and all of it gone!"

Maria-Grazia was up on a ladder painting the front of the bar when she felt the first real shudder. A sideways tugging, like a fishing boat going aground. Descending, panic stifling her so that she could not have cried out if she wanted to, she collided with her brother. "Gesù!" said Flavio. "Gesù Dio!" He was barefoot, still in his nightshirt, as he ran across the square. "Flavio!" she called. "Come back!"

The earth subsided; the island once again lay calm. She pursued her brother across the piazza and cornered him in the shade of Gesuina's empty house. He cowered, on his knees. A crowd had gathered. "Flavio," she said. "It's safe. The earthquake has passed over."

Flavio, turned in on himself, shook his head and keened. He rubbed and rubbed at the stumps of his right hand. When she got up close and looked in his eyes, she could see that they were filmed like the elderly Gesuina's had been: Before him was not the sunlit piazza or the House at the Edge of Night but some desert place. It took her a long time to persuade him to take her hand.

As she led him back to the bar, shivering, clutching his flapping nightshirt to him like a girl caught in a high wind, someone let out a jeer. But a spirit of defiance had come over her now since the gossip over Andrea; she hauled Flavio along behind her without lowering her head. "Come on," she said. "It's not everyone who fought as bravely as you, Flavio."

After that day, the gossip about the island was that the Esposito boy had without a doubt come back from the war damaged in the head — but no one would hear anything said about Maria-Grazia.

AS THE TREMORS PERSISTED, the island was afflicted with a religious fervor. It gripped Flavio worst of all. No one noticed until the Sant'Agata bric-a-brac from beside the bar's front door, to which none of them had paid much attention for a quarter of a century, began to go missing. First the holy water, then the rosaries, and at last even the great gruesome statue of the saint with bleeding heart. The statue was spirited away one night in April, leaving behind only a dust-free circle on the hall table to mark its passing. Pina, searching the house, unearthed the relics under a cloth in a corner of Flavio's bedroom, between two blackened candles. At nights Maria-Grazia heard him in his room below hers, mumbling prayers. Soon he began to absent himself from the bar for long periods, and could be found following Father Ignazio about the church, hounding him with earnest questions.

"Oh, I don't mind," said the priest, when Amedeo apologized. "Sant'Agata knows I've always liked your children, Amedeo — though I'm afraid I can't teach Flavio anything very orthodox. I've forgotten most of it myself!" The priest set Flavio to work polishing the great brass crucifix behind the altar, a chore Father Ignazio had never relished. But Flavio applied himself with solemn devotion each morning, bending reverently over the tin of brass polish with the old shirt rag the priest had given him, pausing to look into the face of the metal Cristo on his cross and murmur private appeals.

Every lunchtime, Maria-Grazia would shut up the bar and walk to the church to retrieve Flavio—otherwise, he would have forgotten to eat. During these walks he harangued her without pause on the miracles of the saint, beginning and ending midsentence, as though the words were merely an eruption of his own disordered thoughts: ". . . and that's the thing about Sant'Agata, you see, the mystery, that no one knows who she was, perhaps a poor peasant girl, or a farmer's daughter, and yet she saw visions, true visions . . ." He had joined the Committee of Sant'Agata, sitting primly on Saturday afternoons in the widows' parlors with their dark wood and rose-scented handkerchiefs, discussing the candles to be ordered for the saint's festival, or the new kneeling cushions to be sewn for the Madonna Chapel. Among the boys who had once been his friends, now fishermen and laborers and shopkeepers, Maria-Grazia knew that Flavio was a laughingstock. "Leaving his sister to run the bar while he prays to Sant'Agata," she had heard, "shutting himself up in secret with those old women." Flavio sat alone now at the table under the palm tree—fasting, he drank only a little lemon water, sucking his teeth.

"It's a guilty conscience," someone muttered. "It's the ghost of Pierino haunting him."

For Flavio was still blamed by many for the beating of the fisherman. In those first earthquake-racked days, old Pierino had died. Though in the end he had reached a decent age, he had never recovered his speech, never gone out again in his boat, and several people swore they had seen the old man since his passing, kneeling beside his headstone in the cemetery, trying to dig himself back into the grave.

Now Flavio seemed to be retreating deeper and deeper inside himself, narrowing to a point. But sometimes, on their journeys home from the church, he would take hold absently of Maria-Grazia's forearm as they walked, and she let herself believe that he was getting better. And yet he had begun to be preoccupied with escaping the island. "I'll leave this place," he told her once, clear-eyed. "I'll go back to England. Even if some of them treated me like a dog, they

treated me better there than I'm treated here, among my own people."

And Flavio, it emerged, had seen the ghost of Pierino, too. "He's
green—transparent," he muttered. "He wants me gone. I'll leave this
place. I'll take flight." What he meant by this, he would not say. But
when Pina heard his muttered pronouncements, she wept, believing
that her son meant by it some spirit world, some heaven. "I'll be
bound by these shores no longer," muttered Flavio cryptically, waxing
the statue of Sant'Agata until it shone.

WHEN THE ISLAND SETTLED after that first tremor, a small miracle
came to light.

Il conte's peasants, coaxed and bullied by Bepe, still tended the
rocky southern field they had occupied two years before. Wheat had
come up during the second year, the green blades scorched at the
edges, starved of nutrition. This the peasants harvested, daringly keeping everything for themselves rather than delivering a quarter to *il
conte*. A second crop had come up. Now it was time to thin it. As they
marched up to the fields, no *organetto* now and fewer in number,
glancing at *il conte*'s villa as they rounded the bend in the road, Bepe
exhorted them from his elevated position on the back of his uncle's
donkey, trotting it back and forth along their ranks as though commanding an army. "March forth, comrades," he urged. "The land is
ours."

But the land, when they got to it, had shifted, altered. A great
eruption had occurred at its center, and something was attempting to
surface. The seedlings lay scattered, uprooted, already burned dry in
the sun. Young Agato made the sign of the cross. "A warning!" he
cried.

"No," said Bepe. "A natural phenomenon. We must investigate it
further."

But this phenomenon, whatever it was, was not natural. Digging
in the sandy earth, throwing aside rocks, the peasants brought to light,

by slow degrees, a wall of stone. Not a wall, no (as they dug further): a kind of seat or enclosure. It curved in a semicircle. Its touch was cold. When they went running for mattocks and spades and dug deeper, they unearthed a second ledge, and another beneath it, narrowing toward the bottom of a bowl like the stripes on a shell. "Look here!" cried Agato, digging a short way off. "An altar."

The islanders drew back a little at this hint of heathenism and human sacrifice, but Bepe seized upon the corner Agato had unearthed and scraped bravely with his mattock. "It's not an altar," he announced. "It's a stage. This is a theater, I'm sure of it. Greek, or Roman. I saw them on the mainland postcards when I visited my city cousin, little ones like this and great big ones the size of a football stadium."

Shrewdly, Mazzu said, "This might be worth something."

"*Il conte* doesn't know anything about it," observed Bepe, "and it's our land by rights now."

The peasants stood around the ghost of the amphitheater, holding this knowledge before them like the image of the saint.

BEPE CAME FURTIVELY TO the bar that night, clutching his *organetto*. "I need to speak to *signor il dottore*," he told Maria-Grazia. "Urgent business. Very important."

"Are you here to play?"

"No, no," cried Bepe. "This *organetto* is merely a cover. Fetch your father."

Maria-Grazia summoned her Papà. She heard Bepe muttering at him behind the curtain of the bar: "We must find an archaeologist to come and tell us how much it's worth. This could be a good thing for the island, an important thing, only we need an educated man to explain it to us. It could bring wealth to Castellamare. *Lire* and *lire*."

"And will you be redistributing the wealth fairly?" Her father's voice, a little teasingly. "Or will you be forming a vanguard party to establish a dictatorship of the proletariat first?"

"Both, both," said Bepe, in earnest. "But I need your help. You're an educated man, *signor il dottore*—educated enough, anyway. You must know an archaeologist we can ask. Back in Firenze or Roma, or wherever it is you come from."

But Amedeo knew no archaeologist. Neither did Father Ignazio, whom Bepe cornered on his entry into the bar that night and ushered mysteriously behind the curtain. "I've been on this island as long as you have," said the priest. "I don't know anyone in the outside world any longer. I've become one of you, for my sins."

The one person on the island who knew an archaeologist, to everyone's surprise, was Pina. "But we all know him," she said. "Have you forgotten? Professor Vincio."

"Who?" Bepe was brusque, expecting some joke.

"Oh, you were only a boy then, Bepe—you won't remember. Professor Vincio, the archaeologist from Bologna. He was a prisoner of war here. He repaired the veranda of our bar."

"That *idiota* who put the beams on back to front?" said Bepe. "Signor Pierino had to fix it afterward, I remember."

"Professor Vincio was an important archaeologist. He worked in Cyprus before the war, digging up early cities. He told me once that he dug up a woman and her child, skeletons in gold jewelry, perfectly preserved. An awful, wondrous thing, digging up the past like that. A thing you should respect, young Bepe. Why, anything might come to light. I don't know what's become of him now."

"We'll write to him," counseled the priest. "Care of the University of Bologna. And see if he's still living and whether, God and Sant'Agata willing, he can come and take a look at this ruin you've found. Say nothing about it to *il conte*, Bepe—not until we know more."

The priest wrote a letter that night, and Bepe delivered it to the mainland. The amphitheater was buried again with mattocks and hoes, covered over with tarpaulins. All that month, the islanders held their secret close, going about with a thrill of expectation in their hearts while the island thrummed beneath their feet.

———

NO ONE RECOGNIZED PROFESSOR VINCIO. He arrived at the untidy end of spring, with white hair and a distinguished umbrella and an assistant to carry his bags. The archaeologist chartered Rizzu's donkey cart. But, as they climbed the hill, he bade Rizzu halt outside the walls of the town. Here he climbed down and stood for a long time before the former prison camp, which had returned to its old mess of scrub grass and thistle, haunted by lizards, bearing no trace of the past. At the House at the Edge of Night, he embraced both Pina and Amedeo with tears in his eyes.

Shortly after the archaeologist's arrival, *il conte*, who had somehow got wind of the appearance of an important city man in their midst, interposed himself. Sweeping into the piazza in his motorcar, he greeted the professor with one raised hand as though they were old friends. "Signor Vincio, allow me to extend a welcome," he called, from the car window. "I have a proposition for you." The archaeologist must stay at the villa, he insisted, where things were more comfortable. And he would dine daily at *il conte*'s expense.

Professor Vincio said that he had already been installed quite comfortably at the House at the Edge of Night.

"Very well," bristled *il conte*. "Then come for dinner."

"No," said Professor Vincio. "Thank you. I remember my time on this island well, *signor il conte*."

Il conte, crushed and enraged, drew his head back into the motorcar and drove away.

The following morning, at dawn, the peasants escorted Professor Vincio to the buried amphitheater. The elderly professor got down on his hands and knees and began sweeping up the dust with a fine brush. Occasionally, he paused to cut away a piece of grass or soil, or to point something out to his assistant. The assistant carried a wooden crate like that in which the islanders transported chickens. Out of the crate came strange objects: something like a pasta colander, a set of toothpicks, a scrubbing brush.

Some of the islanders were indignant at this, suspecting ridicule. But Professor Vincio continued his scraping. "Is that all he's going to do?" burst out the boy Agato at last, unable to hold his disappointment. When it became clear that it was, the islanders drifted away.

Meanwhile, *il conte* had heard about the excavations. The next morning, when the little party from the House at the Edge of Night arrived at the site, escorting the archaeologist, *il conte*'s two land agents were waiting for them. Between them stood Andrea d'Isantu. "This land is private property," he said. "No one's to enter or leave it without my father's permission."

"I certainly mean to," said Professor Vincio, in that calm city way he had of speaking as everybody's equal. "We've excavations to do."

Andrea took his walking cane in both hands. His eyes strayed toward Maria-Grazia as he spoke, then returned to the old professor. "No one's to enter this patch of ground."

Bepe, enraged, dropped from his donkey and advanced three paces into *il conte*'s land. "There you are, Signor d'Isantu," he declared. "Someone just has."

Andrea took the stick and tapped him across the shoulder. "Get back, Bepe. I've told you, no one's to enter."

"It's common land now," murmured Father Ignazio. "And in any case, Signor d'Isantu, wouldn't it be better to resolve this cordially, without coming to blows over the matter?"

Andrea advanced on the priest as though the man were one of his father's peasants. "I'll come to blows with anyone who tries to take my father's land!" he cried. "If any *stronzo* of you crosses this fence, I'll come to blows with him, as Sant'Agata is my witness! See if I will!"

Bepe took another subversive step forward. Andrea swung the walking cane, and with its silver-topped handle sent Bepe flailing into the dust.

"Everyone involved in these land occupations is dismissed," Andrea told the assembled peasants. "You're to find other work. You're to be sharecroppers on my father's land no longer, you *stronzi*, you *figli di puttana*, if you won't respect it as you ought to!"

"Where's your father, Andrea?" said the priest, putting a hand on the boy's shoulder. "Isn't this his business? Don't act so rashly— dismissing families who've worked for your family for generations—"

"I won't be ridiculed like this. The amphitheater is ours, the land is ours—"

Andrea swung the walking cane again in white-faced fury. The peasants scattered, breaking up into their separate groups. Bepe's donkey, braying wildly, cut free of the boy Agato and went at a loping canter down the road, his master forgotten. All was disorder. Behind Andrea, *il conte*'s agents had grown watchful, and shouldered their guns. "The land occupations are over," said Andrea. "You're dismissed."

"THE AMPHITHEATER WAS AN inferior example of the type either way," consoled Professor Vincio later, while Amedeo bandaged poor Bepe's bruised head over the counter of the bar. "From what I could see. Roman, small, rather damaged. Still, I'd have liked to get a proper look at it—and I'm sorry that you were struck on my behalf, Bepe. And I'm more sorry than I can say for the loss of the peasants' contracts."

Bepe fumed in outrage. "I'll go to sea again," he vowed. "I'll be a fisherman. I'm done with this island and that *stronzo* of a *conte*." The following day, Bepe rolled up his Communist flag and went to sea in an old boat of Pierino's, which he had repainted and named the *Santa Maria della Luce*. Roaming the squally depths, he was gone for whole weeks at a time. "If I'm not to improve things here," he was fond of repeating, on his brief and bitter returns to the bar, "then I shall go elsewhere."

But the breaking up of the land occupations contained its own strange blessing—for it was what led Professor Vincio, indirectly, to make a much more important discovery.

As a prisoner, Professor Vincio had never heard tell of the caves by the sea. They were only mentioned to him by chance during his fifth day on the island, when the professor sat on the veranda of the bar, sipping Gesuina's best *limettacello* and studying Amedeo's book of stories. Gesuina had left twelve bottles of *limettacello* behind her when she died, which were brought out only for the most important visitors: Ten were still left. Now, as the archaeologist, warmed by its glow, read Amedeo's story of the caves, a thought lit upon him. He leaned forward and touched the doctor lightly on the inside of the arm. "These catacombs?" he asked. "Are they real, or mythical?"

"Real," said Amedeo, a little surprised at the question.

"Yes, yes," said Rizzu, overhearing and interposing himself eagerly between them. "Square caves. With skulls and bones and things in them. All sorts of relics."

At this news, the professor became as excited as a boy. Spilling his *limettacello*, he went running up the stairs for a flashlight, then came blundering back down again with his odd scrubbing brush instead and had to be sent back up; he drove his assistant flailing about for equipment: "Bring the screens, the brushes, both trowels—no, no, just come at once—we'll get all that later!"

Rizzu escorted the professor to the caves in his donkey cart, wondering if the disappointment over the amphitheater had driven the old man insane. "There's not as much to see as maybe you think," he cautioned. "Just a few skulls and bleached bones. Perhaps I exaggerated a little."

But as soon as they reached the caves the professor immersed himself in the dark. Caressing their walls like the curves of a lover, he declared the place to be a necropolis, a city of the dead. "A rare thing," he said. "An important site. A place where people in ancient times buried their dead. There are very few others so well preserved. Signor Rizzu, this is much more exciting than an old Roman amphitheater! This is a site of worldwide importance. It may be thousands of years old."

"A city of the dead," said Rizzu, in wonder. "That explains the curse of weeping." The islanders reeled with pride at the professor's judgment of Castellamare as a site of worldwide importance—always suspected, now confirmed by a clever city man!

The following week, a whole team of archaeologists arrived from Bologna and set up an excavation site with tents, fences, stakes, and bits of string. The earth tremors had dislodged the skulls from their places and opened up a passage in the second cave. Now, digging out the soil from this passage with what still looked to the islanders like shaving brushes and toothpicks, the archaeologists discovered a system of burial holes, a cache of pots, two gold coins. Rizzu had put it about that the foreign archaeologists were going to solve the mystery of the curse of weeping once and for all, and the islanders were disposed to be helpful. Old Mazzu appeared at the caves on the third day, offering a set of hoes and spades. "You'll be wanting these," he said. "It's a damned shame you can't afford any equipment, so we've agreed to make you a present of them."

The archaeologist accepted this gift with a bobbing little bow, but when old Mazzu passed by the caves the following day, he found to his disappointment that they were still scraping away with those scrubbing brushes. The following month, a team of German archaeologists arrived to join them. From dawn until nightfall, the foreigners could be heard chipping at the rock, scraping in the dirt, exclaiming in their northern languages as treasures were brought to light.

MEANWHILE, SINCE THE BAR and the island were destined to be her lot in life, Maria-Grazia hauled herself from the cave of her self-pity and decided she might as well make the best of them.

Bepe had abandoned communism. But now he had another scheme in mind. Marching into the bar one night, absently flinging upon the counter a small, rather bloody tuna, he announced his intention to start a ferry service. "*Il conte* makes sure no one on the island does business with anyone except their neighbors," said Bepe. "I've been puzzling it all out. He ensures that we make no money, while all the money he earns goes off the island, to be spent in the restaurants of Palermo, in Paris, in Roma. We haven't even got a proper ferry. I'd like my children to go to high school on the mainland. And why shouldn't the ferry bring people to the island as well as carry them off it? I'd like tourists to come here and buy Vincenzo the artist's pictures and drink coffee in your bar and look at our sights, just as they would in Athens or Valletta or Palermo. Now that we've got a proper archaeological excavation."

At this, Agata-the-fisherwoman snorted her coffee all over the table.

"What?" cried Bepe, enraged. "Haven't we got a church, and a saint, and a set of ruins, just like the best of them? Things to stare at! Things to buy! That's what they like best, the tourists—I've seen them in Siracusa! Greek ruins! Postcards! Little plaster models of the Colosseo! We've a city of the dead, haven't we? Isn't that just as good? Already half of you are making money out of this discovery, boarding the archaeologists in your houses. There's more to be made! If we're not to be communists, we must be modern people instead, and beat *il conte* that way!"

"I agree with you, Bepe," said the priest, unexpectedly, from the corner. "I think you're right. Visitors must come and look at the caves by the sea, and witness the Sant'Agata festival. Our children must go to high school on the mainland. We must get the resources to take people to the hospital when they are sick—you know that's been a long obsession of mine. *Il conte* and his family have shown their hand over the occupations. If we want to modernize, we must do it on our own."

"We could have a committee," said Maria-Grazia, surprised to find herself weighing in on this debate when a moment before she had only been polishing the coffee machine. "Like the Committee of Sant'Agata, only for making improvements to the island."

"That's a good thought," said Bepe, seizing upon her idea. "That's good, that thought of Mariuzza's—a committee. We'll have that."

"You mean to drag me into more cooperation," muttered Mazzu, but when Maria-Grazia passed a page of the accounts book around the bar that afternoon, to make a list of prospective members, even he signed.

On the fifth of July, a week after the Sant'Agata festival, the first meeting of the Committee for the Modernization of Castellamare took place. In attendance were Amedeo, Pina, Maria-Grazia, Father Ignazio, the artist Vincenzo, the two farmers Mazzu and Rizzu, and half the dismissed peasants of *il conte*. And Agata-the-fisherwoman, for since her brother's return she was a fisherwoman no longer, and felt herself somewhat relegated. Agata, who had not married, remained alone in her little house submerged in trumpet vine, with only the dog Chiappi; she had serenely resisted her mother and brother's attempts to dislodge her. "A husband would be the death of me," she was fond of saying, though it was well known that Bepe had been trying to win her since the end of the war.

At the meeting, it was agreed that tourist tours would be advertised, and a ferry service established with twice-daily crossings. The money that was made would pay for improvements to the houses damaged in the earth tremors, and, if things went well, new nets for the fishermen's cooperative and an extension to the school.

"Look here," spoke up Amedeo, when the discussions were almost concluded. "We're to be careful how we approach this. Haven't we always swapped and bartered, helped our neighbors out in times of trouble? I remember how you rallied around me with baked aubergines and *pasta al forno*, when Mariuzza was so sick as a child. I didn't appreciate it then, maybe, but this island mustn't change its ways because there's money to be had. You must be the same Castellamare people I've always known."

Maybe so, said Bepe, but money was money and it was time Castellamare became a modern place.

The following Saturday, Bepe and Agata rowed to the mainland with a newly painted sign advertising historical tours of the "Ancient Necropolis of Castellamare." For a hundred *lire*, or a dollar bill, tourists would be ferried over to the island and borne in Rizzu's donkey cart to the caves by the sea to watch the archaeologists at work. "Historic bars!" their sign proclaimed, putting everything on the island ambitiously in the plural. "Old churches! The shrines of Sant'Agata!

Donkey rides! Ice cream!" (The ice cream had not arrived yet, but it was hoped that the new influx of tourists would allow the House at the Edge of Night to install its first ice cream machine by the end of the year.)

Visitors came. Not an influx, but a few, lured by the rustic sign, by the romantic aspect of the island across the water, by the fantastical colors of the ferryboat *Santa Maria della Luce*. Finding, after their long and rattling ascent in the donkey cart, that at the heart of the island was a bar in which they were offered tea and pastries, where the BBC blared from an old wireless, the tourists felt themselves to be both adventurous and safely within reach of the civilized world, a gratifying combination. Besides, half of the visitors were scholars, attracted by Professor Vincio's preliminary research on the recently discovered Cave Necropolis of Castellamare, which had just been published in the *American Journal of Archaeology*.

One of these first visitors was the former prisoner, the poet Mario Vazzo. A man now gilded with a little fame, hung about with literary honors, he nevertheless arrived alone, climbing the hill to the House at the Edge of Night on foot. From her customary seat at the edge of the veranda, Pina rose to meet him. The two of them recognized each other at once. Mario climbed the steps and took both Pina's hands in his own. They remained like that for a long time.

Mario Vazzo had lost his wife at the end of the war, he told them, but his son had survived. A university student now, his son read law in Torino. Mario's chest puffed with pride at any mention of the boy. Mario had also brought with him a paper parcel, which he put into Pina's hands. "My newest book," he said. "You'll see that I found at last the words to write about the war. I've been meaning to come back and bring it to you in person, and been putting it off, and then I saw the newspaper article about the excavations, and it seemed too much like a sign to ignore. This island, on the world map at last."

The book was named, simply, *Odissea*. "Is it a verse epic?" asked Rizzu, no longer mocking now that he saw the thing in printed form and the price on its cover, one thousand *lire*.

"It is," said Mario Vazzo, with a little acknowledging bow of the head. "It's a modern version of the *Odyssey*."

"That sounds interesting enough," conceded Rizzu. "As long as there's a sea battle or two, and you've kept those parts about the naked ladies on the rocks." For everyone on the island knew the story of the *Odyssey* as well as they knew their own island tales. Pina herself had read it to the children in the schoolroom on hot afternoons, opening the windows first to make a sort of backdrop of the noise of the sea.

Later, when she and the poet were alone on the veranda, Pina drew the book from its wrappings. According to the book's cover, Mario Vazzo had been shortlisted for two important prizes: the Bagutta and the Strega, neither of which Pina, to her shame, had heard of. *Odissea* had sold tens of thousands of copies, a *"fenomeno nazionale,"* wrote the professor from Rome whose remarks were printed on its front cover. "That story used to preoccupy me while I was here," said Mario Vazzo. "And when I left, it haunted me. So I retold it. With Fascist guards for the Cyclops and prisoners for Greeks, trying to get home."

Pina sat on the veranda and read it slowly, making it last like a glass of *arancello*, while the poet lay beside her drowsing in the sun. Pina approached the reading of the book with great seriousness, pausing to mark passages in pencil as she had as a schoolmistress when she pored over Dante and Pirandello. She finished the book moved beyond speech, with tears in her voice. "A work of genius," she declared.

Amedeo read the book, too, guiltily leaping through the pages the next day while Pina took their guest to inspect the excavations at the necropolis. The thing was good, Amedeo admitted grudgingly to himself; perhaps it was even a work of genius, as Pina said. He recognized incidents, transformed from the sordid, shameful shape they had taken during the war into struggles of a mythic quality, like those belonging to the island tales he loved. The beating of Pierino became an epic battle, the arrival of the *americani* a godlike deliverance. All very clever.

One section, though, troubled Amedeo. It described how the prisoner Odisseo, who Amedeo assumed to stand for Mario Vazzo himself, fell in love with an island woman. On a night of "black water and
many stars," these two characters made love in the caves by the sea,
"rolling among the skulls, within the walls of the city of the dead."
Mustn't that mean Castellamare's caves? Amedeo felt the description
to be vivid, almost indecent, stamped with the lurid mark of truth. It
brought back to him, with a hot shame he had not felt in twenty years,
his own assignations with Carmela. Here were the facts of the place:
bones digging into the spine, sand in the hair, cold water seeping
beneath the entangled limbs so that they became puckered with
gooseflesh. And which island woman had Mario Vazzo known or
cared about but Pina? Pina who had employed him, defended him,
gathered his fragments of verse and kept them in the drawer of her
nightstand, tied up with string? Amedeo had seen the yellowed paper
napkins there himself not six months ago, surprised to discover them
preserved so carefully. Pina had never spoken of Mario Vazzo after he
left the island, but the napkins had troubled Amedeo then; their
memory provoked him again now.

So, too, did the way his wife had greeted the prisoner, silent with
emotion. Now doubt began to work at him, too absurd to articulate
but not yet ridiculous enough to dismiss altogether. He would find
himself staring at the poet over the beans and *sarde* of the dinner
table, or across the crowd in the bar, his soul run ragged by the very
possibility of the poet and Pina engaging in such shameful acts in the
caves by the sea. Had there been some affair between them? Strange
if, after his years of guilt over Carmela, his wife had carried out a betrayal of her own. Peculiar rumors were about now, that the two of
them had been observed together on the cliff top above the caves by
the sea—and it was true that Pina had taken to returning at odd times
from long walks across the island, with disarrayed, windblown hair.
Amedeo had heard his wife speaking with Maria-Grazia in the room
at the top of the house after dark, her voice going up and down like a

motorboat as it had during the war, pouring out some secret or some story, too far away for him to hear. He could make out none of it, no matter how he pressed his ear against the door.

Many of the islanders were exhilarated at this turn of events, calling it a kind of poetic justice.

Not knowing what to say, Amedeo said nothing.

Still, he was glad when the poet departed. He took *Odissea* and hid it away in the Campari liquor box at the top of the house, pretending to his wife not to know where it had gone. Unperturbed, and without displaying any outward sign of guilt, Pina merely crossed to the mainland on Bepe's ferryboat and bought another copy from the bookshop in Siracusa.

AT THE END OF THE SUMMER, a meeting was called in the town hall to present the findings of the archaeological team. The hall was as crowded as the church during the Sant'Agata Mass, for everyone wanted to hear what was to be said about the curse of weeping. Though no one had heard the weeping in their lifetime, all knew of someone—an aunt's aunt or a cousin's cousin—who had heard it, who had solemnly sworn to the truth of its existence, who had suffered madness or disturbed sleep because of it. Perhaps these foreigners could illuminate the mystery.

Amedeo sat with his red notebook open before him, ready to record the story. Rizzu occupied, eagerly, the first seat of the front row. The meeting had to be delayed by an hour because more people kept arriving: the fishermen in their tweed trousers and oily white vests, the shopkeepers in white aprons, the peasants, with faces set like death masks from the dust of the fields. Bepe had suspended his ferry service especially to attend, but was still twenty-five minutes late. Agata-the-fisherwoman followed him, still in her greasy slacks and man's *borsalino*. Still more people kept coming. The girl Concetta, who had got away from her father and mother, ran, straggle haired, along the rows of benches to squeeze herself in beside Maria-Grazia.

Two widows of the Sant'Agata Committee, who had claimed to be scandalized by the excavations and all this talk of the curse of weeping, attempted nevertheless to slip in unobserved. The members of the town council arrived together, self-important, led by Arcangelo. Still the islanders kept coming, until there were no more benches left and some shuffling had to take place, some ejecting of the young to make space for the old, some jostling for position.

This disregard for time and appointment troubled the northerners. Eventually, the doors were shut and a woman archaeologist stood up to speak, sweating, a German with a frizz of gray hair and bare freckled arms. She spoke; Professor Vincio translated.

"The caves by the sea," the islanders were told, "are catacombs, a necropolis of over a hundred tombs. The smallest were for families, with between two and seven bodies in each. The three larger ones were originally . . . how shall I put it? . . . rock-cut dwellings, we believe, later also used to house human remains. The earliest date from prehistoric times, the larger ones to the time of the Byzantine Empire. There are also a small number of natural caves, but the majority of the site is a man-made necropolis. And it's a great discovery, an important discovery," Professor Vincio added, "just as I first suspected. Apart from the site at Pantalica, this is the only example of such a necropolis that we know of in the Mediterranean. We've found several objects that will be displayed in important museums in Milano and Roma, which we hope will attract other scholars—and visitors to your island, too, of course."

Here the German archaeologist gave a gracious little nod. Her assistant, gloved, came forward and held up first a rusted knife, then a pin so oxidized it was like some barnacled thing from the bottom of the sea, and a few fragments of glass. The islanders beheld them as though they were the relics of the saint. At last, Bepe said, "How many visitors will come?" and at the same time Rizzu spoke: "But what about the curse of weeping?"

"To answer the first question," said Professor Vincio, "we can't yet say how important the site is. But once we present our second, more detailed, paper at a conference in Heidelberg in November, I expect at least a year of further excavation, with a larger team."

Another voice echoed Rizzu's, more strident—Agata-the-fisherwoman: "What about the curse of weeping?"

The professor glanced at the German archaeologist, but with a little nod of her gray frizz she deferred back to him. The professor got to his feet and wetted his lips with a methodical circle of the tongue. "We believe we've satisfactorily solved that mystery," he said. "The rock out of which the caves are formed is permeable, porous." The faces turned up to him remained respectfully blank. In his formal Italian, the professor groped for words that would make sense to these islanders, for he spoke no dialect except his own Bolognese. "Water runs through it," he continued. "Air passes through. When I first entered the caves, I felt a draft. That's an odd thing, a draft underground."

Now, at last, a collective murmur of recognition. Yes, everyone who had entered the caves had felt the strange draft, and that word was the same in their language.

"Being so close to the sea, the rock in that region of the island was already eroded before the tombs were built," said Professor Vincio. "Worn away. Which is the reason for the natural part of the necropolis. The Byzantine islanders must have excavated the man-made chambers. But the rock has worn away further in the many centuries since, so that now there are tunnels and fissures connecting the burial chambers. Countless tiny openings. You'll notice by the fact that even if you go deep into the caves, you can feel drafts, breathe fresh air. Isn't that right?"

Here, some nodded. But the islanders had always assumed this phenomenon was part of the caves' natural air of miracle. "When the wind blows at a certain angle," continued the professor, "a curious phenomenon occurs. The wind is funneled through these narrow chambers and it causes an odd howling sound. We've heard it, too, on several occasions. Possibly the phenomenon was already known to the prehistoric islanders, and that was the reason they chose the site for their burials. A fitting place for mourning."

"But what about the houses?" said someone else. "All the rock of the island makes that weeping sound, when you dig it up and build with it. Everyone knows that."

But here, doubt interposed itself. A couple of the islanders expressed murmurs of dissent. "I don't know," spoke up Mazzu. "We extended the farm in '38, and I don't remember any sound of weeping then from any of the rock we used."

"What about *signor il dottore*'s house?" spoke up Agata-the-fisherwoman. "That house carried on the weeping long after everyone else's. Who's heard it? There must be someone here?"

But no one spoke up. Some had been told of the sound of weeping emanating from the House at the Edge of Night in times of trouble, others thought they had faintly heard it, on stormy nights leaving the old bar when it had belonged to Rizzu's brother, but no one could solemnly attest to having heard the weeping stones.

"There's one other unusual fact about the caves," said Professor Vincio. "We believe that the islanders buried there died not one by one over the years but all at once, within a matter of months or years, not centuries. The burials seem to be oddly uniform, and the bodies were all put in at once—at least, there's no sign of any reopening of the chambers to admit more bodies as one would expect in such a necropolis. The one at Pantalica, say. In the larger caves, from the position of the bodies that haven't been disturbed, we can see that they've been put in quickly all at once, suggesting some crisis on the island, probably a plague. Perhaps some tragedy took place here. It's natural that the islanders would start to believe after that that their island was a sad place, a melancholy place, even cursed. That's probably the origin of the tale."

The islanders looked helplessly to *il dottore*, that great gatherer of folktales, but found him nodding in agreement with everything the professor had said.

In the days after the report of the archaeologists' findings, bitter disagreement seethed on Castellamare. To those who had always believed in the curse of weeping, the archaeologists' flat, unmythical explanation was a personal offense. "There's more to it than they say," Rizzu insisted. "There's more to it. I can't deny I'm disappointed. Catacombs. Chambers. What kind of talk is that? The curse of weeping isn't just some trick of the wind. It isn't just a matter of air funneled through holes, like a great big fart!"

"What difference does it make?" said Concetta from behind the counter of the bar, spooning hot chocolate into cups beside Maria-Grazia. "I've never been frightened of those silly caves, and if they can bring visitors here to stare at old bits of glass and rusty pins and pay us for it, then I for one am glad there's no curse of weeping anymore." For already the bar was making good money from the feeding of archaeologists and the entertaining of visitors—enough to make the down payment on an ice cream machine very soon. And, secretly, Maria-Grazia still saved a few *lire* a week in the empty bottle behind her bed.

Bepe inclined to the same view as Concetta. "I'm glad, too," he said. "A curse of weeping's no good for tourism, is it? It's just as well there's none anymore."

"There *is* a curse of weeping," said Rizzu ferociously. "There *is* a curse of weeping. Just because they say there isn't, doesn't mean anything—those foreigners with their big Italian words and their toothpicks and scrubbing brushes!"

"It's still a beautiful story," said Amedeo, "whether or not it's strictly speaking true." Which made Rizzu huff crossly and spill his coffee.

Indeed, though Signor Rizzu, already past ninety, was to live in perfect health for another four or five years, he never overcame his disappointment. He remained personally offended to the very last by the solving of the mystery of the caves.

V

THAT SUMMER OF THE ARCHAEOLOGISTS, FLAVIO BECAME MORE haunted, more ghost-riven, more determined than ever to leave. "I'll be bound by these shores no longer," he muttered as he went about his daily work, and Pina wept to hear him speak so, for all the world sounding as though he had resolved to die. Now Maria-Grazia found herself fierce with indignation at the injustices that had been done to her brother.

On the morning after the meeting in the town hall, he had come home wild-eyed and shuddering, with prickly pear buds stuck all over him like the statue of a martyr. He would not say who had flung them, or who it was who gave him a black eye the following day, or ripped the seat of his trousers open with a fishhook on the road up from the sea the day after. But Maria-Grazia, bathing his face, soothing his wounded skin with calamine lotion, became as fierce as her mother, Pina. "Someone's trying to drive him from this island," she said. "Someone's trying to drive him mad. I mean to find out who."

For the ghost of Pierino had been seen again since the festival, digging in the earth with its green translucent hands.

The day after the meeting in the town hall, the bar remained closed. When Flavio woke up, at a quarter to five in the afternoon, Maria-Grazia summoned him to the kitchen. Dismissing the others — for her mother was too apt to weep when it came to matters of Flavio's sickness, her father to shuffle and mumble — she sat her brother before her at the great table and commanded him to tell her the truth about the beating of Pierino.

Flavio sat with both elbows on the table, his head suspended between his hands, and a great shadow came over him. Undeterred, Maria-Grazia shook the *melanzane* in their colander, making them sweat, and waited for his story to emerge in its own time. The evening breathed its coolness in at the window. On the Terazzus' farm, the German shepherd barked once, twice, three times. "I never did anything," said Flavio at last. "Mamma and Papà think I'm mad. I'm not. I've seen him, too, the green ghost. I saw him down at the caves by the sea, walking with lobsters in a trap, covered in green motorboat oil. Even he thinks I did it. But I never did anything."

"Tell me, *caro*," said Maria-Grazia.

Flavio brooded for several minutes, gazing into the depths of the tiles between his feet. Then he said, "I was sent home early from the *Balilla* meeting that night. You remember. I had that cough."

"Yes, I remember."

"We were supposed to go on a special night exercise. We weren't to tell anybody about it. Then Professor Calleja said I wasn't to take part in the night exercise after all. So I left, in a bad mood because I wasn't to be included. I came home the long way, by the prickly pears. You know the goat path, through the scrub grass—"

"*Sì, sì.*"

"That's all I have to tell you. Professor Calleja dismissed me at half past nine; I came home; I met no one. Next thing, they were accusing me of beating Pierino, saying I'd been dismissed at nine o'clock and had the time to go and get a horsewhip and follow Pierino home and beat him. All of which was lies."

Maria-Grazia abandoned the aubergines. Rubbing the salt from her hands, she gripped Flavio by both shoulders. "So tell the truth," she said. "Tell the island. You had no part in it—you must tell everyone so."

"Who would believe me, in a town as full as this one of spies and gossips? No, there's no point telling. They've all made up their minds about me."

Flavio gave a great gravelly cough, which brought something up from deep in his chest that he spat, precisely, out the kitchen window.

Maria-Grazia decided to pay a visit to Arcangelo.

The grocer's was a little cavern off the main street, cool and wood smelling, whose varnished shelves and counters had not been altered since the nineteenth century. Maria-Grazia stood before the bulk of Signor Arcangelo and moved her eyes over the boxed pasta and tinned vegetables and mainland wine in bottles, the tins of anchovies and the great legs of dusty *prosciutto* that hung like clubs about his head, the cheeses that sweated upon the counter, each enthroned upon its square of greased paper. At last, summoning her courage, she said, "Signor Arcangelo, what do you know about the beating of Pierino?"

Then the grocer, incoherent with rage, rose up like a sea monster from behind the counter and drove her from his shop. "I've nothing to say about it to you Espositos!" he roared, as she fled down the street. "You're lucky I don't take off my belt and beat you, *puttana troia!*"

With Professor Calleja she had no more luck, for as soon as she approached the old schoolmaster, where he sat on a wooden chair before his house, he retreated into the dark and banged all his shutters closed.

Meanwhile, the customers in the bar had heard what she was up to, and were indignant. "What does the girl mean, dragging up that Fascist past?" asked the elderly *scopa* players. "Pierino's dead, and these things had better be left to rest," coaxed the fishermen who had once been his comrades. And some of the customers were so incensed at what the widow Valeria called "that Esposito girl's poking and prying" that they staged a temporary boycott of the place. Only the ferryman Bepe seemed to agree with her. "Someone's got to bring it to light," he muttered over the counter. "If you don't manage it, Signorina Maria-Grazia, I'll do it myself. He was my friend, and someone killed him, and it's time the truth came out and the guilty were punished. Why else is his ghost hanging about? I agree with you."

———

THE FIRST PERSON TO break silence was the girl Santa Maria, Pierino's youngest daughter. Now twenty-eight and a widow, she beckoned Maria-Grazia from behind her apron, terrified, one Sunday morning after Mass. "I hear you've been going around asking about what happened to my Papà," she murmured, drawing Maria-Grazia up the steps of her house, shepherding her between the pots of overgrown basil. "I've something to tell you—a little at least. Perhaps it'll help—who knows?"

In the parlor, much faded, where the widows had once prayed for Maria-Grazia's soul, the old fisherman's chair still stood in a corner, the velvet worn bare in the heart shape of his behind—for he had never left it, besides when he slept, except on the particular Tuesday morning on which he had decided at last to die. Santa Maria sent her mother Agata-the-baker's-daughter downstairs for a stale *cassata* cake, which the old woman served to Maria-Grazia with solemnity. The house was empty now. The misfortune of Pierino had driven his elder children away in the years after the war, to America and to England, Switzerland, and Germany, until Santa Maria was the only one who remained—and now her husband was gone, too, lost at sea, leaving the family childless altogether. The house no longer billowed with the washed linen of the fisherman's great family, and the widows of the Sant'Agata Committee, finding Agata's parlor too gloomy even for their somber tastes, had taken their meetings elsewhere. Pina visited occasionally, with gifts from the bar, for Pierino had been a relative. Otherwise, the cool of the parlor was undisturbed.

"Signorina Esposito, I remember that night of my Papà's injury very well," said Santa Maria.

At this direct mention of her poor husband's beating, Agata-the-baker's-daughter was overcome, and buried her face in her skirt. "Go downstairs, Mamma," said Santa Maria. "I've important things to discuss with Signorina Esposito."

The old woman obeyed. Santa Maria leaned forward and said in a whisper, "I don't believe it was your brother at all."

Relief made Maria-Grazia giddy. "Then you don't—you don't think Flavio is guilty—"

"I'm sure he isn't."

Maria-Grazia attempted to swallow the *cassata*, but found it cleaved to the dry roof of her mouth. "Go on," she said. "Tell me what you know."

"We were in the kitchen that night," said Santa Maria, "my mother and I—we were plucking a chicken, salting the *melanzane* for the next day while we waited for Papà to come home. Also my eldest brother Marco, who'd been out fishing with him. Marco said Papà would be home late. They'd taken a big tuna—Papà was down at the *tonnara*, celebrating, as he always used to. Though he was no drunkard," she added. "God rest his soul."

Again, Maria-Grazia tried to swallow but found herself choked.

"Anyway," continued Santa Maria, "we heard an odd scrabbling at the door. It was late—nine or ten—and my mother thought the noise was stray dogs making trouble. She went upstairs to fetch the carpet beater. She was always afraid they'd bring the rabies after my Zio Nunziato on the mainland got bit and died in '09. But it wasn't stray dogs—it was poor Papà, struggling to get up, scrabbling about the walls. We opened the door and in he fell. They'd beaten his chest with something. I don't know—a stick, a belt. And we heard them fleeing—big footsteps, at least one of them a grown man."

"And that's all you remember?"

Santa Maria nodded, and allowed the force of memory to overcome her at last. "Poor Papà," she wept. "Poor Papà. He never spoke; he never went out in his boat again, after that day."

Maria-Grazia forced down her *cassata* in great chunks, stifled by the melancholy of the room. As soon as she could, she made her retreat.

When she got home, the bar was astir with excitement. The ghost of Pierino had been seen again, wandering the cliffs of the sea. Arcangelo had shut his shop in a fit of rage and was threatening to take the Esposito family to court for slander, and all was disorder and fighting. "Be careful," Amedeo advised his daughter. "You've your mother's determination, and it didn't always go well for her, Mariuzza."

But a fierce hunger for the truth had possessed Maria-Grazia, and she couldn't have stopped even if she wanted to.

BEFORE DAWN THE NEXT MORNING, Andrea d'Isantu came uninvited once more to the House at the Edge of Night.

He drove up to the bar in his father's motorcar, so that Maria-Grazia found him already waiting outside when she came to open the door at half past seven. There he stood, like an apparition, in his faded English suit. "*Salve*, Signor d'Isantu," she said.

Without rising from the car, Andrea d'Isantu said, "I've kept away, haven't I?"

"Sì, Signor d'Isantu."

"While you considered—while you made your decision. Six months you said. It's been eight."

"Sì, Signor d'Isantu."

"When am I to get my answer? I can't sleep, Maria-Grazia— I can't eat."

In the fierce thirst for justice that was now possessing her, how could she think of such a thing? How could she think of marrying anybody? "When the truth about the beating of Pierino has come to light," she said, "that's when I'll think about marriage. Not before."

Andrea, she saw when she looked at him properly, was stringier, worn thinner, like a man of forty-five. It plucked at her heart a little to see him like that, but not enough to break her resolution. "When the truth about Pierino has come to light," she said, a little guilty that the months had elapsed so quickly, without her noticing.

But Andrea seemed satisfied. With a small nod he swung the car around, away from her, and left the square.

THAT NIGHT, SHORTLY AFTER half past seven, *il conte*'s son confessed to the murder of Pierino.

The elderly *scopa* players arrived early at the bar, in a lather of excitement, for the widows of the Committee of Sant'Agata had told them everything. That afternoon, *il conte*'s motorcar had drawn up before the church, with Andrea d'Isantu alone at the wheel. By all accounts an inveterate heathen, he had nevertheless taken off his hat, entered the church, seated himself in the confessional, and summoned Father Ignazio to attend him. The members of the Committee of Sant'Agata, at the time, had been engaged in the polishing of the saint's statue and the replenishing of the offertory candles. Thus they had heard, quite distinctly, Andrea's mutter as Father Ignazio seated himself behind the little purple curtain: "I confess to Almighty God and to you, *padre*, that I have sinned. It's been fourteen years since my last confession. Since then, I have committed one mortal sin and several venial. But it's the mortal sin I want to talk to you about."

The widows of the Committee of Sant'Agata, only a little ashamed of themselves, stopped polishing and wholeheartedly listened. By the time the bell chimed for the noon angelus, everyone on the island knew that it was Andrea d'Isantu who had beaten the fisherman.

The gossip in the bar that evening threatened to cause a civil war. "I won't believe it!" cried the widow Valeria. "He's trying to cover for his friend, that's all—he and Flavio Esposito, who have been so thick together since the war."

"Nonsense!" cried Bepe. "Why can't you believe it was d'Isantu? Look at how the *fascisti* on this island treated him as a boy—as though he were a hero! Destined for an important career overseas. They knew, believe me. Everything makes sense to me now."

"And I suppose," said Valeria, "that Flavio Esposito really is innocent?"

"I knew," breathed Agata-the-fisherwoman. "I knew it was never young Flavio."

Maria-Grazia, meanwhile, was furious at what Andrea had done.

Confiding in the girl Concetta—for there was no one else—she raged in the storeroom of the bar: "Andrea's only done this to force an answer out of me—and if he thinks I'll marry him now he's utterly mistaken, the *stronzo*, the fool!"

"Quite so," said Concetta, unperturbed by this display of fury, sucking an *arancino*. "You're waiting to marry Signor Robert anyway. *Signor il figlio del conte* hasn't a hope."

But either way, the deed was done, and as day became evening the inhabitants of Castellamare became convinced of Andrea d'Isantu's guilt.

Then, in indignation, Bepe and the fishermen, the widows of Sant'Agata, and all the other arbiters of justice in the town stormed the gates of *il conte*'s villa and demanded that the murderer show himself.

But Andrea d'Isantu had nothing more to say. His father would accept no visitors to the villa at the end of the avenue of palms, and refused to answer their knocking. The islanders, enraged, demanded that Andrea d'Isantu be brought to trial instead—that he kneel before the grave of the fisherman and beg mercy of his green ghost—that he leave the island like Odisseo, never to return. Their demands became more and more outlandish as the night wore on. Perhaps he should be made to go about the island on his knees, following the statue of the saint, suggested the Committee of Sant'Agata. Perhaps, growled Bepe, he should be shot. "Now, now," counseled Father Ignazio, who had never been good at moralizing but attempted a little now, "all this is getting out of hand. We must leave this war behind and come out into the light, practice a little charity."

But Andrea d'Isantu, the islanders had decreed, must, at the very least, leave the place.

LATE THE FOLLOWING NIGHT, Maria-Grazia was woken by the thud of wet sand on her window. Opening it, she looked down into the moonlit piazza and beheld Andrea again, leaning on his stick, his face raised like a moon in the dark. In one hand he held his walking cane, in the other the cardboard suitcase with which he had returned from war. "Where are you going?" she whispered.

"To the mainland. A friend of my father's is taking me. Come down, Maria-Grazia. You promised me an answer. I won't see you again, after tonight."

Maria-Grazia, indignation and regret troubling her in equal measure, threw on a shawl and went down to him.

The bougainvillea made great cloud shadows in the moonlight. Beneath its shelter, Andrea d'Isantu brooded, kneading the pommel of his walking cane. "You owe me an answer," he said at last. "You promised me one."

"No," said Maria-Grazia. "I don't owe you an answer, for I don't believe this is truth at all, what's come to light. It's some game you're playing, covering up for Flavio in the hope it'll make me love you. Well, it won't. I don't believe you did it."

Then, in the shade of the terrace, Andrea d'Isantu told her the true story of what had happened on the night of the beating of Pierino.

THERE HAD BEEN THREE BOYS that night at the *Balilla* meeting: Flavio Esposito, Filippo Arcangelo, and Andrea d'Isantu. Also the two *Ballilla* leaders: Dottor Vitale with his great bass drum, and the schoolteacher Calleja. In the dusty schoolroom, underneath the portrait of *il duce* that Professor Calleja had snipped out of the newspaper after his March on Rome, they rehearsed their marching songs. There was some disagreement: Flavio Esposito was racked with coughing, producing only ridiculous honks from his brass trumpet, spoiling the dignity of the thing. At twenty minutes to ten, Professor Calleja lost his temper and dismissed the boy.

("And that was the last Flavio had to do with it?" asked Maria-Grazia.

"That," said Andrea d'Isantu, "was the very last.")

Now that the Esposito boy had been dealt with (for his father was known to be a northern Bolshevik and could not be trusted), the drums and trumpets were abandoned. Professor Calleja put on his black shirt. They were going out on their special night exercise, he told the others. A local communist needed to be taught a lesson. They were to make their way to the Mazzus' olive grove, and lie in wait there for the communist to come up from the sea.

The two boys sniggered, knowing who was meant, and picturing the ignominious dosing with castor oil.

"One of us," said Professor Calleja, eyeing each one of them in turn, "needs to make damn sure that he's taught a lesson. That's what *il conte* and Signor Arcangelo, your Papàs, told me."

Professor Calleja brought out his shotgun from among the chalk and lead pencils in the school cupboard. He gave each boy a flashlight. "You're to go one at a time," he said. "Reconvene in the olive grove in thirty minutes."

As soon as Andrea was dismissed he ran, flashlight bobbing over the stones, toward his father's house. He had no plan except to arm himself, in his excitement, like Professor Calleja with the marvelous shotgun. But the outbuildings were dark, the bailiffs' guns locked away for the night. The lone donkey, the watchman Rizzu's, stamped and brayed eerily in the farthest stall. Andrea, hauling away great garlands of cobwebs from the wall of the stables, came upon antique mattocks, a rust-barnacled pitchfork, and, at last, an ancient horsewhip. Seizing this, he extinguished his flashlight and ran for the Mazzus' olive grove.

The olive grove at night was a place of oceanic shadows. Andrea took up position behind the great abandoned stone of an olive press that had stood at the entrance to the grove for three hundred years. Farther off, he made out the moonlike face of Filippo, sequestered in a thicket of hazelnut branches, and the black shape of Professor Calleja, his shotgun a ruler-drawn line pointing upward in the dark. Dottor Vitale, comically wedged up an olive tree, attempted a boy-scout owl call and made both boys convulse with silent laughter. In the dark, they waited. Then, on the road above them, they heard the unmistakable burr of *il conte*'s motorcar.

Through the scrub, someone was moving. He was drunk: Andrea could tell by the rolling of his walk, the grunting of his breath as he came closer. "Papà?" Andrea murmured, thinking his father must be coming down from the car to join them, a little intoxicated as he often was on such summer nights. The figure released a deep sigh, and Andrea watched it, all dark legs and arms, unbutton itself and aim a stream of piss into the depths of the hazelnut thicket. Not his father after all. Papà must be farther off. Only Andrea was within striking distance of the man.

Andrea raised his head from behind the stone and, with tiny steps, approached the figure through the hot dark. In that moment, he did not intend to strike, only to get a closer look. Sure enough, it was the fisherman Pierino, swaying a little, leaning on his tuna gaff. Andrea thrilled with terror and elation.

But now Pierino seemed to prickle. He turned his great hangdog eyes this way and that. "Who's there?" he said.

Andrea was caught in the fury of his glance. The wily Pierino spun, raising his tuna gaff. "Is it you *fascisti* again?" he roared in drunken bravado. "I'll fight you all—I'll spear you with this tuna gaff!" He made one lunging grab in Andrea's direction, and Andrea stumbled backward. Scrabbling in the thorns of the undergrowth, he felt the fisherman grasp at his ankles. Pierino in the dark seemed a great thing, terrible, as big as the demon Silver Nose. Andrea swung blindly with the horsewhip, yelling, whipping and whipping at the great chest of the fisherman to keep him at bay. Losing his balance, Pierino flailed and went down, too. A deep crack. His limbs opened like a sea star. He lay still.

"Signor Pierino," called Andrea d'Isantu, into the dark, in his high schoolboy's voice.

No answer came.

Now, with their flashlights, the others converged on him—

Professor Calleja, Dottor Vitale, his father, *il conte*. With shame, Andrea found his *Balilla* knickerbockers clinging to him wetly. The horsewhip had fallen somewhere in the dark. "I'm sorry!" he cried. "I'm sorry! I didn't mean to do it—"

Il conte raised one hand and lifted the flashlight. Now, the cause of Pierino's silence was apparent. The fisherman had hit his head, going down, on the great olive stone. He lay spread out as though melted, his left eyebrow disgorging a stream of blood. "*Bravo*, Andrea," said *il conte*. "Good boy. This is nothing to be ashamed about."

Filippo Arcangelo could be heard gaining the safety of the road with low whimpers of terror. Now Dottor Vitale fled, too, up through the scrub grass, sending his flashlight rolling and bouncing through the dark until it lay, extinguished, at the foot of the hazelnut tree.

"Neither of you is to go anywhere!" ordered Professor Calleja. "You're to help me." Professor Calleja hauled Pierino up under the armpits. "Take his feet—Andrea, *signor il conte*. We've got to carry him back home."

Il conte seemed to consider for a moment, then nodded. "We'll put him in the motorcar," he said. Before bending to take the fisherman by the ankles, *il conte* turned off his flashlight with a snap and stowed the horsewhip inside the jacket of his English linen suit. "Come on. One—two—three—heave."

They bundled Pierino into *il conte*'s motorcar. Andrea, in the backseat, kept his face turned away from the unconscious fisherman beside him.

They left the motorcar under the archway at the entrance to the town. Through the hot dark they manhandled Pierino, by the alleyways and *vaneddi*. None of them spoke, but occasionally the two *fascisti* gave Andrea a thoughtful, approving glance. That walk under the stars, carrying the bleeding fisherman, was the longest journey of Andrea's life.

They deposited Pierino in the alley beside his house. Perhaps his father, *il conte*, or *il professore* had intended to knock at the door. But the fisherman came alive a little at that moment, turned over, and grasped at the dirt. Then their courage failed them and they fled, through the alleys and passageways in their separate directions, feeling already the grip of the great silence they must keep, their awful complicity in what Andrea had done.

Driving home beside his father, Andrea hunched over and wept. "It was an accident," he said.

His father put a hand on his shoulder. "It *wasn't* an accident," he exhorted Andrea. "It was the correct thing to do. Sit up straight. You mustn't be ashamed."

Running the motor before the House at the Edge of Night, *il conte* reached inside his jacket and took out the bloodstained horsewhip. He threw it, and it arced high over the palm tree and the piazza and came to rest a long way off, in a loop of the bougainvillea, outside the bar's front door.

"What if it's found?" said Andrea.

"Let the Espositos worry about that."

GREAT SOBS RACKED ANDREA D'ISANTU after he had recounted this tale to her. He stood for a long time looking over the wall at the cacti, which were gaining their solid shapes at last in the dawn, and continued to weep at what he had done. "I loved this place," he told her. "I wanted to belong. I wouldn't have beaten him at all except out of fear. But the *fascisti* all believed I'd done it on purpose. They all believed I was a kind of hero. My father was *proud!*" He brought forth the word with disgust, as though coughing it up. "They never let me speak the truth. They made me believe I'd really meant to do it. I didn't, Maria-Grazia. I'm not like my father. I'm not like him, believe me. Now you know what I am, and you won't love me, but there it is if you'll believe it, at last, the truth about Pierino."

Now, in the cold light, in the dripping quiet of the piazza, Maria-Grazia believed.

"I'll give you my answer," she said.

Andrea raised one hand. "No—no—don't tell me. I already know, Mariuzza."

Muffling his overcoat about him, he touched her arm once and was gone. She watched him cross the piazza, with his stiff old-man's walk, his narrow shape like a ghost's, and it seemed to recede and recede before her, to undergo a narrowing without end as his mother Carmela had done a quarter of a century before when Pina had driven her from the bar. So Andrea d'Isantu went on walking, out of Castellamare, and vanished across the ocean. He left his mother defeated, shrunken, never to recover the stature she had possessed in the years before the war. He left his friend Flavio more brokenhearted than he would allow himself to admit. And as for Maria-Grazia, it would be another fifty years before the two of them spoke again.

FLAVIO DISAPPEARED SHORTLY AFTER his friend, one morning in September. On that day, Pina went up to his room with his usual coffee and pastry, hauling herself by the bannister, to find the bed unslept in, his nightshirt neatly folded at its foot like the cloths of Gesù in the tomb. Then Pina wailed and dropped the coffee, for she knew at once that her son was gone.

Searching the island, the fishermen and the farm laborers spread out and beat the undergrowth, plunged into the ditches in case Flavio had tried to drown himself, crawled beneath the vines. They searched the quay, the dark depths of the old *tonnara*, and the outbuildings of the Mazzus' farm. Reaching the caves by the sea, they came upon a trace of Flavio: His shoes, the dirty English brogues he had worn since his return from the war, stood on the cliff side by side with the toes pointing out to sea. His war medal with the face of *il duce* was hidden in the toe of the right one, its earth-stained ribbon neatly folded.

Pina lit a candle for her son in the church and knelt before it, under the crucifix that still bore the gloss of his polishing. She and

Carmela acknowledged each other occasionally from opposite sides of the church, kneeling before their separate candles, occupied by their separate griefs—for Carmela also prayed daily for the return of Andrea, who was said to have traveled as far as West Germany now, and to be steadfastly refusing to come home.

Then the miracle. On the tenth day, a letter arrived in Flavio's handwriting. He was alive and well, he wrote, in England. From Castellamare, he had swum out to a mainland fishing boat, and from Sicily had hitchhiked north. "I have a good job a steady job as a night guard at a factory," Flavio wrote, in his usual unpunctuated style. "I needed to start again but God and Sant'Agata willing I'll be back for Christmas or the festival and give my regards to Fr Ignatsio please. So you see I am fine."

Though Pina was to receive a steady supply of misspelled letters—was even to hear his voice, tinny but recognizable, across the telephone wires in later years—Flavio did not come back. After his departure, Pina began in earnest to get old. But Maria-Grazia believed her brother had left for his own private reasons, not all sad ones, and she reconciled herself to his second departure. For, in the end, a kind of order had been restored on the island. "I thank you for what you did," he wrote to her a year later, across the cutout inside of an English cereal box, "I sleep more easily now."

VI

INTO THIS WORLD OF CHANGE AND SEISMIC TREMOR CAME A FOR-
eigner, seating himself in his old place behind the counter as though
he had never been gone.

When Maria-Grazia returned one afternoon from the church, to
which she sometimes walked on days when her heart was melancholy
to speak a little with Father Ignazio about her brother, she knew by
the self-satisfied smiles of the old women outside Arcangelo's shop, by
the blessing the widower Onofrio cried from his upstairs window as
she passed, even by the unusual quiet of the doves in the palm trees,
that something had altered on the island. Pondering its strangeness,
she went home by the *vaneddi*, the little roads, so as not to be further
gossiped over.

Concetta greeted her in the doorway of the bar. "You've a new
customer!" she crowed. "You'd better come and meet him."

Maria-Grazia, in good humor, took the girl's guiding hand. She
expected one of the archaeologists, perhaps another returned prisoner. To hope for Robert would have been as absurd, by now, as to
expect Sant'Agata herself to be sitting there.

So it was with a great shock that she beheld her old lover waiting
at the counter, smiling in abashed pleasure at the shock he had
caused.

He was older, smaller than she remembered, badly dressed. Her
voice came from a distance and stunned her: "What are you doing
here?"

Robert got to his feet, rubbing a little sweat from his eyebrows. He was speaking to her, making clumsy expressions of tenderness in English and Italian: *cara mia*, darling girl. Expressions that belonged to those hot afternoons of five summers ago, when she had still been a girl, which were not things to be aired publicly in front of the neighbors in the bar. She found herself unable to reply, so extreme were the emotions that broke over her in quick succession: first shock, now joy, now anger. "What are you doing here, Signor Carr?" she said again.

Robert was mumbling, reaching for her hands. "I'm back," he said. "Maria-Grazia, I can't tell you how happy—and you haven't changed—" He spoke Italian now, of sorts.

Unchanged? After five years? She who had picked up snails and gathered bitter greens, who had steered the bar out of the war and into safe waters, who had lit on the idea of the Modernization Committee and proven Flavio's innocence at last? She found herself clenching and unclenching her fists. "You never wrote," she said.

The elderly *scopa* players had turned around their chairs, and now nodded at her in expectation.

Was she to throw herself upon him before them all, to give them the satisfaction of this reconciliation?

She swayed, pressing one hand against the counter to prevent herself from falling. Robert approached, a little anxious now. "I shouldn't have shocked you like that," he said. And then again, more timidly, "All this time, Maria-Grazia, I've loved you. I'm back. I'm back for good now."

She looked up and met his eyes. His hair had dulled, grayed, in his absence; the skin that had once been as translucent as tissue paper had coarsened and reddened. She wanted to speak, but still these waves of rage and joy were breaking over her, violent as a fever, so that she shuddered. "Is it that you love someone else?" he murmured, when she maintained her silence. "Is it that you don't care for me anymore?"

As they stood face-to-face before the counter, the earth gave a sudden sidewise jolt. So extreme was the disorder of her mind that it took her several seconds to locate it outside herself. Again, another tug. "Tell me what's wrong," Robert pleaded.

"You never wrote," she said again. But before he could form a reply, a great crowd had barged into the bar. The congregation leaving Father Ignazio's twelve o'clock Mass had got wind of the Englishman's return, and now they came to pay their respects. Robert was separated from her, absorbed in a noisy crush of delight. "Signor Carr! Signor Carr!" "The *inglese* is back!" "Praise-be-to-Sant'Agata-saint-of-misfortunes-and-praise-be-to-all-the-saints!"

Here came Father Ignazio, seizing Robert by both hands. "There'll be a wedding now," announced a widow Maria-Grazia barely knew, nudging her in a sidelong fashion, delighted with her own wit. "Prepare to read the banns one more time, *padre!*"

They must get away from these crowds! She felt nauseous, light-headed—she could not think, with their damned noise. But as she struggled toward the door, seizing the wrist of the Englishman, another wave of islanders appeared, swarming up the steps of the veranda. Old Mazzu, driving his goats before him with a metal washing pole, followed by a crowd of *il conte*'s peasants. Mazzu held both hands aloft at the sight of Robert and anointed the Englishman on both shoulders with his stick in spontaneous blessing. "Signor Carr!" he cried. "Signor Carr! Thanks be to Sant'Agata, you've returned at last! And here's Maria-Grazia, to be made a bashful bride!"

"All of you leave us alone!" Maria-Grazia cried. "You with your gossiping, your orchestrating, your interference!"

With that, she fled through the curtain of the bar. She took refuge in the courtyard, among the sunlit flapping of the sheets Pina had washed that morning. Now she heard the door bang: Robert had followed her, as she had hoped he would. "Maria-Grazia?" came his voice. "*Perché mi fuggi?* Why do you run away from me?"

Then the wave of rage in her broke, swamping temporarily the joy that had risen at his faltering Italian, his murmurs of "darling girl." "Because you didn't write!" she cried. "Because you didn't send me anything for five years, except that damned postcard! Because you've subjected me to ridicule, to humiliation—"

"But *cara* . . . "

Wrestling his way through the sheets, he found her and stood before her. "You didn't write," she said. "Nothing but that postcard: *Sto pensando a te.* Do you think that's adequate? Do you think that's just?"

"No," he said, bringing forth each Italian word with care, "I don't think it's just."

"Then what explanation can you possibly give me now?"

"When I sent you that postcard," he murmured, "I intended to overtake it, and be with you in a matter of days. Otherwise, I swear to you, I would have written more."

She turned—not to run again, but perhaps to provoke him a little with the fear that she might. "Wait!" he cried in anguish. "Wait, Maria-Grazia. At least let me explain. It takes me time to find the words—I'm trying, *cara.* I can explain, if you'll just give me time."

Indignation took the breath from her lungs. She seized the washing basket, upturned it, and flung herself down. "*Bene.* Very well. Explain yourself."

MEANWHILE, IN THE BAR, a mutiny was threatening. A strange fierceness had come over Amedeo, and he was refusing to let anybody follow Maria-Grazia and Robert into the courtyard. More islanders were converging on the bar by the minute in search of the Englishman, and Amedeo would let none of them go. "Where's he hiding?" demanded the widows of Sant'Agata, marching in formation up the steps. "We've a welcome bottle of *limoncello* to present to him, and a pennant of the saint."

"No," ordered Amedeo. "You're not to disturb him. I absolutely forbid it."

In this matter, too, Pina Vella was adamant, and stood guard over the curtain of the bar in case anybody should attempt to pursue Robert and Maria-Grazia. "They haven't spoken in five years," she said. "In the name of Sant'Agata, you're to leave them alone, all of you! If you so much as try to go after them, I'll lock the doors of this bar and keep you prisoner here. There'll be time enough to see Signor Carr after they've had a chance to speak to one another."

The neighbors resigned themselves, and sat muttering about the bar and the veranda awaiting the Englishman's reappearance.

But Concetta could not bear such uncertainty. Waiting until Pina was distracted, she crept through the door of the bar and escaped by the alleys. Hauling herself up on top of the courtyard gate, she made out the figure of Signor Robert, a figure behind the sheets like a puppet in a shadow theater, making gestures with his hands. And there was Maria-Grazia, seated on the washing basket, her arms knotted, her face turned away. Concetta, a declared heathen, nevertheless offered a secret prayer to Sant'Agata that Mariuzza would turn around.

ROBERT HAD BEGUN HIS STORY, falteringly, at the moment of leaving Castellamare. He told her how the ships had borne him away from her: the fisherman's little rowing boat and a great gray transport and a hospital ship whose cavernous holds were full of sighs and groaning. From Siracusa to Catania, from Catania to Tunisia, from Tunisia to Southampton, and then, at last, to the hospital with gray curtains where he had sweated out the rest of the war. Always, on that journey, he had felt himself to be looking back over a widening stretch of gray water, searching in a blur of fever for her face among the crowd.

As Maria-Grazia sat unmoved, he found that the words came more easily. Now, in desperation, he laid them all before her.

For months his shoulder had wept pus, he told her, bled, refused to heal. It had remained unhealed until the day the fighting ended. The wound had prevented him from parachuting into Arnhem after D-Day, from dying in the churned mud outside some Dutch village like almost everyone else he knew. His shoulder had cost him the rest of the war. But as May 1945 began, the wound began to pucker and heal, and the fever abated. As the fighting ended, he found that there was no longer anything wrong with him.

"That's when you wrote to me," said Maria-Grazia. "That's four years ago. What about the rest of that time?"

"*Lo so*," said Robert. "I know, *cara*. I'm coming to that."

The trouble had begun with his recovery, he told her. For he had found himself not discharged from the hospital, but ordered to Holland to rejoin his regiment. The soldier in the next bed, a melancholy captain, had told him it might take years to be discharged. He could not wait for that. He packed his belongings and absconded. On the way out of the hospital, he penciled Maria-Grazia a note in the only Italian he remembered: "*Sto pensando a te.*" I'm thinking of you.

"I couldn't write more," he said. "I had to leave."

He fled the hospital and made for the sea, walking along the road-side with his belongings in his arms, wearing the same mildewed uniform in which he had been admitted to the hospital. He felt the motorcars at his back slowing to regard him with curious eyes. Half-way there, a woman ambulance driver picked him up. She was driving as far as the docks, she said. She could take him there. But she didn't know where he could buy a ticket for Sicily. Besides, Robert had very little money. After the ambulance driver left him, he was obliged to go into a bank to withdraw it, and he had been uncomfortably aware there, too, of the attention that his rumpled uniform got, the stares directed at his bundle of belongings wrapped in a hospital towel. As he left the ticket office, having bought at last the precious ticket across the channel (Sicily he would get to by degrees), he was intercepted by a pair of military policemen. They wanted to see his discharge papers.

He told her the rest in odd moments, anxious not to inflict on her the desperation of that time and yet desperate all the same: to plead his case, to win her over. They had ordered him tried for desertion, he told her. They had confiscated his ticket. He told her how, at the court-martial, he was defended by a major as thin as rope, a stranger, who had sat with him in the entrance lobby of the court and ran over his case, making misspelled notes. How Robert's trial had been the seventh in a series of twenty-nine that week. How, meanwhile, London and Paris swarmed with deserters; they roamed about stealing trucks, robbing cafés, waging war. "You should have made for London," said the major wryly, as he wrote underneath Robert's name ("Carr" spelled with one "r" and "Private" for "Paratrooper") the fact that Robert had been "treated by a native doctor in Castle Amary, Sicily, afterward at Netley Park."

The court-martial was a divided affair, since it was felt that somehow for a simple shoulder wound to open and bleed, to weep pus, to cause shivers and fever, and to heal on the last day of the war, was a circumstance suspicious enough to have some psychological root. And yet clearly, at some point, the man had been unfit to fight, for it was there in his medical notes.

"What about this Sicilian doctor?" asked the colonel who presided over the panel. "Can we get some record from him? Have we any assurance that you were really so ill as you say you were, too ill to rejoin your regiment, during the years 1943 to 1944?"

"There wasn't enough time to write to the native doctor for a statement," said the major, with perfect truth—for he had met Robert two hours previously.

"Are you willing to go back to the Third Battalion until your discharge?" asked the assistant counsel for the prosecution.

Robert was not willing. It was only when he was sentenced to ten years with hard labor that he understood the great error he had made.

In the first days of his imprisonment, thinking of Maria-Grazia, who had been a girl when they were lovers and would be almost thirty when he returned to her, Robert had given himself over to despair. "For how could I write to you?" he said. "How could I ask you to wait for me, to wait ten years, even supposing they'd have given me the paper and the pen and the foreign stamps, which they wouldn't? You were just a girl when we met—I spoke none of your language—we were lovers for a few months, during the war. How could I presume that what you felt for me was the kind of love that would make you willing to wait, to forfeit any other chance of happiness? How could I presume that anything would be the same in peacetime? How could I have asked that of you?"

"What about the love you felt for me?" asked Maria-Grazia, very coolly. "Was it that kind of love?"

"Yes, *cara*. It was—it is—of course it was. But I wasn't sure of your feelings. It was all such a long time ago."

"I loved you, too," said Maria-Grazia, stung. "I was just a girl, but I loved you. I would have waited if you'd asked."

Now buoyed with a little hope, he forged on. The only thing he told her about the glasshouse, the military prison where he had served his sentence, was that a kind church woman had talked to him, a charity visitor, and asked him about his arrest, and that afterward, some months later, she sent him the books with which he learned Italian. "Couldn't she have sent me a letter?" demanded Maria-Grazia. "Couldn't you have asked her to?"

And Robert said, startled, "But, *cara*, I did. She did. She sent ten or fifteen letters."

But apparently, those letters had never reached Castellamare. Now he began to understand her indignation.

"What are you doing here?" she asked now, still unbending. "You've six more years to serve in prison, according to your tale."

So he should have had. But four years into his sentence, a colonel had come to the glasshouse requesting prisoners with good conduct who might be deployed to the north to work in the undermanned coal mines. A northern man, born in a mining village, eager to earn himself an early discharge, Robert was put forward. He received a slip of paper to be exchanged for a train ticket. "You can go home now," said the colonel.

Robert hitchhiked to Dover and boarded a ship for Calais. This time, he met no military policemen. He begged lifts, he walked when no lifts were forthcoming, and he made his way down the continent. Before crossing to the island, he had washed in the ocean with a bar of carbolic soap, trimmed his hair and shaved in the mirror of a motorcar, and purchased from a peasant for a few *lire* a set of new clothes. It had been Bepe who had carried him across the ocean. Timid with hope, Robert had asked the old man about Maria-Grazia, and Bepe with a shout of joy had recognized the Englishman. "I'm not here to cause trouble, if she loves somebody else," Robert murmured. "Only tell me, is she married? Do I have any hope? She never replied to my letters."

"Go up to the House at the Edge of Night and see for yourself," counseled Bepe.

By the ferryman's continuing roars of joyful laughter, by the welcome he had received as he disembarked at the quay, he had understood that there was some remnant of hope. Now he was less certain.

Strange what short work he had made of those years, when he told them. "I'll be wanted as a deserter if I'm found," he said. "That's the difficult situation I'm in. I should have done my time in Holland, and waited to get discharged properly—that was my mistake, and even if I could have written I wouldn't have dared to ask you to wait ten years for me because of it. But it was never lack of love, Maria-Grazia. Don't accuse me of that."

He had chosen the particular word for a difficult situation, *frangente*, which was also the word for the long white breakers of the sea, and she found herself stirred with emotion at the way he laid it before her, tenderly, hesitantly, as Andrea d'Isantu had once offered her a flower. "You can't go back?" she asked at last, a little timid at the rage she had flung at him.

"No, *amore*. I can't go back to England."

She bent and touched the cool tiles before her, without knowing why, until it came to her that it was the ground of home that she was touching. His predicament frightened her: to be condemned never to return home to the earth that had made you, never to be lulled by the familiar noise and hush of its ocean, never to be comforted and infuriated by the narrowness of its walls.

But she must have spoken some or all of this aloud, for Robert said, quietly, "This island is the earth that made me. Not there."

And now a strange thing happened. Now she found that her impatience to leave, that pain that had goaded her for years, like the sting of invisible cactus needles in the hands that persists for days after gathering prickly pears, was healed in her, was gone.

"Do you believe me?" he said.

"Yes," said Maria-Grazia. "I believe you."

Robert, moved, said, "Dear Mariuzza, *cara mia.*"

"I believe you," she said. "But you haven't made amends yet. Not nearly."

She would not kiss him, would not embrace him, but she consented to take his hand. After she took it, she found it very difficult to let go. So they stood like that a long time, formally, as though newly acquainted. "Do you think you ever could love me again?" asked Robert.

"I don't know," said Maria-Grazia. "But stay here."

Concetta, still concealed behind the gate, saw their two shadows approach and capered in silent joy.

VII

WHEN ROBERT AND MARIA-GRAZIA CAME BACK INTO THE BAR APPARently reconciled, hand in hand, there was a great eruption of joy in the House at the Edge of Night. But it soon became apparent that there was no wedding fixed, no imminent return to their old status as lovers. It was even rumored that Maria-Grazia had exiled the Englishman to the top of the house, to sleep on the old velvet sofa to which Amedeo had once been banished, instead of inviting him to her little room with the vista of palm trees.

This was the perfect truth. Over a bottle of *arancello* that afternoon, Amedeo attempted to console Robert a little. "She's a fierce girl, my Mariuzza," he murmured. "She always has been. She needs time. She loves you. Only she's making you wait a little, as you made her, while she examines her own feelings on the matter. She isn't one to be rushed or bullied into making up her mind."

"I made her wait five years," said Robert. "Surely she doesn't mean . . ."

"Give her time," counseled Amedeo.

Robert sipped the *arancello*, and it seemed to cling to his mouth, a coarser thing than the bright liquor he remembered. "Speak to her," said Amedeo at last. "Tell her all the things you could never have told her before, when you couldn't speak our language. Tell her about your childhood, your youth. The ordinary things that lovers talk about. You're a stranger to her now, at least a little. Tell her your stories. Bring her round to you that way." For Amedeo had never discovered any means more certain of winning a person's heart.

———

MARIA-GRAZIA WOKE THE FOLLOWING morning in the middle of a
sort of argument with herself. She dressed calmly, washed her face,
braided her hair, and descended the stairs with resolution, ready to
bear the truth that Robert's return had been a hallucination. And instead there he was, seated between her parents, peeling figs with his
steady, rough hands. He leapt from the chair and drew hers out as she
approached. "Good morning, *cara mia*," he said carefully, studying
her face.

Maria-Grazia took the tea Pina offered. Then, as her parents left
the table with hasty excuses, she found herself assailed by stories.
Robert was laying before her a great rush of Italian, telling her of his
childhood, his infancy, his youth.

He began with his home in the north, in a mining village, two
straight terraces of houses set upon a patch of green, under a gray sky.
Its name had been Aykley Moor. The story of his family was that he
had none, except an elderly aunt and uncle who had brought him up
halfheartedly between them. His mother, a repertory actress, had
died of the Spanish influenza when he was a few months old. Robert
had been there at the time, sleeping in his baby carriage in the corner
of some provincial dressing room. In the rush to cart the dead woman
off without causing a scene, he had been quite forgotten. It was only
the caretaker, locking up, who was drawn by the ghostly wails and
found the boy. After this, the child's mother was identified as the poor
dead actress, and her aunt and uncle had been summoned to fetch
him.

Maria-Grazia set aside her tea, for she could not drink it. "Why are
you telling me this story now?" she asked him.

"Because, *cara*—" He took her wrist. English in all things, he had
always held her tentatively, as though it were an imposition. Even
that first day on the beach. "Because I intend to ask you to marry me,"
he said. "And it's only fair that you know me a little better than you
did last time."

The upsurge of joy that accompanied these words threatened to reduce her to tears. Instead she beat it down, suppressed it. She allowed him to continue his story. He told how his aunt and uncle had considered abandoning him. On the long train journey north, while the boy stared at them with cold blue eyes, they resolved to deposit him in a boys' home in Newcastle. This they had related to him many times, as though it were proof of their kindness in the face of his cold nature. For reasons never disclosed to Robert, they had relented at the gate and brought him home. As though to make up for this weakness, they never afterward allowed themselves to show him generosity. They were to treat his presence as an imposition until the day—aged seventeen—that he left their home, a cardboard suitcase in one hand and a new-pressed suit on its wooden hanger in the other, in search of a better life.

"What is Newcastle?" asked Maria-Grazia in English.

And Robert said, in Italian, "A great city in the north, full of arches and bridges."

Later, though she would never have admitted it, when he had gone out to pay his respects to those islanders who had not yet heard the news of his arrival, she ran upstairs and searched for the place in her mother's schoolroom atlas. For the story had stirred something in her. Quite suddenly, stacking boxes in the little storeroom of the bar, she found herself weeping and weeping for joy, bent double over a crate of *arancello*, both hands pressed over her mouth to stifle the noise.

That evening, across the counter of the bar, she asked him, "What kind of a boy were you? When you lived in Aykley Moor?"

Robert scrambled for language, desperately grateful at this sign of her favor. "Small," he said. "Quite narrow." He meant thin, she understood, from the pinching motion he made with his hands. "I was always as white as chalk," he added, and she found herself marveling: What an odd, schoolroom figure of speech he used, when on the island they would have said "as pale as *ricotta*."

"What else?" she asked.

And Robert, who had been assembling phrases with a desperate fever, now poured forth all the Italian he could muster at once: "I had an eye which wandered. I had to wear a big sticking plaster over it. When I didn't get up quick enough in the mornings, my aunt would make me scrape the ice off the inside of the windows. She'd pull me from window to window by the ear."

"The inside of the windows?" said Maria-Grazia, and Robert said, "Sì, cara."

"Then what happened?"

"Then I got strong," he said, "and quick enough that she couldn't catch me. To get away on Saturdays, I began to run cross-country. Out on the moors, on the hills, for hours. I got to be the best student in the school—I had the highest marks—and I decided to get out of that place."

By these and other fragments, which he murmured to her later that evening at dinner and over the washing-up in the stone kitchen, and as they climbed the stairs to bed—he keeping a respectful distance—she began to understand that he, too, had once been a child, an adolescent, a youth. Always, before, his air of miracle had been part of her adoration for him: a stranger who had appeared out of the ocean fully formed and returned to it again, like some wayfarer in her father's book of tales. "May I?" he said at the door of her room, trembling a little as he touched her wrist, and she said, "No, caro." But that second night, when she heard him move about in the room at the top of the house, she saw the many younger Roberts he had been and stirred again with tenderness: a boy with a patched eye, scraping ice in that arctic place with little chalk-white hands; a youth running across gray English wastelands, coiled with a fierce determination to get out of that place. She had never told him of her leg braces, had burned with shame whenever she thought of them lying in the Campari liquor box during those months when they had been lovers, though he must have noticed how she limped. She had not yet told him anything about the bottle stuffed with banknotes down the side of her bed. Now she felt that he might have understood.

———

HER MOTHER AND FATHER regarded them each morning over the breakfast table with cautious eyes, breathless with expectation. And the bar was no better, for whenever Maria-Grazia tried to speak with Robert, as he sat bearing her steadfast company each day behind the counter, the elderly *scopa* players turned their chairs around and stared, as though this return of Signor Carr had been laid on for the sole purpose of their entertainment. How could anyone speak freely in such conditions? "I'm going to the scrubland," she murmured to him, the next afternoon. "To harvest prickly pears."

Allowing a respectable time to elapse, he followed her. While Maria-Grazia, hands wrapped in rags, salvaged the fruits from the cacti, he began to speak again of his past life. Now he told her of his youth, his flight from the village. A grammar school pupil, while the rest of the boys from his village went down the mine, he had abandoned home and ridden his bicycle east toward the ocean, holding his suit high with one arm to protect it from the mud of the road. He was apprenticed to the drawing offices of the Furness Shipbuilding Company. Here he had lived alone in the back room of a senior clerk. In the evenings he had bicycled along the seafront to a place of learning he called the Literary and Mechanics' Institute, where he read books on engineering and physics, and studied pictures of the stars.

Half comprehending, self-conscious, he had devoured the works whose names had been revered by his grammar school masters. He was determined to travel, to be an educated man. He seized upon every object that tasted of learning: Dickens, Shakespeare, a second-hand box of engineer's tools unearthed one rainy Saturday in a junk shop. It was in memory of this that he had almost wept when he first encountered Pina's translated *Opere di Shakespeare* and *Racconto di Due Città*.

In 1939, he confessed to Maria-Grazia, he had even applied to take the entrance examination of the University of London. He had never been to London, and it was for this reason that he chose it.

Everything about his childhood and youth seemed drab to him, a thing without consequence, a thing best recounted in a paragraph. That was how he recounted it to her now, and she found herself turning away, not in anger this time but at his capacity still to stir her to tenderness, something that she did not want to admit to him just yet. She had never once spoken to him of her prize books, put away before she had even opened them, the pictures of mainland universities in the encyclopedia over which she and her mother had once pored. The war had put an end to all that. While she hesitated, unsure whether to bring forth these confessions, he unbuttoned his shirt and caught in it, gallantly, the prickly pears that were overflowing from her hands.

AND THEN, AS SHE climbed on a chair to hang the garlands for the Sant'Agata festival, he told her of the war. For war was really at the heart of all this. It was war that had bundled him away from his life in the north, leaving the examination for the University of London forever unsat, his apprenticeship forever uncompleted, and his library copy of *Bleak House* forever abandoned at chapter five. War had interrupted that paragraph of a life, made of it merely a preamble to some greater, unrelated history. War had ended everything, and yet not everything, for it was war that had brought him to her. It made her reel a little to hear him, in his approximate Italian, describe this war in the same way she had always thought of it: as a great monster that had swallowed cities, islands, men, and then, in the end, given one thing back only—the Englishman, appearing like a strange blessing out of the sea. War had ended everything, and war had brought him to her.

Now she found herself curious about the kind of war it had been for him—what he had suffered, while she was diluting the coffee with chicory and water, navigating the separate silences of her parents, digging for snails.

He spoke to her about the long hard slog of El Alamein, and the desert camp where everybody went about dust caked, squinting. He told her of his friends, briefly, without describing them, for they were gone and it was safer to refer to them only by name, not attribute. Jack Snapes, who had first told Robert of the news that they were looking for men from all battalions to form an airborne division. Robert's application for transfer had been accepted, Jack's rejected on account of his imperfect eyesight. That was the last Robert saw of him. Jack, he learned later, had died of gangrene in Normandy. Paul Dodd, who had leapt beside Robert from fifty gliders, a northern man, too, a Newcastle man, their paths through the war eerily aligned until the night when the storm had drowned Paul and spared Robert. It had been Paul, mostly, he had thought of during the hours that he had spent drifting toward Castellamare, believing the hazy rock before him to be some odd hallucination, some fevered dream.

"You've never seen the island from the outside," he told her. "But it looks strange, *cara*. A sort of apparition. As though it's covered in fog."

"It's the heat making the water evaporate," she murmured. She had seen it before: The fishermen's boats when they got far out were often shrouded in such vapor. But it was his other words she marveled at: *You've never seen the island from the outside.* It was true. She had never left its shore, except once or twice to orbit it by boat on a summer swimming expedition. And didn't it seem an odd thing, she murmured aloud, that she who had never left this place and he who had been buffeted about the continent by the tides of war should ever have coincided on its shores?

"Sì, *cara*," he said. "*Un miracolo lo era.*" A miracle it was.

It cut at her heart a little, how he spoke of it as belonging to the past. She set aside her garlands of trumpet vine and looked down at his impossible, straw-colored hair, his thin shoulders, turned slightly inward as they always had been, his spectacles. Spectacles! For days she had been trying to place what was altered about his face. There it was. Not some dark difference, some sinister alteration, but merely spectacles. "You wear glasses now," she said.

"Yes, *cara*. All that reading."

Tenderness moved her. She reached down and touched the side of his head, where the arm of the spectacles rested on one ear. This touch was witnessed, for the bar was illuminated like a lantern at this hour across the dark piazza, and by morning it was known all over the island that the Englishman had begun, a little, at last, to regain Maria-Grazia's heart.

VIII

AFTER ROBERT HAD TOLD MARIA-GRAZIA HIS STORIES, HE HAD ASKED her to recount to him everything that had happened to her since his departure. And now, telling her own story, Robert caressing the hand she permitted him to hold as they sat together in the little room at the top of the house, she understood that the girl who had loved him, a girl barely free of the trappings of adolescence, had been superseded altogether in her by a woman of greater stature. She was the mistress of the bar now, and the one who had laid the ghost of Pierino to rest and started the Modernization Committee. Here a difficulty presented itself. For who was a woman like that to be made a wife, like Giulia Martinello, who went about with pinned-back hair, hunched over a baby carriage, or the widow Valeria's daughter, one of the lipsticked beauties who had once simpered over Robert at the counter of the bar, whom she had seen out on her step with lye soap and a washboard, her hands scraped raw? No, that was not Maria-Grazia's intention.

And yet she loved him. That had become plain to her, she told him, when he had recounted to her the tales of his boyhood: The old feeling had returned, to make her restless at nights when she heard him moving about in the little room at the top of the house, so that she found herself unable to sleep, so carefully was she storing up in her heart every familiar sound. To hide this love any longer, to maintain her composure, was almost too much to bear.

"But then," he said, "we aren't to be married?"

"No," she said. "Not yet."

"I'll wait," he said. "I'll wait five years for you, if that's what you have in mind—I'll sleep up here, and be patient, and respectful, and wait five years to be your lover again."

"But *caro*," said Maria-Grazia, a little mischievous. "I never said anything about that."

Robert glanced up into her face and saw that she was laughing, uncertain, like the girl she had once been. She took his other hand, and something in the way she seized it must have been different, more tremulous, for Robert allowed himself for the first time to kiss her, not on the face but on that hand she had offered, leaving a single burning impression on the palm.

Maria-Grazia, hardly knowing what she was doing, got up, turned the key in the door, and drew the curtains shut.

This had been their signal, before, during the siesta hour, and he half understood and came toward her, palms upraised, deferent, allowing her to unhook the back of her dress, to remove the pins from her hair one by one. But when she at last embraced him he was overcome: In a fever he was tugging all at once at his belt, his shoes, the braid that still fastened her hair. Half-dressed, they collapsed together on the mildewed velvet sofa, pulling the tarpaulin over them to keep out the autumn drafts. And now it was as though time folded like a heat haze and became less substantial—so that the hour they now inhabited might belong to that very first afternoon in her girlhood room, or else to some evening of their old age, fifty years from now. He worked at her in exaltation, inhaling deeply from her hair, finding their old rhythm. In this joyful silence, they remained locked together a long time.

Afterward, as she dressed, Robert said, "And you don't want to marry? You're certain?"

"Well, can't we be lovers, like before? What's the difficulty in that?"

Robert replaced the new spectacles and blinked through them in abashed surprise. "What about all the gossip, *cara*?"

"The gossip I can take," said Maria-Grazia. "I've suffered worse."

Without shame, she returned to the bar and served tables all that afternoon, meeting Robert's eyes from time to time when he lingered in the kitchen doorway. That night, she invited him back to her little room with the vista of palm trees for good, laughing a little at his great joy, his professions of adoration. "I'll accept a ring," she told him. "I'll be your lover as before. I'll love you always, as I always have. All of that I'm happy to do, *caro mio*. But we'll marry some other time."

And in the years that followed, though no one on Castellamare could have doubted that she loved him, though it was rumored scandalously that they lived as man and wife, though they ran the bar between them, making up the accounts in companionable quiet every night on either side of the counter, for all the world like a long-married couple, that was the only answer she would give to the prying of her neighbors: "We'll marry some other time."

IT WAS NOT UNTIL the spring of 1953 that she changed her mind. Maria-Grazia, on that particular morning, had returned to the bar from the widow Valeria's house behind the church, where she had successfully made a deal for a dozen bottles of *limettacello* to be ready in time for the festival. On that particular morning, she found Robert bent over the wireless radio, in tears, the customers clapping him on the shoulders as they did with the bereaved and drunk. "What is it?" she cried, seizing his wrist. "What's wrong?"

The wireless radio was tuned to English. Bepe nodded in its direction. But in her consternation she could not make out the words: They were utterly foreign to her once again, as they had been when she was a girl.

Eventually Robert heaved himself up on his elbows and wiped his eyes. Seeing her, he took both her hands and kneaded them between his own. "The deserters have been pardoned," he said at last, in her ear, getting her face all wet with tears. "The deserters have been pardoned."

"Signor Churchill has pardoned them," said Agata-the-fisherwoman, "and Signor Robert can go home."

Then Maria-Grazia found herself, too, in tears, without at first knowing why. "Do you want to leave?" she said at last. "Will you go away again?"

"No," said Robert. "No, *cara*. I promise you, I'll never leave this place."

"More fool you," said Agata-the-fisherwoman, not really meaning it. "But Maria-Grazia, even I think you'd better marry poor Signor Robert now."

Sì, sì, the elderly *scopa* players protested—hadn't she made him wait almost four years, nearly as long as she had waited for him? Still, the thought made her despair a little, as it had in the midst of her joy when he had first returned. "I don't want to be a wife," she cried, "and have to wash and clean and cook all day, and trail around with a baby carriage, and never be in charge of this bar any longer, this bar that's been in my family since the end of the first war—and who will take care of it then? You aren't a wife, Agata, for you've always sworn it would be a kind of death to you, and what if I feel the same way? What then? None of you think of that. If I marry, I'm forced to give up the bar."

"If that's the only thing that troubles you," said Robert, a little giddy, when they lay together that night in her room, "then *I'll* wash and cook and clean. *I'll* trail round with the baby carriage. Run the bar if you want to! Anything, Maria-Grazia, if you'll just say yes."

"In that case," she said, trying and failing to suppress her elation, for she knew he meant every word, "I suppose we had better marry after all. There's only so much gossip a person can bear in a lifetime."

MARIA-GRAZIA AND THE ENGLISHMAN were married by Father Ignazio, like her mother and father had been. Afterward, Robert signed his name in the grimy book the priest offered. To cut the thread of his old life, he took her name: Robert Esposito.

Then, for the first time since the war, there was dancing on the terrace of the House at the Edge of Night. *Il conte* did not attend to give his blessing and drink a sip of *arancello*, as was customary at the islanders' weddings. After the departure of Andrea, *il conte* and *la contessa* had entered a period of mourning. The shutters were kept closed, the façade of the house left unpainted, and the servants were under permanent orders to report to the villa in black. But nothing could disrupt the festivity of the House at the Edge of Night. Maria-Grazia had to be hauled away from serving the drinks and counting the takings. Then there was Robert, very English and flustered and a little drunk, holding out both hands for her to dance. As she whirled about in his arms, the island beyond him narrowed, became less significant than the man before her. "I'm glad," she murmured.

"Of what, *cara?*"

"To have married you, in the end."

By the light of the moon, to the strains of the *organetto*, they went on whirling, pinned in each other's arms. Inside her dwelt already the fingernail of life that would become the next Esposito.

PART FOUR

The

TWO BROTHERS

...

1954–89

TWO BROTHERS WERE FISHERMEN UPON THE SEA, BOTH VERY *handsome and so alike that nobody could tell them apart, and both very poor. After a day of fishing without luck, they caught at last a tiny little sardine, hardly worth eating.*

"Let's eat it anyway," said the elder brother. "It's worth a few mouthfuls."

"No," said the younger. "Let's spare it. It's not worth killing."

They spared the fish and it brought them good fortune: two white horses and two bags of gold, with which to journey about the world, and a pot of magic ointment with which to cure all wounds. Since this could not easily be divided, the elder brother, who was braver and stronger, gave it to his younger brother to protect him from harm.

The brothers rode away in opposite directions. The younger brother had no adventures—at least, if he did, the story does not mention them. The older brother rescued a princess from a sea serpent, cutting out its seven tongues and hacking off its seven heads, and for this labor won her as his bride. He saved a valley from the curse of an evil sorcerer. He journeyed to the bottom of the ocean in an enchanted ship and dug up pearls. His hair grew long, he married the princess, and he no longer looked like his brother anymore.

Then, still not content, he went in pursuit of a witch whose evil was enchanting a whole country, whom no one could manage to kill. Riding up to her castle with his sword, he threatened to cut off her head. But this witch was cunning. Looping a single strand of her magical hair around the boy's throat, she took him prisoner. "Now," thought the witch, "I will make him my slave, and he will defend me from these troublesome knights who come riding every day to cut off my head, and I will sit and eat roast meat and pastries all day."

Meanwhile, the younger man, growing lonely, was riding about the world in search of his brother. For many years he rode, asking everyone he met whether they had seen the man on the white horse with a face like his own. At last he came to the witch's valley, and heard tell of his brother's capture. "Now," said the younger brother to himself, "the moment has come, and I must rescue him."

On the way, he met a little old man who asked him where he was going. "To free my brother," said the younger brother, "who is under the power of the witch."

Then the old man told him what to do. Since the witch's power was in her hair, he must seize her by it and keep hold, and that way he might overpower her. "Then cut off her head," said the little old man, "and do us all a favor."

The young man rode to the witch's castle. Out came a fearsome knight with flowing hair, swinging his sword, roaring in anger. With one blow the terrified younger brother cut off this knight's head. Then, seizing the witch by the hair, he drove his sword through her body and killed her, too.

But now that the spell was broken, he saw that the fearsome knight he had killed, the witch's slave, had something familiar about him. Bending near, he recognized the face of his brother, and wept and wept at what he had done.

All at once, he remembered the magic ointment. He ran to his horse, and returned with it to the place where his brother's headless body lay. Kneeling beside it, he rubbed the ointment on the body, and the skin healed and the dead man sat up. The two brothers embraced each other, and the younger asked forgiveness for the terrible crime he had committed. *Then they went back to the older brother's palace side by side, and never again were they parted all their days on this earth.*

AN OLD ISLAND TALE, *as told to me by the widower Mazzu, which bears similarities to the Sicilian tale of the same name and probably derives from it. Recorded circa 1961.*

I

YEARS LATER, WHEN BOTH OF THEM HAD GROWN UP AND CEASED TO
have anything to do with each other, Maria-Grazia would struggle to
remember a time when her two sons had not been at war.

The boys were born what their English great-aunt and -uncle, in
the stiff congratulatory letter they sent to the island after their second
nephew's birth, called "Irish twins." They emerged at the bracket
ends of the year: Sergio in January 1954, Giuseppino the following
December. The arrival of Sergio was prefaced by a forty-hour breech
labor. In its worst throes, at four in the morning of the second night,
Maria-Grazia swore again and again to Robert that she would never
have another child.

But the day she carried Sergio home from the hospital in Siracusa,
the three of them bundled in Robert's overcoat on the thwart of the
ferryboat *Santa Maria della Luce*, he tenderly stroking her bruised
sides, she changed her mind. "We'll have another one after all," she
said. "Only we'll have to hurry, before I lose my nerve."

If Robert was alarmed at this news, he did not say so. "*Cara*," he
said, "we'll do whatever you like." Before the infant Sergio could sit
up by himself or take solid food, the elderly customers of the House
at the Edge of Night had reason to gossip once more at the balloon-
ing of Maria-Grazia's ankles and her sudden rushes from the bar to
plunge her head in some lavatory or wastepaper basket. "That Englishman of yours is a force to be reckoned with," said Agata-the-
fisherwoman, prodding Maria-Grazia in the side, eliciting sniggers
from the elderly *scopa* players.

But nothing now could shame Maria-Grazia. "These island men can take note," she said, eliciting a chorus of hooting laughter from the fishermen in the corner.

Giuseppino emerged on his due date, obligingly headfirst. The delivery took less than an hour. Afterward, relatives and neighbors would never cease to point out this difference to Maria-Grazia, as though it revealed some profound fact about the character of each child. And perhaps that was where the trouble began.

The first thing that Sergio did, when the second baby was brought home, was crawl over to its cradle. Dragging himself to the foot of the crib, the infant Sergio hauled himself up by its bars and looked in. "Oh," cried his grandmother Pina, moved. "See—he wants to greet his new brother."

Instead, Sergio roared in the face of the other baby, startling it into tears. Sergio would not stop roaring until Pina had borne him away.

This was odd, for as Maria-Grazia remembered it, her younger boy, Giuseppino, had been the one who had started every argument ever since.

ROBERT HAD PLANNED, in the joy that had followed her consenting to marry him, to take sole charge of the bringing up of the two children while Maria-Grazia handled the affairs of the bar.

But the care of the boys was not a thing that could be parceled out to one adult. It was a messy, disorderly thing, liable to engulf every nearby relative, to deprive all of them of sleep. The two babies could not be left alone together. Very quickly they wore both their mother and father out. In the spring of 1955, Concetta came in search of Maria-Grazia and found her asleep behind the counter of the bar, the customers having resorted to getting their own coffee and liquor. Rousing Maria-Grazia, the two of them traced Robert by the scream-ing to the red-tiled upstairs bathroom, where he was close to tears in a mess of baby shit and talcum powder, while Sergio was striking Giuseppino great blows to the head with one fist. Concetta considered all this with narrowed eyes. Then she knelt, retrieved Sergio from the puddle behind the toilet cistern, wiped Giuseppino's soiled backside, and supplied Signor Robert with a handkerchief.

"Oh, Concetta!" wept Maria-Grazia, who had followed her up the stairs and now witnessed the rage of her two sons. "These babies hate each other!"

"Now," said Concetta, in the tone she had first learned from Pina Vella. "That's silly."

"We can't manage any longer!" cried Maria-Grazia. "I can't get down to the bar, and Robert can't take care of both of them all by himself, and my mother and father are too old—" For Amedeo was eighty now, Pina close behind him, and she was afflicted by a swelling of the feet that had diminished her at last, so that she could only limp and hobble after the babies. "The business will be ruined," said Maria-Grazia, "and these boys will kill each other before they're ten years old."

"It's just fighting," said Concetta. "All children fight. When I was a child I fought everything that moved. Other children, dogs, lizards. Your brothers must have fought, too, didn't they?"

"But not like this," cried Maria-Grazia.

"Now, now, Mariuzza," said Robert, putting a hand on her back comfortingly. "We'll find some way to resolve things."

But their mother's despair had penetrated even the enraged consciousnesses of the two brothers. They ceased their warring for a moment and looked up at her, gazing with matching opal eyes from beneath peaked English eyelids. Sergio was a sage infant, with a curiously oversized face that gave him the look of a statue, some bald professor or diplomat from a nineteenth-century bust. Giuseppino, meanwhile, was a red little thing, alert, watchful, constantly spoiling for a fight. Concetta seized him and bore him out of his brother's sight, into the doorway, where she fastened the diaper with admirable speed and lulled him into calm.

But Concetta, despite her command of the warring babies, was not herself, Maria-Grazia saw now. Her shoulders were a little bowed down, her usual bright face somewhat pallid. The girl had been suffering troubles of her own. All spring, the island had been aflame with rumor about the girl and her father, Signor Arcangelo.

It had been known for some time that Arcangelo was vexed with his wayward youngest child. Concetta, according to her father, was supposed to be at an age when she put on long skirts and began to consider a husband. And instead here she was running about the island with the teenage sons of the fishermen, lighting fires and plunging into the sea in ripped-off slacks. She appeared to have grown out of her childhood seizures. And now she refused to be prayed for any longer, and had—during one particularly fierce argument, audible through Arcangelo's open windows all over the southern part of the town—flung her rosary out into the courtyard, announcing herself a heathen like Agata-the-fisherwoman.

This had gone on from Epiphany to the festival of the Presentation. On that night, after another particularly ferocious argument, Concetta had staged a rebellion. She left her father's shop in the midst of the last streaming storm of winter and proceeded, with a neat burlap sack containing all her belongings, along the main street, past the green fountain, through the Fazzolis' alleyway and up the poky passage grandly named Via Cavour, to arrive at the door of her greataunt Onofria's house at a quarter past twelve. During her solitary march, which it seemed the whole town had witnessed from behind their curtains, everyone had observed the red marks running like a ladder up the backs of Concetta's arms and the bruises under her eyes. Concetta would not say where she had got them, claiming they had merely appeared like the stigmata of a saint, but any fool knew that when the backs of the arms were faintly lashed like that, the shoulders in between would be a mess of belt strokes.

Now, those islanders who had always sided with Arcangelo swung the tide of their favor toward Concetta. For the grocer, it emerged, had been beating her since she was a child. And other odd rumors surfaced: The girl had been made to sleep on the floor at her father's house, it was said, and had been ordered to hide away in the storage cupboard or the outside bathroom whenever a fit came over her to avoid alarming the shop's customers. Concetta did nothing to deny these rumors or confirm them. She merely shut herself up in the back bedroom of the widow Onofria's house and refused to come home.

"She's shamed me," raged Arcangelo to *il conte.* "Can't you do something—bring her home, stop these lies about me spreading any further?" For his other children had always been so obedient: Filippo, who had followed him into the shop and now all but managed the place, allowing Arcangelo himself an easy retirement; and Santino, who worked as a land agent for *il conte* and rode about daily, swelling his father's heart with pride, beside *il conte* in the island's motorcar.

But *il conte* was not interested in the plight of his former friend. Since Andrea's departure, the count went about in distraction and seemed hardly to be listening at all. "Hasn't everyone beaten a stubborn child?" pleaded Arcangelo. "Hasn't everyone had to punish a son or a daughter? Am I to be held up for rebuke and shame because I've admonished my child—out of love, mind, not cruelty—merely in order to set her on the right path?"

"My wife and I never once beat Andrea," said *il conte.* "You must solve your family troubles yourself. But"—here he extended a small scrap of comfort—"I daresay Concetta will come back once she's starving, for God knows the widow Onofria doesn't have enough about her to keep the girl." For Onofria was one of *il conte*'s dismissed peasants, and poor as a plowed field in winter, subsisting half on her wits and half on charity.

"Yes," said Arcangelo, soothed. "Yes, yes—that Concetta'll be back soon, damn her, in time for the visit of her cousin Cesare for the Sant'Agata festival, and with any luck he'll consent to take her off my hands this year. She'll be old enough to marry."

"Face down this shame," counseled *il conte.* "And deal with Concetta once she comes home."

But Concetta had other ideas. Now, kneeling beside Maria-Grazia with Sergio held prisoner by the scruff in one hand, Giuseppino squalling in the other, she said, "It's this business with my father I want to talk to you about."

"Yes, *cara*. Tell me."

Always, Maria-Grazia had loved the girl. Now Concetta, embarrassed and anxious for once in her life, proceeded with a little clearing of the throat: "I need work if I'm to keep myself and my old Zia Onofria. But who'll employ me after this disagreement with my father? People aren't fools. They know he's a great friend of *il conte*."

"Work?" said Maria-Grazia. "What about school?"

Concetta straightened herself. "I left school last summer. I'll be eighteen."

Eighteen. She had utterly missed the growing up of the child. Guilt burned at Maria-Grazia when she considered the beatings she had failed to notice, the odd marks she had always dismissed as belonging to the girl's wild adventures among the scrub grass and prickly pears. "I'd like to work here in the bar," said Concetta. "Couldn't you employ me?"

Now Maria-Grazia understood the matter. "Go on."

Concetta continued, all in a rush, "You need help—you've just said so yourself, you and Signor Robert—and I love the bar and I know how it works. I know how to make the coffee and the chocolate and do the accounts. Or I could take care of Sergio and Giuseppino. I'd be like Gesuina was, looking after you and your brothers when you were babies, except I'm not a hundred and twenty years old and blind like she was, God rest her soul."

Maria-Grazia knew it would be a comfort to have the girl about every day, as she often had been as a child.

"Please, Maria-Grazia. Say yes. See how well I cleaned Sergio's ass just now—"

"That one's Giuseppino."

"It doesn't matter—I'll learn which one's which. Please say yes, Maria-Grazia."

"Yes," said Maria-Grazia, and Robert said, "Of course, Concetta, you must work here. If Maria-Grazia agrees, you can begin at once."

The following Monday, in a new black apron commissioned especially from the tailor Pasqualina to fit Concetta's small waist, in her one good dress pressed and sprinkled with lavender water, her cheeks gleaming with pride and a little anxiety, Concetta moved between the tables of the House at the Edge of Night for the first time in her official capacity as assistant to the bar. She heaved plates above her head with newfound grace, and listened to the tourists' orders with respectfully folded hands. "A miracle," said Agata-the-fisherwoman. "Concetta tamed by you Espositos, when everyone else had given up hope."

Meanwhile, Arcangelo went about with a face like bad weather, knowing he was shamed in everybody's eyes.

WITH CONCETTA IN THE HOUSE, things began to proceed more calmly. She learned to startle the boys with a cry of *"Basta!"* just like Gesuina, and occupied them for hours in wild games of her own devising, until they were so exhausted that they forgot to be enemies. Proudly, she pushed them about town in their matching baby carriages, which Robert had yoked together with a broom handle so as to be able to propel both at once while keeping the boys separated—for even the sight of the other boy sharing his baby carriage filled each child with rage. Meanwhile, the bar had never been better tended, for Concetta had grown up in and out of the place, and she could carry a tray of drinks in one hand, heave the bawling Sergio in the other, and still remember an order of twelve pastries for Maria-Grazia behind the counter. More important, she loved the House at the Edge of Night. Maria-Grazia, looking back, didn't know how they had ever run the bar without her. Now, on every night on which she and Robert were able to sleep soundly, or retreat to their little room with the palm trees at the window and become again, for a few hours, the careless lovers they had been during the war, she offered the saint a silent prayer of thanks for the girl.

Concetta's father was seldom seen behind the counter of his shop any longer, leaving the running of it to his son Filippo. He spent his days in a vacant patch of earth beside the old Arab *tonnara,* where the young builder-fishermen 'Ncilino and Tonino had been employed to dig. "A new house," speculated Agata-the-fisherwoman. "Why, the man's so shamed by the gossip about his daughter that he's decided to leave the town altogether."

"A second shop," said others. For it was well known that Arcangelo's business had done well since the arrival of the tourists, better even than the House at the Edge of Night.

On clear nights that summer, the sound of sawing could be heard rising from the patch of earth by the harbor, as Tonino and 'Ncilino worked late, raising the beams.

The day before Sant'Agata's festival, workmen from the mainland arrived in a boat and unloaded crate after crate. These Arcangelo ushered inside the building, chasing away anyone who stopped to look in. The last object to arrive was a long wooden box shaped like a coffin. The foreign workmen could be heard drilling until the early hours. While the women of the island bent among the damp hedgerows to gather petals of bougainvillea and oleander, preparing their baskets for the rain of flowers, something ignited briefly and glowed purple in the darkness, an infernal, miraculous fire.

By morning, it was clear what sort of work Arcangelo had been engaged in. A neon sign, the island's first, beamed from the front of the new building, making the children and the elderly alike stop and gaze up, enthralled by its liquid fire. The building had a new red roof and a curlicued balcony. Its cement terrace had been swept clean and fitted with a dozen tables. Inside, refrigerators hummed and a wireless radio broadcast English voices; a new ice cream machine glimmered in the gloom like a reliquary. The neon sign, American-style, proclaimed the building's title: "Arcangelo's Beach Bar."

MARIA-GRAZIA ONLY BECAME AWARE of this new development when, opening early before the Sant'Agata Mass, she found their own bar empty. Usually the islanders would queue on the terrace to take a glass of *arancello* or *limonata* before church, in honor of the saint's day. But now, gone were the elderly *scopa* players, gone were the fishermen with their cigarettes behind their ears and the shopkeepers who usually hung about to read the morning newspapers. The bar breathed the quiet noise of the surf. Robert, carrying a baby on each hip, appeared at the curtain.

"What's happened?" he said. "Has somebody died?"

"I don't know, *caro*."

A little preoccupied, he leaned over to kiss the side of her hair. "You mustn't worry," she said. "I'm sure there's some reason."

But he was still anxious. Handing her Giuseppino to nurse and setting Sergio down between the empty tables where he was now learning to stagger about, he kept her company a little while in the bar.

Agata-the-fisherwoman and Bepe arrived half an hour later. "There's something you'd better see," said Agata. Grimly, she led the Espositos—Maria-Grazia, Robert with the baby carriage, Concetta, who had just arrived, Pina, and Amedeo—along the path through the prickly pears. From behind a cactus, Maria-Grazia made out Arcangelo's neon sign and a crowd of people milling about on the concrete veranda; she heard the blare of music and the clink of glasses. Concetta burst into furious tears. "Damn my *stronzo* of a father—he's trying to ruin the House at the Edge of Night!"

Yet by evening, the House at the Edge of Night was once again occupied. Shamefacedly, the usual customers crept back by ones and twos, to take up their usual positions. The dancing on the veranda was only a little thinner than usual. "You should have seen the price Signor Arcangelo was charging for coffee," muttered Signora Valeria. "It's a wonder any of us were taken in."

But some had remained at the new beach bar. When Maria-Grazia and Robert walked out to the *belvedere* sometime near dawn, she made out figures dancing there, too, down by the black ocean, in the blaze of neon light.

"The twenty-eighth of June, 1955," noted Amedeo in his red book that morning, feeling himself to be recording an omen, "opening of Arcangelo's Beach Bar."

THIS OPENING OF A RIVAL business was a challenge that the Espositos felt must be answered. "We must have an ice cream machine of our own," said Amedeo. It was duly ordered, paid for with the stacks of foreign currency that now stuffed the cashbox of the House at the Edge of Night. For the archaeological remains still brought visitors. Visitors took possession of the veranda of the bar from morning until night: visitors with pale foreigners' legs; visitors who lunged alarmingly at the children with the blinking eyes of their cameras; who sat out in the sun even at noon; who wore specially purchased summer clothes, indecently rucked-up beige shorts and white socks and great flopping hats, as though they were exploring Africa. These visitors, who came really for the archaeological excavations, might now prove to be a kind of salvation, for without them how would an island five miles long support two bars?

A catalog of neon signs was brought from the mainland and pored over. "Everything he does, we must do," said Amedeo. But Pina quietly disagreed. "This is the real bar, the old one," she said. "People will come here all the same."

Maria-Grazia concurred with Pina, and no neon sign was purchased to adorn the front of the House at the Edge of Night. But from then on, whenever business was a little depleted, or archaeologists thin on the ground, or when some other misfortune struck the House at the Edge of Night, it was only a matter of minutes before someone would raise their eyes to heaven and fix the muttered blame on Signor Arcangelo. It became a familiar game between Maria-Grazia and Robert in those early years of their marriage. Lying awake at night, fretting over a troublesome tooth of Giuseppino's, or a fever of Sergio's, or a bad month's figures in the accounts book, Maria-Grazia would murmur, provoking her husband to reluctant laughter, "It's all the fault of that Arcangelo and his beach bar."

II

SERGIO AND GIUSEPPINO HAD BEEN BORN IN THE VERY FLOURISH-
ing of the island's prosperity. As they grew up, Maria-Grazia marveled
at the life they inhabited. To her sons, the caves by the sea had never
been anything other than an archaeological site with a little shed at
the entrance, in which Salvatore Mazzu sat and sold tickets. They did
not remember a time before Bepe's ferry or a time when the island
had possessed only a single motorcar, and they would not believe that
the Greek amphitheater had once been a cobbly field, occupied only
by goats (for *il conte* had dug it up and put his own fence around it
and his own little ticket booth manned by Santino Arcangelo, determined to profit in his own way from the new popularity of Castellamare). To Sergio and Giuseppino, the House at the Edge of Night
had always been a place where foreigners took tea on the veranda and
snapped photographs. And to Maria-Grazia, too, the island seemed
once again a place heady with possibility. It was Robert who had
cured her of her restlessness, in the end. Robert to whom no happiness was greater than to plunge into the ocean with their sons on
Sunday afternoons, to lie folded in the curve of her waist on hot
nights, listening to the palm trees breathe beyond the window, to sit
on the veranda after the day's work was finished and, totaling the figures in the accounts book, lay before her all kinds of glittering specu-
lations. His hopes were touchingly modest. "The boys might go to the
mainland high school," he told her on such nights, "and you might
make this bar an air-conditioned place, with a television, better than
Arcangelo's."

For in those years of modernization, Castellamare had gained many foreign curiosities, including a television. The ferryman Bepe, who had earned so much money out of his new ferry, the bar's elderly customers muttered disapprovingly, that he couldn't think of anything sensible to spend it on, had purchased it in an electrical shop in Siracusa. He bore it across the ocean in a box wedged in with newspaper, as though it were some archaeological relic. Workmen from the mainland installed an aerial on the top of his blue house behind the church, and now the islanders gathered in Bepe's mother's old parlor with its velvet curtains, its sorrowful figurines of the saints, to watch black-and-white foreigners roll precariously from the top to the bottom of the screen and report the news. ("I thought they'd speak our dialect," said Agata-the-fisherwoman, disappointed. "At least some of them.")

On Bepe's television, Sergio and Giuseppino, hunched between their parents' knees, saw the state funeral of the American president Signor Kennedy. They were promised that when the foreigners who launched rockets into space, the *russi* and the *americani*, succeeded in walking on the moon, that would be broadcast, too. Maria-Grazia marveled that on the same island where she had picked up snails and ground chicory for tea, in the same place where Robert had been washed up, fevered, lacking penicillin, her sons would watch men catapulted into space. But seeing the outside world only through Bepe's television and the pages of the newspapers, she struggled not to picture every other part of the world except Castellamare in black-and-white.

The bar now had the latest ice cream machine and refrigerators that hummed coolly and gathered condensation. Sometimes the tourists would open the cabinets and stand before them in relief a while, seeking the cold of their native north. Meanwhile, Bepe replaced his little motorboat with a great flat-bottomed modern ferry, the *Santa Maria del Mare*, capable of carrying five cars.

The islanders' hopes swelled like heat mirages—became immoderate and soaring. "Perhaps we'll have nightclubs, like in Paris," speculated the young fishermen in the corner of the House at the Edge of Night. "A whole row of bars, not just two old-fashioned ones full of domino players. A proper store with new clothes from Milano." For it was hard to be content any longer with the usual clothes, ordered in brown paper from the mainland or bought from the widow Valeria's hardware store, where the same faded underpants and socks and funeral trousers had been known to hang in the window for decades at a time.

What the island got, eventually, was a savings bank.

No one could remember there ever having been a bank on Castellamare. Though the Arcangelo family had been known to lend their neighbors the money to repair a roof or buy a fishing net, though the ancestors of Pierino had once run a kind of racket whereby they lent ships and nets to fishermen whose boats had gone down, taking half of the fish in return and none of the risk, though the cousins of the Mazzu family, now deceased, had hired out suits for funerals at ten *lire* an hour, profiting from the protracted wakes of the nineteenth century to make the values of the suits back twenty times over— though the island had known all these manifestations of capitalism in its past, a bank was a very different matter. "There's no need for all that," said Agata-the-fisherwoman. "Haven't we always managed?" For always, the islanders had kept the takings from their businesses in metal cashboxes, seldom padlocked, and under the mattresses of their beds. It was as common to be paid in tuna or in oil as it was to receive actual money, and this system had always kept the island's population housed and fed. ("Unlike those *americani* during their Depression," observed Agata-the-fisherwoman darkly.) But now there was to be a bank, a building with gleaming glass and gold door handles, fashioned from the remains of Gesuina's house in the piazza, facing the House at the Edge of Night a little challengingly across the expanse of dust and sun.

It had all started with the death of *il conte*. Amedeo's old enemy had died quietly in the spring of 1964, without ceremony, behind the wheel of his ancient motorcar. It took eight men and three donkeys to haul the car out of the ditch into which it had plunged after his death, but the body of *il conte* was intact, without a scar. He seemed, to all appearances, to have merely fallen asleep at the wheel.

He was buried with honor, surrounded by white-gloved pallbearers from the mainland, other former *duces* and *contes* from that passing world into which he had been born. His old doctor friend read the eulogy. Carmela, tearless, in her ancient funeral veil, stood alone at the head of the grave.

Then, too late for the funeral, Andrea d'Isantu came home. Maria-Grazia did not see him that first day, for he arrived after nightfall and shut himself away in the villa with his mother. But the customers in the bar reported that he now wore a glossy suit and glasses without rims, like a foreigner. *Il conte's* last elderly peasants had presented to him at the quay the signet ring belonging to his father, but there had been some disagreement, some shouting about the ghost of Pierino. Carmela had clung on her son's arm. The estate—what was left of it—would pass to him now. Carmela rejoiced so openly at the church the next morning for the return of her son—"my boy . . . my handsome boy . . . praise be to Sant'Agata and all the saints"—that it was embarrassing to hear her, said the widows of the Sant'Agata Committee, so soon after her husband's death.

"He means to stay," muttered the builder Tonino to the crowd at the bar. "He's paid me and 'Ncilino to fix up half his empty houses. We've so much money now we're going to replace our toolboxes and buy a new set of ladders."

Maria-Grazia could not have said why this made her uneasy or why, when Robert asked, "What's all this talk about *il conte's* son coming home?" she did not know how to reply. Her husband knew that the count's boy had once loved her. It did not trouble him. Why, then, did she fear Andrea's return?

Soon the builders working on Andrea's houses were obliged to hire half the out-of-work laborers on the island. And by the end of the summer Tonino and 'Ncilino could buy not just the toolboxes and the ladders but the van to keep them in and three acres of land on which to park it. For *il conte*'s son had returned to the island a rich man, and with grand plans for its future.

The bank, with its whitewashed windows and a sun-yellow and ocean-blue sign shrouded in a sheet, was treated with suspicious interest. The day before the Sant'Agata festival, while nobody yet knew what the new building was, Andrea d'Isantu announced a grand opening. Frightened to stand before the islanders (or so the elderly *scopa* players claimed), he sent his mother instead to do the honors. Carmela stood at the door before the islanders, in her faded aubergine suit, and cut in half a pale blue ribbon. The land agent Santino and his father Arcangelo rushed forward to drag down the dust sheet from the sign and expose its lettering: "Castellamare Savings and Loan Company." "You've all begun to profit from the interest of tourists in our beloved island," announced Carmela, mimicking *il conte*'s strident style of oratory. "Now you'll have a safe place to invest your new riches, and if you want to replace your old houses with new ones, well, come to us and we'll see about lending you the money for that, too."

Filippo Arcangelo was the first customer each evening, standing nervously before the counter with his takings in a burlap sack. Soon the baker and the florist followed. And when Agata-the-fisherwoman asked, timid for once in her life before the new bank's mainland assistants in their glossy suits, whether she might be eligible for a small loan to repair the earthquake damage to her floor, Andrea d'Isantu's bank offered her the money to knock the house down and build in its place a concrete villa—all free of charge, all to be paid later. For Agata-the-fisherwoman had been persuaded to join Bepe's ferry business as a partner, handling the accounts and bookings for him as well as piloting a quarter of the ferry's journeys, and was likely soon to become as wealthy as he was.

"As if I'd want to knock down the house my great-grandfather built," scoffed Agata. "But I'll take the money to repair the floor—that I'll accept, for I'm tired of the rain getting in in wet weather."

Now word got round that Andrea d'Isantu's company was not just lending to his father's friends, but to everybody, indiscriminately. And while Agata-the-fisherwoman might be perfectly happy with her great-grandfather's drafty house with lizard nests in the walls, others seized the opportunity to get out of the poky ancestral homes they had been living in for decades. On Castellamare, houses had always been an inherited thing, a kind of lottery of birth: You rejoiced if the windows were large and the view of the sea enticing, or mourned and patched the place up as best you could if it was narrow and dark like Bepe's house behind the church, his dead mother's. If there were no descendants to inherit a place, or so many descendants in so many foreign countries that they could not agree about how to divide it, then the house merely stood empty, valueless, until its shutters caved in and vines crawled over the mess of rubble inside. This was what had happened to Gesuina's house before the bank replaced it. But now, announced the new *conte*, anyone with a good job and savings in his bank could apply for a mortgage to buy a patch of unused land and build on it a concrete villa of his own.

"Shouldn't we put our savings into the new company?" asked Robert one night, caressing Maria-Grazia's wrist. "For I'm always tripping over cashboxes and envelopes of money about the house. We're getting wealthy, *cara*. Only last week I found a bottle of old *lire* stuffed down the side of the bed."

Her savings, shored up against some future escape. She had almost forgotten about them. She reached behind the bed, retrieved the bottle, and unscrewed the cap. Out came a faint tang of Campari, an odor of dust. Digging inside with a bent hairpin, she pulled out *lira* after *lira* in a slippery torrent of banknotes. "What were these for?" asked Robert.

Smiling a little at the recollection, she told him. "But *cara*," he murmured, half-mocking, half-serious, "how could you ever have wanted to leave this place?"

When she returned to bed, he drew her near, as though she were cold. "What do you think?" he murmured. "About what I said. The savings bank."

"No," said Maria-Grazia. "I don't want to put the money there."

"I wouldn't mind if you did," said Robert. "I've no difficulty with your dealing with d'Isantu. I don't fear him."

Sometimes, in Italian, he still brought forth these odd expressions: I don't fear him. Her husband—strong, as brown as Maria-Grazia herself, with the shoulders of a fisherman from heaving the boys about all day—what fear need he have of the new *conte*, with his shattered leg, his sallow aspect, his fussy, old man's gait? She kissed Robert's hands one by one, and said, *"Lo so, caro.* I know."

But still she did not deposit the bar's savings in the bank.

"There's a reason it's called a savings *and* loan company," said Amedeo, dampening the murmur of excitement that had filled the bar in recent days (for he found it hard to be charitable in any matter concerning his old enemy *signor il conte*). "Andrea d'Isantu is borrowing your money with one hand and lending it with the other. If Arcangelo puts his takings for the month into the bank, say a hundred thousand *lire*"—here he moved a set of salt-shakers to demonstrate— "all that Signor d'Isantu has to do is take that hundred thousand *lire* and lend it to Agata-the-fisherwoman to fix her floor. She pays him back at high interest—he pays Arcangelo back at low interest—and keeps the rest. That's what he's doing."

"Whatever he's doing," said Agata-the-fisherwoman, "it's worked, and while he's been overseas he's become a wealthier man even than his father." For Andrea d'Isantu had begun refurbishments and alterations to his father's villa, installing proper electricity in every room, tearing down the dilapidated outbuildings, ripping off the buckled shutters and replacing them with new. He had sent the old motorcar away for scrap metal, and Carmela now drove around in a West German sedan with an impressive growl that had been shipped especially on Bepe's ferry. As for the new *conte*, he remained locked up in the villa, where nobody could see him.

Pina, too, railed against the new developments. "That line of concrete villas," she said, "why, they aren't worth anything, not like these old houses in the town. Anyone can see the first earthquake will knock them flat. And before long there'll be no view of the sea left, and no bay, and no space to graze goats, and more tourists in this place than islanders. And that new *conte* with his city ways will own everything."

But Maria-Grazia could not deny that money flowed more easily in the bar now, that the cashbox (though its contents were still transferred to the backs of bookshelves and slipped between mattresses and pillows each Friday, not deposited in the new *conte's* savings bank) was fatter and more quickly replenished. The walls of the house were painted, the coffee machine replaced, and Concetta from her rising salary overhauled the furnishings of her Zia Onofria's house, painted it a pale blue all over, and planted orange trees in its front yard. Meanwhile, Robert worked long hours each Saturday repainting Tullio's and Aurelio's rooms, which Amedeo had finally relinquished, for Sergio and Giuseppino: discussing with the carpenter new furniture to be specially manufactured, sanding the doorframes, waxing the floorboards until they shone.

MARIA-GRAZIA NEVER ONCE SAW Andrea during the months he spent on the island on that first visit. At the beginning of the second week, she had gone very early in the morning to the gate of the villa and rung the bell, with no clear intention. After some five or ten minutes' delay, the agent Santino Arcangelo appeared behind the wrought ironwork. "Sì," he said. "What do you want?"

"I'm here to see Signor d'Isantu," she said.

Santino disappeared. Without hurrying, he walked back up to the house, pausing to whip the long grass with a stick at intervals as though to demonstrate to her his utter unconcern for haste. It took him twenty-five minutes to return, and when he did, it was with an odd, satisfied sneer. "He won't see you," Santino announced from behind the gate. "You're to leave at once, Maria-Grazia Esposito, for *signor il conte* has nothing to say to you."

Walking home, she wondered why her steps were so heavy. What would she have found to say to Andrea d'Isantu anyway? They had not spoken in fifteen years. She had wanted him to know that she had never thought any the less of him after his confession about the beating of Pierino, that Flavio was happy in England, to judge by his unpunctuated missives, that the ghost of the fisherman was no longer seen on the island except under the influence of the widow Valeria's extra-strength *limettacello*, that all here, in short, was well. But how would she have brought forth the words to say all those things?

Back at the bar, she found Robert arbitrating a disagreement between Sergio and Giuseppino in the courtyard, his thin hair blown vertical by the spring breeze. "I know where you've been," her father, Amedeo, said quietly. "It's all over the island already. Be careful, *cara*. Your husband's a good man not to question you about it."

"Damn this place," she said. "Damn the gossips and the spies—haven't they any proper work to go to? Must they always be poking about in other people's concerns?"

Then, for the first time, she fought with her father. "I don't understand what you can possibly have to say to that man," said Amedeo. "And what business you can have going to visit him at dawn, in secret, in your best clothes. While your husband is here taking care of your boys, minding the bar—"

"He doesn't suspect me of anything, Papà. Maybe you should do the same!"

"Robert," said her father, "has the patience of Sant'Agata. We all know that."

Stung, she cried, "*Cazzo*—must I report everything I do to you? Are you my jailer as well as my father?" Which was unfair—even she felt it to be so. And yet, to save herself the humiliation of apologizing, she found herself storming instead into the bar, and starting up the coffee machine in a knot of fury.

So the argument was carried on in mutters about the bar all that day, and resolved only when she saw Robert walking toward her across the piazza at dinnertime, distorted by the heat mirage, a boy on the end of each arm. Then she ran out to him and buried her face in his neck and said, "I'm sorry, I'm sorry. It didn't mean anything, my visiting him." And Robert said, "I know." And Amedeo, witnessing, patted his daughter's arm in consolation as she returned to the bar counter, resolved to say no more about *il conte*'s boy.

In a few months, Andrea d'Isantu was gone again. Maria-Grazia never once saw him, and in years afterward she would struggle to believe that he had ever really visited the island, picturing him only as a figure in the shadows, appearing and vanishing like the ghost of Pierino.

THE DEVELOPMENTS THAT ANDREA had set in motion, however, were of a concrete nature. For instance, the matter of tourist accommodations. Currently, all visitors were obliged to make a great pilgrimage to get to the island, like devotees of the saint. To get here from the nearest mainland places, Noto and Siracusa, most had already traveled for a whole day from the airports in Catania and Palermo or on slow ships from northern seaports. So it was that the average visitor to Castellamare was still something of an explorer, interested in the history of the necropolis, attempting a little faltering Italian. "If only there were a proper airfield right here on the island, or just across the sea in Siracusa," said Bepe. For he had heard from the foreign fishermen that the accessible islands of Greece, a short air-conditioned airplane journey from London and Paris, now lured thousands upon thousands of tourists to their blue waters.

Sometimes, in those heady years of development, great white liners passed on the horizon, blaring into the sea air, making the island children whoop and stamp in greeting. Through Flavio's *Balilla* binoculars, you could see little gold heads in sunglasses moving about on the deck, long pink bodies extended on recliners. "If only they'd stop here," said Giuseppino. Both of Maria-Grazia's boys loved the tourists, with their air of other places and their cursory, brisk northern languages that seemed to speak of cities where important things happened, where things must be said in a hurry. Not like the dialect of the island, which dragged on and on by its nature, went round in epic, exhausting circles.

It was rumored that the new *conte* had bought the old farm belonging to the Mazzus, which had fallen into ruin when the old man died and the last son left for America. Carmela had hired mainland builders on her son's behalf to dig up what had always been the island's best field, the flattest one with a view of the harbor. The Mazzus' old farmhouse was knocked down.

"They're building a villa, I daresay," complained Tonino, put out at being passed over for the contract in favor of those foreigners with their new cement mixers. "When it's finished, I believe our new *conte* is going to move there with his mother and knock down the old place altogether."

"Not if I have anything to say about it," said Pina. "Why, half the tourists stop by the count's villa for a glimpse, for don't you know it's partly Norman, Tonino, one of the oldest buildings on this island?"

The new building, a vision in pink concrete, was raised by degrees. At sunset, the light fell between its empty pillars and steel girders, making of it a burnished silhouette. By day, the builders labored under the full force of the sun. The building gained not only balconies and cornices but a swimming pool in the shape of a kidney, stained blue on the inside; a garden with palm trees, which were wrapped for protection in brown paper until the building dust settled; and, in the shade behind, a concrete wasteland for parking motorcars. The spaces in this American-style parking lot, reported Concetta, who had spied, were large ones, for foreign motorcars, twice the size of the little Cinquecentos and three-wheeled Ape vans favored on the island. And why should the new *conte* need so many spaces for his guests, for not a soul had visited him or Carmela since the death of his father (even supposing, muttered the elderly *scopa* players, he had the courage to come back to the island a second time)? Now the building rose and towered over the line of little concrete villas, which from the veranda of the bar looked no bigger than cigarette boxes. By the following summer, the great new building was ready to open its gates.

No one was clear on what the new building was meant for. "It's *signora la contessa's* new summer home," speculated Agata-the-fisherwoman. "She'll drive down the hill in that motorcar of hers in April to spend the summer by the sea, and that will save her the fifteen minutes' switchbacking up and down each day." For Santino Arcangelo bore Carmela back and forth daily in the German motorcar to her favorite spot at the end of the bay, where she sat alone under a parasol rubbing lotion on her papery arms.

"There's no telling what these rich people like to spend their money on," said Bepe.

"Televisions, for instance," needled Agata-the-fisherwoman.

"It's another bar," said Concetta. "*Il conte* means to cut out our business, like Arcangelo."

The pink building stood on the horizon, its gates open, its parking lot deserted.

"It's a hotel," announced Tonino, settling the matter that evening. "I've seen the sign, and a little reception desk with a brass bell."

ON THE ISLAND, there had never been so many jobs as there were in the weeks before the hotel's grand opening. Jobs cleaning and polishing and sprinkling the grass of the new hotel with water out of a hose ("A shameful waste," grumbled Pina), jobs carrying in the beds and wardrobes and dining tables the new *conte* had ordered from the mainland, jobs preparing island delicacies and foreign food in the great silver kitchen. Even the island's ancient band was hired, to provide a touch of local color. One morning, when the islanders woke, a great white liner hung like a miracle just outside the harbor, riding the calm waters of the bay. The children ran down to meet it. While they capered, the band tooted nervously through their island songs. The visitors were borne ashore, clutching suitcases and bags and boxes as though they had been rescued from some disaster at sea, muttering in their odd northern languages, unsure whether they should tip the ferryman or offer the children coins.

HERE A PROBLEM PRESENTED itself. These new tourists preferred the air-conditioned salon and neon-lit veranda of Arcangelo's Beach Bar to the dark, old-century interior of the House at the Edge of Night. *Il conte*'s company had partitioned a section of the bay for them, on which they lay on plastic recliners. The beach bar served American cocktails, and whiskey in crystal glasses. Between the luxuries of the hotel and Arcangelo's air-conditioned bar, there was no need for the new breed of tourists to make the hot climb to the town at all.

"But I can't understand why anyone would choose that bar over this one," maintained Bepe. "Arcangelo charges a hundred and fifty *lire* for a coffee, and his tastes like donkey piss."

"Seek out those tourists," urged Robert to Maria-Grazia, ambitious on her behalf. "Encourage them to come here. They'll love the island, as I did when I first saw it, if only you can persuade them."

One morning, two of *il conte*'s tourists at last braved the climb up to the town. They were sighted in the piazza shortly after the Mass bell stopped ringing, hanging nervously about the palm tree. Emboldened, Maria-Grazia went to the door. "Welcome," she called, in English. "Come in."

After some heated discussion, the couple crossed the threshold of the bar. "Coffee?" offered Maria-Grazia. "Tea? Pastry?"

The new guests, gold-haired, a little sunburned, glanced at the elderly *scopa* players in the corner, at the wireless radio, tuned to a Sicilian station, at the sweating cold cabinets full of rice balls and pastries, at the coffee machine. The man made a gesture like opening a book.

"Menu?" he said.

"No menu," said Maria-Grazia. "But we make whatever you want. A coffee, perhaps? A rice ball?"

The man shook his head and eventually asked the price of a tea. "Thirty *lire*," said Maria-Grazia. "Three American cents."

But the couple, after examining the rice balls one last time, merely shook their heads and wandered back out.

The House at the Edge of Night, Bepe explained, was charging too little. "Arcangelo has two price lists," explained Bepe. "One for the tourists, one for the fishermen."

"We couldn't do that," said Robert, scandalized at this calling into question of his wife's honesty. "The House at the Edge of Night isn't that kind of business."

"The tourists don't *like* to pay less than they expect. You've seen them yourself—the ones you get on your veranda, the archaeological ones who come to see the caves. You've seen the tips they give you—paying thirty *lire* for a coffee and leaving you eighty on top of that. You charge less than they expect, they think you're giving them inferior coffee. Or else that you're living in poverty, like some goatherder from before the war, and either way it makes them uncomfortable, Mariuzza."

"We couldn't charge two different prices," Maria-Grazia said. "It wouldn't be right."

Arcangelo with his two price lists did a steady trade.

III

IT WAS TRUE, AS AMEDEO HAD JUDGED, THAT ROBERT POSSESSED the patience of Sant'Agata. This became evident in the early years of the boys' growing up. For Robert, who had lived three years in a military prison, who had waited five to return to the island, and another four to be Maria-Grazia's husband, evidently had something steely in him that could not be broken by a little childhood bickering. When his sons fought, he would listen in calm to each outpouring of discontent, arbitrate and mete out punishment, and remain composed throughout, as unbending as the schoolmistress Pina Vella had been before the disputes of her pupils. After such tiresome afternoons, he still had the capacity to seize his wife in an embrace behind the counter, or hum island songs as he went about straightening the tables, while Maria-Grazia felt herself worn thin just by listening to them.

Perhaps Robert's patience was the difficulty. Perhaps if he had been less tolerant of the boys' warring, perhaps if it had made him more miserable, they might have behaved better. But then again, they might have been much worse.

Meanwhile, Amedeo found himself seized by a kind of fever at the way his grandsons goaded each other, having forgotten the cruel battles that had once been waged between his own three boys in the courtyard and corridors of the House at the Edge of Night. He loved Sergio and Giuseppino more fiercely than he had loved any of his own children, except perhaps Maria-Grazia, and yet they had a far greater capacity to drive him to exasperation.

By four years old, Sergio could often be found puzzling over the pages of his grandfather's book of stories. His brother, still only three, had begun to decipher the words. To make them equal, Amedeo read the stories aloud to both of them on the veranda of the bar, plying them with ice cream and tales in equal measure. Sergio listened, his eyes on the horizon, spooning ice cream thoughtfully into his mouth and—occasionally—down his front. Giuseppino, meanwhile, swung his legs against the chair, refusing to sit still. He swung and swung until he kicked his brother and the storytelling dissolved in yells of rage. Yet when Amedeo questioned Giuseppino about the stories afterward, he would remember every one and could recount them at length: "And that was the one about the parrot—and he flew in at the window—and he told the girl about ten white horses with ten black-armored riders who were riding off to war—"

"That Giuseppino's an intelligent boy," said Amedeo.

"They both are," said Maria-Grazia fiercely. "Both of them just the same." Then he saw that he had hurt her maternal feelings, and attempted to change direction: "Sì, sì. Of course, both of my grandsons are intelligent. I didn't mean that."

But wasn't this part of the problem, this treating them both exactly alike? For the two boys seemed oddly separate at times, as though they were brothers by accident rather than blood.

From the time they started school, Sergio had been praised as a great scholar, and it was true that he achieved the higher marks. Amedeo knew this because he had scrupulously recorded every victory and milestone of each boy's life from the beginning: "Sergio now 65 cm in length," he would write in his red notebook, with satisfaction, marking the date, or "Giuseppino first solid food: a pea and a spoon of mashed *carciofo*." Then later, when school began: "Sergio 7 in arithmetic test (addition and subtraction)"; "Sergio appointed class pencil monitor 1961–62"; "Giuseppino awarded sports day running prize." In all their endeavors except those of a sporting kind, Sergio emerged the victor. But it was Giuseppino, a formidable athlete like his father, who gave the impression of intelligence, who seemed to take everything in from behind eyes languidly half-closed, as though, if he went to the trouble, he could outstrip them all.

WHEN THE BOYS MADE their First Communion, Amedeo presented them—half-jokingly, half in earnest—with a children's picture book which retold the Sicilian story of *The Two Brothers*, ordered from the bookstore in Siracusa and wrapped in red paper.

Sergio and Giuseppino loved the tale, as Amedeo had known they would. True, they dwelt more upon the parts about the sea serpent and the witch than on the miraculous reconciliation, which was the part with which Amedeo had hoped to capture their attention and instruct them on the futility of their tiresome quarreling. But he believed that this understanding would come. "The hero of the story is the younger brother," maintained Giuseppino. "He was the one who showed mercy to the fish and he was the one who saved the day." And, "No!" cried Sergio. "Wasn't it the older brother who won the princess in the first place?"

When each boy had listened to his grandfather reading the story, an urge came on him to possess the book exclusively. They fought over it, tugged it, and eventually tore the pages clean in two. Too late, Amedeo was sorry that he had given them only one copy to share. He ordered two matching replacements, but the damage had been done, and now both boys wanted the original, the one with their grandfather's looped schoolroom handwriting inside the cover: "To Sergio and Giuseppino on the occasion of your First Communion, with love, Grandfather Amedeo."

This incident of the book was only one example of the way that, somehow, they all managed to get it wrong again and again, this matter of raising the two boys.

And yet, some of the time—mostly under the influence of their father—the boys were calm, and Amedeo wondered what he was getting so agitated about. Pina was inclined to agree. "What's a little childhood fighting?" she said. "I trust Mariuzza and Robert to manage them right."

Like the villagers in the story, the islanders of Castellamare struggled to tell Sergio and Giuseppino apart. Despite Sergio's long face and Giuseppino's small red features and constantly searching eyes, the boys slept and woke at the same times, walked with the same gait, twisted the fronts of their hair with the same motion when they were reading, and quite separately decided to study at the same university in London, one or the other of them having seen its picture in Pina's encyclopedia as a small child and folded down the corner of the page. On Sunday afternoons, plunging into the sea at Robert's heels, glancing back to check that they were observed by their adoring mother and their Zia Concetta, they occasionally consented to play together and would remain immersed in intense, private games for hours at a time. Giuseppino, who roundly humiliated his brother every school sports day, who was the best football player and the fastest runner, had only one fear, embarrassing enough on an island of this size: the ocean. He would not stray out of his depth. Sergio, once, was observed taking his brother's hand and leading him out, and for days afterward Amedeo and Pina discussed it, as though it were the sign of some great change in the boys' comportment toward each other.

But both children disliked the island, to Amedeo's dismay. It was as though they had been born out of place—perhaps their English father's fault, he thought privately, though he would never hear a word openly said against Signor Robert. For really Robert was a kind of angel, the son who had come to them out of the sea when no other son was left, the only husband he could ever have pictured being the equal of his Mariuzza. But it must have originated somewhere, this dissatisfaction, brooded Amedeo, forgetting the restlessness that had driven him to seek his own life here on the island, and that had possessed his own teenage sons.

These two grandsons were forever complaining, this Sergio and Giuseppino! The bar was too stuffy for them in summer; the house too drafty in winter; they railed at the lack of books and the absence of a cinema and the endless, relentless sea. Besides, both boys were sensitive enough to be troubled by the gossip of the town, the tireless exchange of rumors at every shop counter and street corner, rumors that very often concerned the Espositos. For instance, people claimed that their grandfather had been involved in some scandal between two women, years ago, that their father's role in the war had been less than honorable, that Uncle Flavio had gone mad and run about the island naked, wearing nothing but his war medal. These rumors, which were really only the ordinary currency of gossip that had been circulating for half a century, depressed Sergio and infuriated Giuseppino; both were overcome by a great impatience to be gone from the place. As they grew older, Giuseppino began to talk only in formal Italian and Sergio only in English—"as if," lamented Amedeo, "the dialect of this island wasn't good enough for either of them."

"These are different times," soothed Pina. "They've seen motorcars and tourists from England. They've seen moving pictures of men from America flying into space. It's natural that they want to be part of the rest of the world. You mustn't go taking it so hard, *amore*."

But how could he take it anything but hard, when he had watched his sons depart one by one from the island, never to return? In Amedeo's mind, a plan began to form. "Supposing I instructed them in how to run the bar?" he proposed. "Like I did with our own boys? And put them in charge of it?"

"They'd hate it," said Pina. "And besides, they want to see the world outside, these boys, and we'd do better to let them than to fight it and drive them away for good."

Of course, as in all things, Pina was correct.

Nearly immobile now on account of her swollen feet, she sat on the veranda each day and read and reread the books she had loved as a schoolmistress: Shakespeare and Dante and Pirandello. Also new volumes that they could afford now to order from the mainland: *Il Gattopardo* and Danilo Dolci's work on poverty in Palermo, which made her suck her teeth, glad to belong to a smaller, kinder place. Though her feet pained her too much to walk about, she traveled great miles in her reading as Amedeo once had in his recording of tales. And in all disputes between Sergio and Giuseppino she had the capacity to reduce each rebellious boy to a meek infant with her schoolmistress's stern gaze. Things might have gone much worse in their infancy if it hadn't been for their healthy respect for the fierce judgments of Grandmother Pina.

NEVERTHELESS, BY THE BOYS' eleventh year, Amedeo had begun to fear that there really was some great ill erupting between them.

It came to light, as all things seemed to, during the Sant'Agata festival in June. But the trouble had really begun that February. Just after Sergio's birthday, the boys had seen snow for the first time. When they woke, it lay dustily on the piazza. All was disorder beyond the doors of the House at the Edge of Night: The teenagers were waging violent war in the streets, the elderly customers refused to step out even into their courtyards, and six of the island's motorcars had rolled down the slopes and crashed into the houses at the bottom. Also, Arcangelo's Beach Bar had been flooded out by the winter storm, a victory for which the adults of the House at the Edge of Night refused to congratulate themselves.

The snow made the air odorless, and as sharp as glass splinters. His grandsons, Amedeo could tell, were enchanted. As the sun entered the courtyard the leaves of the oleander dripped a little, like the leaves of some alpine village. In the newspapers, which Robert brought in from the step in a snow-damp bundle to show his sons, they discovered photographs of English houses with snow piled on top like slices of *ricotta*, cars buried on the roads so that only their shiny roofs were visible. "Why couldn't I have been born there?" cried Sergio. "Instead of only a stupid English passport, which I never get to use! Why can't you take me there to see the snow?"

As Maria-Grazia poured the coffee for breakfast, Amedeo, wounded at Sergio's words, sought feverishly in his red book for tales of snow belonging to their own island. But the boys weren't interested. They kept jumping up at the window, jostling for space, and left their breakfast uneaten. Robert raided the disused pantry where they kept their winter coats, and came struggling out with his arms full of old knitted caps and gloves and furs from Pina and Amedeo's youth, into which he proceeded to stuff the two boys before setting them loose into the snow. "Play together nicely," called Maria-Grazia after them, with an optimism Amedeo found admirable, given their record so far.

Sure enough, after little more than half an hour, Giuseppino trailed in sobbing, flinging off his gloves and scarf in a passion. Sergio—fuming in his wake—followed with a bloody nose. The boys, it emerged, had fought over a bucket of snow.

"He took it all!" sobbed Giuseppino. "He went out into the court-yard and took all the snow before I could get any!"

"But you only wanted it for snowballs!" raged Sergio. "And I was going to make a snow statue, and I'd gathered it all up, from the steps and the tiles and the leaves of the oleander, and you came and snatched the bucket and made it fall in the dirt!"

"Where's the snow now?" demanded Robert, getting to his feet.

"Go-o-one!" roared Sergio in a passion.

Giuseppino, kicking the baseboard, muttered, "There's no need to be such a baby about it."

As usual—Amedeo judged privately—Giuseppino was the unhappier, Sergio the most wronged party. Limping outside, leading each of the boys by one ear (something Robert would never consent to do, not even when provoked), Pina found from the scene of the crime that they had fought in the pile of spoiled snow, rolling over and over, until there was nothing left. Pina attempted valiantly to make a lesson of the situation. "You see," she said. "You fight over something, and in the end no one gets it."

"I hate him," hissed Sergio, through his punched nose. "I hate him. I want to kill him."

All that morning (the school furnace had broken, and lessons were canceled), Amedeo roamed the town in search of more snow for the disconsolate boys, who had been confined sulkily each to his own bedroom. But the snow was gone or else spoiled, the town disgorging its remains soggily from every roof and branch. By afternoon Giuseppino seemed to have forgotten the argument. But Amedeo observed that something had altered in Sergio. All that spring, rage against his brother boiled and seethed in him, threatening to explode. They fought over everything that season: their marks at school, their places at the table, the games of football in the piazza. Behind it all, he feared, was some graver, deeper ill.

IT WASN'T THAT SERGIO hated his brother—not really—just that there didn't seem to be space for the two of them in a place as narrow as the House at the Edge of Night, and that when they tried to settle matters between them everybody seemed to lament over it, as though there were some terrible omen in their fighting. It had been that way ever since he could remember, and none of his relatives seemed to understand it. It was clear from what everybody said that the natural destiny of the two of them was to become, like every other set of siblings on the island who stood to inherit a business, the joint proprietors of the House at the Edge of Night. Sergio loved the bar, but if he were forced to share it with his brother for all eternity he felt he would go as mad as his Zio Flavio and run about the island in his nightshirt, too.

That year, the day before Sant'Agata, the *scirocco* came. A wind from North Africa with a voice full of gravel, it sifted red dust over the town and made everybody's eyelids prickly and everybody's tongue dry and sour. It huffed on the back of the neck like bad breath and turned even climbing the stairs into an ordeal. In the bar, the ceiling fan was jammed with dust, and sweat ran down the refrigerator doors and condensed on the gleaming levers of the new coffee machine. The boys, irritable and niggling, were sent out of the house and down to the sea so that the adults could finish their preparations in peace.

Even their father, their usual ally, was immersed in making an inventory of the stock in the back room and sent them away.

On their bicycles, bought by their mother out of the cashbox last summer in matching red—as though they were twins, fumed Sergio privately!—they dropped down the switchbacking road to the bay. The wind huffed in their faces at each bend but provided no relief.

Even the sea seemed listless today, rolling oily over itself to break against the red-silted rocks. It made Sergio's head ache to hear it. The boys wore homemade bathing shorts that bagged embarrassingly when wet. Sergio put his on and plunged into the water near the caves. A scattering of tourists lay across the beach, roasting their white skins. Giuseppino sat on the shore and eyed the sea warily, flinging stones.

Some impulse to provoke his brother brought Sergio back, swimming his best crawl. "Here," he said. "Come in with me. There's nothing to be scared of. It's time you stopped being afraid of the sea, Giuseppino. You have to get over it."

A short way off, on the sand, a cluster of northern tourists lay immobile. Now a girl with gold hair, awkward and lanky in a too-small pink bathing suit, turned toward them. Sergio had spoken in English, hoping to shame his brother a little. The girl detached herself from the others and approached. Shyly she flung a stone into the sea.

"Lots of people are scared of the water," said the girl at last to Giuseppino. English, with a southern flatness, unlike their own accents, which belonged, by several degrees of separation, to the north. And yet to Sergio the girl's seemed the most beautiful voice he had ever heard. "How old are you?" Giuseppino said, evidently drawing the same conclusion.

"Eleven."

"We're eleven, too," said Giuseppino.

"I am," said Sergio. "He's not."

"Twins?"

"Brothers."

"I'll swim with you," said the girl. "I'm the best swimmer in my school. I won the house cup last year."

Giuseppino did not know what this meant, but he agreed to follow the girl into the water a little way. "Maybe if you take my hand it'll help," he tried, but the girl only laughed and flipped over in the shallows, giving them a glimpse of her skinny, inadequately covered backside. She surfaced again, streaming seawater. "Let's go to the tunnel," said Sergio, seizing the girl by the arm.

"No," said Giuseppino. "Wait. I'm not properly in yet."

"Come on," Sergio told the girl. "If you can swim well enough, I'll show you a tunnel."

The tunnel, a natural archway in the rock, was dark and full of underwater shadows. Through this archway fish with blue and yellow stripes and staring silver eyes drifted on the currents, grazing on the rock's slimy underside. If you dived, it was possible to plunge through the arch and come up on the other side. Sergio knew full well that Giuseppino was frightened of the place. He swam ahead with the girl beside him, letting his brother splash and trip after them through the shallows, crying, "Wait! Wait!"

"Come into the water," Sergio goaded. "Swim, Giuseppino. Don't splatter about on the edge."

They reached the pool, at whose center Sergio trod water. "Wait for me!" called Giuseppino.

Already they were getting away from him. Giuseppino lowered himself into the water, curling his stomach in, and let go of the rocks. With a great ungainly splashing he descended and gained a purchase on the edge with one toe. Sergio, with a toss of his hair, dived and vanished, coming up on the other side of the tunnel, from which his voice penetrated echoingly, like it was floating up from the crypt of the church. "Come through!" he called to the girl. "There's a great big shoal of fish here!"

The girl dived. Her bare feet splashed and labored on the surface for a moment, then she, too, was gone.

Giuseppino balanced on his rock, alone now, listening to their shouting on the other side. He observed how the *scirocco* left a dusty film on the water, how the sky was becoming overcast and the waves were pounding a little stronger, so that his toes struggled for purchase. "Come on!" called Sergio's strangely echoing voice on the other side of the tunnel. "Come through, Giuseppino!"

A big wave buffeted Giuseppino; curling back off the rocks called Morte delle Barche, it hit him with a hard slap. The water was cold here in the shade, deeper than he had first expected. Giuseppino did not want to swim through the tunnel; he did not want to go near it. It made strange sucking and slapping sounds. Sea anemones like red jellies pulsed on the dark underside of the archway. He was tugged close enough to touch and drew back again in terror: It was icy, like the walls of the freezer in the House at the Edge of Night. The water here was endowed with a powerful undertow. His father had almost drowned in this ocean, years ago.

But he could hear his brother splashing on the other side, the girl's English laughter. "Swim through!" Sergio yelled. "Swim through! You can almost touch the bottom here!"

"Sergio!" Giuseppino called. "Come back!"

"Swim through! The sea's calmer on this side, I promise."

Another big wave. The girl's high laugh. When Giuseppino put out his feet for the rock again he could not feel it. His feet kicked at nothing, dizzily, and he was slipping out and down, into the pool where he came up against the tunnel roof with a smack. He gulped water, sinking, scrabbling to get through the arch in the rock—yes, he would make it through the tunnel now!—he would show them!—and up again the sea brought him, grating his back against the barnacles, and down again, and under, and he was shouting and crying and gulping, flailing against the cold sea, and where was his brother? The sea had changed: It had become a fierce thing, the thing he had always feared it was at heart.

Sergio grabbed him around the waist and hauled him, pushing his head out of the water so that he heaved and honked and spluttered. "Swim," Sergio was grunting, dragging him back toward the shore. "Swim, damn you. If you hadn't panicked you would have made it."

Sergio hauled him out of the water and up across the sand and stood over him, black over the sun, hands on hips. "Why didn't you try properly?"

Giuseppino heaved and coughed. When at last he could speak, he said: "You left me. You didn't help me at all."

"It's not my fault you're ten years old and can't swim."

Giuseppino began, falteringly, to cry. He *could* swim. Hadn't he swum? Lungs burning from his ordeal, eyes hot with tears, he glared at Sergio and at the English girl who was hopping from foot to foot, embarrassed to be caught in the crossfire of their enmity. "You left me," he accused. "I heard you splashing and shouting on the other side. You didn't care what happened to me."

All at once they became aware of a chugging, and now a shout made them both turn. The fisherman 'Ncilino was out there beyond the rock; he had cut his motor and was bobbing up and down on the sluggish waves, his face wearing a startled, naked look without his sunglasses. "Boys!" he called. "Is this girl called Pamela?"

The girl nodded. "Her parents want her back. You two Espositos are going to be in trouble—the whole island's looking for her."

"Look what you did!" cried Sergio. "I was taking good care of her, but you delayed us with your splashing and your crying and now we'll both be in trouble."

Sanding himself off with the gritty towel their mother had sent, hauling his bike up by the handlebars, Giuseppino turned and began to run barefoot toward the road, shedding sand and water. Driving his bike ahead of him, sobbing, he climbed the hill to the town, Sergio following close behind, a little abashed at his brother's grief.

When they reached the bar, Giuseppino buried his head in their mother's waist, and naturally Sergio got the blame of it. And though Robert listened and listened to both sides of the tale, he felt he could no longer arbitrate between them, as though the boys had descended into some private battleground in which they must fight until one, at last, emerged the victor. "We should never have sent them to the ocean," lamented Amedeo in private to his wife, that afternoon.

"There are some things that children must fight out alone," said Pina, which only confirmed his worst fears about the matter.

THE TWO BOYS WERE sent that evening to make their confession to the priest. Grandmother Pina had always been adamant about the Sant'Agata festival, and she felt that a little Catholic fear might improve matters now. "Go and talk to Father Marco, like your grandmother says," Maria-Grazia ordered. "And come back ready to get on with each other. Didn't you agree at the beginning of the summer to be friends?"

Sullenly, both boys went to church. Father Ignazio was gone now: He had retired to his little house with the oleander bushes, replaced by a new and earnest man named Father Marco just out of the seminary. Father Ignazio's eyes, always a little mischievous, had been a reassurance during the long and protracted confessions preceding the Sant'Agata festivals of other years. They had reassured you that no sin was unredeemable if only you were to confess it. The eyes of the young Father Marco were pious and impossibly sad. Even before you confessed your sins, he looked disappointed in you. When Sergio found himself on the other side of the grille, behind the little silk curtain, looking into the mournful eyes of Father Marco, sobs of guilt rose up in his throat. He blurted out a confused, choking confession: "And I didn't mean to—I didn't want to kill him—only I was so angry at him that just for a moment I hoped, I actually hoped a little bit, that he would dro-o-own—"

Every widow of the Sant'Agata Committee was engaged in the ceremonial polishing of the saint's statue at the back of the church, and the separating of sprigs of oleander for her starlike crown. Thus, every widow of the Sant'Agata Committee heard Sergio's grief-stricken sobbing, and his long howl, and by nightfall it was known all over the island that Sergio Esposito had tried to kill his brother.

Like the rumor about Uncle Flavio and Pierino, it was one from which Sergio was never fully to recover.

"Why don't you both go to high school on the mainland?" suggested Maria-Grazia. "Bepe can take you across each morning on his ferry. There's a whole big world out there, and Lord knows there's space enough in it for both of you, if you can just bear each other's company until then."

Why, mourned Amedeo, must everybody always be encouraging them to leave?

AFTER THAT YEAR'S SANT'AGATA FESTIVAL, Giuseppino became quiet and secretive. He locked himself in his bedroom each afternoon, refusing even to play football with his friends Pietro and Calogero anymore, and studied with such ferocity it was as though he and the schoolbooks were engaged in a fight to the death. Sergio began to complain that his own books were going missing in those months, that Giuseppino was stealing them. But this was never proven, for the books were always found in their proper places when the house was searched. Giuseppino became so immersed in his studies that he emerged from his room only to eat and visit the bathroom, and even that he did reluctantly, rushing up and down the hall with a line between his eyebrows and a newly developed scholar's hunch. At the end of the year he passed his exams so conclusively and astoundingly, exclaimed the new teacher, Professoressa Valente, that she recommended he be moved up a year. He was the cleverest boy she had ever taught.

When Giuseppino's report was delivered to his parents, there were firecrackers on the veranda of the House at the Edge of Night. The tourists cheered and capered, believing it some local festival. Sergio stood at the edge of the party. For when had he ever been given such a celebration—when had firecrackers lit up the dark for him?

Thus, when the time came, Giuseppino went ahead of his elder brother to the mainland *liceo*, seated alone on the thwart of the *Santa Maria del Mare*, a neat parcel of books in his lap.

"I'll go to university," declared Giuseppino, to approving murmurs from his elders. "I see that it's better to study hard now."

"What about me?" raged Sergio to his mother. "I wanted to go to university, but Giuseppino's got ahead of me now, on purpose, to stop me doing it. I know he has."

"Well, can't the two of you study?" asked Maria-Grazia. "Why does his studying stop you from studying?"

But Sergio, in some obscure way, still clearly felt that his destiny hung upon his brother's. The two of them were separate now, Maria-Grazia saw; they had undergone some irreversible schism the summer of the almost-drowning, so that now they merely coexisted under the roof of the House at the Edge of Night, no longer really brothers. And now, too late, Sergio wanted Giuseppino back; now it was he who roamed about disconsolately with their slingshots and marbles, hoping Giuseppino would leave his books and join the games in the piazza, desperate for some friendly word.

"Did I do something wrong?" Maria-Grazia murmured in her husband's ear the night after this disagreement. "Should I have been with them more as children? Was it a mistake to put so much of myself into the bar?"

But how could she have given them more? She had felt herself stretched thin as wire in the boys' first years, torn between the demands of the business and the demands of her children until hardly a scrap remained of the girl who had once presided over the counter of the House at the Edge of Night, who had gone fearlessly about the island in pursuit of justice for Flavio, who had been the only island girl to win Robert Esposito's heart.

"But what if I'd been the one in the bar?" reasoned her husband now. "What if I'd been the one putting aside the money in the cash-box to buy them new bicycles, saving to send them to university? And you'd been the one to care for them as babies? What then? What difference would it have made?"

"It would certainly have been more usual," said Maria-Grazia, who had endured her share of scolding from the island's widows, and the incomprehension of the fishermen who wondered why she stood at the counter while Robert wandered about the island with a baby carriage.

"Do you love them?" Robert asked her now, a little stern.

"Sì, caro. Of course."

"Well, then."

"You know what the widows say in the bar."

"Oh, to hell with the widows in the bar!"

She laughed, and he seized her around the waist, as though they were still fresh lovers, as they had been during the war. "What they need," said Robert, "is love. I didn't have it, and I know that. Anything else is just incidental."

And yet—though she never could have brought herself to articulate such a feeling out loud, or even in her own mind—she had never loved her sons as much as she had loved Robert. It had been her initial, guilty thought, on seeing the infant Sergio, that the suspicion she had held during her pregnancy was now confirmed: Yes, she loved her son, but no rush of affection had displaced Robert from his place of honor in her heart. Nothing had: no absence, no humiliation. Not her children's births. As she watched the boys grow up, this secret had become blacker and more awful to her, a thing she felt certain her sons must sense, that was perhaps responsible for their constant warring, their dissatisfaction with everything. "It will all come right," murmured Robert, as though he understood.

AMEDEO WOKE ONE MORNING IN 1971 TO FIND PINA TURNED AWAY from him a little, one hand gripping the blanket. Ordinarily, her side of the bed would be abandoned before seven, her hobbling footsteps audible in another corner of the great house, moving about her early morning tasks. Now Amedeo touched her and found her cool. His cry woke the rest of the house. The others came running, and Maria-Grazia held before her mother's face the spotted mirror from the bathroom shelf. The mirror remained clear.

All that day, the House at the Edge of Night was full of weeping. Amedeo wandered from room to room, his head bowed, his hands searching the walls, inconsolable. The death notices were put up, pasted with their black borders to every flat surface in the town, and mourners came to sit with Amedeo on the veranda. No one had been as loved on the island as Pina Vella.

The poet Mario Vazzo returned for the funeral; so did Professor Vincio and a handful of archaeologists, and those emigrants of Castellamare origin who remembered the schoolmistress from their humbler days: sons and daughters of the island who now wore loud foreign clothes and drove foreign cars. The church was so full that Father Marco was obliged to open both doors and shout the funeral Mass over the heads of the congregation to reach the crowd outside. Afterward, Pina was buried in a plot not far from Gesuina's grave, and the islanders fought decorously for space to lay their particular flowers. The florist Gisella had been up all night winding funeral wreaths of trumpet vine and bougainvillea and blue plumbago, Pina's favorites. Always, Pina had loved the native flowers of the island, for never in her life had she lived away from it.

That evening as the sun set, Maria-Grazia roamed alone about the island, limping in the uncomfortable shoes purchased from Valeria's hardware store for the funeral, gathering more flowers. For, as decked as her mother's grave was, it still did not seem enough to her. Maria-Grazia wandered until nightfall, allowing herself to weep, seeking greater and greater armfuls of plumbago and oleander. At eight o'clock, when she had piled the grave with a hundred boughs, she saw Robert coming to meet her across the fields. He stopped before her, and rubbed the tears from her face with his thumb. Bending, without speaking, he helped her arrange the boughs about Pina Vella's grave until every one was used, a great canvas of island colors. "Is that enough?" asked Robert at last.

"*Sì, amore,*" said Maria-Grazia. "That's enough."

Now she composed herself a little, took a handkerchief from her pocket, and wiped the tears from her cheeks and the pollen from her hands. Robert put his arm about her, and together they returned to the bar to meet the crowd of mourners.

That night, Mario Vazzo sought out Amedeo, and sat beside him at the edge of the veranda. Amedeo clung to a bottle of *arancello*. The poet was to return to the mainland tomorrow. "I don't know if I'll come back here again," said Mario Vazzo. "I'm getting old. But I wanted to be present today—for Pina—to honor her. A great woman, she was, a woman unlike any other I've met. . . ." Mario Vazzo attempted a few more words about Pina, then fell into a contemplative silence, massaging his chin.

Amedeo anchored himself with both hands by the bottle of *arancello*. He had never said anything to Pina regarding his suspicions about the poet. Now he accosted Signor Vazzo instead, eyebrows bristling: "You loved my wife, didn't you?"

The poet, elderly and stiff of motion, drew forward a little toward the doctor. He thought for a long time, watching the lights of a liner ply the horizon in search of some other, larger island, and eventually decided to remain silent.

This maddened Amedeo. Eyes puffed with weeping, gripping the bottle of *arancello* by the neck, he spoke at length about Pina—the grace of her, the strength—until the poor poet was reduced to tears. There had never been a better woman born on the island, persisted Amedeo. By Sant'Agata and Holy Gesù, how could she be gone? "And you loved her, too, Signor Vazzo," he declared, some coldness in him making him repeat the accusation. "You're weeping for her right now, and yet you won't admit it. All that stuff in your poetry book about making love with an island woman in the caves by the sea. An island woman making love with Odisseo in the caves by the sea. An island of black water and many stars. You meant Pina, and that's what you did with her, and you won't do me the decency of admitting so."

Mario Vazzo swept this accusation away with one fierce motion. Rising from the table, he left, and departed from the House at the Edge of Night, never to return.

Now Maria-Grazia, who had witnessed this altercation, sat down beside her father. "Mamma told me all about her friendship with Mario Vazzo," she said. "They used to walk about the island. They sat on the cliff above the caves by the sea and read poetry. Nothing more than that. You have been an old fool, Papà, to brood on it all these years."

"Did they love each other?" asked Amedeo.

"Not the way Mamma loved you. It wasn't a matter of rolling about in the caves by the sea, if that's what you mean. No wonder Signor Vazzo left like that."

"But why didn't you tell me so? If she talked to you about it, *cara*."

"She asked me not to. Not until after her death."

An innocent liaison, then, or innocent enough—walking about the island, reading poetry. Had a part of Pina wanted him to believe in the truth of the affair all these years, to believe she was as capable of betrayal as he, just once, had been? "And that's all?" he said.

"That's all."

So, in the end, she had been better than him. He had always suspected it to be the truth; now he saw it confirmed. Tears of remorse stung the corners of Amedeo's eyes, mingling with those of grief. "We can remedy this," consoled Maria-Grazia. "I know where Mamma used to keep his address."

AMEDEO WROTE TO MARIO VAZZO the following week, begging his pardon for the offense he had caused. Mario wrote back, and for the rest of that year he and Amedeo found themselves corresponding, mailing each other twice-weekly letters in which they extolled the virtues of Pina: her beauty, her fierceness, her grace. From this, oddly, Amedeo derived a vestige of comfort. Otherwise, for several weeks after Pina's death, he was as lost, as constantly searching, as he had been when he was a foundling, or when his sons were first missing in the war. He walked each morning to the cemetery, taking a child's camping stool that had been Sergio and Giuseppino's. On it, he installed himself at the foot of Pina's grave. There, his white eyebrows blown by the sea winds, his hands calcifying around the end of his walking stick, he would address Pina, exhort her, murmur expressions of tenderness. From the graveyard he moved restlessly on to her other haunts, and it was in vain for Maria-Grazia to try to persuade him home. The path Pina had taken to Mass each Sunday, the schoolhouse, her old chair under the bougainvillea, the stone room by the courtyard where she had loved him, brought forth their children, and at last died. This place was her, its air, its light. He spoke constantly to her as he crossed and recrossed the island. Then, one day, as though Pina had at last spoken back from the faraway world she now inhabited, Amedeo gained a kind of resolve.

That night, Maria-Grazia found him sorting his belongings, stowing the most important in the old Campari liquor case where he had kept his medical instruments during the war. He became irritable when questioned, though previously he had sought out her company whenever he was in the house, unable to bear her leaving him alone. "I'm tidying, that's all," he said. "Now shouldn't you be minding the bar, Mariuzza *cara*?" He could still be heard thumping about behind the door when the bar closed, muttering to himself as he deliberated over each object before either packing it in the liquor case or setting it aside.

Once his belongings were in order, he became careless about the ones that had not made it into the liquor case, as if they were no longer his. Sometimes he would come upon some object in the house with a start of scientific interest—the bloodstained statue of Sant'Agata, say, or a lesser family photograph not consigned to the box—examining them as though they were new to him. Soon after, he began to go through his book of stories and his other papers, discarding some pages and annotating others, pausing to note in the margin the circumstantial details of the records: "Tale recounted to me in widow Agata's house, autumn 1960," or "An interesting truth-comes-to-light narrative belonging to my time as a *medico condotto* in Bagno a Ripoli." Those pages that were discarded he burned, with serene abandon, in an old tin can in the courtyard, and as he poked the flames with a stick he, too, seemed aflame, and almost happy.

During these weeks, his grandsons abandoned the aloofness of their late teenagehood and became small boys again, tearfully following him about the house. Sergio even took the much-abused copy of *The Two Brothers* and repaired it with tape, and Maria-Grazia found him in a corner of the veranda one day after school, poring over its pages. "Read to us again, *nonno*," Sergio begged his grandfather. But Amedeo merely wandered up to his room at the top of the house to continue his packing. "If you want a job to do, Sergio," he said, a little sternly, "you can help me transcribe these stories. I've a few about the place on scraps of paper that want copying into the book." This Sergio did, hunched over the desk that had once been the old doctor's, adding his scratchy handwriting to his grandfather's elegant script. While Sergio was engaged in this labor, Amedeo hauled his old medical periodicals off the shelves and threw them away. "Nothing is now true that was true when I studied as a doctor," he announced. "So I might as well get rid of this old stuff."

The following evening, he called both Sergio and Giuseppino up to his study. The boys stood before him, keeping an arm's length apart. Sergio was bowed, a little awkward. Giuseppino tapped one foot against the lion's foot of the mangy sofa and frowned at the floor.

"Boys," said Amedeo. "I want to talk to you about my will." Though the plan had been forming in him since the beginning of the boys' enmity, he was nervous now in bringing it forth, and found himself puffing for breath, delaying a little.

Giuseppino kept looking at the floor; Sergio raised his head in respectful attention.

"When I die," said Amedeo at last, "I'm going to leave you two things. Don't tell your mother or father. This is only for you to know. Firstly I'm leaving you my book of stories, and secondly the bar. You're to take good care of both." Amedeo heaved himself upright in his chair, and tapped Giuseppino's knee with the end of his walking stick. "Do you hear me, Giuseppino?"

For Giuseppino was still sullen, kicking the lion's foot. But when he raised his head, his grandfather saw that he was staving off tears. "You aren't to die," Giuseppino said. "You aren't to die, *nonno*. Stop talking about it."

Fear united the boys, temporarily. "He's right," said Sergio. "You mustn't die. You mustn't talk to us like this about dying. We'll bring you to the hospital."

Amedeo raised his hand. "I'm ninety-six," he said. "I'm not about to go to the hospital. To tell them what? That I'm dying. That will be news to them, I'm sure, that a man of ninety-six years is dying. Ha!"

"You aren't to die," continued Giuseppino, kicking and kicking at the lion's foot until the varnish was all scuffed away.

"The two of you have a duty, when I leave you the bar," said Amedeo, endeavoring to steer the conversation back in a sensible direction. "Your Mamma and Papà can't run the place on their own forever. One day they, too, will be old. Then what's going to happen to this business we've all tended for fifty years? That's why I'm leaving it to you now. To ensure its future. Do you understand?"

"But which one is to run it?" said Sergio.

"Both of you," said Amedeo. "I'm dividing it between you evenly."

Sergio felt a little light-headed, picturing the two of them condemned to spend eternity on either side of the counter, fat island men like Filippo and Santino Arcangelo, perpetually tethered one to the other.

After that day, neither brother spoke about the conversation with their grandfather. But Giuseppino became more tightly wound, Sergio more bowed and hunched, more endlessly apologetic.

By the time Sant'Agata's festival came round, Amedeo had cataloged and parceled up his life. Without farewell, he went to sleep on the sofa, and was found that night, long after dark, resting on his back with hands folded, as though to save his family even the trouble of positioning him for the grave. He had waited just four months to follow Pina, and since no other islander had died in the interim, he had the victory of being buried—in the giant coffin specially made for him—in the adjacent grave.

In the hollowed-out grief that followed the passing of her mother and father, Maria-Grazia felt weightless, as though the ceiling had been ripped off the House at the Edge of Night, leaving her pitifully exposed. Besides, a second wound had opened in her heart after her father's passing, a wound that she would allow herself to admit to no one but Robert: that after all the years she had tended the bar in his honor, her father had not left it to her. The boys did not want the place. This matter of the will would cause nothing but trouble. Pina would never have allowed it. And now once again she, Maria-Grazia, felt herself at the helm of a wayward ship, obliged to steer carefully on others' behalf, while only rough waters lay ahead.

Robert, to her surprise, agreed in some respect with Amedeo. "He's forcing them to bring this enmity of theirs out into the open," he said. "Perhaps it's for the best. We're both of us more than forty. Every other business has some younger relative lined up, and how could your father have chosen between Sergio and Giuseppino? How could any one of us have done that?"

"But why," she wept, feeling like a slighted girl, "didn't he leave it to me?"

And yet, as winter passed over, her father's presence began to hang about the bar on cool nights, overseeing the adding of the accounts, guiding her hands as she plied the levers of the coffee machine, stepping in with a clearing of the throat as though it could settle the debates between the fishermen and the elderly *scopa* players once and for all, if only it could make itself heard. In deference to this new household spirit, Maria-Grazia hung a photograph of Amedeo above the counter. She chose the first picture that had ever been taken of him, by his bride, Pina Vella, his medical bag in one hand and his book of stories under one arm. Thus her mother was present, too, by implication, in the glance of startled love the young Amedeo directed beyond the lens. The picture, spotted now with age, followed Maria-Grazia with its eyes about the room like a *Cristo Pantocrator*, fixing her with that same look of blindsided love he had once bestowed on his young wife. Now she thought she understood. If her Papà had left the bar to her, the time would have come when she herself would have been forced to choose between the boys, and she never could have done it. "Papà," Maria-Grazia prayed, forgiving him, "watch over this place."

V

THE BOYS KEPT PEACE JUST LONG ENOUGH TO BURY THEIR GRAND-
father. Then they made bitter war—first over the bar, which neither
of them wanted, then over the book of stories, which both of them
coveted. Now, in the face of their grandfather's absurd, good-hearted
gift, the unrest that had simmered for years inside the walls of the
House at the Edge of Night at last came forth into the open. Maria-
Grazia, climbing from the courtyard to the top of the house with a
bundle of dry sheets, pausing to dry her eyes on one corner of a pil-
lowcase (for she allowed herself to cry for her Mamma and Papà a
little as she went unobserved about the household chores, though
never in the bar), heard them hissing imprecations at each other behind the door of Sergio's room, and feared this intense, private war
they were waging. For days the boys remained locked in battle, pursuing each other through the house whose air was still thick with the
scent of Amedeo's funeral flowers, until Concetta confiscated the
book of stories and carried it away to her house on Via Cavour.

The following Monday, Concetta's front window was found shattered in the early hours. Nothing was missing but the book, which
had been taken from the old cashbox in the bottom of the dresser. *Il
conte*'s land agent Santino Arcangelo, her brother, attended the scene
and wrote everything down in a notebook as though he were a real
poliziotto. Whoever the criminal might be (here Santino held up a
shard of glass shrewdly, as he had seen a detective do once on the
television), he had clearly known Concetta well enough to understand where to search for the book. It was the first robbery to take

place on the island in living memory. To everyone but Maria-Grazia and Robert, it was evident that the younger Esposito boy had done it, especially when Sergio came running to report that his brother could not be found. Maria-Grazia and Robert, for their part, closed the bar and searched the island.

In the House at the Edge of Night, nobody slept.

Giuseppino called them three days later from Uncle Flavio's house in Surrey, a place that had always been mythical to Maria-Grazia, now made oddly real by the tinny, insubstantial voice of her younger son calling from the other end of its English phone line. The voice that reached her was small and a little frightened. "I'm here with Uncle Flavio," he said. "Yes, yes, I'm fine. Mamma, you don't need to worry. Only, I'm not coming home for a while." A pause, a crackle. "I'll find work in London, yes. Or study at university. Uncle Flavio's helping me with all that. I've got my English passport—I've finished school—why shouldn't I?" Another pause. "I'll be home for Christmas, if I can."

"And what about the book of stories?" said Maria-Grazia, trying to speak to him calmly, as Robert did. Giuseppino took a long time to answer, and when he did his voice came a little stronger. "Oh, that. Don't worry, it's safe and sound. I'll mail Sergio a copy."

Sergio, throwing himself facedown on his bed, wept and wept with rage.

Sure enough, a parcel arrived with an English postmark, addressed to Sergio. Giuseppino had made a photocopy of their grandfather's book. The copies were smudgy and rippled as though they had been written underwater. Maria-Grazia knew that Giuseppino was ridiculing his brother; it was the original book that both of them wanted.

She watched with concern as Sergio steeled himself, determined to claim the sour victory that was left to him, the victory of being the better son. "You can leave, too, if you want to," she told him. "You've always known that. There's no problem with the two of you leaving, both at once, and our managing the bar."

The islanders had always muttered darkly about Sergio, since the summer of the almost-drowning of his brother, but now the tide of opinion had turned in Sergio's favor. "That Giuseppino always thought he was too good for Castellamare," said the elderly *scopa* players. And Agata-the-fisherwoman: "If Sergio really did try to drown Giuseppino when they were children, at least I'm beginning to understand why."

MEANWHILE, SERGIO SURPRISED EVERYBODY by refusing to leave. That autumn, he went to the Castellamare Savings and Loan Company with ambition, for the first time, in his heart. He wore the suit he had worn for his grandfather's funeral, already straining at the crotch and stomach after his latest growth spurt, flapping comically at the ankles. He carried in his hand an old attaché case of Amedeo's with the bar's accounts copied out in neat pencil on five sheets of school graph paper. Inside the bank, he waited on a carpet-covered sofa, hoping no neighbor would spot him through the great glass windows. An assistant from the mainland called him into the little box of an office where Gesuina's kitchen had once been, and poured him mainland coffee.

"I'd like a loan," Sergio said, when he had explained the workings of the bar's accounts.

"To modernize your business?" asked the mainland assistant, running a pencil down the figures, nodding in approval.

"To buy my brother's share."

"How much do you own now?"

"Half. But I'm going to be the one who runs it from now on—he's left—and look at the way our profits have been rising, year on year." For Sergio had drawn a graph for the years 1960 to '71, with an arrow marked "projected growth" shooting beyond, into the future, full of tightly coiled promise.

The assistant made a calculation on a sheet of watermarked notepaper and nodded in satisfaction. "We won't offer a loan without security," he said. "My advice would be to mortgage your share and pay your brother off with that. We'd value your business at about six million *lire*. We could offer you a mortgage for half that sum, plus a little extra for refurbishments or a new car."

"Extra?"

"Yes. Say three and a half or four million total. Wouldn't a van be convenient, like the other business owners have?"

"And when would I repay?"

"Over the next thirty years. At a rate of seven percent."

Sergio leaned forward and cleared the gravel from his throat. "Who owns the bar if I do that?" he said.

"You," said the assistant, "own it all."

The assistant drew up the papers. Sergio carried them back to the House at the Edge of Night. The irony of mortgaging one-half of the bar to pay off the other did not escape him. And yet the thought of Giuseppino's face at the news was a grim kind of satisfaction in itself.

Giuseppino, on the other end of the telephone, indeed exploded with such loud rage when the plan was announced to him that it was as though he were back on the island for an instant, filling the house with his noise. But Sergio spoke over him with quiet persistence. "I've valued the business for you. I've done it fairly, based on the rule the bank gave me—the value of half the house plus half of three years' profits. You'd get a lot of money, Giuseppino. Millions of *lire*. You could go to university, like you wanted. You could do whatever you liked with it."

"You're driving me off the island!" cried Giuseppino. "You mean to get rid of me! I didn't say when I went to see Zio Flavio that I was leaving for good!"

"You left! You took the book, you ran off, you didn't want the bar."

Giuseppino, in a small contrary voice said, "I might want to come back. How can I know?"

"Then come back," said Sergio, "if you want to." All at once, his chest was a barrel of longing—for what, he did not know at first, until it came to him from a long way off that what he missed was his brother.

"Come back," said Sergio, a little pleading. Giuseppino huffed in tears or anger, and put down the phone.

The bar was mortgaged. Giuseppino sent back the papers fully signed. It was Maria-Grazia who opened them, and wept in rage when she got out of Sergio, by slow degrees, the whole sorry story of what he had done. "You've risked the future of the House at the Edge of Night," she cried, as fierce as her mother Pina, "mortgaged it to the d'Isantus, your grandfather's old enemies, and for what—some schoolboy feud, some quarrel with your brother? Seven percent? Do you think interest rates have always been at seven percent, Sergio? Do you think they'll be so for the next thirty years? Is this the kind of mortgage a good businessman would ever take out?"

Sergio, who in truth knew nothing about interest rates or good business, hunched behind the counter and muttered, "I mean to pay it all back."

But in burdening himself with this mortgage, he had only shackled himself further to the place.

Giuseppino did not come back. He mailed them a photograph of himself when he graduated from university, looking fierce in a black gown and card-lined mortarboard, standing before a screen on which was printed a square of grass, a brick building, an impossibly cyan sky. In spite of the fact that he was still a little in disgrace on the island, it was added to the array on the stairs.

That summer, Sergio increased the business's opening hours, replaced the old coffee machine, and with the profits from sales of ice cream—more than he needed to make his payment to the savings bank—had a neon sign installed at last. It was hoisted onto the front of the bar with ropes by the builders Tonino and 'Ncilino. Now, the veranda glowed with a mystical green light. This light drew the local wildlife in all its eerie variations. Lizards basked beneath the neon tubes as though in the heat of an alien sun, and great velvety moths bumped up against them, making sparks. Sergio ordered a football table, and sat up all night putting it together with a screwdriver and

270 little white screws that blistered his fingers. Now tournaments were held every Saturday afternoon and Tuesday evening.

Sergio replaced the ancient wireless radio with a color television, subscribed to the sports channels, and in a single stroke, as his mother had done a generation ago, restored the bar to the heart of the island. For now, the neighbors crowded to the bar to watch the mainland football matches and the dubbed dramas belonging to the Italian channels, the advertisements for washing machines and window-cleaning solution, the multicolored announcements of the BBC News. With the extra money the savings bank had offered, he had already bought a little three-wheeled Ape van like the one the builder Tonino drove, and repainted the whole of the building. The place seemed to be entering an era of prosperity, as it had when Amedeo first opened its doors. And yet, to Maria-Grazia, it seemed that nothing changed any longer in the House at the Edge of Night. Sergio had settled down behind the counter to pay off his debt. Giuseppino, meanwhile, in London, collected about himself effortlessly the trophies of a successful life, and mailed each one back across the sea in a triumphant photograph: girlfriend, wife, house, motorcars. He seemed immune to his parents' professions of forgiveness over the staticky long-distance telephone line; he would not come home even to visit. Behind the counter of the bar, Sergio waited, still in his high school shirts and short boyhood trousers, refusing to let Maria-Grazia mend the holes in his vests or cut his hair.

And again, oddly, she felt that she was losing herself a little, as she had when she was first a mother. For hadn't it always been her bar?

"If only he'd make up his mind to marry," Maria-Grazia lamented to Robert in the stone room by the courtyard, which was now theirs. "Or if only Giuseppino would bring that English wife to meet us, and make his peace with his brother. Any change would do." But Sergio, stubborner than his brother in the end, persisted in his loneliness, sitting like a martyr behind the counter as Flavio had once knelt in self-abasement before the statue of the saint.

And now, until some change came to shake the bar from its slumber, Maria-Grazia felt that it would remain as hopelessly locked in time as it had been in the last years of the war—Giuseppino absent, Sergio absent in his mind, and everything out of place.

So it was that for a long time nothing happened at the House at the Edge of Night.

VI

THE CHANGE THAT AT LAST CAME TO THE BAR, AND TO SERGIO ES-
posito, was the arrival of the child Maddalena. She was born feetfirst
like her father, Sergio, had been, disconsolate and roaring, in the
same week that the bar's three televisions broadcast the toppling of
the Berlin Wall.

It had been an odd year to begin with. In January, between *Santo
Stefano* and the festival of the *Epifania*, Carmela d'Isantu had died.
Andrea d'Isantu had returned to Castellamare for the funeral. He refused to see Maria-Grazia, but all the same the islanders had revived
the ancient gossip about his throwing of sand at her windows, his tossing and turning in bed sick with love for her for days at a time; they
whispered about it in the corners of the bar in a way Maria-Grazia
found tiresome and infuriating now, forty years after it had been interesting news to anybody. She had glimpsed Andrea this time, across
the funeral crowd at the windswept burial of *signora la contessa*, a
small thin man with extravagant eyebrows, more old than middle-
aged.

"How can that be Andrea d'Isantu?" she marveled to Concetta, as
the two of them walked home arm in arm.

"But we're all getting old," said Concetta. "Haven't you noticed
lately? Bepe, who used to be so handsome, has a paunch the size of a
wine barrel, and Totò's hair is all gone, and Agata-the-fisherwoman
wears a housecoat and slippers and shuffles about just like Signora
Gesuina used to."

Maria-Grazia was forced to concede that this was the truth.

But still, how could she and Robert be old? The two of them, who still slept entwined like teenagers in the stone room that she continued to think of as her mother and father's, who danced at the Sant'Agata festival with the same abandon with which they had danced on their wedding night. Her life seemed to her an odd thing, a thing that had dragged all the time when happiness still seemed far off, when she was a girl in leg braces, and at last, when happiness had been afforded her, seemed to have rushed over at a breathless speed, leaving no room for thought.

Even Concetta was past fifty. She had never married, but all the same she had recently acquired the custody of a child. This child, a formidable boy of five named Enzo, had been her brother Filippo's— still was, if truth be told. But the boy had lost his mother, and as soon as he could walk he had begun to roam the island, catching lizards, hitting things with sticks, launching himself down the steepest and most rock-strewn of the island's hillsides on a blue plastic donkey with red wheels. By four, he had become quite ungovernable, the elderly *scopa* players reported, for Filippo Arcangelo's raised voice had been heard all about the south part of the town from his open windows, exhorting the child down from ladders and out of cupboards and off the great towers of boxes in the grocer's back room.

Now Concetta herself, who had not spoken with either of her brothers in thirty years, became stern. "I'll go over there," she told Maria-Grazia, "and see that they're treating him right."

Filippo, it emerged, had not mistreated Enzo. Rather, it was Enzo who had the upper hand. Concetta found her aging brother seated on the back step of the grocer's, while the boy ran roaring circles in the yard around him, covered in syrup and flour. "So you've heard, too, sister," he said, raising his hangdog eyes to her, "that I can't control my child, and here you are to pass judgment."

"I didn't come here to pass judgment, you fool," said Concetta, "but to offer you help, for Lord knows I was wild, too, when I was that age. Enough of this silly argument between us. The boy has no mother, and I came here to tell you that he's got an aunt, even if you and I can't be civil to each other. Whenever he's too much trouble, you're to send him to me. However wild this boy is, I was much wilder. Enzo—come here!"

The boy, startled, obeyed. "You're to come to visit me sometimes," said Concetta. "Would you like that?"

"Sì, Zia," said Enzo meekly, for he had heard a hundred stories about his fearsome aunt. The following weekend, with his little grocery bag full of belongings, riding his blue plastic donkey, he came to spend the day at the blue house with the orange trees, trussed and buttoned in his Sunday clothes. A little dark boy, as undersized as she had been, with thin wrists and ankles, he moved his aunt to tenderness, and she decided to occupy herself with bringing him up.

Concetta had not attained any great height or breadth, but in all other respects she was a large person. The life in her radiated forth when she was troubled just as when she was merry, a fierce kind of energy that made her hair frizz out from her head, her cheeks gleam like a girl's. She was the equal of the boy Enzo, and Enzo sensed it from the beginning and behaved.

Industrious in middle age, Concetta had thrown her energies into the planting of a garden. It engulfed her house on all sides, so green it hurt the eyes. An ingenious system of perforated hoses watered the rows of vegetables each morning. Concetta had planted vines of *zucchine*, rows of tomatoes and aubergines, and pots of basil. The basil grew at alarming speed, each clump tall and wide enough to swallow up the child. Along the front of the house grew tangled, floor-creeping vines of watermelon whose tendrils encroached under the windows and edged eerily round the doors. Between the orange trees grew asparagus, fennel, mint, and great artichokes bristling with silver spears. Concetta let Enzo loose in this jungle. "Scream and hit things with sticks all you want," she told him. "I don't mind what you do." Placing a man's greasy *Borsalino* on her head, she began serenely to cut a row of bull's heart tomatoes from their spidery stems and left the child to his own devices.

Soon Enzo came creeping back, all his roaring and hitting used up now that no one much minded whether or not he did it. "The *cuori di bue* are coming ready all at once," Concetta said, without turning to look at the child, for she knew he was as timid as a lizard despite all his noise. "We'll make great salads out of them, and rice balls with mozzarella. Will you help me?"

"Sì, *Zia*," said Enzo. All afternoon he worked by his aunt's side, rolling rice balls and working bread dough and lifting the great colander to shake the bitter dew from the salted *melanzane,* until he was quite exhausted.

"There," said Concetta with satisfaction, delivering the boy back to his father in his filthy Sunday clothes. "He's calm. You're to send him to me whenever you want."

From then on, Enzo spent half his time at his father's and, when he couldn't be trusted to behave tamely, he packed up his little bag and came to spend the day or the week at his Zia Concetta's house. Though he loved her as well as a mother in the end, he never quite lost his awe of her. Even when he was at his wildest she could still outstrip him in running and roaring, still push him with alarming speed on his blue plastic donkey, whipping the air from his lungs. Having met his match in his formidable *zia*, Enzo resolved, in her presence at least, to be calm.

In this way, the feud between the Arcangelo brothers and their sister, Concetta, which had simmered ever since she defected to the House at the Edge of Night, became a thing with less sting in it, still carried on for old times' sake, but no longer worth speaking about. In deference to his sister, Filippo Arcangelo even began sending spare tourists up the hill from Arcangelo's Beach Bar to the House at the Edge of Night, though Santino Arcangelo, furious, did his best to catch them and bring them back again, "For," as he said, "there's family feeling, and then there's plain stupidity, brother."

In February the child Enzo turned five, and became calmer still. The final descendant of Vincenzo the artist on his mother's side, he had discovered pencils and paper. "Good," murmured Concetta to Maria-Grazia, watching Enzo feast on a handful of *cassata* at the counter of the bar, a stick of chalk in the other hand, sketching the elderly *scopa* players in unflattering detail. "He'll be good now, and go to school quietly, a thing I never managed to do."

"How did you calm him?" asked Maria-Grazia, for even she had been a little alarmed at the child's roaring.

Concetta said, startled, "But Mariuzza, with kindness—the very same way you tamed me."

And strange it was, thought Maria-Grazia, that the little straggle-haired girl in the white sundress, gobbling *arancini* and sour *limonata*, had grown to a woman of such strength, the most enduring friend of her life.

IN MARCH ANOTHER GREAT EVENT had occurred. At last, when everybody had given up hope in him, Sergio Esposito had brought home a girl to the House at the Edge of Night.

Sergio was thirty-five, and for seventeen years Maria-Grazia and Robert had begged him to leave the island to seek his fortune, to marry, to do whatever he wanted except sit hunched behind the counter in his graying high school polo shirts, looking as though he wanted to be elsewhere. If he did it to spite his brother, the real pity, Maria-Grazia felt, was that his brother, immersed in a life of his own two thousand miles away, did not seem to have noticed. Now, without any word of warning, Sergio led a girl through the door of the bar, stood her before them, and informed his parents and the assembled customers, "Mamma, Dad, this is Pamela."

Neat, small, Maria-Grazia noted approvingly, a little person with red-dyed hair that clung to her head like a bathing cap, the girl stood before them and said, "*Buongiorno, piacere*," over and over, for those were the only two words she knew.

"You are American?" asked Maria-Grazia, and the girl said, "No, no—English."

"Pamela and I have been seeing each other for a while," announced Sergio, as though he had only just recalled the fact, "and we're having a baby."

At this, a great rejoicing erupted in the House at the Edge of Night. The elderly customers would have greeted anything in female form, Maria-Grazia knew, from a goat to a *riccio di mare*—but, still, the girl was charmed. A little overwhelmed, she consented to let herself be placed at the best table, and plied with rice balls and presented with flowers. Meanwhile, Maria-Grazia watched her son across the bar and saw him for the first time alight with happiness, possessed by it, no longer hunched and apologetic as he had been since a boy.

BUT SOON, DIFFICULTIES HAD EMERGED. Pamela wanted to have her baby in England. This was the first disagreement that Maria-Grazia overheard between the young couple. Then there were others. Why hadn't he sent out applications for jobs in London, as he had promised? Why did he speak to the baby only in Italian? Where was the money for the plane tickets home?

By "home" the girl meant England. Maria-Grazia listened to these hissed arguments, and worried for her son.

Sergio loved Pamela. Of this Maria-Grazia was certain, for they had come into the bar on that day in March lit up with the auspiciousness, the particularity of their affection, as she and Robert had been. That illumination had continued in Sergio for a little while, suffusing his long face with a youthful sheen as he flung himself into new enterprises in the bar: the installing of a larger television, the systematization of the last half century's accounts, the repair of the cracked veranda tiles. And, inwardly, she and Robert had rejoiced, too, at first. Sergio had occupied too long that odd, shadowy position between childhood and adulthood that on Castellamare could be extended indefinitely, leaving him an overgrown boy in everybody's eyes. She knew what they muttered about him: a man of more than thirty still sleeping in his childhood room, still eating his mother's *ri-*

sotto and baked *melanzane,* dressed in an odd assortment of his high school clothes, keeping company with his childhood acquaintances: Nunzio, the baker's son; Valeria's boy, Peppe, the manager of the hardware store; Calogero, the lawyer. All of them were still children by the rules of Castellamare, stranded behind the counters of family businesses, subjected to the scolding of the grandmothers and the gossip of the elderly *scopa* players, embroiled in weeks of scandal if any one of them should bring home a girl. So the English girl, Pamela, had at first seemed a deliverance to everybody. In Maria-Grazia's experience, the only way to escape such a position was to get married, make money, or leave.

But she had begun to be uneasy when Sergio had poured forth, shortly after their wedding, the story of their love affair. "We met each other before," he cried, exuberant, slopping more wine into everybody's glasses. "As children. I never told you, Mamma, Dad, Zia Concetta. We met in '65."

"How can that be?" said Robert, inclining his head in the direction of the beaming Pamela, but here Sergio spoke again: "Pamela was here as a girl. She came with her parents for a holiday."

Then Sergio recounted how the two of them had become acquainted again, last summer, on the stretch of sand outside *il conte*'s great hotel.

Sergio had the habit of swimming early every Sunday morning from the rocks in front of *il conte*'s fenced square of sand. On this particular morning, Sergio had arrived a little earlier than the others. He had thrown down his bicycle beside the quay as usual and crossed the hot rocks at a run, removing his shoes, his jeans, and the graying polo shirt with the holes under the armpits that Maria-Grazia was always trying to throw out on his behalf, until he stood in his trunks in the hot sea air, ready to plunge. Only then, with acute embarrassment, had he become aware that the nearest plastic recliner was occupied by a young woman, and that she was crying.

Pamela, nodding, laughing a little now, confirmed this account. "My husband and I had just divorced. I came out here for a little holiday. I'd been here as a girl, you see, with my parents, and I re-membered the island."

Sergio had done the only honorable thing to be done in such a situation: He had retrieved his shirt, retrieved his jeans, buckled his belt, sat down beside the stranger, and attempted to comfort her. "A real gentleman," Pamela said, in English. "He asked me about when I last visited the island and I told him, in '65, with my mother and father."

"I was eleven at the time," said Sergio. "And she said she was about eleven, too, and then I asked her name and it was Pamela."

Then he told them how it had come back to him, like a vision: Pamela of the pink bathing suit, plunging beneath the waves to come up streaming seawater, Pamela of the *scirocco* and the caves.

"What Pamela?" asked Concetta, who did not know the story.

"Remember, *Zia*," said Sergio. "The girl we were swimming with the day Giuseppino almost drowned."

This story had troubled Maria-Grazia, though she could not have said why. Only it seemed to her that her son was attaching too much importance to the tale. He had even telephoned his brother to re-count it to him. "What Pamela?" said Giuseppino, too, claiming no knowledge of the angel in the pink bathing suit. When Sergio an-nounced the news of the baby, Giuseppino, on the other end of the telephone, had gone very quiet. He and his own wife, Maria-Grazia knew, had never been able to have a child. "Congratulations," he said in English, and nothing more.

But at first, all had gone well. Then Sergio, in those storm-troubled early days of spring, had attempted to talk to his wife again of the *sci-rocco* and the pink bathing suit and the tunnel through the rocks. Now, it seemed, Pamela was no longer interested in miracles. "Why does it make any difference either way?" was all she said.

"But, Pam, don't you remember it yourself?"

"When was it?" said Pamela. "At the beginning or end of the sum-mer?"

He had always assumed that the incident must stand out to her as

it had stood out over the years to him, a moment of special importance. "The day before Sant'Agata," he said. "Nineteen sixty-five."

Pamela seemed barely to be listening. "I don't know. We went to
Mediterranean places every year—in my mind they get mixed up. I
suppose it must have been me." She shrugged off the question.
"Would it have made a difference?"

And how could he tell her that it would have made a difference,
her not being the real Pamela? She was already a little irritated at his
asking. He became incoherent in his desperation to lay it all before
her. "Don't you remember swimming through the tunnel, the *scirocco*? And then think—what was the chance that I would find you
again? Just like one of my grandfather's stories."

But, "You and your stories!" she hissed now, in inexplicable rage.
"You Espositos and your damned stories! Of *course* it wasn't me!"

They were eye to eye now in the dark of his boyhood room. "I
wasn't even eleven in 1965. Surely you know that." She was the one
who accosted him with words now, while he lay mute, unyielding.
"In the summer of '65 I'd have been *sixteen*, Sergio. I wasn't even
here on the island. We never could have met. You *know* that! Don't
be a child about it. We submitted a marriage application with our
dates of birth."

"Then why did you go along with it? If it was all so ridiculous in
your eyes?"

"I found it *flattering*, Sergio," cried Pamela. "For God's sake! You
pretending I was five years younger than I am. I didn't think you really
believed it! You didn't, did you?"

Sergio felt washed up at the edge of something, hopelessly unrav-
eled; he could not say. There was the baby, he confessed to his
mother, and besides, did it really matter, her being the real Pamela?
No, they would marry either way.

And Pamela, in those weeks, had still loved him. In their wedding
photograph, taken outside the Siracusa registry office on the damp
morning in April when they had held their twenty-minute ceremony

with Maria-Grazia and Robert as witnesses, her little red-dyed head emerged from a puff of white organza, resting affectionately on Sergio's shoulder. She had even let Maria-Grazia teach her how to make *limoncello* when they returned from their brief mainland honeymoon, with alcohol and sugar and a sack of lemons from the tree in the courtyard, and Maria-Grazia, watching the girl stir the cloudy liquor, had allowed a great tenderness to come over her for this unexpected daughter-in-law.

All that had changed when autumn came. Now, Maria-Grazia saw, Pamela wished to go home. "We need our own place," she overheard her whispering. "There isn't enough room here."

And Sergio, meekly, misunderstanding, "But love, there are plenty of rooms."

Maria-Grazia, for her part, inclined toward the girl's point of view. For how could she fail to be oppressed by the indefinable boyhood smell of Sergio's bedroom, by the noise of the bar rising through the open window when they retreated upstairs together on warm summer evenings? Privately, she agreed that Sergio must follow the girl to England, or lose her.

Now, as things grew strained, their marriage seemed a last-ditch thing, a union of two separate lonelinesses. "Visit England," Maria-Grazia urged her son. "Take her on a visit at least. Introduce yourself to her family."

But Sergio, in his indecision, had never booked the tickets. He attempted to talk with her family on the telephone. But Sergio found himself incoherent in English when he had to speak it with these strangers—why, he grasped for quite ordinary words, threw out wild guesses, calling toes "foot fingers," the highway the "autostreet," translating literally from the languages he knew better, as though he weren't English at all! He had always spoken English without trouble to his father and his brother. But now, Maria-Grazia understood that Sergio was cleaving to the island, that some formidable stubbornness had emerged in him at the thought of being forced to leave it. "He's being a child," she raged in a whisper to Robert that night. "If she wants to live in England, he must let her. Didn't you come all the way here for me?"

On this matter, Robert—who had returned half for Maria-Grazia, half because he had never been able to imagine loving any other place but Castellamare—found himself utterly divided. And Maria-Grazia, too, if she was forced to be honest, was a little discouraged at the thought of a foreign country with no sea hush, no cicadas, a land composed of black and white. But they would visit him there, and the grandchild, and Giuseppino, and perhaps if they found themselves on the same island again the two brothers would find some means to reconcile.

EVEN THE CUSTOMERS IN the bar had noticed that Sergio Esposito's English wife was growing discontented. Meanwhile, Sergio threw himself with new vigor into his old concerns that autumn: the pouring of coffee, the rolling of pastries, the gathering of grimed *lire* at the end of each night on the counter of the bar beneath the photograph of his grandfather Amedeo—ostensibly in order to save the money for tickets to England. But really, his mother saw, he did it for love. This was a life, it seemed to her now, that he would not be persuaded into leaving. For at last he seemed to have decided, seventeen years too late, that the island was the place to which he belonged.

Maria-Grazia was adamant that they must deal with the mortgage on the bar as soon as possible, if Sergio were to leave before December when the child was due. Still half of it was left to pay, with interest—a sum of three million *lire:* ten thousand coffees at the bar's current rate of profit, as she put it, in an effort to get him to understand, eight thousand rice balls. The flow of tourists that had been so steady for twenty years had begun to slow. Fewer visitors had checked in to the hotel than expected this year; by September, they were all gone. The archaeological site was shut up for the winter, the amphitheater covered over with black tarpaulins. The fences around the caves by the sea became disordered, assaulted by early autumn storms; some fell down altogether. This year, no one bothered to fix them, for there would not be any visitors to pay the two thousand *lire* entrance fee until, God and Sant'Agata willing, they returned next spring. The local teenagers colonized the caves with their bicycles and what Concetta called "those American booming-boxes." The catacombs became again a place haunted by the sea. And yet Sergio seemed to think all at once that to pay the debt would be an easy thing, a thing of little significance. And, he confided in his mother hopefully, perhaps by the time it was paid Pamela would have come to love the island and the bar.

Giuseppino had not come back for Sergio's wedding. Instead, by way of consolation, he sent them a check for two million *lire* to refurbish the House at the Edge of Night.

The roof had begun to leak in the usual places. Maria-Grazia telephoned the builders Tonino and 'Ncilino and asked them to come and repair it. "Could you cash that check from your brother?" she asked Sergio.

Meanwhile, Pamela hissed urgently, "Pay off the rest of the mortgage with it, and you'll be free of your obligations and we can leave for England before the baby is born."

The check lay on Sergio's nightstand for several weeks, untouched. How could he explain it to either of them, that he still felt wrong-footed by his brother? Giuseppino sent regular checks to keep the bar afloat, to pay for refurbishments and alterations. Giuseppino had paid for the new three-wheeled van that had replaced the original Ape and which now stood in the piazza and was used to bring the cigarettes and coffee tins back from the mainland. Giuseppino had paid for the second football table, the newest television. But the bar hadn't been Giuseppino's for seventeen years, and it wasn't his now.

Work on the bar began during the second week of October. A week afterward, when the builders Tonino and 'Ncilino had stripped off half the roof tiles, Sergio tore up the check from his brother and threw it into the sea. He would pay the cost of the building work himself. He had coaxed the bar into making a profit in the past, and he would do so again.

He counted it as a mark of Giuseppino's excessive wealth, his carelessness, that he never noticed the check had not been cashed.

On the island, the absent Giuseppino was a kind of celebrity, a fact by which Sergio tried to prevent himself from being infuriated. It was always Giuseppino, Giuseppino in the bar, from morning until night, or so it seemed. Two years previously, the butcher and his wife had gone on a package tour to London. On the way back to their hotel after a visit to Buckingham Palace, they had taken a detour with the special purpose of viewing Giuseppino's apartment. The butcher had come back with a grainy set of pictures of the gated apartment complex, taken from behind a dumpster. In one photograph, Giuseppino was visible, very blurred and miniature, getting into one of his cars. In another, the whole building was captured, identified on the reverse simply as "Giuseppino's house." These pictures were still brought out and pored over in the bar when other news was slow. "To think," marveled Agata-the-fisherwoman to Sergio, "that your brother made all that money telling fortunes. Millions of *lire*, just from telling the future. Why, Concetta's great-aunt Onofria used to do that, with a pack of *tarocco* cards, and no one ever paid her anything much. Of course," Agata-the-fisherwoman added, "that was partly because she wasn't any good. But still, think of your brother making all that money from telling the future, thousands of pounds!"

"Not *telling* the future," said Sergio. "*Selling* futures. It's different." In truth, he was hazy as to how. "It's something to do with finance," he said. "Stocks and shares. Trading." But what Giuseppino did, he knew, was also in some obscure way related to houses—or had that been merely a side project? "I think he sells contracts for houses that haven't been built yet," he finished, satisfying no one.

The preferred rumor on Castellamare was that Giuseppino was a famous fortune-teller.

"And what is it you'll do in England, Signor Sergio, when you and your wife leave?" asked Bepe the ferryman. "Will you sell futures, too? Or own a bank like *il conte*? All kinds of good jobs there are, in a place like London."

"I'd always have liked to be a librarian," admitted Sergio.

This job, which Sergio had coveted since he first opened his grandfather's book of stories, captured Bepe's enthusiasm. "A librarian!" he cried. "That's a fine job—a good job. Why, everybody needs books." The elderly *scopa* players nodded in agreement—yes, yes, they all needed books.

"But no one needs to go to fancy cities, to Londra and Parigi, to be a librarian," said Bepe. "You could do that very well here."

Bepe himself had a special affection for literature. Every book on the island had to be ordered from Siracusa, and made its journey to Castellamare on his ferry. When shipping was delayed, Bepe opened the packages and read every one, taking care not to break the spines. Romances, family sagas, crime thrillers. Nobody on the island could get enough of them. And nobody could accuse him of reading them, for he kept the brown paper in which they had been wrapped and returned them to their packaging before delivery. But a library would be better.

"Why shouldn't you be a librarian here on Castellamare?" said Bepe. "We've never had a librarian. You could carry your books about in a little van. Or keep them here in the bar for people to borrow. Five thousand *lire* a read," he added enterprisingly. "Or else charge a monthly fee for membership. That way even the greatest *idioti* on this island will sign up, for fear of looking stupid before their neighbors, and half of your customers won't even borrow the books, and that way you'll get rich."

"No one wants a library," said Sergio.

But the elderly *scopa* players shook their heads at this. "Every town wants a library," Bepe repeated. "Here—I'll even lend you the money to set it up if you'll make me a shareholder."

"I need to talk to my wife," murmured Sergio. "She doesn't want to stay long-term."

"What's 'long-term'? You could run it twenty, thirty years and still go to England to retire when the baby is grown up—keep her happy that way." Bepe hauled a stack of notes from his back pocket and deposited them on the counter.

The next day, he brought Sergio a bookstore catalog from the mainland, zipped carefully into a plastic freezer bag to protect it from the damp sea air. "Here," he said. "You can choose all the books, and I'll ship them over for you. Why, you were the one who last modernized the bar, Sergio. You installed the first television, and the football table. Everyone remembers that."

Then something stirred in Sergio and he remembered how, driven to ambition for the first time in his life by the departure of his brother, he had worked all night to put together the first football table with a screwdriver, and climbed on a stepladder to oversee the hoisting of the neon sign. Why not a library, too? And maybe, by the time the library was established, Pamela would have come to love the island. "The idea of a library is a good one," said Maria-Grazia, gratified despite herself to find that her son was, after all, a businessman. "But you must have Pamela's blessing first."

"You go through the catalogs for me," said Sergio. "Then it won't be as if it was all my own idea."

Maria-Grazia, against her own better judgment, agreed. "We could have books of folk stories for the children," she said, turning the catalog's pages. "And Sicilian books—*Il Gattopardo*. Pirandello. English books, and history. We'll draw up a list."

Sergio and Maria-Grazia sat up late that night going through the catalog, and the next day he ordered two hundred books. He arranged them at the back of the bar, under the spotted photograph of Amedeo. Thus the business became the House at the Edge of Night Bar and Lending Library: membership one thousand *lire*. On the first day, fifty islanders signed up. By the end of the month, Bepe was repaid for the first two hundred books.

"How long do you expect me to stay?" Pamela confronted him that night, brittle with fury. "We were supposed to leave for England. The baby's due in eight weeks."

Sergio found himself pleading. "I might as well improve the business while I'm here. The library will start making money, and we can put it toward anything we like—the plane tickets to England—"

"If that's so," she said, "you've got a month to buy the tickets. And we can't go by plane anymore."

"We'll go once everything is in order here," he pleaded. "I can't put a time limit on it."

Pamela walked away, slapping up the stairs in the sandals she had been wearing since the summer.

At nights, she cried on the telephone to her mother, weeping in fast English while her mother's staticky voice on the other end could be heard, over and over, embarrassingly amplified by the echo in the hallway: "Come home, love. Leave him. I never thought he was right for you, love. Come home."

THE PROMISED BABY WAS forecast for the end of the year, and arrived during the second week in November. On that morning, Maria-Grazia found herself pacing anxiously between the door with its Chiuso sign and the kitchen where Pamela stood bent over a chair, cut through with labor pains. Back and forth Maria-Grazia paced, looking for the doctor. Sergio knelt before Pamela, massaging her back, caressing her hot arms.

"She'll come," soothed Sergio. "She's on her way."

Below, at the bottom of the tumble of scrubland, the sea was wild, showing its white breakers. "The ferry won't be able to carry the doctor back in time," Maria-Grazia fretted to Robert, concealed behind the curtain of the bar, "and the baby will be born too early, like all the Esposito children have been since time began, no matter what we do to stop it."

"No, cara," said Robert. "She's here."

For here came the doctor at last, windblown, at a run, with her bag and her little plastic shock machine in case of emergencies, and the midwife after her. Sergio's daughter, baby Maddalena, was delivered half an hour later, born like her grandmother all in a rush, within the walls of the House at the Edge of Night.

PART FIVE

The

WRECKED SHIP

...

1990–2009

ONCE THERE WERE TWO ELDERLY PEOPLE WHO WERE VERY loyal to Sant'Agata. Every year they celebrated her feast. They had no money, only a little grandson whom they loved more than anything in the world. But one year, after a bad harvest, they found themselves penniless and with nothing to sell in order to celebrate the saint's festival. So they decided to take the little boy across the sea and sell him to a foreign king, to raise a few lire and ensure that the child had a chance of a richer life. The king offered them a hundred gold pieces and took the little boy in.

The little boy, 'Ncilino, grew up in the king's palace alongside the king's daughter, and very soon she fell in love with him. The king, seeing this, grew anxious, for he didn't want to marry his daughter to a penniless youth from an island at the edge of the known world, and so he resolved to send the boy away.

When the boy was eighteen, the king told him, "Now listen, 'Ncilino, I am going to send you on a trading expedition, and you have a day and a night to load your boat." Then the king took out his oldest boat, full of holes, and gave it to 'Ncilino to sail.

On the following morning, 'Ncilino set off. But no sooner was he out upon the open sea than his boat started leaking and began to sink. 'Ncilino wept. "My poor grandmother and grandfather," he cried. "My poor island, which I'll never see again." Then he thought of the saint whose festival his grandmother and grandfather had always celebrated. Surely she must have been a great and powerful saint, for they had sold him, the thing they loved most in the world, in order to celebrate her

*feast. The boy decided to ask the saint to rescue him: "Dear Sant'Agata,"
he cried, "please help me!"*

*Then all at once the saint appeared in a solid gold ship, and lifted
up 'Ncilino and bore him away to the island, where his elderly grandmother and grandfather were waiting to welcome him, and from which
he would never stray again all the days of his life.*

A STORY I HAVE *heard many times in various versions, which seems to
have its roots in a tale of Saint Michael belonging to the west of Sicily.
This version was told to me by Agata-the-fisherwoman, circa 1970.*

I

IT WAS THE CHILD MADDALENA, IN THE END, WHO BROUGHT THE
bar back to Maria-Grazia.

The change of year had been tempestuous, dominated by crisis.
Sergio and his wife had not been able to reach any kind of accord,
and now there was some graver, darker difficulty. In the weeks after
the baby's birth, Pamela sat on the windswept veranda looking toward
England. In her arms lay the infant Maddalena, staring at the sky.
Even when Pamela consented to sit with her family-in-law in the
kitchen, she placed herself a little way off from Sergio, allowing the
baby to feed from her without encouraging her one way or the other.
Often, the baby went disregarded. Then Maria-Grazia took the child
and sang to her, "*Ambara*-bà, *cic*-cì, *coc*-cò!," the song her father,
Amedeo, had sung when she was a child. Or Robert would chant for
her English songs with their odd nonsense words: "Pat-a-cake, pat-a-
cake," "Rock-a-bye baby." The baby's face would light with recognition, with a sudden dazzling smile. They turned to Lena as to a bright
fire, feeding off the distraction that the baby provided from the trouble that was hanging over their house.

Before Christmas, Maria-Grazia was so concerned for poor Pamela that she summoned Concetta from the blue house with the orange trees. While Enzo prodded baby Maddalena, Maria-Grazia and
Concetta drew Pamela from the shadows and set her to work with
them rolling rice balls for the Christmas Eve celebrations. Maria-
Grazia offered the girl an early gift, a pearl bracelet that had once
been Pina's, and when Maria-Grazia fastened it around her wrist,

Pamela's eyes welled at the kindness. "England very beautiful at Christmas," Concetta said. "England I like. Lovely place. Kensington Gardens Park. Queen Elizabeth. Yes?"

Pamela, tearful, told them that she wasn't used to the loneliness here, the dust, all the vegetables, plates and plates of them covered in oil and salt, which they were obliged to eat each evening, the ferocious stray cats that ambushed Maddalena's pram as she pushed it about the village, the island dialect she couldn't understand—though she had *tried* to learn Italian when she and Sergio were first married! Soon, her voice became wailing and insistent, unlocked by the two older women's sympathy, a rising tide of grief: "The truth is I hate it here—and I can't look after the baby—and Sergio doesn't understand—and the lizards everywhere, the dust, the sun, and so cold in the winter—I'm sure I've never been colder, not even in England—all those old women staring at us when we walk down the high street—I don't love the baby—I don't love Sergio anymore—"

"I'm sorry for the vegetables, *cara*," said Maria-Grazia in regret. "I would have cooked you English things."

"It's not that," wept Pamela. "It's not that."

"Postnatal depression," said Concetta knowledgeably, dropping the rice balls in breadcrumbs. "Also my mother she have this problem, though no one diagnose it properly in the old times. But you get help from proper doctor, maybe you feel better, *cara*. And the old women not mean any evil, you know, when they stare. And the cats, they timid really. You give them one flick with your handbag and they no bother you no more. They learn."

"I know," cried Pamela. "I know. But I can't stand it here any longer."

"Then you must go to England," said Concetta. "What game is Sergio playing, not letting you?"

Maria-Grazia had asked herself again and again the same question. "Now, Sergio," she told her son at last, early in the new year, "you're to talk to your wife one way or another about when you're going to move to England."

Then, too late, Sergio attempted to make amends. "Be patient, Pam," he murmured into the warmth of her unresponsive back that night. "Give me another month or two."

Pamela huffed over the narrowness of the bed, pulling the covers this way and that. He found himself desperate, pleading, like a hurt child, "Don't you love me?"

"I can't stay here," she said at last. "That's all."

"Just for a few months more."

"But you won't ever come with me to England," she said. "That's the truth of the matter. You won't ever leave this damned island. At least do me the decency of admitting that."

"I can't," said Sergio, his stomach constricting. "I can't leave, Pam. I'm sorry."

The next morning, Sergio was aware of Pamela's weight leaving the bed beside him, and the water in the bathroom turned on and then off again, leaving a dim echo in the pipes. By the time his mother woke him properly, Bepe's ferry had sailed, with Pamela on board. She had taken everything with her except the baby.

NO ONE HAD CONSIDERED that Pamela might leave without her child. That night, Maddalena was afflicted by a bad case of colic; she screamed and screamed, blotchy faced, for relief. It was Maria-Grazia who took the baby's soft weight. She shut up the bar, pulled the blinds, and carried her granddaughter from room to room. The baby had peaked English eyelids and lovably oversized ears. And yet her eyes belonged to Castellamare, eyes of an indeterminate opal color with bristling lashes that seemed the softest thing, like the legs of a caterpillar. Maria-Grazia found herself reeling with love for the child.

"Pam will come back for her," said Sergio. "And I'll sort everything out then."

But what if Pam didn't come back? Maria-Grazia asked herself this half in fear, half in hope. Didn't the baby, for her part, love the island? Already she had grown fat, her skin a little burnished. She wrestled spiritedly with Concetta's Enzo, and grasped for the lizards as they traversed the walls above her cot. The sounds she had begun to make, Maria-Grazia believed, were half English, half those of the island dialect, and she tilted her head and listened to both languages with equal attention. She would soon sit in thrall to the island's stories if she were allowed to remain—she would run on the goat paths with Enzo and the other children, plunge fearlessly into the ocean, and learn every one of the wailing Castellamare songs.

She was destined to remain, in fact, for Pamela did not return to collect her.

When the baby finally quieted that first night—this Maria-Grazia never told anyone except Robert—she stopped before the picture of her father, Amedeo, and took in her heart a private vow to protect Maddalena.

SO, FOR EVERYBODY'S SAKE, Maria-Grazia resumed once again her old post behind the bar. While Sergio carried the colicky baby from room to room and Robert attacked the chaos of the past decade's bookkeeping on his wife's instruction, determined to get the accounts in order now that they had a child's future to worry about, Maria-Grazia took over the running of the House at the Edge of Night. She instigated a strict schedule for the posting of *lire* into the little box with the crucifix each Friday, in order to get the mortgage paid off sooner, and systematized the contents of the lending library. She also replaced the old spluttering coffee machine with a new one that made *americano* and *caffè macchiato* and great soupy bowls of *cappuccino*, for that was what the tourists wanted now.

Often, Maria-Grazia thought Lena must have been born with a love for the place in her veins, a side effect of having been accidentally born between its four walls. The infant staggered her first steps between the tables and chairs, was lulled asleep under the counter by the blue hiss of the sea and the rattle of the swinging door. Once she was up and running, she tore in and out of the rooms of the old house and unearthed strange objects—Amedeo's forceps and surgical scissors, Uncle Flavio's war medal with its Fascist insignia, the leg braces in which her grandmother had once been imprisoned. Maria-Grazia took the braces in both hands and showed Lena how they had fitted. She told the child the story of Flavio's war medal, and Robert's.

Seated beside her grandfather in the great stone kitchen, Lena polished and repolished the medal with a little Brasso on a tissue until the face of King George was shiny and zealous again. And Robert, who had never spoken of such things since the summer when he told Maria-Grazia the stories of his youth in order to win back her heart, consented to talk a little again about the war. "Why did you never tell me these things?" asked Sergio, entering the room to hear Robert recounting the sinking of the glider. "That you jumped from planes, that you were wrongly imprisoned for three years?"

And Robert, blinking, said, "I never knew you wanted to hear."

A change had come over Sergio since the birth of Maddalena. He had emerged from the ruins of his marriage no longer an overgrown boy, no longer discontented. After Pamela's departure, he had thrown out the graying polo shirts of his high school years, and when the widow Valeria had prodded his stomach with a mocking tone one Sunday afternoon, he had taken the matter rather too much to heart, in his mother's opinion, swimming lengths of the bay each morning until the fat around his middle was all gone. Now everyone was forced to admit that a steadier Sergio had emerged, a man whose marriage might have disintegrated and whose business sense might never have matched that of his mother, Maria-Grazia, but who was possessed with an earnest desire to acquit himself as a father. He taught his daughter to read, and carried her to school on his shoulders, and the elderly *scopa* players and the widows of Sant'Agata stopped referring to him as *il ragazzo di Maria-Grazia*, Maria-Grazia's boy, and instead called him plain Sergio Esposito. Even—occasionally—*signor.* Perhaps it had been the child, not the wife, that had been lacking all along.

For a wonderful thing it was, thought Maria-Grazia, to have a child like Maddalena in the house, so alive with the future and yet so in love with the past. From the photocopied sheets that were all that remained to them of Amedeo's book of stories Sergio read to her Amedeo's fantastical tales. Lena heard tell of the girl who became a tree, became a bird, became an apple. She heard of giants cut up in pieces; of a demon named Silver Nose and a sorcerer named Body-No-Soul; of brothers who repaired each other's severed heads with magical ointment; and—in a little-known story Amedeo had gathered from Concetta's great-aunt Onofria just before she died—of a boy whose head got back to front somehow, and who was so alarmed at the sight of his own backside that he fell down dead. At this tale, the girl screamed in horrified delight.

Lena and her Papà lay on winter afternoons among the shelves of the lending library, immersed in its volumes. The library's patrons filled in little pink request forms, on which they ordered from Maria-Grazia romances, thrillers, and long and protracted epics of great foreign families in which everybody seemed to have the same name. But though the elderly islanders consumed these books with a fervor, none of the foreign stories ever seemed to Lena quite as good as those belonging to Castellamare. By the time she was five, she knew by heart each one of Amedeo's tales. She knew in detail, too, the episodes belonging to her own family, for Maria-Grazia herself had told her granddaughter as soon as she was old enough about the time Uncle Flavio plunged into the sea in escape from the island, the time her uncles, one by one, left for war. The day her great-grandfather Amedeo had first set foot upon the island. The twins born by different mothers. The man from the ocean. The warring of her father and Zio Giuseppino. If only Lena herself had been alive when those legends walked the island—Gesuina and old Rizzu and Father Ignazio and the ghost of Pierino, Pina the schoolmistress with her rope of black hair and Amedeo with his book of tales! To her, their spirits still hung about the goat paths and the alleys, as important as the presence of the saint. For the island itself seemed alive to her, a place where the earth heaved with stories.

The day before the Sant'Agata festival of her sixth year, the enterprising Lena wrote a cardboard sign, "Museo dei Miracoli," in felt-tip capitals, and arranged a handful of precious family relics beneath it on the veranda—the two war medals, the leg braces, the little tin medallion that had arrived at the foundling hospital with Amedeo, the photocopied pages from the book of stories. "A thousand *lire!*" Lena yelled at the tourists, in English and Italian. "A thousand *lire* to see the wonders of the island! A thousand *lire* to see the Museum of Miracles! Or a dollar, or whatever you have." Enzo knelt on the pavement beside her and sketched with chalk a reproduction of the *Mona Lisa,* which he had seen a real artist doing when he had been sent to visit his mother's family in Rome.

Whenever the tourists stopped to look, Lena went up to them with her relics and artifacts, and explained to them the stories belonging to the objects: "This was what my grandfather Robert won from the English government, during the war, before he was shot down in the ocean. . . . This one my uncle won from Mussolini. . . . This was the book of stories my great-grandfather wrote, when he used to be a *medico condotto.* . . . This lucky Sant'Agata rosary is mine. . . ." By midnight, when the two children fell asleep under the museum table to the whirling of the *organetto,* she and Enzo had made thirty-seven thousand *lire,* two dollars, and a British pound. After that, they repeated the enterprise every year.

For Lena seemed to be the first Esposito who had been born with no wish to leave Castellamare. In the bar, her grandmother let her carry the round trays with the logos of the coffee company, which she heaved above her head in both hands to get between the tables. Solemnly, she took orders on a little hologrammed notepad she had won as a school prize. Robert drove her in the three-wheeled van to the cash-and-carry warehouse on the mainland, and together they rode back on Bepe's ferry with the van full of cigarettes and coffee jars and mainland chocolates. "Will the bar be mine one day?" she asked her grandmother, when she was six years old.

Maria-Grazia thought of the mortgage to the d'Isantus, which had become a tiresome, rolling thing, never quite repaid. "Yes," she said. "Of course."

WITH EACH PASSING YEAR, they became more certain that Pamela would not return to take Lena. Maria-Grazia had watched her granddaughter carefully for signs of damage—for the child's beginnings had been inauspicious, the girl barely three months old when her mother had departed across the sea. But Lena seemed a robust child. Though she had developed a habit in her infancy of following Maria-Grazia about the bar, which she never quite abandoned, she seemed otherwise mercifully solid. Besides, she had found a hundred protectors on the island. Even from the customers in the bar she received special treatment: The elderly *scopa* players, around whose legs she had played without fear of scolding since her infancy, brought her historic potsherds and coins from about the island to add to her museum; the widows of Sant'Agata prayed for her every week, garlanding her with more charms and rosaries than she could carry; and the members of the Modernization Committee (who had, without Maria-Grazia's knowledge, sworn themselves the child's protectors at the very first meeting after Pamela's departure), reported back to Maria-Grazia by telephone the child's comings and goings about the island. "She's just walking up through the Mazzus' olive grove," the widow Valeria would hiss furtively, like a detective. "She's awfully sandy, Maria-Grazia. Catch her and make sure she gets a bath." Or, "She's on her way home from school," Agata-the-fisherwoman would report, from her little house beneath the vines. "Walking as good as a little *santina*, Maria-Grazia, and she'll be home in five minutes or less." With such careful attention, how could the child do anything but grow and flourish?

But, of course, as Maria-Grazia was to reflect in years to come, it was no use congratulating oneself on the raising of a child to ten years old, for most of the real trouble came later.

Once a year, at the beginning of the summer, Lena was dispatched to England to spend a month with her mother. Pamela seemed, to Maria-Grazia's relief, to have recovered, as far as Sergio had, from their brief and stormy marriage. Lena had two small stepbrothers, and a room of her own with pink curtains. Pamela, Maria-Grazia knew, hoped each year that Maddalena would decide of her own accord to stay. Always, for a few weeks, there were long evenings of tearful telephone calls between the two of them after Lena had come home. But the girl had confessed to Maria-Grazia that in London her stomach always ached and she slept badly, listening to the strangely muted English traffic, with no *put-put-put* of *motorinos*, no seething back-and-forth of the sea. This was her curse: to miss her mother all year, and then to sleep badly and lose her appetite until she was back on the island, running between the prickly pears or plunging with Enzo and the other children into the foaming ocean. Thus Lena came to believe that it was her personal destiny to remain on Castellamare, to become the next proprietor of the House at the Edge of Night.

IMMERSED IN THE STEERING of the bar across the difficult period of Lena's growing-up, Maria-Grazia found her life once again accelerating giddily, the century drawing to a close. She was more than seventy years old. Robert said, when she informed him of this fact in wonder, "Well, and doesn't it seem a long time to you, all these years we've lived?" And it did, but not that long. Not seventy years.

To the child Lena, the change of year was nothing to be marveled at. To Lena, things on the island stayed perpetually the same. But for Maria-Grazia, the closing of the century in which she had lived most of her life recalled to her the inescapable truth that she was growing old.

That year seemed full of portents. During the summer, Maria-Grazia watched with her granddaughter a solar eclipse. The event was over in a minute or two, the eclipse itself merely a black fingernail of shadow that could only be looked at indirectly, on a sheet of white paper or through a special pair of cardboard glasses. In the autumn, a great storm carried several tons of sand up the beach, depositing it in the mouths of the caves, leaving behind a small miracle: the wreck of a ship, lying beneath the water of the bay. The children dived, and made out the name: *Holy Madonna*. Somehow, Agata-the-fisherwoman's boat had made its way back to the island, dragged by the currents, little by little, until the storm did the rest. That winter, at the House at the Edge of Night, the islanders celebrated the new year, and watched city dwellers set off fireworks, shrieking as the television cameras swooped low over their heads. Inspired, Lena and Enzo let off a few firecrackers in the piazza, startling Concetta from her chair. But as the light dwindled, the islanders returned in the dark to their separate houses, leaving the island unaltered, swept by the same hot breezes, lulled by the same hush of the sea.

THE FIRST MODERNIZATION OF the new century, when it came, threatened to provoke outright war. "Why," demanded Agata-the-fisherwoman one morning over the bar, "have you got two prices beneath the *arancini* in your counter?"

"We're having a new currency," explained Lena, who had learned about it at school. "You're to swap your *lire* for the new coins."

"Says who?"

"The government in Rome."

"Oh," said Agata, relieved, for it was well known that no one listened to them.

But the new currency was coming. Bepe's ferry had a new tariff, and Arcangelo had also introduced two sets of prices in his shop, based on a favorable conversion rate of his own devising. Meanwhile, the islanders who still mistrusted the savings bank were outraged at the news that they would have to bring all their savings to the bank in order to exchange them. "How will I know I'm getting the right amount?" demanded the widow Valeria.

"And I'm certainly not putting my money in those accounts of theirs," said Bepe. "For I don't trust *il conte* any more than I did his father."

On the appointed day, the exchange took place. The islanders came slinking from all corners of Castellamare with buckets and crates and sacks full of *lire*, millions upon millions, a small hoard. The elderly *scopa* players, for all their complaining, had five sacks between them; Agata-the-fisherwoman had ten of her own; and Bepe and his nephews were obliged to borrow Tonino's van to haul their two hundred million to the bank, for it could not be carried. In return, they received plastic pouches full of coins and new paper currency.

"I never knew our island was so rich!" cried Lena in wonder.

But the island had, in its quiet way, continued to prosper. And in those years, it seemed anyone could get a loan from the savings bank. Sergio, creeping across the piazza, borrowed a little more to stave off the tiresome mortgage, still not entirely paid. Others bought motorcars in monthly installments, televisions, complicated pension accounts guaranteed to grant them a luxurious retirement. *Il conte*'s concrete villas, which had cracked as predicted in the first earthquake, were shored up and extended out of the savings bank's funds. "It borrows the money from bigger banks overseas," said Bepe knowledgeably, for one of his nephews worked there. "They can get as much as they want. But for my part, I'd rather keep my money where I can see it."

To interest Lena in the opportunities of the outside world, her father borrowed the money to buy a computer, and had it shipped to the island; this borrowing displeased Maria-Grazia, for she was inclined to distrust the savings bank, too. It was the first computer to arrive on Castellamare. Sergio would pay for it, he assured her, in twenty-four monthly installments. And how could she be angry with him? For he did it, as he did all things now, out of love for the child. As Bepe's nephews carried the computer in its black-printed box up the main street, a procession of children followed them. Sergio unpacked the computer, examined its separate parts, read and reread the English instructions, then sat defeated on the floor of the bar. It took an afternoon's labor on the part of Enzo and his friend Pino, who had already seen a computer at their mainland high school, to assemble it and bring it to life.

To connect to a thing called the Internet, the thing that had most interested Sergio in the first place, for he had heard it was like a great encyclopedia, there was a special black box with a line of red lights that flashed on and off. "Come, Lena," Sergio called. Lena came, barefoot, leaning affectionately against his shoulder. Curious, Robert and Maria-Grazia, too, bent over the thing. "How do we make it work?" Sergio asked at last. "Do we type commands? I've seen that on television."

"No, no," said Enzo. "That's old-fashioned stuff. You just click on the Internet icon now, and the Internet appears."

"Icon?" murmured Robert, thinking of saints' images, candlelight. Maria-Grazia squeezed his wrist, an old signal between them. Now what she meant by it was this: *Caro*, we're growing old.

Enzo hunched over the keyboard and moved an arrow across the screen, too quick for Maria-Grazia to follow. The computer made a series of beeps as though it were telephoning to America, a static noise, a couple of low tones, a weird growling, a whirring like that of the cicadas. "It's broken!" cried Sergio in dismay. "They've sold me a faulty one!"

"It's dialing," said Enzo.

Words appeared. "There," said Enzo.

"Is that all?" said Sergio, crushed. "Is that the Internet?"

"It can do other things, too," said Enzo. "You just have to learn how to do them."

"We should charge people to use it," said Lena. "I saw it last year, when I went to England. An Internet café, it's called."

Sergio blinked a little, divided between pride in his daughter's great knowledge, and regret that she had already encountered such things.

Maria-Grazia, however, studying the computer's instruction manual, found that it was quite straightforward to work. She took Lena's advice, and after she had learned how to use it, she hired it out to the island's teenagers and foreign visitors at fifty cents an hour.

In one plunge, the House at the Edge of Night had entered the new century. After that, to Maria-Grazia, it seemed no time at all before Lena had finished growing up.

II

MORE THAN HALF A CENTURY AFTER HE HAD FIRST LEFT THE ISLAND, Andrea d'Isantu, now past eighty, returned to Castellamare. He came by sea, and when Maria-Grazia saw him she was struck with terror—for she saw, quite clearly, that death rested upon his shoulders, as she had seen it once rest upon the shoulders of the fisherman Pierino, and upon the shoulders of her father, Amedeo, in the autumn before he died.

This time, she had been given a day's warning of *il conte*'s return. She heard Bepe whispering about it over the *scopa* table. "He's coming alone," Bepe hissed, "and I think he means to stay."

The following evening, she walked down to the quay to witness the ferry coming in. A few of *il conte*'s old retinue stood assembled on the concrete. The brass band played. She made out Andrea's narrow form, inscrutable in his great foreign overcoat. The ferry rolled in toward the quay. As Bepe's youngest son put the engine in reverse, *il conte*'s thin hair was sea-blown, and he seemed to shudder in the wind like a suspended husk, not really there at all.

That night she went by the side roads and *vaneddi* to the d'Isantus' villa once again.

Santino Arcangelo appeared behind the gate as usual, wearing his customary insolent grin, though he struggled to swagger now on account of his two hip replacements. "Signora Maria-Grazia," he said, maneuvering himself up to the gate on his crutches. "It won't do. *Signor il conte* won't see you. Surely you know that after all this time."

Maria-Grazia had brought with her a plate of grilled aubergines wrapped in foil, as though this were merely some conventional visit. "Then I'll wait," she said, "until he's ready. These *melanzane* are for *signor il conte*. Will you please tell him I sent them?"

For the time had come, she felt, to put all this silliness to rest. Maria-Grazia, sitting down upon the old hitching post before the gate, slid the aubergines under the wrought ironwork and settled down to wait with neatly folded hands.

Santino left the aubergines where they were and turned to make his way back toward the villa.

On the road, the fishermen passed, returning from the sea. "Maria-Grazia!" hooted Bepe. "What is it you're doing here, sitting at Signor d'Isantu's door like a lovesick girl?"

"Nothing but minding my own business," said Maria-Grazia. "What are you doing, Signor Bepe, walking up the road? On the way to a tryst with Signora Agata-*la-pescatrice*?"

Bepe, a little shamefaced, left off his teasing and hobbled out of sight in the wake of his nephews, and the road was once again empty. Night fell with a great plunge of the sun over the edge of the sea. Maria-Grazia shifted her position, to let her hot neck cool. Well, now, that was the worst of it, and she might as well wait here until something happened.

SHE MUST HAVE SLEPT, or half slept, for she woke to a full moon burnishing the leaves of the palms, to the vanishing of the song of the cicadas. The aubergines on their foiled plate were gone, and someone stood in the shadow beyond the gate. "What have you come for?" he said at last. It was the first time Andrea had spoken to her in half a century, and the breaking of the silence, or perhaps her abrupt awakening, made her dizzy. Had his voice really been so dry and insubstantial, so much like an old man's?

"Signor d'Isantu," she said. "I want to speak with you."

Andrea stood for a good long while behind the gate, working at something with the side of his mouth. He fretted on the other side of the bars, sucking his teeth. Then, at last, he took three steps forward and unchained the gate. His hands were too weak to lift the great chain; it went rattling to the ground as he tried to grasp it. Maria-Grazia lifted it. Carrying it in both hands, she followed him through the gate.

SHORTLY AFTER ANDREA D'ISANTU'S RETURN, Lena heard the widow Valeria, whose hardware store was opposite the Arcangelos' grocery, whispering about her grandmother on the veranda late one autumn night. "She's visiting him every Sunday after Mass," Valeria hissed at the elderly *scopa* players, with mischievous intent. "Drinking port wine from Palermo on his veranda, and laughing, and reminiscing about the past. She stays for whole hours at a time. I don't know how Signor Roberto stands for it. And at their age"—Valeria herself was nearly ninety—"at their age it's indecent, a damned shame."

Lena said nothing about this to any of her elders, but she contemplated it in her heart. She did not have to wait long before she heard more. "I've been told Signor d'Isantu's remaking his will," muttered the florist Gisella, whose shop was next door to the solicitor Calogero's office. "And it's no secret these Espositos will benefit, for he's said to be quite as smitten with her as he was as a boy."

It was true that Lena's grandmother often went out now on Sundays, in her best clothes, leaving the bar to the care of Sergio and Robert. And sometimes she did not return until five or six in the evening. Meanwhile, Lena found her grandfather exasperatingly calm about the matter, merely spreading his hands and sipping his *arancello*, unwilling to say anything about what he knew. "I trust Mariuzza," he said. "I know it's no love affair. She's told me so herself. Why should she have to justify herself to these gossips in the bar?"

But Lena found herself impatient with such capitulations, such weak acceptances. In those days, it seemed, she was impatient with everything: she would find herself beating the unwieldy vine with a stick when she was supposed to be pruning it, flinging the glasses into the dishwasher in a passion, without knowing how or why she found herself so out of sorts. The elderly customers had their own suspicions on the matter. The boy Enzo had left for art school in Rome. With a safety pin through one ear, a rosary of Sant'Agata swinging from the rearview mirror of his car, and the radio tuned permanently to foreign stations on which American bands shouted exuberant songs, he had been the island's taxi driver until he had at last outgrown Castellamare and left in a plume of exhaust smoke the previous summer. Since then, though Enzo sent Lena hasty letters assuring her he still thought of her entirely as a sister, nothing had been right on Castellamare, and Lena found herself entering her sixteenth year with restlessness in her heart.

Like her great-grandfather Amedeo before her, she remedied this by plunging herself headlong into stories.

"What's got into you?" complained Concetta one evening, helping her wash out the heavy ice cream vats while her father, Sergio, swept the bent *scopa* cards and cigarette ends from the floor. "You're the same, you and Enzo. He wouldn't be content until he left the island. And look at you, Lena, reading and rereading those foreign books of your Papà's as though you were meaning to leave us, too."

Lena, humiliated, turned *War and Peace* facedown. "It doesn't mean I'm going away," she said.

"Whenever a person reads great big books like that," said Concetta, "they're thinking about going away."

Over the sink, Lena fumed silently, swilling the ice cream in its rainbow variations down the drain.

"Sometimes I think I'd go if I could," said Concetta. "Sometimes I think I'd have liked to get away from this island to a proper city, like my Enzo. But then I remind myself that I'm old, and this is my home, and the feeling passes."

———

THAT SUMMER, ON CONCETTA'S suggestion, Lena went to visit Enzo in Rome, carrying the cardboard suitcase that had once belonged to her Zio Flavio stuffed with his aunt's *melanzane* paste and *limoncello* and *marmellata*. She found him lovably pleased to see her and un-altered, except for the fact that on their long walk around the archae-ological excavations, during which he slung his arm over her shoulders like a brother, he confided to her that he was in love with a boy from Torino whom he had met at his art history class. This she was not to tell anybody ("Except my Zia Concetta and your *nonna* and Signor Roberto, for they'll understand"). The story of the boy from Torino, which Lena poured out between sobs on the telephone to her *nonna* that night, had not—she swore furiously—broken her heart. All the same, Lena spent the whole remaining three months of the school holiday with her mother in England.

In other years, Lena had telephoned her father each evening with a homesick pain in her stomach just to listen to the sounds of the bar: the roar of triumph as an elderly *scopa* player gathered in a hand, the hiss of the coffee machine, the swing of the door on its axle. She would stand by the phone in the hall with closed eyes, holding the sounds of the island before her like a glass of water, careful not to lose a single one. But this year, the telephone calls made her impatient. "I'm going to lose her," mourned Sergio. "Her mother's going to keep her there. I know it."

"No, no," consoled Maria-Grazia. "She just needs time."

But Maria-Grazia, returning from *il conte*'s great villa one Sunday evening, slipping off her shoes, which were as misshapen now as Pi-na's had once been, setting her Sunday handbag on the table before the statue of Sant'Agata, heard the telephone ring and knew with premonitory certainty that it was her granddaughter with bad news.

"*Cara*," she answered. "Now tell me, when are you coming home to us?"

"I'm not," said Lena, her voice very thin and small. "I'm staying here for a while."

LENA, WHOSE ELDERS HAD always praised her intelligence, was going to remain in England and study, like her great-grandfather Amedeo, to be a doctor.

And now the House at the Edge of Night seemed a hollow place; now, its walls contained within them the absence of Maddalena as they had once held the curse of weeping. Everyone mourned her departure: the elderly *scopa* players, who sought about for the girl bustling with her upraised tray; the widows of Sant'Agata, who had no beloved child on which to hang their rosaries any longer; Sergio, behind the counter, who felt once again that the island was too small, too narrow, and who had become again merely *il ragazzo di Maria-Grazia*; and Robert, whose medal, forgotten, grew tarnished on the hall table beside the statue of Sant'Agata with no one to take it up and polish its bronze face. Maria-Grazia even caught Concetta weeping about it, the very first time she had ever seen Concetta cry about anything. "I've been an old fool," confessed Concetta, "for I hoped the two of them would marry, Mariuzza—I did—and that they'd take over the House at the Edge of Night!"

"Well," said Maria-Grazia. "And can't Lena and Enzo run the House at the Edge of Night between them, all the same? Why must they be married to do it?" For she found herself, as she had in the weeks after the departure of her brothers, furiously refusing to believe that the girl would not return. No, she told herself, as she had told Sergio—Lena just required time.

Meanwhile, weeks passed, months passed, until the girl had been gone almost an entire year. Maria-Grazia found herself existing from Sunday to Sunday, when the girl would telephone with her news. She had made progress in her studies, passing a series of important English exams with grades Maria-Grazia understood to be impeccable. There was talk, to Maria-Grazia's relief, of some other boy. "She'll come home," Maria-Grazia murmured to Robert on Sunday nights, as she lay sleepless in their bed in the stone room by the courtyard. And Robert gripped her wrist as he had in sleep on summer afternoons when they were first lovers, and murmured, "*Lo so. I know.*"

IN THE END, IT was a kind of vision that called her back, or so Lena would explain it to her grandmother, years later. On that particular evening, ascending from the Underground station in a gust of hot air, a strange thing happened: She was assaulted by the scent of bougainvillea. At first just a trace of it, in a woman's perfume. Then it was everywhere, an invisible rain of flowers, at once near and far off. The force of memory brought her to a halt. She had missed, for two years in a row, the Sant'Agata festival.

This fact, as it came over Lena in the darkening street, seemed to her so awful that she began to weep.

A van swerved; a motorbike passed with a long blare. She gained the safety of the curb, and the scent was gone.

She didn't resolve to come home that day; not yet. But from that day onward, a great unease lay upon her, so that she was as irritable as Agata-the-fisherwoman before bad weather. The island had forced itself upon her attention, as though something were badly wrong. The way she had recounted it to her grandmother, it was as if she had sensed that the bar was in trouble. That was odd, thought Maria-Grazia, for if there had been any trouble simmering during those last months of 2007, it was like the shudders that came before an earthquake, too faint to detect without special gauges and needles, and no one had yet been aware.

THAT AUTUMN WHILE LENA was still absent, Concetta's Enzo had returned to Castellamare. "Why?" asked Maria-Grazia, when Concetta came running to the bar with the news. "I thought he wanted to get away."

"Homesick!" cried Concetta, half in joy and half in frustration. "He said he was homesick! He wants to drive his taxi again, and make statues of the saint. Maria-Grazia, I fear he's gone entirely mad."

But the truth was, Enzo had made his peace with the island. For, shorn from Castellamare, a strange affliction had come over him. At art school in Rome, to his dismay, every sketch he attempted turned under his hands into a scene of the island: its church, its piazza, its lines of prickly pears, the goats grazing on the slopes of its bay, the boat *Holy Madonna* with its rusted keel, the avenue of palms leading up to *il conte*'s villa, and over and over again the image of Sant'Agata. So he had returned, one windswept day three years after he left, to drive his taxi again.

"Why come back here?" Concetta harangued, though she had wept when he left, cursing his ambition. "You were going to be a fancy artist, in Roma or America, with exhibitions and galleries and I don't know what else."

Enzo, instead, began work on what was to become his masterpiece. In his ancestor Vincenzo's old studio, a rough-hewn block of stone had stood for as long as anybody could remember: a rock belonging to the caves by the sea. Vincenzo had commissioned the fishermen to haul it out with winches at some point in the last century, intending to make from it a life-size image of the saint. Now Enzo resolved to complete the statue.

Working the edges of the stone with a chisel, he frowned, pale and distracted, his hair bristled through with some ashy substance. "It won't come right," he said, speaking through his Zia Concetta rather than to her. "I can't get it to work."

Concetta, narrowing her eyes, said, "What's it supposed to be?"

"Sant'Agata." Enzo touched a fold of the saint's robes. "And here at her feet, this is supposed to be a map of the island. Here are the fishermen's boats with all their names—the bottom of her robe becomes the sea. Look, here's *Trust in God, Holy Madonna, Sant'Agata*

Salvatrice, the *Santa Maria della Luce. Maria Concetta* here, and *Siracusa Star.* All the boats that ever sailed to or from this island, the surviving and the wrecked." Gesticulating, reaching toward something, Enzo gave up and dropped his arms to his sides. "The volcanic rock's too porous, too brittle. But Vincenzo specified that it must be made from this particular block. He must have had something in mind. It's all somewhere inside the stone."

Concetta didn't know whether to rejoice or despair over her nephew. There he sat, hunched over the saint's form, and late at night the sound of his chisel could be heard from the old studio's open windows.

"Perhaps," murmured Maria-Grazia to Robert that night, afire with expectation, "Lena, too, will come home."

SO SHE DID, at last, crossing by Bepe's ferry at the beginning of the following summer. She had been gone two entire years. Sitting on the varnished wooden seat at the prow of Bepe's boat, she felt worn thin, as though time had traveled twice as fast since she had left the island. Her skin was no longer well armored; she had forgotten the way it stung you, this sun, the air that came over you in hot waves, the bare white to which all colors turned under its glare.

The ferry swung against the tide, water pooling under its left flank, and before her reared the island. And now she was down on the quay, and now climbing the old hill, and the island assaulted her with the force of memory: the sea's hydraulic hiss, its familiar hot-dust smell. And yet she saw it through her mother's eyes, too: saw how the streets she climbed were full of stale air, the pavements crusted with dog turds, the façades of the church and the shops peeling, and every inhabitant in some phase of advanced age. The kind of place one could not love without effort, and yet, she understood now, the only place on the face of the whole earth that she herself loved.

On the row of chairs outside Arcangelo's shop, people stared. "Is that Lena Esposito?" hissed the widow Valeria, quite audibly. "Is that Maddalena Esposito, Sergio's girl?"

"Yes, Signora Valeria," said Lena, trying on this day of homecoming not to be irritated with anyone. "I'm home."

"Isn't she so much taller—and so pale, like a little ghost?" hissed Valeria to the pharmacist, raising her hand in innocent greeting to Lena.

But now here was the piazza. Here was the veranda with its mat of bougainvillea. Here was her grandmother—and yet she doubted a little, as she approached: Was she really so neat and small, so old? Maria-Grazia set down the tray she had been carrying. Then all at once she was running as though for her life, arms readied in an embrace, crying, "Lena! Lena! Lena!"

Her cry reached Robert, who came out, too, disbelieving, shielding his eyes against the white sunlight with one hand. And here was her father, Sergio, abandoning a tray of drinks to run and run and get there before either of them. Lena allowed them to bury her in embraces, with no thought of leaving now.

"Lena's here!" Maria-Grazia cried to the watching customers. "My granddaughter is home! Didn't I always tell you she would come?"

So it was that Lena became the first Esposito to leave Castellamare and return again. "I'll stay here," she told her grandmother. "I'll be a doctor some other time."

III

ONE MORNING IN SEPTEMBER, MARIA-GRAZIA TURNED ON THE TELE-vision in the bar to find strange images of unrest: men in glossy suits, emerging from great glass buildings into the green-lit New York night, with boxes in their arms. "An attack?" cried Maria-Grazia, fearing fire or murder, for the men moved slowly, with stunned eyes.

"No, no," said Sergio. "They've lost their jobs."

"Why are they walking out with boxes like that?" said Agata-the-fisherwoman. "What's that you say? Englishmen like Signor Robert, are they, or *americani*? Turn it up—I can't hear!"

"*You* can't hear?" retorted one of the elderly *scopa* players, with spirit. "Why, it's we who can't hear, with you turning and turning up that television every day, and those boys rattling on the football table—"

Here an argument broke out, and the facts of the matter were missed altogether. By the time Maria-Grazia got the customers under control, the men with their boxes were gone from the screen, to be replaced by more familiar calamities.

Maria-Grazia went out to Robert, who was taming the bougainvil-lea on the veranda, an almost monthly task once the summer began. "There's something strange," she said, sitting down beside him, taking his hand in hers. "Something odd happening in the world outside."

"This house has survived trouble before," said Robert, kissing the palm of her hand.

Lena was worried, too. All that week, though she was supposed to be making—under her grandmother's orders—an application for a medical school in Sicily, which, after all, wasn't too far from home, she scrutinized the newspapers for an explanation instead. By degrees, she understood that the English and American banks were beginning to founder. "Like '29," said Agata-the-fisherwoman. "A Great Depression."

"No, no," said Bepe. "Nothing like that." For though he mistrusted *il conte*'s bank on principle, he had a great respect for those towers of finance across the sea.

In the bar, there was some disagreement over how the trouble had started, for all the newspapers seemed to tell them different things. Some of the customers maintained that it had begun with two rich Americans, Freddie and Fannie, others that it had started with two brothers called Lehman, still others that it was something to do with a city called Northern Rock. A few recalled that, late the year before, the savings bank had stopped giving out loans. The money that had poured forth like miracles a decade ago was now being withheld. But could that really be related to these troubles across the ocean? In the bar, Maria-Grazia studied the newspapers and kept the television tuned to the news channel.

Slowly, the crisis moved toward them, like a tidal wave.

"You'd better be careful," counseled Agata-the-fisherwoman. "A business like yours can be gone in eighteen months, and in another eighteen there's no trace of it left."

"Now, you know that's silly," said Bepe. "Think of all the storms this bar has weathered. Both wars, and any number of scandals, and two earthquakes, and that *stronzo* Arcangelo opening his rival business right at the bottom of the hill. We hardly noticed when the *americani* suffered their Great Depression. What did it matter to us?"

Agata-the-fisherwoman said nothing. Always, her family had possessed a prodigious gift for predicting the weather.

THE FOLLOWING SPRING, trouble came to the doors of the House at the Edge of Night.

Lena was behind the counter, half scanning the papers for news of the crisis, half listening to the small morning noises of the island. Already the bar was populated. Fishermen; the elderly *scopa* players; Father Marco, who came in to check the football results each morning. Also Tonino the builder, who was waiting for a contract with *il conte*'s hotel to be finalized and occupied himself meanwhile with daily study of *La Gazzetta dello Sport*. Robert, on the veranda, paused over the accounts book to watch Filippo Arcangelo come striding up the steps, full of some private rage. So it was that Signor Arcangelo had several witnesses as he blustered into the bar in his striped apron and plastic slippers, fresh from the counter of the grocery store, and announced, "I've come about a debt. Is Signor Tonino here?"

The builder, shamefaced, got to his feet, already suspecting humiliation. "You owe me"—here Filippo Arcangelo paused to read off a long receipt, calculating with the fingers of one hand—"eight hundred and eighty-nine euros, and seventeen *centesimi*. To be repaid in full by the close of business today. I've given you your groceries on credit for a full three months, and enough's enough, Tonino."

"I haven't got it," said Tonino. "I'm still waiting for that contract to come through on the new hotel. You know that, Signor Arcangelo."

At this, a few of the elderly *scopa* players got to their feet in the builder's defense. "Coming here in front of everybody, without any shame!" "Don't you know he's waiting for his contract?"

"Am I not to be paid?" Filippo Arcangelo swung his body, stout as his father's now in middle age, from side to side in his passion for justice. "Do I not have my rights, too? I've sent Signor Tonino warnings. He's been avoiding my shop for months since he racked up this enormous bill—he refuses to answer the door when I call at his office or his house. These are his personal debts to my shop. Do I not deserve to be paid for the food he's eaten and the wine he's drunk?"

Here, the tide began to turn a little. "Yes," murmured Bepe from the corner. "Signor Arcangelo should be paid one way or another, that's true."

"It's no good asking me for money when I've not got it yet," cried Tonino, wounded into retaliation. "How was I to know the contract with the hotel would take so long?"

"I'll have what's due to me!" shouted Arcangelo in a frenzy. "All of you are running up accounts at my shop, telling me you'll pay at the end of the summer. It's not just Tonino. How am I supposed to order stock, pay my own bills? Haven't any of you thought of that? I've got a debt come due at the savings bank myself, and I must pay it."

"Signor Arcangelo," said Sergio. "Business is bad for everyone at the beginning of the season. You know that. Every year, you've allowed us to run up accounts and pay them at the end of the tourist season. That's how things work. The tourists come and our businesses prosper and we pay."

Arcangelo glanced around, drawing everyone into his confidence. "There's something happening overseas, in case you fools haven't noticed. At the end of the summer, half your businesses might be gone. There might not be any more tourists. I want my money now."

And then a strange thing happened. The bar came to life with indignation, as the islanders remembered other debts they owed their neighbors, and—more important—the debts their neighbors owed them. "What about my ten thousand *lire*!" cried one of the elderly *scopa* players. "Why, I lent them to Signor Mazzu to buy a goat in 1979, and now I recall that I never got them back!"

"What about the money I put into Signor Donato's house when it was damaged in the earthquake?"

"What about the investment I made in Signor Terazzu's lemon grove in '53, in return for marrying his daughter to my son?"

A kind of madness now came over Castellamare, as it had at the end of the war. The owners of each of the shops—the printing shop, the baker, the tobacconist, the butcher, the electrical goods store, the pharmacy, the hairdresser—went into battle with one another, loudly and in public, over who owed how much to whom. Frightened by these displays of panic, the widows of Sant'Agata in their respectable black made a raid on the savings bank, having heard from a reliable source that it was about to meet the same fate as those giants of finance across the sea.

Bepe's nephew, the only islander who worked in the Castellamare Savings and Loan Company, was sent out to talk to the customers. Though he was forty-three, Bepino seemed a boy again in his suit and cheap tie; the sun shone through his large ears, his nose sweated. "You can't take your money all at once like this," he said. "What are you doing here?"

The widow Valeria spoke up at last: "We've heard the bank is going to close its doors."

"Is it true?" demanded Bepe of his nephew. "You're to answer me honestly. Is the savings bank failing?"

"Sì, *zio*," said Bepino, who could not have lied to the widows of Sant'Agata even if he had wanted to. "It's true."

"What does that mean, 'failing'?" cried the chief widow, Signora Valeria. "If there's something wrong at the bank, I want it back now, in full, the money I put in."

"You've about seven thousand saved with us, haven't you?" said Bepino.

"Seven thousand, two hundred and twenty-seven euros." She brandished a savings book with the yellow-and-blue insignia of *il conte*'s business. "You can take it out of the pile you've got locked up in that great safe of yours. I've seen it, in your back room that used to be Gesuina's parlor, God rest her soul."

"Take it out of the safe?" said Bepino. "There's not enough money in that safe. A few thousand euros at most."

The widow put a hand very firmly on the door, ready to give it a shove as soon as Bepino got it open. "That's all right," she said. "A few thousand euros is enough for me for now."

But here a clamor arose: "What about my pension savings?" "What about my investment account, with almost eleven thousand euros, that *il conte* sold me personally in '92 and that I've been filling up ever since?"

"Oh," said Bepino, understanding the problem. "We don't keep that money here. We can't give it all back at once like that. Don't worry. The money will find its way back to you eventually, one way or another."

"But where is it?" said Bepe. "You're to tell us at once. If you're borrowing from one neighbor to lend to another, without having enough to go round, that's a damn dishonest trick you've been playing, Bepino, and I'm sorry to hear it of you."

"It's not like that. We don't keep it here at all."

"Where does it go?"

"Abroad," said Bepino, whose own knowledge was incomplete on the subject. "To foreign banks, bigger ones."

"Then get it back from *them*," cried Bepe in frustration. "Gesù, Bepino, haven't you the sense you were born with?"

"But it's not like that—they haven't got it," said Bepino. "They've probably given it to other people, too, for all I know."

"*That's* how you do business?" cried Bepe, in a rage. "Why, I'm glad I've kept my money in a bag under the mattress, even when I had two hundred million *lire* of it, and I don't mind telling you so, Bepino!"

"It's not my fault," protested Bepino, hot with embarrassment before the accusing eyes of the islanders. He struggled against the tide of their incomprehension, their disappointment. "It's just how it works," Bepino pleaded with them all, his voice cracking a little in shame.

"You shouldn't have invested in the place!" cried Bepe. "None of you should. How many times do I have to tell you that *il conte* is a bad man?"

THE LUNCHTIME HEAT IN Castellamare had a force of its own, and today it tempered the fury of the island. It drove the shopkeepers indoors, the stray cats into the shade, and slowed the widows in their impractical black almost to standing point. Inside, the usual quiet of early afternoon presided over the bar. But Maria-Grazia's outrage at this contemptible bickering over debts would not be calmed. She marched along the road to Concetta, whose day off it was, and found her seated on her doorstep with a copper pan of beans between her knees, stripping off the spines. While Maria-Grazia lamented, Concetta, without pausing in her deft knife work, consoled. "Never in the town's whole history has there been such squabbling over a thing like money," Concetta said. "Because no one's ever had any, and we've always got along fine. Think how many coffees you've given on credit. Why, Father Marco never pays, for instance. It wouldn't be right. Tonino, too—how could we charge him while he's waiting for that contract? This will all pass over."

But as the restless days of April wore on, it began to become clear to Maria-Grazia that things would remain out of sorts on the island for a long while yet. Filippo Arcangelo had sent out blustering letters to everyone who owed him so much as fifty cents. The baker was in trouble, also the butcher, for they relied on supplying *il conte*'s great hotel, and the food for the Sant'Agata festival, both of which were diminished this year. And half the islanders, it emerged, had mortgaged their shops years ago in the general fever for cars and televisions that had swept Castellamare, cars and televisions that were now broken or worthless.

Even the tourists, this spring, were thin on the ground.

"Will the bar survive?" asked Lena. "Is the business in trouble? That's what I want to know."

Lena and Maria-Grazia got out the accounts books, and with Robert's help—for he had always had a cool head for such things—they tried to calculate. But now, in this uncertain world without the savings bank to shore up the island's economy, anything might happen.

As for *il conte*, he had refused to speak to anyone about it. But two weeks after the trouble began he summoned Maria-Grazia, by scrawled note, to the villa. In the bar after she departed, there was some arguing and muttering over the *scopa* tables. "She oughtn't to be associating with him," claimed Bepe. "It isn't right."

"Oh, hush now," said Agata-the-fisherwoman. "Maria-Grazia must have her reasons."

"Think of poor Signor Robert," mourned the elderly *scopa* players.

Lena, finding her neck feverish with indignation, interrupted and risked a scolding. "I can hear what you're all saying," she said. "And you must speak to my grandmother about it, not go gossiping behind her back."

"I will speak to your grandmother about it," muttered Bepe, "at the very next meeting of the Modernization Committee."

Though she never would have admitted it, even Lena felt a little impatient with her grandmother, at the way she skulked about with Andrea d'Isantu, as though they really were carrying on some secret affair. That night, she sought her grandmother out in the stone room by the courtyard, where Maria-Grazia was applying night cream before the spotted mirror. *"Nonna,"* said Lena, laying her head on her grandmother's shoulder. "Everyone is gossiping about you."

"I know, *cara,*" said Maria-Grazia. "I know. But I've been gossiped about before, and I daresay I'll bear it this time."

"Why does he call you to the villa?" Lena found herself lamenting. "What can he have had to say to you? And why must you obey him all the time, as though he still had some hold over you?"

Maria-Grazia merely murmured, *"Cara, cara,"* and stroked her granddaughter's hair. "I'll tell you in good time," she said at last. "I'm not free to speak about it now."

Meanwhile, *il conte* was expecting other visitors. Rumor had it that the savings bank was awaiting representatives from a foreign bank across the sea, who were to come and make arrangements to take it over. Sure enough, at the end of the month they arrived, and were admitted to the villa, where they sat in conversation with *il conte* on the terrace, turning over great sheaves of paper. Apart from the foreigners and Maria-Grazia, *il conte* would speak to no one.

Now once again Maria-Grazia found herself the keeper of the island's secrets. For, over the counter of the bar, her neighbors poured out to her their troubles: the mortgage payments missed, the businesses whose takings were lower than they should be, ruinously low for this point in the season, the sons and daughters thinking of departing for the continent, as their ancestors had between the wars.

By the month of the festival that year, Maria-Grazia knew the difficulties of every one of them.

MEANWHILE, MARIA-GRAZIA WAS DETERMINED to resolve the matter of the bar's mortgage to the savings bank. "We've only a few months left on that loan," she told Robert. "Thirteen months, and it will all be paid off. Three and a half thousand euros. Couldn't we ask Giuseppino?"

"I don't know," said Robert. He had never approved of asking their younger son for money. "Better to leave him alone, and try to fix the problem ourselves. Lena's home now, and she's got a good head for business. Between us we'll manage."

But Maria-Grazia invited Giuseppino home for that year's festival all the same.

In the first months of the tourist season, Tonino's building company lost its contract with *il conte*'s big hotel. An extension to the building had been started, but now it was abandoned, and another building, the block of tourist apartments that was supposed to keep five island men employed all summer, was halted before it was properly begun, remaining just a skeleton of girders against the sea.

IN THOSE UNCERTAIN DAYS of early summer, Concetta was a little ashamed to find herself praying to the statue of Sant'Agata with the bleeding heart. She was never quite sure afterward what had come over her, except that she saw it there in Maria-Grazia's hall, gathering dust, and was seized with pity: for the bar; for her nephew, Enzo, whose taxi sat unused among the artichoke spires for whole weeks at a time; for the girl Lena who at this rate would never be a doctor.

Kneeling in the entrance hall, she lit a candle and addressed a few words to the saint. "I haven't asked you for anything in my life," she said, "not for you to bring Robert home during the war, or to end the feud with my brothers, or to help the Espositos when all their sons went away across the sea. But I ask you now to help the bar, and the island. It's years since you've done any miracle for us, Sant'Agata. You brought us the miracle of twins born by different mothers, to Professoressa Vella and Signora Carmela, and the miracle of Robert's rescue from the sea. You brought Maddalena home from England, and my Enzo from Rome. Just a small one now, please. Just for Giuseppino to return for the Sant'Agata festival, and reconcile this silly feud with his brother, as Maria-Grazia longs for him to, I know, and to give the Espositos enough money to keep the bar going another year. And the other businesses, too—Valeria and Tonino and even my brothers Filippo and Santino. Don't let them fail."

The saint stared down, head tilted, one hand raised as though directing traffic, the candlelight rolling over the painted face that was, in this half darkness, gentle and impossibly sad.

In the weeks that followed, others began praying to the Espositos' statue of Sant'Agata. For someone had remembered that it had been an auspicious object, once housed in the little chapel beside the *tonnara*, and that it held at its heart a holy relic, the right thumb of the saint herself.

Whether or not this was true, the widow Valeria one day, too, decided to pray to the statue, and only a few days later a startling and troubling miracle occurred.

Valeria, close to a hundred, had asked the statue for 220 euros to make her mortgage payment to the savings bank. She was almost entirely deaf, and the customers of the bar heard her quite distinctly as she lamented in dialect: "And *pi fauri, signora la santa*, two hundred and twenty, just enough to make the payment on my mortgage, for Lord knows Carmelo has found it hard to get work, and poor Nunziata with her bad knees . . ."

The following morning, rising before dawn, the widow Valeria's granddaughter Nunziata roused half the town with her shrieking. She had discovered, stuffed down the side of the pot of basil outside her grandmother's front door, a wad of banknotes. Exactly 220 euros, as though the saint knew.

"It's a miracle," cried the elderly *scopa* players, when Valeria came shuffling enraptured into the bar to thank the saint's statue.

Agata-the-fisherwoman was inclined to be skeptical. "We all of us heard her going on and on about the two hundred and twenty euros. Why, it might have been anyone in this bar who left it there."

But that afternoon, inspired, a queue of islanders formed before the statue all the same.

The next person to receive a miracle, however, was the fisherman-mechanic Matteo, who had not prayed before the statue at all and, as Valeria observed in outrage, hadn't attended Mass since he was a boy. Matteo, who drank a coffee on the terrace of the bar each afternoon after coming in from the ocean, had been stranded onshore several weeks for want of a new outboard motor, lamenting its loss to anyone who would listen. Now he found a brand-new one, wrapped in plastic, wedged under the little shed outside his mother's front door. Someone had left it there in the night. It was true that Matteo had not attended Mass since his childhood, and had never knelt before the statue of Sant'Agata. But as the days passed, a spate of other odd miracles occurred: wads of money shoved under the doors of failing businesses; new parts for broken vans hidden in courtyards in the dead of night; tiles for damaged roofs left on doorsteps before dawn, so that when the inhabitants of the house awakened they were simply, unsettlingly, there.

Some attributed these strange happenings to the saint. Others, like Agata-the-fisherwoman, were inclined to put them down to earthly causes. "Someone knows," she maintained, "what everybody needs, and is sneaking about the island with kind intentions."

"But who would have the money?" said Concetta. For really it was becoming a great sum, when Lena totaled it in the back of the accounts book, more than they had thought their island held.

"Maybe it's Signor Arcangelo," said someone, and the whole place became one yell of laughter.

No miraculous gift was ever found on the veranda of the House at the Edge of Night, though Concetta and Lena searched it carefully each morning before opening the bar, a little drunk on the air of miracle that hung over the island.

"This trouble over finances will pass, one way or another," soothed Concetta, for Lena was inclined to be disheartened at such moments. "Giuseppino will come through, as he always has, with the money to make things right—and Sergio will just have to swallow his pride about the whole thing."

But inside Maddalena, doubt had taken hold. What if it didn't pass? What if this crisis, not war, not earthquake, was to be the end of the House at the Edge of Night?

"Now don't talk like that," counseled Bepe. "This isn't a real crisis. By 2010 it will be over, and everyone will have forgotten it ever took place."

IV

IN THE WEEKS BEFORE THE SANT'AGATA FESTIVAL, A SPECIAL MEET-
ing of the Modernization Committee was called. That night, while
the islanders were assembling, a great storm broke over the island. It
assaulted the windows of the House at the Edge of Night so that they
shuddered; it poured with a guttural din down the drains and off the
swags of bougainvillea on the veranda. It grew so loud that Maria-
Grazia had to get to her feet and shout. "We need to make this
Sant'Agata festival as good as any other," she said. "Even if we've no
money to pay for it anymore."

For the Castellamare Savings and Loan Company had always par-
tially funded the Sant'Agata festival. The bank had paid for it for so
long that the islanders had all but forgotten where the money came
from—but now who would cover the bill for the flowers in the church,
the procession of traditional musicians shipped over from the mainland, the stalls with their sugared nuts and plastic souvenirs, the vans
full of fencing and generators and spotlights and amplifiers that must
be brought across the ocean on Bepe's ferry and installed in the piazza the day before? In the past two decades, in pursuit of more tourists and eager to please the former islanders who returned every year
to mark Sant'Agata's Day, the festival had become a grander and
grander affair, which must now be maintained.

As preparations for the festival began in earnest, the rain intensified. "Sant'Agata is angry," muttered Agata-the-fisherwoman in the
corner of the bar, her eyes moving to and fro, tracking the football
players on the screen of the television. Juventus versus Inter. In her

old age, Agata had become something of a football fanatic. "That's what we always used to say when we came across a localized squall," she said. "Sant'Agata is angry. A storm like this comes over a fishing boat when someone on board has a guilty soul."

One or two of the elderly *scopa* players glanced at Maria-Grazia, for it was no secret that she was still spending Sunday afternoons at *il conte*'s villa, for reasons she refused to declare to anyone except Signor Robert.

"I think there's a miracle coming," said Concetta. "I think that's what it means. There's no need to be so gloomy about it, Signora Agata."

In a rare spell of gray calm, two weeks before the festival, a strange half miracle did occur. As Bepe's ferry plied the churned waters between Siracusa and Castellamare, a shadow approached under the water. Closer and closer it came, making the tourists restless. "Sharks," murmured someone. All at once, the shadow burst through the surface. A bullet of moving water, it soared for a moment, then crashed on the deck. Not a shark; a dolphin. As gray as the rain with a pink underside, it flopped on the rusted metal of Bepe's ferry, croaking and squeaking in its own strange language, scattering the tourists. "Quiet!" cried Bepe. "Quiet. Let me approach him and see what he wants from us."

Bepe had last seen a striped dolphin as a young man, from a distance, from the bow of the *Santa Maria della Luce*. Now that this creature with its fishy smell had invaded his modern ferry, snapping unpleasantly with its teeth, he was not certain what should be done about it. Seizing his boat hook, he cut the engine and approached. "There now," he murmured. "Hush, dolphin. Stop snapping. Good boy. *Stai bravo*."

The dolphin turned one glossy eye on Bepe. With cautious prods, Bepe slid it toward the side of the boat. Then all at once the dolphin gave a furious flip with its tail and sent Bepe staggering backward. It plunged over the side of the boat and hit the water. As the tourists crowded to the railing, they saw it bob up again to hang below the surface of the water, looking up with its little black eye. Then, with a twist, it was gone, leaving only empty sea.

By the time the ferry reached the quay of Castellamare, the passengers hardly believed it had been real. And when Bepe brought the story to the bar, no one believed him there, either. "No, no, that never happened in my time," said Agata-the-fisherwoman, clicking her tongue in disbelief. "A striped dolphin would never jump into a boat in that shameless way, like a performing seal at a zoo."

"It did," insisted Bepe. "It jumped into mine."

"Right up onto that great big ferry of yours? You're getting old," said Agata-the-fisherwoman. "With all respect, Signor Bepe, your memory is getting tangled."

"It was real," cried Bepe. "I really saw it. And who are you to call me old, Signora Agata, when you yourself were born the same winter I was?"

The two of them had never married, but it was no secret that they had carried on some kind of discreet affair for the past fifty years, and now in their old age they argued with the familiarity of an ancient couple. "You silly *stronzo*," said Agata-the-fisherwoman affectionately. "You damn fool. A striped dolphin leap into a boat!"

But that night the youngest fishermen, Matteo, and Rizzu's youngest great-grandson, whom everyone referred to simply as Rizzulinu, arrived with strange stories of their own. They climbed the hill to the bar that evening in their ripped-off jeans and their sea-stained T-shirts with printed faces of American bands, and murmured in agreement at Bepe's story. Yes, yes, it was certainly possible. They, too, had seen dolphins surfing a rogue wave off Morte delle Barche, two days ago. Also a great shoal of flying fish like hailstones had fallen one dawn on either side of their boat, the *Provvidenza*. And once, fishing late at night with their lights out, they had cut the engine and heard in the depths below them the mourning of a whale.

"Everything's turned strange," said Agata-the-fisherwoman, who believed wholeheartedly in Bepe's story now that it had been confirmed by other sources. "Like there's a miracle coming. The fish must know it, too."

MEANWHILE, THERE WERE ODD RUMORS circulating about *il conte*. Though he still saw no one except Maria-Grazia, strange parcels had begun to leave the villa at the end of the avenue of palms. Square ones that looked like portraits wrapped in brown paper, and great packing cases, and once even a box that jangled as though there were brass candlesticks inside.

"He's selling his possessions," reported Bepe, who had heard it from the housekeeper. "Everything that belonged to his mother and father. The ancient portraits, the silver with the d'Isantu crest engraved on it, the French tables and chairs. Even the frescoes off the drawing-room walls. He's become a communist in his old age, I suppose, since the failure of the bank."

"He must have gone mad," said Agata-the-fisherwoman.

"He has no respect for the old *conte*, his father," murmured the elderly *scopa* players. "That's what it means."

The storms continued. The fences for the Sant'Agata festival were blown down; the makeshift stage that the builders Tonino and 'Ncilino erected grew so heavy with water that, when it was tested, the middle of it fell away, dropping the brass band on their backsides in the mud. One morning, Maria-Grazia and Lena opened the blinds of the bar to find half the veranda down. The beams with their garlands of soaked vegetation were too heavy to lift back into place.

The house itself seemed to be disintegrating. The roof leaked, dripping rain all over Amedeo's velvet sofa so that its surface was permanently misted with water droplets. One of the upstairs windows had been left open overnight and now the wood had swollen and it would not close, so that any visit to the bathroom had become a rainy, windswept affair. The paint in the entrance hall had turned scabrous, and half the books in the library buckled. Sergio sat behind the bar counter blasting each one with Lena's hairdryer to save it from permanent damage.

Never before had the islanders faced the problem of rain at the Sant'Agata festival. Nevertheless, said Concetta, there might be a miracle approaching, a softening of the weather after all these days of tumult. "There hasn't been a great miracle since Robert came from the sea," she said. "It's overdue—it's time."

All week the rain continued. Meanwhile, the numbers of tourists continued to diminish—a small tragedy, in a summer already so pinched and disappointing.

"You're to call your brother, Sergio," said Maria-Grazia. "If you call him yourself, if you invite him to the festival, maybe he'll come this time."

But the phone lines were down, torn from the corner of the House at the Edge of Night when the bougainvillea had made its abrupt descent onto the veranda. There was no calling Giuseppino.

Lena wandered the rooms of the house, but Maria-Grazia was ferocious with determination. "I'll not leave the island," she said. "It's my intention to die here, like my father, Amedeo, and my mother, Pina. I'll die in this house that's been ours for ninety years. This house my father's spirit still inhabits, this house where I was born. And Robert can't leave. He's bound to this place."

"Figures are figures," said Sergio gloomily. "Numbers are numbers. We can't make money out of nowhere."

"That's what everyone else seems to have done," said Maria-Grazia, and stalked to the room at the top of the house to gaze from her father's old desk at the gray, roiling sea.

Since no one else seemed willing to do it, Lena began to go through their things and make the annual inventory, fearing the bailiffs belonging to the big bank from the mainland who had reportedly been seen on the other side of the water, knocking on doors, threatening to extract microwave ovens and televisions. For their next payment to the savings bank was due at the end of the week, and they risked falling behind. Beginning early in the morning, Lena hauled out sacks of papers and outdated stock catalogs for the rubbish, polished the coffee and ice cream machines until they shone, prepared the boxes belonging to the television and the football table so that they could be packed again at short notice. She went through the supplies in the storeroom—peach juice and paprika chips and hard little almond biscuits to accompany coffee; *arancello, limoncello, limettacello.* Yes, there was enough for the festival. These things were noted in the accounts book. Maria-Grazia watched her with pressed mouth and a frown like that of her father, Amedeo.

"Now, until the preparations for the festival are over, we're not going to say anything more about what happens after," Maria-Grazia declared, when Lena was finished. "We've too much to do. The whole bar must be decorated, three thousand pastries made. We need to scrub the windows, put up the lights in the bougainvillea. Clean the tiles of the veranda and do something about that fallen vine dripping all over everything where the dancing was supposed to be. Prepare the bottles of *arancello* and *limettacello* and *limoncello.* Get out the jars of coffee from the store cupboard. Churn the vats of ice cream, or they'll be spoiled. When Giuseppino returns for the festival, we'll ask him for help with this debt, and that will buy us some time."

If Giuseppino returns, thought Lena, but did not say so.

Sergio stayed up all night making rice balls and pastries, working in silence in his apron and rolled-up sleeves. Around eleven Enzo arrived to help them for an hour, and ended up staying until morning. Enzo worked the dough as though it were clay, with delicate artist's fingers, and his pastries all took the form of the saint. Meanwhile, Lena and Concetta ran into the rain to cut garlands of bougainvillea, which they hung inside the bar. The branches dripped onto the floor, making dark puddles. From the ceiling the three women, balanced on chairs in the darkening bar, hung pennants of the saint.

There was no florist anymore to provide the petals for the festival; Gisella's shop had been the first to close. So that night, the women of the island went out with buckets and baskets and shopping bags, under flailing umbrellas, as they had after the war, and stripped every plant and hedgerow of its flowers. Lights were rigged up on the wreck of the *Holy Madonna* and on the arches of the fishermen's *tonnara*. As Maria-Grazia and Lena climbed the hill again they saw now that the festival would come off after all, was already beginning, its magic hush suffusing the rain-washed dark.

INTO THIS HUSH WALKED Giuseppino, off the day's last ferry, trailing his belongings in his hand. In his glossed gray suit, hauling his wheeled suitcase over the cobbles, he made an odd, diminished figure. The islanders did not recognize him as he climbed through the waterlogged town, as furtive as Zio Flavio had been on his return from war. It was only when Concetta came running into the bar— "Your son is here, Mariuzza! Your son!"—that Maria-Grazia stepped off the veranda into the darkness and knew her boy. He stopped before her and wiped the rain from his sparse hair. Lena shyly dried her hands on her apron, for she had never met Giuseppino and did not recognize him either. "*Salve,*" he said stiffly, in the Italian he had not spoken for decades. "I'm home."

No joy before or since could match the joy of Maria-Grazia in that moment of her son's return.

Summoned by the noise of exultation, Sergio came to the edge of the veranda, squinting into the rain. He descended the steps and consented to shake his brother's hand. Concetta and Lena hung back, feeling a miracle at last draw close—for now Sergio spoke in a rush, fumbling with the strings of his apron: "A loan, Giuseppino—a thousand euros, or two thousand—enough to pay the savings bank and keep the bar going over the winter—otherwise we'll lose everything— I'm behind on my payments—I know I shouldn't ask."

Giuseppino sat down. He massaged his chest, propping his case against a sodden chair. At last he said, "I can't help you, Sergio."

"*Pi fauri,* Giuseppino."

"I can't help you. I've no money. My business is gone."

Maria-Grazia stepped forward now, took Giuseppino by the shoulders. "What do you mean?"

"I had to file for bankruptcy—the company closed—"

All at once, Maria-Grazia seemed a great-sized person, a giant like her father, Amedeo. "Bankruptcy!" she cried. "Look me in the face, Giuseppino! Explain to me what you've done."

Her son, under the accusing eyes of his mother, became clipped and irritable. "I used to trade in futures, and now I don't, and the money's gone. The crisis. The business failed."

"Your important job," murmured Maria-Grazia, uncomprehending.

"It's not an important job," said Giuseppino. "I buy and sell contracts. You islanders, thinking I'm some wealthy man! I've only ever been at the edges of all that! What do you think I can do—some miracle?" His voice became brittle with contempt. A few neighbors had gathered at the edge of the veranda now, drawn by the air of scandal.

"The apartment," continued Maria-Grazia. "The big cars—"

"I bought all those on credit!"

"*Ai-ai-ai*, Giuseppino!" cried Concetta, in spontaneous lamentation. "What's become of you since you left this island?"

Giuseppino's head bent lower and lower, exposing the great bald circle on the crown that matched Sergio's. "Oh, Giuseppino!" cried Maria-Grazia. "If your grandfather Amedeo were here now, what could he possibly have to say to you?"

"Haven't I always sent you money?" cried Giuseppino, stung at last into retaliation. "That two million *lire* for the refurbishment. All the times I've put my hand in my pocket for repairs, to make up a shortfall in the profits, again and again, though Sergio shut me out of everything to do with this bar from the beginning. You've profited, Mamma! You and Sergio and Dad and all the rest of you! You wanted a van and you wanted to repair the roof, to buy new televisions—all of you wanted to be in on it, not just me!"

Sergio, who had been lingering in the doorway without speaking, now found himself fixed by the spotlight of the neighbors' attention, thrust into the unfamiliar position of the more successful son. He saw his brother cowed, reduced, and the triumph tasted sour in his throat, like spoiled wine. "Mamma, Zia Concetta, that's enough," he murmured. "Giuseppino, come inside."

Giuseppino rose from his chair. Into his mother's hand he put Amedeo's book of stories. "Here," he said. "I brought this back. At least no one can accuse me of stealing it, for I always said I'd return it the next time I came to the island, and now I have."

And in the end, it was a kind of relief to him to follow his brother through the door of the bar, embracing this homecoming like some wanderer in his grandfather's book of stories, diminished, penniless, cut down to his original size.

V

MARIA-GRAZIA COULD NOT SLEEP. INSTEAD, SHE SAT AT THE COUNTER of the bar and turned the pages of her father's book of stories. The story of the parrot and the girl who became a bird; the stories of Silver Nose and Body-No-Soul. And as she read further, seated behind the counter of the bar that cold dawn under her father's old damp-spotted portrait, she discovered, too, a strange wonder: stories she had not read before—tales her father must have remembered in the last days before his death, recorded in Sergio's scratchy teenage handwriting, carried off the island by Giuseppino before any of the rest of them had seen.

Maria-Grazia woke Giuseppino, who was sleeping on the velvet sofa in the room at the top of the house. "*Caro*, what's this?" she asked, indicating the unknown tales.

Giuseppino's neck turned red and blotchy, as it always had as a boy when he was caught out. "I didn't photocopy the last ones," he muttered. "I ran out of money before it was finished printing. And I figured Sergio remembered those ones anyway. He was the one who wrote them down."

But *she* had never known about them! And now Maria-Grazia discovered the last stories belonging to her father, as though he were with her again for a spell, whispering his island tales to lull her to sleep as he had when she was a small girl in leg braces. Turning over the pages, she read tales of the island, of donkey auctions and rescues at sea, of feuds between neighbors, of a spectacular catch of fish in 1913 ("told to me in 1922 by Signora Gesuina"), of a great landslide in

1875 ("passed down in the Mazzu family"), and then, on the final pages, a tale belonging to the saint. This one was marked with no date and no teller, and forever afterward she would associate it only with her father and with the festival, convinced he had written it for her to discover at this precise moment on the eve of Sant'Agata's Day, ninety-five years after the first one that he had witnessed.

Sant'Agata was once, wrote her father, sighted in the cemetery beside the swamp, when she appeared in a vision to the grave digger, rather alarmingly, hovering above the gateway with outstretched hands. When he went back to the grave, he found his shovel gone and the hole closed up as though it had never been opened. Most inconveniently, he was forced to give up his work and go home.

Those were earthquake-troubled times. Though the grave digger tried to dig again, he found the earth uncooperative, hard as marble, and one day, after a great tremor, he woke to find all the graves opened and gaping, a fearsome sight.

By this, he understood that the saint had either grown contrary, or else intended the burial of the dead in some other place.

The islanders called a meeting, and decided to obey the saint and move their dead to some safer lodging. But in those days, there was a great fear of disease, and the islanders refused to have the dead buried near their houses and their wells. And yet, refusing to obey the saint's wishes, the island became troubled anyway. The islanders were once again afflicted by a plague of weeping.

One morning, the saint appeared again to the islanders, on the road outside the cemetery. She seemed to be gesturing, and a group of fishermen followed. She led them all over the island, on a miraculous journey through fields and ditches and olive groves, until at last they came to the caves by the sea. Here the saint took up post at the back of the cave, and waited. The islanders, after some deliberation, decided there was nothing to be done but move their dead to the caves.

Here they found a second miracle: little compartments, full of bones already, in which to house their ancestors' coffins and funeral urns, and great stones, ready cut, with which to close them up.

The day of the procession was stormy. The islanders were uncertain, but the saint appeared all about the island, insisting that they carry their dead to the caves. The whole town gathered, and the procession took most of the afternoon, but at last they reached the caves.

Then, while the islanders were shut up inside the caves, an earthquake shook Castellamare to its roots. Great jettisons of lava sprung up beneath *il conte*'s villa, and the island heaved and convulsed. The islanders, cowering in the caves, emerged to find their town on the horizon flattened, not one building standing except the church and the villa and the House at the Edge of Night.

Then they understood that the saint had protected not only the dead but the living, for not one islander died in that earthquake, and all of them were sheltered by the ancient rock of the caves.

And when the islanders had finished burying their dead, a third great miracle occurred. The rock at the back of the cave, which had tumbled during the earthquake, held the form of the saint. The artist Vincenzo cut it free, to make of it a statue, and forever afterward the islanders knew that the caves were not a cursed but a holy place.

"And that, Mariuzza *cara*," her father wrote, "is how the islanders ended the curse of weeping."

THERE WAS ROBERT. He stood in the doorway, puffing a little at the exertion of walking the corridor—at last, she was forced to concede, an old man. Maria-Grazia put the book into his hands. "Someone should have written down all the other stories," she said. For after her father, Amedeo, who had remembered to do it? What about Agata-the-fisherwoman's rescue from the ocean? What about Robert's own appearance? The day of the ships, when she and her father had witnessed them arrayed on the horizon like raindrops on a wire? The ghost of Pierino? The taming of Enzo; the building of the great hotel;

the miracle of the bundles of money appearing after dark at the islanders' doors? What about all the tales that had gone unrecorded? Someone should have made remembrance of these things.

"Well," said Robert. "Can't you write them?"

"*Caro,* I'm too old for that now. We both are. Look how the time has passed. There's barely time for anything left now."

Taking him very lightly by the wrist she led him back to their stone room by the courtyard. As they walked, Robert leaned on her a little, a fact that still disconcerted her, for it had always been the other way around. But now she understood that her time had nearly gone over. Robert seemed to believe so, too, for he had his spectacles on, the reading lamp beside his bed was lit, and he had clearly been awake, too, thinking. Maria-Grazia closed her father's book and laid it on the nightstand. "Couldn't you sleep either?" she said.

"No, *cara.* I've been making plans."

"What about?"

"We've got both the boys in the same place now, at last, and it seems to me it's time we talked to them about the future of the business."

"What about the future?" said Maria-Grazia, a little startled.

"If Maddalena wants it," said Robert, "they should hand it over to her. That's what I think now. She's loved the place since she was born. She's tough enough to navigate it through this crisis. The bar should be hers, as it should have been yours all this time. I always loved your father the old doctor, but that was one thing he got wrong."

Some stubborn pride in her, some trace of the spirit of Pina Vella, still wished so fiercely for the girl to go to medical school. But, "She won't go," he informed her, very gently, when she raised this objection. "She's working up the courage to tell you, *amore.* She's already told me."

And something in her had known it already, that Lena, in her heart, was as ambitious as her grandmother and her great-grandfather before her, capable like nobody else of protecting the bar.

SANT'AGATA'S DAY DAWNED COLORLESS, THE SEA OBSCURED IN mist. The morning's Mass, outside the church, was conducted under a phalanx of umbrellas. "Praise to be to Gesù and Santa Maria!" cried Father Marco, against the wind, shielding the plaster saint with his spread soutane. "Praise be to Sant'Agata and all the saints!"

The procession was a slippery, muddy affair. The statue, ancient, made in plaster by the great-great-great-great-grandfather of the artist Vincenzo, had never been out in the rain before. On the gravelly path down to the caves by the sea, a small tragedy occurred. The statue began to melt, her face tracked with black tears like those that had once fallen from the eyes of Carmela, her robe shedding its purple in rich streaks.

"Quickly, Rizzulinu, Matteo!" cried the priest. "Get the saint in at once out of the damp!" For Father Marco, in his old age, had become as great a devotee of Sant'Agata as any of them.

The fishermen, at a run, made for the caves by the sea. Scrambling in over the rocks, they bore the saint into the dry darkness, the rest of the islanders in pursuit. "Is she damaged?" cried the widows of the Sant'Agata Committee. Cigarette lighters flamed; mobile phones were illuminated. The saint, by a hundred lights, glimmered mournfully, her face shifting as though alive, a little paler than it had been before the storm.

"We can't bring her back out into this rain," said Father Marco. "The paint will run; the plaster will fall apart. We'll have to keep her here and wait until the storm dies off."

So it was that when the bailiffs from the mainland arrived on Castellamare to begin calling in the islanders' debts, they found not one house inhabited, not one knock answered, the whole island empty and every shop shut up as though the place were abandoned—and at last were forced to put away their warrants and papers and briefcases and leave.

MEANWHILE, IN THE CAVES, there began to be some disagreement. "We'll be here until the end of the world," warned Agata-the-fisherwoman.

"Another half hour," said Father Marco.

The half hour became an hour, an hour and a half. An argument was just beginning to threaten when Concetta spoke up. "Enzo has a statue," she said.

All at once, Enzo found himself at the center of the crowd's attention. A few people who had seen his great stone figure of Sant'Agata nodded in approval. Yes, yes. That was also a statue of the saint.

"Fetch Enzo's Sant'Agata instead," said Concetta. "It's waterproof. It was planned by his great-uncle, the artist Vincenzo. It's almost finished. We can make the procession with that one."

The elderly *scopa* players nodded. The other Sant'Agata could be used. After all, wasn't it an image of the same saint?

"It's too heavy," said Bepe. "It's made of stone. The normal Sant'Agata is plaster. How are six fishermen going to lift it?"

"It can be lifted," said Enzo. "It's volcanic rock. It's porous, like pumice. We'll find some way."

At this, there were some mutters about the curse of weeping.

"Let's go and see the statue," said Father Marco, guiding the old one farther back into the dry safety of the caves, where no squall could reach it.

It was another half hour before the fishermen returned across the bay, and when they did, there were cries of wonder. The fishermen had loaded Enzo's statue onto Rizzu's old donkey cart, which no one had thought of in twenty years. Now the cart came into view across the bay, slowly, falteringly, emblazoned with its green and yellow island tales. Between them they hauled her, the fishermen and their descendants: Tonino, Rizzulinu, Matteo, 'Ncilino, Calogero.

ALL AROUND THE SHORES of the island, in the storm, the islanders bore their saint. Past *il conte*'s villa, shuttered and closed. A few of the islanders glanced up at the windows, expecting to see *il conte* there to nod his blessings on the procession as his father used to, but no face appeared. The statue was borne on, the fishermen heaving at the back of the cart, bracing it against the slopes. Past the rocky south end of the island, past the Greek amphitheater, now overtaken by scrub grass and thistles, along the cliffs, above the caves by the sea, past the gates of the new hotel where the Mazzus' farm had once stood. The hotel was subdued, its plastic recliners by the pool overturned, its parasols heavy with water. But a few tourists appeared at the doors and joined the procession. Meanwhile, the saint, the water making rivers and torrents in the folds of her stone robe, swayed in the back of the donkey cart with one hand upraised. "Come on," coaxed Maria-Grazia. "Not far now." For she found herself breathless with anxiety, willing the statue to complete its pilgrimage as though it were the saint herself who swayed there in the cart, as though some metamorphosis had occurred during the miraculous hush of the night.

At the quayside, before the old *tonnara* and the rusted remains of the boat *Holy Madonna*, Father Marco prayed for the saint's good grace. Babies were brought forward for a blessing. The farmers' crops, moldering in the constant storm, were consecrated anyway. Father Marco tipped a bottle of holy water into the general downpour over the prow of the island's one new fishing boat, Matteo's *Provvidenza*.

The rain drove trade to the bar that evening. "Why so many people?" wondered Maria-Grazia. "Has everyone taken pity on us and decided to buy an *arancello* each, to keep the place open another summer?"

Concetta came edging through the crowds, eyes lit with suppressed mirth. "I've just heard," she whispered. "Arcangelo's place has been flooded out, just like the winter of '63 when we had those storms! My poor brother!"

"A miracle!" cried Agata-the-fisherwoman. "I told you! That's what all the rain was for!"

The bedraggled clients of Arcangelo's bar, a little shamefaced, sidled through the door in search of liquor and hot tea. Filippo Arcangelo hung about the veranda until Concetta took him by the arm and hauled him inside.

But it was not enough, Maria-Grazia understood as she watched her sons and her granddaughter tend the overcrowded tables. They needed more than a few ninety-cent coffees, a few single-euro glasses of liquor. The rain had made the veranda impassable, and the ice cream crystallized in the vats, unused. Even the tourists didn't want it in this weather.

In the square as night fell there was dancing all the same, wildly among the great pools of water, beneath the sodden pennants of the saint, which poured their lukewarm cascades onto the heads of the revelers. Under the great hired spotlights on their stands, the islanders whirled to the music of Bepe's *organetto*. Maria-Grazia, seated at the edge of the veranda beside Robert, under Giuseppino's great striped golfing umbrella, told him of her father's first night on the island. The story he had made of it for her as a girl: how he had marveled at the statue surrounded by a hundred red candles, the magical hush as *il conte* parted the crowd. How different from the festival now with its growl of generators, the flash of colored lights on the stalls, the pounding music to which the young gyrated in a corner, no longer enamored of the wailing island songs. And the tourists with their cameras taking a hundred thousand photographs when on her father's first night there had been only one, the very first, the photograph that held within it everything that was to come after. No *conte* this time. Though no one but she would admit it, least of all the members of the Modernization Committee, the festival was hollowed out somehow, without his presence.

But now, into the wet disorder of the piazza came Bepe and his nephews, running like young men. "There's an emergency," Bepe cried. "The ferry has broken down!"

"Broken down?" asked Tonino.

"Damned flying fish—a great shoal of them—stuck in the motor. This *puttana* of a storm!"

"Leave the *Santa Maria*," counseled Tonino, clapping old Bepe on the shoulder. "You're soaked through—I'll order you an *arancello*. We'll fix it tomorrow, when we're all sober and the rain has stopped."

"No, no!" cried Bepe. "You don't understand. The *Santa Maria del Mare* has broken down, and there are people—lots more people—waiting to come across! We must fetch them!"

There was some confusion at this. Tourists, from *il conte*'s big hotel? "No," puffed Bepe. "All sorts. Visitors from the mainland. Islanders coming home—some third cousins of the Mazzus, so I've heard, who've traveled all the way from America to be here, and the Dacosta uncles from Switzerland! I think I even saw Flavio Esposito. Tourists, too. They've heard about our festival. They're queuing at the quay. They want me to bring them to the island to see the saint. And now the ferry has broken down and I can't."

Maria-Grazia rose, possessed with a fierce conviction. "Flavio? My brother Flavio? He must be brought here—we must send out the little boats. Where are the fishermen? Matteo? Rizzulinu?"

Rizzulinu extracted himself from the dancing, wringing the ends of his wet jeans. "We can only bring five or six in the *Provvidenza*," he said, when Agata-the-fisherwoman explained the difficulty.

"How many are there, Bepe?"

The old ferryman puffed out his cheeks. "I don't know. Far more than that."

"Who else has a little boat?" cried Maria-Grazia. "Who else can help?"

The youngest Terazzus stepped forward, one or two others. That was all.

Now Agata-the-fisherwoman rose to a great height, hauling herself by the bar's counter. "We'll take the old boats," she said. "We'll launch the ones stored away in the *tonnara*. The old boats, painted, with the white stones, that we used before the war. There are ten or twelve in there."

The islanders began to stir themselves. Down the road to the quay they hurried, in cars and vans, on bicycles, on foot, bearing lanterns like little white stars. Maria-Grazia seized Flavio's *Balilla* binoculars, and together she and Lena took the three-wheeled van and followed them. In the dark that was all at once less storm-tossed, less rain-washed, the young men of the island launched the boats. On the waters of the harbor they rode again: the *Sant'Agata Salvatrice*, the *Trust in God*, the *Santa Maria della Luce*. The *Provvidenza*, the *Maria Concetta*, and the *Siracusa Star*.

Lena and Maria-Grazia were left onshore with the rest of the islanders, watching the lights sail away from them. And here on the edge of the ocean, Maria-Grazia seemed to see the island as it looked to those ships leaving it, and must have looked to those Espositos who had left it: her son, her brothers, her granddaughter—a rock in a haze of water vapor, receding on the clouded surface of the water like a ship cast off. "Didn't you want to go in the ships, too?" she asked Lena.

"I'm going to stay here," said Lena, "and prepare the bar for when they get back."

But Maria-Grazia, finding herself pensive, wanted to watch the ships awhile longer in case, by some miracle, her brother really was brought back on one of them. Lena left her with the keys to the van and went home on foot, at a run, through the last of the rain. So it was that when the land agent Santino's son came running with a sodden note in Andrea d'Isantu's handwriting, summoning Maria-Grazia to the villa one last time, Maria-Grazia found herself alone.

WHEN CONCETTA STEPPED INTO the piazza, to the abandoned music and the upturned chairs of the veranda, looking for her friend, she found a strange alteration. The savings bank was lit fluorescent white, its sliding doors open. Behind the counter sat Bepino.

The widows of the Sant'Agata Committee led the charge through its doors. The remaining islanders followed. Rain-soaked, jostling, they came to rest before the yellow counter. "Now what's all this, Bepino?" cried Valeria. "You're doing business, in the middle of the night, during the festival?"

"The bank is just open for an hour or two," said Bepino, with a ceremonious little clearing of the throat. "I'm supposed to tell you that you'll get your money back. The money from your accounts that you all deposited here."

"But the bank was failing," said Concetta. "It can't be unfailing."

"The bank is failing. But you'll get your money, as we promised you."

But who could have paid so much? In wonder, the widows of Sant'Agata began withdrawing their savings and pensions. "Is it the foreign bank?" persisted Concetta. "Talk sense, Bepino. Is it them?"

"Not them."

"Then who? Is it someone from overseas, investing money in our island?"

Bepino gave a quick flick of his head, for what foreign investor would have done that?

"I know who it is," cried Agata-the-fisherwoman. "That same person who hid the money outside everybody's doors, the same person who gave 'Ncilino the tiles for his roof and Matteo the outboard motor."

"Sant'Agata," breathed one of the elderly *scopa* players.

Into this scene of consternation came Maria-Grazia at last, in the three-wheeled van. She stopped beneath the palm tree and got out, and Concetta was dismayed to find her weeping. "What is it, Mari-uzza?" she cried.

But Agata-the-fisherwoman, who had not noticed Maria-Grazia's tears in the general damp of the night air, merely seized her by the shoulder and said, "Come and help us puzzle this mystery out. Some-body's given us back all our money, Signora Maria-Grazia. You're the one who's always known everybody's secrets. You must know who it is, if anybody does."

"Sì," said Maria-Grazia, without ceasing in her weeping. "*Il conte.*"

Bepino's translucent ears turned a fierce pink. "No one was sup-posed to say anything about it," he whispered.

"Now, Bepino," cried the ancient Valeria, seizing him by the wrist. "You're to tell us everything."

"I'm not supposed to," said Bepino. But Valeria was the oldest person on the island, and neither did he dare to disobey her. "He sent Santino Arcangelo down here with a lot of cash," he confessed at last. "To give back to everybody. So you don't lose what you're owed when the bank fails."

"Why?" asked the widow Valeria.

"Aren't all your businesses in difficulties? Don't you all need this money back?"

It was true—but all the same, *il conte*?

"He beat the fisherman Pierino," said Agata-the-fisherwoman, in blank incomprehension. "He's not a good man. Not like his father, the old *conte*. If he means to make amends, it's much too late."

All at once, Maria-Grazia was seized with a pity so profound she felt she could taste it, like a storm coming in off the sea. "He's never been such a bad man as you all think," she murmured. "He doesn't deserve this blame."

"You should know that best, Maria-Grazia," said Valeria. "If he's a good man, why have you been wandering up there at all hours of the day and night, skulking about in the alleyways and *vaneddi* like a lovelorn girl?"

But now here was Robert, a little breathless, who had come up unobserved at the edge of the crowd. "Now, Signora Valeria," he said. "What kind of accusation are you making?"

The old woman reeled a little, for never had Signor Robert spoken so forcefully to anybody on the island. "Nobody here is making accusations," she mumbled.

"Mariuzza," said Robert, touching her wrist. "Tell her the truth."

Maria-Grazia said, "*Il conte* is sick. He's dying. I went to him because I was anxious about him, and as it turned out he needed my help, so I kept visiting. He has no family. He'll be the last *conte*. He has no one to leave his belongings to, and so it will all be seized—the villa and his father's hunting ground and the bank and the buildings around the piazza that have belonged to his family for three hundred years. And when he came back to the island and saw these troubles coming from across the sea, he decided to sell everything, to help everybody a little with their debts. Perhaps to make amends for the beating of Pierino, for Lord knows how everybody's made him suffer for it."

"Go on," said Robert. "Go on."

"It was he who had the idea of leaving gifts about the island in secret, the tiles and the outboard motor and the stacks of money, so that you'd think it was the saint. But how could he do that on his own, when he's been confined to bed for months? How could he know who was in trouble on the island, who needed his help, when none of you speak to him any longer—when none of you have, since his father died almost fifty years ago?"

"But why you, Maria-Grazia?" complained Valeria. "For he could have asked anybody. Santino Arcangelo, or his foreign assistants."

Concetta, understanding, said, "None of them would do. It had to be someone who knew everyone else's troubles. Who else but Mariuzza?"

For always, from a girl, Maria-Grazia had been the repository of the island's secrets, since she had led the wild Concetta into the bar and tamed her with kindness and *limonata*.

"And you've been doing this, Signora Maria-Grazia?" said Valeria.

"Signora Maria-Grazia and I," said Robert.

Valeria was still dissatisfied. "There's some ungodly connection between the two of them," she mumbled. "Something not right. You've been visiting him, Maria-Grazia, since long before these troubles started. Every Sunday afternoon, if rumors are to be believed."

Maria-Grazia, drawing herself up like her mother, Pina Vella, said, "Of *course* there's a connection between us. We're half brother and sister. And all of you know it, so you might as well come out and say it, instead of gossiping about it in corners as you have for ninety years."

The elderly *scopa* players, feeling themselves to be very modern, murmured about the need for DNA tests and blood samples before any judgment was made on the matter. "We've done all that," cried Maria-Grazia, allowing her irritation to get the better of her. "We did a DNA test three years ago. It's all done with. Robert knows. Now can't you all just let us be?"

"Well," said Valeria, launching a final halfhearted challenge, "what were you doing there tonight?"

"I went to the villa because *il conte* is dying," said Maria-Grazia. "And there's not one person in this godforsaken little place who's willing to visit him."

Maria-Grazia felt herself to have gone too far in her anger, to have been uncharitable—for really she loved the island as much as any of them. But Robert took her gently by the wrist. And the fact remained, Andrea d'Isantu was dying. Eighty-eight years old—the same age to the day as the ghost of Uncle Tullio, whose youthful portrait still hung on the stairs of the House at the Edge of Night, whose presence haunted the goat paths on still evenings—Andrea had been diagnosed with a persistent cancer of the liver, and now it had all but used him up. He had been too sick even to attend their festival.

Now the widows of the island murmured in pity, thinking of the dying man in the villa at the edge of the town, unvisited, unmourned.

The music had stopped, and no one knew anymore what to do or say. Even Valeria fell back a little, chastened.

"We must go and see him, Mariuzza," said Concetta at last. "We must bring him gifts, as we used to do for his father, *il conte*. How can we have neglected that part of the celebrations?"

"He's very sick," said Maria-Grazia. "The priest and the mainland doctor are there with him—it's too late now—they won't want us all there."

"We must go anyway," said Concetta. "It's the proper thing to do."

IN THE PINK AND AMBER ROOM with the cherubed ceiling, Andrea d'Isantu lay in the same bed in which he had been born. A rosary wound his right hand. Father Marco proffered holy water. Beside him, the doctor was making ready to leave, unlooping her stethoscope with an old weariness Maria-Grazia recognized from her father's late-night returns when there was nothing more to be done. Into this room came the islanders, unannounced, dripping rainwater over the tiles. "*Signor il conte*," cried the widow Valeria. "We're here to bring you our festival offerings. We know the truth now. We know the truth about what you've done for us."

Immensely old, like a tortoise, Andrea d'Isantu strained up from his pillow, his neck a rigging of taut wires. He surveyed the islanders before him. Then he fell back and closed his papery eyelids again. All at once, someone broke ranks and came forward with a tray of baked aubergines, depositing it in his lap. Someone else advanced, bearing a chicken in a cardboard box, and shoved it into the arms of the doctor. Concetta held forth a great slice of tuna wrapped in plastic. And then a tide of islanders, bearing gifts, braved the disapproval of their neighbors to approach the ancient man, Castellamare's last *conte*.

The old man raised his head again briefly and gripped in turn each of his islander's hands.

So it was that the bailiffs who lurked across the ocean, when they returned at last, would find in Andrea d'Isantu's great villa not one stick of furniture to be seized, not one ancestral painting or silver candlestick, not one crystal remaining on the cut threads suspended from the chandeliers—for all had been sold, all had vanished into outboard motors and patched roofs, fishing boats and ancient houses. The villa at the end of the avenue of palms was to be sold to developers, and the bank and the hunting ground and the empty houses cut into pieces and turned over to other hands. But the remnants of *il conte's* great wealth had been swallowed up in the earth that made them, returned to the descendants over which his father had once ruled, and nothing now remained of them anymore.

MARIA-GRAZIA AND ROBERT WALKED home arm in arm, by the alleyways and *vaneddi*. The rain had stopped at last. A procession of lights was advancing up the road from the harbor. The visitors from the mainland. Enzo had got ahead of them. "Quick—get ready!" he cried, from behind the counter. "It's going to be the biggest Sant'Agata festival we've ever seen!" Maria-Grazia, sinking down on the edge of the veranda, sat for a long time instead with her hand in her husband's. He gripped her wrist with a calm pressure, as he had once gripped it when he was a young soldier and she a girl just out of leg braces, in the shadow of the war. "I've only ever cared for you, you know," she said.

"*Lo so, cara,*" said Robert.

MEANWHILE, LENA, WORKING IN a great frenzy, had prepared the bar. She had mopped the rainwater from the floor, stacked bottles of *arancello*. She had heaved tables and chairs. She had polished the condensation from the mirrors until each one shone. Now, one by one, she dropped the rice balls into fat so that they should be crisped and burnished to perfection. Her father and her uncle she ordered about like schoolboys, to the great amusement of Zia Concetta, who busied herself with setting out the veranda chairs on her return from *il conte*'s, so as to be out of the way.

Into the piazza, slowly, as though making a pilgrimage of their own, the visitors came. They plunged into the night that now whirled again with the music of the *organetto*, surrounding themselves with the warm dark. They saw what Amedeo had seen a century before: a small shut-up place, fragrant with wet basil, beyond the dark edge of the world. And miracles, too: a saint lit red from beneath by a thousand candles; an extraordinary house balanced at the edge of the town. In their faces, Lena saw the wonder he, too, must have felt, the old doctor, to find at the end of his long journey an island such as this.

The visitors crossed the threshold of the bar. Lena plied the tables. She served coffee, chocolate, *limoncello*, *arancello*, *limettacello*, the *limonata* her grandmother had taught her how to make—unsugared, fragrant with honey, belonging to the war. She served endless *cappuccinos*, which had never before been ordered after eleven in the morning in the House at the Edge of Night. She served, in spite of the chill that still lingered a little, so much ice cream that Sergio and Giuseppino had to be set to churning a new batch, in a rush, in the bar's back room. She served rice balls and pastries, which the visitors lapped from greased paper, as greedy as the girl Concetta.

"Why so many people?" marveled Bepe. "And not even tourists—not all of them—for some are quite ordinary people from the mainland."

"It was like this after the war," murmured Agata-the-fisherwoman. "Any hint of trouble in the world, and people renew their interest in miracles."

It was true that the visitors this year were of a different kind: shabbier, more ordinary. And yet they ate and ate. In tips alone, which Lena amassed in the old box with the rosary and wax candles, she found that she had made up almost what they owed the savings bank for the month. "I wish we could have served them all for nothing," said Maria-Grazia, a little sadly, her hand in Robert's. "That's what we did in the old days when a person in trouble came to our door."

"Why didn't *signor il conte* give you money?" asked Robert. "That's what I've been wondering all these months. For he helped almost everybody else."

"I think," said Maria-Grazia, "that he knew we'd be all right without him. The bar always has been, after all."

Lena appeared at the edge of the veranda. Setting down her tray of drinks, she approached her grandmother and grandfather. "*Nonna,*" she said, "I'm sorry I believed that gossip about you and Signor d'Isantu. And I've something to tell you. Grandpa knows already. I want to stay here and manage the bar."

The girl could have been a doctor like her great-grandfather. And yet, in the great noisy thrill of the saint's festival, to give things up did not seem to Maria-Grazia the loss it would have been in city places. What could Lena do but return, like a ship cast off upon the waters, like the *Holy Madonna,* as though drawn by an invisible compass to the shores of this place? Something in her granddaughter had settled, altered. Strange it was, that in this island where everybody knew your business before you knew it, where the widows burdened you with prayers and the elderly *scopa* players scolded and the old fishermen knew you by name before you were even born, it was possible still for a person to be as deep as the ocean, as unfathomable as the dark beyond the bar's four walls. She understood now that Lena would go on returning to this place all her life. As Amedeo had, and Pina the schoolmistress, and Maria-Grazia herself—all of them, living and dead. Lena would return always, to walk the same goat paths her great-grandfather Amedeo had walked, with his medical bag in one hand and his head full of stories, foundling, founder, drainer of swamps, healer of sicknesses, sworn protector of this place.

All at once, with a gray brightening, the night became crepuscular. And then, at every window, a great unfurling. Into the rain, the islanders hurled fistfuls of bougainvillea and white oleander, trumpet vine and plumbago. Flavio Esposito, who stood trembling on the edge of the piazza, came forward at last into the hail of flowers. The air was clogged with them; the hired spotlights were extinguished.

The dancers stumbled in the onslaught, blind, reeling. The *organetto* sang in the depths of it all. Wild with the noise, the two youngest Dacosta children flung firecrackers. And through the freshening dawn, the ghost of Pierino and the spirit of *il conte* took flight together, green, translucent, in search of other shores. The stone saint was heaved aloft by slow degrees, borne up on the shoulders of the fishermen—until at last they stood triumphant, slick with rainwater, and Sant'Agata swayed once more over Castellamare, all miracles upheld in her right hand.

ACKNOWLEDGMENTS

The House at the Edge of Night would never have come into being without the work of three great chroniclers of Sicilian and Italian folk stories: Giuseppe Pitrè, Laura Gonzenbach, and Italo Calvino. Pitrè, the real story-collecting doctor whose life inspired the character of Amedeo Esposito, rescued many hundreds of Sicilian folk stories from obscurity and *The Collected Sicilian Folk and Fairy Tales of Giuseppe Pitrè*, translated and edited by Jack Zipes and Joseph Russo, was my first point of inspiration. Laura Gonzenbach's *Beautiful Angiola: The Great Treasury of Sicilian Folk and Fairy Tales* (also translated by Jack Zipes) was another important resource. My version of "The Two Brothers" is an adaptation of Andrew Lang's retelling of Gonzenbach's version of the tale. Italo Calvino's *Italian Folktales* introduced me to many of the haunting and beautiful stories from across Italy that found their way into Amedeo's red book. The story that I have called "The Wrecked Ship" was inspired by Calvino's version of "The Ship with Three Decks," and the story that I have called "The City of the Dead" is an adaptation of Calvino's version of "The Dead Man's Palace." The excerpt from "The Man Wreathed in Seaweed" at the opening of Part Two is taken from George Martin's 1980 translation of Calvino's *Italian Folktales*. The tale of the curse of weeping, however, is my own.

For invaluable help with my research into Amedeo's early life, I am grateful to Dottoressa Lucia Ricciardi and the archive and library of the Istituto degli Innocenti, Florence, as well as the book *Figli d'Italia: Gli Innocenti e la Nascita di un Progetto Nazionale per l'Infanzia*. In *The House at the Edge of Night* I have presented a fictionalized version of that noble and forward-thinking institution, Florence's foundling hospital, and any errors are my own.

My research into life under Fascism was helped enormously by R. J. B. Bosworth's book *Mussolini's Italy*, and by Francesco Fausto Nitti's personal account of escape from a prison island, "Prisoners of Mussolini." For its informative and vivid account of Operation Husky, I am grateful to Rick Atkinson's *The Day of Battle: The War in Sicily and Italy, 1943–1944*, and for its sensitive portrayal of the plight of deserters in World War II, Charles Glass's *Deserter: The Last Untold Story of the Second World War*. Finally, I drew inspiration from two great chroniclers of postwar Sicily, Danilo Dolci and his book *Inchiesta a Palermo*, translated into English as *Poverty in Sicily*, as well as Carlo Levi's *Le Parole sono Pietre* or *Words Are Stones*.

There are several people without whose immense personal support *The House at the Edge of Night* would never have been written. First, I would like to thank my agent Simon Trewin, the book's greatest champion, who has, as always, been part of this project from the very first page. Second, my U.S. agent Suzanne Gluck, whose support and passion for *The House at the Edge of Night* have been incredible. Also Tracy Fisher, international agent extraordinaire, and Matilda Forbes-Watson, for her invaluable and much-appreciated support at every stage of the process. My editors, Kate Medina and Jocasta Hamilton, have championed both me and the book with infinite care and wisdom; I feel very fortunate that *The House at the Edge of Night* has been in their hands from the start. I would also like to thank Derrill Hagood for her support and guidance during the editing process, and Robin Duchnowski for providing important insights. The teams at Hutchinson and Random House, as well as my editors around the world, have been an invaluable support, and I am more grateful than I can say for their belief in *The House at the Edge of Night* and in the importance of telling this story of the financial crisis, the small town, and European history.

Many friends and family sustained me during the long process of writing *The House at the Edge of Night,* and I am extremely grateful for their immense love and support. In particular, I would like to thank my mother, Jane Wheare, my sister, and my father, Michael Banner, as well as Sally-Ann Gannon, Marta Ruth, Roberto Galloni, Michela Joppolo, Alessandro Galloni, my extended family both English and Italian, and those friends who offered me support and help in countless ways during the writing of the book.

Finally, and most importantly, I wish to thank my husband, Daniele Galloni, to whom this book is dedicated. His support has been so unfailing and his belief in me so complete that I feel that this book is as much his as it is my own.

CATHERINE BANNER was born in Cambridge, England, and began writing at the age of fourteen. She has published a trilogy of young adult novels. She studied English at Fitzwilliam College, Cambridge, and has taught at schools in the United Kingdom. *The House at the Edge of Night* is her debut adult novel. She lives in Turin, Italy, with her husband.

catherine-banner.com
Facebook.com/CatherineBannerAuthor
@BannerCatherine